Mona Lisa of the Galilee

Mona Lisa

of the

Galilee

Beth Jacobi

Matador
9 Priory Business Park
Kibworth Beauchamp
Leicestershire LE8 0RX, UK
Tel: (+44) 116 279 2299
Fax: (+44) 116 279 2277
Email: books@troubador.co.uk
Web: www.troubador.co.uk/matador

ISBN 978 1783062 430

British Library Cataloguing in Publication Data.
A catalogue record for this book is available from the British Library.

Typeset in Garamond by Troubador Publishing Ltd
Printed and bound in the UK by TJ International, Padstow, Cornwall

Matador is an imprint of Troubador Publishing Ltd

For all who love the land of Israel/Palestine

 Main Characters

KEZIA: Jairus and Leah's daughter on whom they have doted and over-protected.

JAIRUS: A boyhood in Nazareth and educated in the Temple at Jerusalem. As Ruler of the Synagogue in Capernaum, his life is comfortable and his prospects solid.

LEAH: Born in the fishing village of Capernaum, her late parents were thrilled when she married the handsome Jairus.

ADAH: A slave-girl sold when her father could no longer feed her. Bought by Jairus as his wife's servant.

MORDECAI: An elderly, conservative Pharisee. Jairus' uncle.

SIMON: Fisherman and neighbour to Jairus. Good-natured, rumbustious member of Rabbi Jesus' group.

SARAH: Simon's wife and Leah's close friend.

ESTHER: Sarah's sharp-tongued mother and local 'midwife'; lives with Simon and Sarah and rules the roost.

ZEBEDEE: Owner of the largest fishing business on the Galilee lake. Proud of his family's long tradition in fishing and confident his sons will inherit for the future.

SALOME: Zebedee's long-suffering wife. A mild-mannered woman whose easy-going ways prove essential for the smooth running of Zebedee's household.

JAMES: Zebedee and Salome's eldest son. A fisherman follower of the itinerant Rabbi Jesus.

JOHN: Middle son of Zebedee and Salome. Like his brother James, a fisherman involved with Rabbi Jesus.

JARED: Zebedee and Salome's youngest son. His surly demeanour and fiery temper isolate him from normal friendship groups.

ANNA: Zebedee's widowed sister living in her brother's household.

MIRIAM: Anna's elder daughter.

DEBRA: Anna's youngest daughter.

JOANNA: Leah's younger sister, married and living in Sepphoris.

SETH: A potter in Sepphoris, married to Joanna.

ABNER: Friend of Jairus, a silversmith living in Jerusalem.

JUDITH: Abner's wife.

CAIAPHAS: High Priest at the Temple in Jerusalem. An obsequious collaborator.

CAPERNAUM: A Jewish village on the north-west shore of Lake Galilee. The focal point is the Synagogue and the markets. Traders bring their wares from south, north, east and west on donkey carts, camel trains and on foot. A Roman Garrison is encamped outside the village to ensure peace for the occupying forces in the Galilee region.

SEPPHORIS: A hilltop city with a harrowing past and name changes. The Greek occupation called it Sepphoris, the Jews called it Tzippori. At the Roman conquest, they named it Diocesaraea and the Arabs called it Saffuriya.

JERICHO: An oasis town in the Jordan valley, 800' feet below sea-level.

JERUSALEM: The religious capital for the Jewish nation. King Herod initiated a massive modernisation of the Temple, so that it made a monumental impact to all who approached the city. The Romans laid beautiful stone pavements and built great water cisterns for the battalions stationed to quell the Jewish freedom-fighters.

CAESAREA PHILIPPI

DAMASCUS

LEBANON

CAPERNAUM
SEA OF GALILEE
SYRIA
TIBERIAS

SEPPHORIS
NAZARETH

RIVER JORDAN

MEDITERRANEAN SEA
(GREAT SEA)

CAESAREA MARATIMA
SAMARIA

JERICHO

BETHANY
JERUSALEM

DEAD (SALT) SEA

EGYPT

APPROX MILEAGE

CAPERNAUM → SEPPHORIS   30m
CAPERNAUM → JERUSALEM VIA JORDAN VALLEY 125m
                    VIA SAMARIA   90m

SEPPHORIS → CAESAREA MARATIMA   50m
JERUSALEM → DAMASCUS   150m

Chapter 1

KEZIA lifted the latch. She opened the door a crack and peered into the courtyard. There was only one hand that knocked with such pent-up force, a knock that sent tremors down the door-frame and through her own virgin heart.

Dark clouds threatened rain and a few stray vine leaves skittered in the chill wind. A sullen youth slouched in the doorway, his eyes averted from the door.

"Oh, it's you," Kezia murmured. She was right, it *was* him. Her hand dropped from the latch, the door swung wide and she retreated into the house. From the back of the room her mother's voice called from the loom where she was weaving.

"Come in, Jared," Leah welcomed. For a few halting moments Jared stared into the room before ambling over the threshold. He rubbed his thumb on the side of his nose, a habit that betrayed his tension as he eyed Kezia. There was no other girl in the village more desirable.

"You're not dead then!" A husky voice escaped through lips which barely moved.

Kezia paused before she replied. She tried to decipher Jared's statement. Was it relief, pleasure or disappointment? Her mother had sobbed as she explained to Kezia the severity of her fever, how she had lain tossing and halucinating, so weak and eventually unconscious. Everyone thought she was

1

dead. The village mourners were summoned to the house to perform their ceremonial weeping and wailing. Kezia recalled nothing of the trauma. She remembered aching and feeling hot but she had no idea that she had caused such anxiety. She lifted hesitant dark eyes in Jared's direction.

"I *felt* dead." The flat voice didn't sound like her at all. Twiddling her comb between her fingers, she turned her gaze on the new rush mat by the wall. Leah had left her window-seat at the loom and was talking to Jared but the words failed to register with Kezia. Her mind was preoccupied… what on earth had possessed her loving parents to betroth her, their only daughter, to *him*. If only Jared was like his older brothers. She liked them – everyone liked them – but Jared was different. He wasn't like anyone she knew.

He never mixed, had never joined the gang of children who grew up to romp on the shore, clamber over the fishing boats and chase the furry brown hyrax from their hot-rock siestas.

Try as she might, Kezia could find nothing attractive or even remotely pleasant about the young fisherman destined to be her husband. Her heart clouded with dread at the thought of becoming Jared's wife.

Leah's sister, Joanna, poured the young man a cup of water. The last time she'd seen Jared, he was still a boy, now she detected significant sprouts of dark fuzz down the side of his face and below his spotty chin. 'Hobbledehoy!' she smiled to herself, 'neither man nor boy!'

Despite the boy's gaucheness, Leah had every confidence he would make an honest, reliable husband for her Kezia. She and Jared's mother, Salome, spent hours plotting and planning their children's future as they knelt side by side washing clothes in the lakeside wash pool or pouding grain for the daily bread. Leah felt it was to Jared's credit he had stayed with his brothers in the family fishing business when so many other youths has left Capernaum to seek better paid employment. Jared's father, Zebedee, a man whose voice carried like a shofar in the fog, repeated his joke that his ancestors had been fishermen on Galilee's lake before the great Moses was found in the bulrushes. With three strong sons to carry on the family tradition, Zebedee boasted he could die happy.

"Are you…" Jared shuffled his feet on the flagstone. He sniffed, "…you alright now?" he asked Kezia. Intuitively, she knew his question bore no genuine concern for her health, rather he had only come to find out if she was still fit to become a wife. More to the point, she swallowed at the truth, he wanted to be sure she was robust enough to bear him sons. Suddenly as the blank, humourless eyes returned her gaze, cold realisation gripped her that Jared would never love her in the way she was used to seeing her parents love and care for each other.

Jared stared at the girl he had been contracted to marry from the age of six. He looked at her taut and flawless complection framed with shimmering, thick hair waving into the nape of her neck, and down to her tanned and slender shoulders. Any man would long to run his fingers through that hair. She moved like a graceful willow in the breeze and he noticed where her developing breasts pushed against her tunic. Her composure unnerved him. Jared's eyes rested on Kezia's breasts, but his mind was far away. Another girl filled his thoughts. A girl who blushed and giggled each time he passed her market stall, a girl whose language he couldn't understand but whose pale skin, glossy black hair and almond eyes aroused a fire in his loins that consumed all his waking thoughts.

"Will you eat with us, Jared?" Leah took an extra wooden board from the shelf. Resentment flushed Kezia's cheeks. Why was her mother always so sweet and pleasant with him? She flicked her hair and glared out through the open door to the stone water jars propped up against the far wall of the courtyard.

"No," Jared mumbled a reply. Kezia's shoulders relaxed. A sour odour of sweat drifted to her nostrils. "Damage to the nets last night…" Jared spoke to the loom. "Lots to do." With no further word, he turned and left.

Joanna pulled a face.

"Oh my!" she laughed, "Poor lad hasn't got used to his man's voice yet!" Joanna tried to make light of Jared's uncouth personality. Leah managed a smile in reply. Kezia's expression remained stony. Something about Jared's smouldering presence caused panic in her breast. For a few moments she wrestled to control her breathing and the rolling in her gut.

"Here we are!" The little servant-girl bustled in from the courtyard, a pile of fresh-baked flat bread in a cloth. Barely a couple of years older than Kezia, nevertheless, her bird-like frame and wispy hair gave her an old-fashioned image. Since the shock of Kezia's brush with death, the servant-girl had become fiercely protective of her Master's young daughter and hovered over her like a ewe with it's new lamb.

"Ah, that smells good," Joanna tugged at Kezia's sleeve, "C'mon chicken, get your strength back." She tore a piece of bread, dipped it in the olive oil dish and passed it to her neice. Leah opened a jar of olives, decanted some into a bowl and sat down on her cushion. She watched Kezia eating and laughing with Joanna. Though barely past her twelfth birthday, the bloom of maturity had begun and anyone looking at the two of them together would imagine Kezia was Joanna's sister rather than her neice.

Happy as she was to see her daughter well, Leah was haunted by vivid flashbacks of the limp and lifeless frame beneath the linen sheet, the sallow face wreathed in sweat and the shadow of death around her eyes. Leah relived the panic of watching her daughter slip away. She could not forget her utter helplessness and wild desperation. She had used every herb she could think of to stem the sickness but nothing seemed to work. The terrible memory brought beads of perspiration to Leah's forehead. As she basked in her vivacious daughter's warm smile, her tired eyes filled with tears of gratitude – her prayers had been answered – the Rabbi had come just in time. Kezia was alive. She adjusted her position and put a hand to her belly. Beneath her fingers another life stirred. More prayers to be said… 'Please God, this time, let it be a son.'

Chapter 2

WOMEN in Capernaum held firm ideas on the vagaries of life. With sisterly concern they gossiped how fate had dealt a cruel hand to Jairus' wife and her sister. Joanna's womb remained empty while Leah's womb seemed cursed to shed her babies before full-term. It had been near fourteen years since Leah became Jairus' wife but Kezia was their only child to live. Repeated miscarriages had robbed her of the vivacity and smiling eyes the women now saw in Kezia. Years of disappointment had left Leah wrapped in an aura of dejected weariness and inner pain.

But wherever the women gathered, at the drying sheds by the harbour or at the street corners, the threshing floor or the well, the topic on every lip was Kezia. Her recovery from the brink of death astounded the whole neighbourhood and as they mingled daily chores with chatter, so they balanced their received faith with deeper superstitions. They chewed the report from every angle, flummoxed and exhilerated in turn. Their repetitive snatched conversation began to sound like the vociferous chirping of the ubiquitous sparrows.

"Leah said he only just got there in time…"

"She'd gone, dear of 'er…"

"I heard he and Jairus were boys together in Nazareth…"

"…that's right… and studied together in Jerusalem…"

"…didn't his wife die of the fever back when half Nazareth went to the grave?"

"…you've never seen a man so heart-broken…"

"…how come he couldn't heal his wife…?"

"…Sarah said he used the *stones* on Kezia… "

"…oh yes… I've heard my gran tell of the stones…"

"…whatever dears… t'was a miracle…"

"…my man says he's seen him do miracles…"

Day after day the air reverborrated with recollections, pronouncements and conjecture.

***

With all the worry of Kezia's illness and nervous anticipation for her next baby, Leah's friends urged her to take life gently for the next few months. Joanna, who had rushed down from Sepphoris when she heard Kezia was so ill, now basked in her role of indispensable sister. It was a role she had craved from childhood, a desire to be needed by her serious older sister.

Joanna leaned against the windowsill in the room Jairus and Leah kept for guests. Misty fingers of pink dawn crept over a cloudless sky. The hills of Syria loomed grey in the distance as the sky lightened and pink traces faded into morning yellow, then imperceptively transformed into a translucent duck-egg blue. Joanna absorbed the precious moments for herself. She imagined her husband whistling along the city street to collect his bread… smiles and a nod of his purple turban for all his customers. Seth the Potter in his purple turban was a well-known personality. Joanna sighed. She missed him. But she knew her place should be with Leah until the birth. If only Leah could hold on to full time with this one…

Joanna felt she ought to pray but… prayer was a dim memory. 'Was there a God?' she asked herself. 'If there was,' she mused, thinking back on the times she had stood in the Synagogue silently aching for help, 'he's never answered *my* prayers.' Joanna had prayed so often and so earnestly… and all for nothing.

She shrugged away her thoughts. Egrets chattered in the rising warmth. Another hot day, she decided – time for her and Kezia to whisk the pile of the dirty clothes down to the wash pool before the sun rose too high and the intense heat drove everyone into the shade.

Leaving Leah in bed and Adah, the servant-girl, in charge, Joanna led Kezia out of the courtyard and into the lane leading to the lake. In the morning stillness, the loudest sounds came from croaking frogs and waking birds, especially the swooping cadences of the laughing doves. Cool, sweet air rose off the water – Kezia loved these mornings. Joanna, basket full of washing balanced on her elegant head, strode purposefully along the path towards the wash pool. Keziah, whose stride was not as long as her aunt's, hurried along beside her clutching her basket on her hip, the bag of soaps slung over her shoulder.

Kezia looked forward to this time alone with her aunt. She felt she could say things to Joanna she couldn't ever say to her mother.

The two wove their way along the path hugging the lakeside, unaware that, from behind a shutter, someone was watching. Kezia had no idea that someone was watching her most of the time.

"Won't Seth be missing you?" Kezia asked, thinking of Joanna's husband alone in the fast-growing city.

Joanna laughed; "So you want to get rid of me! Making you work too hard, eh?" She neither turned nor slowed her stride but her voice was amused more than accusing.

"No! No, I didn't mean that." Kezia called over the top of the washing. She thought of Capernaum's two potters. Children loved to gawp in at the pottery, mesmerised as the potters fashioned coils of clay into dishes or threw lumps of clay with unerring accuracy onto the spinning wheel. Their wives stacked all the pots, filled and emptied the kilns and served customers. Kezia wondered how the gentle Seth could possibly manage glazing, firing and selling his work without his business-like wife.

"Seth's got too much to do to miss me, dear," Joanna continued. "And he's got a good boy who'll take pots down to the market for him. I reckon he can spare me a while longer." They reached Job's Pool, the area where, for centuries, women from the village gathered to do their washing and share the latest gossip. It was called a 'pool' but was more a sheltered inlet where, in winter, seven springs gushed into the lake, and even in high summer the trickle was still enough to fill jars and wash garments. Kezia crouched opposite her aunt, took her father's tunic out of the basket and pushed it gently into the water. They were so early, no-one else was yet in sight.

"I really like you being here," Keziah confided, "it's so much more fun with you around."

"I've never called 'washing' much fun!" Joanna gave a fond wink. "You're going to have to prove to me you can wash well enough to look after a husband!" she teased.

Pleasure drained from Kezia's face. The memory of Jared's icy stare sent shivers down her spine. She wanted to pour out her misgivings to this woman who always appeared so confident and capable.

She looked sideways at her aunt's strong hands plunging into the fresh water… would she understand? There wasn't much time before other women would be sure to join them. Kezia took a deep breath and grasped the moment:

"I don't want to marry Jared!" she announced.

Chapter 3

"KEZIE – what *are* you talking about!" The clothes in Joanna's hand flopped on the washing stone. She rolled her eyes to the sky in exasperation.

Kezia, startled by the sudden brusqueness in Joanna's tone, felt heat rise in her cheeks as her aunt launched a counter attack.

"You're *betrothed*!" Joanna spluttered. "Why, it's all arranged… for years… don't you understand…? You're betrothed to Jared, my girl, and that's that. You… you *have* to get married."

Joanna's mouth stayed open as she looked out across the water for inspiration. After a pause she turned her gaze on her neice. "You know the Commandments – 'honour your father and your mother'," she emphasised, "and, well… it's your duty. Heaven knows, your mother and father have chosen a *good* family for you…" Joanna was picking up speed. "Salome's a kind woman, you don't know how lucky you are to have a mother-in-law like her… and don't you forget, Jared's father owns the biggest fishing company on the lake – you'll never go short." Joanna frowned at Kezia in disbelief. "I don't think you realise what that means." Her mouth screwed up in frustration.

"Kezia," when Joanna called her Kezia, it was a sure sign she was serious, "your parents have *guaranteed* you a secure future." She came to an abrupt halt. Joanna knelt quite still, her gaze now lowered to the wet clothes in front of her.

When she spoke again the steam had gone and her tone was gentle, "What's made you think like this, chicken?"

"Don't like him," Kezia's voice was weak. "He's… oh… he's so different to Father and…"

"…and Rabbi Jesus?" Joanna finished Kezia's sentence. She knew full well Kezia idolised the Rabbi, and even more so after he cured her of the fever. Kezia's eyes lowered at her aunt's perception.

Kezia attempted to explain herself. "Jared's so… I don't know… I just can't imagine…" her voice trailed away as her body wriggled. She hunched in despair, peering at her aunt with the eyes of a trapped rabbit.

"Why do things have to change?" Kezia whimpered. "Why can't I stay at home with Mother and Father?"

Joanna picked up her washing and assumed a crisp, matter-of-fact tone, "It's called 'growing up'," she retorted. "It happens to everyone. It's not a perfect world Kezie, and the sooner you get used to that, the better." The tunic in her hands was in danger of being scrubbed in half as she went on, "And don't forget – Jared's young too. He's got a lot of growing up to do." She splashed vigorously as a group of women came into sight along the path headed by the slight figure of Salome. "I expect he's every bit as nervous as you – it's natural to wonder about these things but…" she threw Kezia a disarming smile, "Oh, chicken… it'll be alright… you'll see."

Kezia soaped her father's tunic before immersing it in the soft, cool water. The familiar hint of incense that impregnated all his clothes was the scent of the man who made her feel safe and special, the sweet perfume that made her feel proud and loved. But on this particular morning, kneeling by the water's edge, the scent of incense made her want to burst into tears.

***

Jared could buy no more rope. His father's hired men had made enough snide comments already, such as, 'we'll soon be selling nets to Syria'. He'd bought so much the coils of rope piled high in the back of the salting shed. It had not escaped the men's notice that the rope seller was next to where merchants from the east had their material stall. Each day Jared made excuses to pass the material stall and the bright-eyed, doll-sized girl behind it. Intoxicated by lust, the desires of burgeoning manhood dominated his every conscious moment. He *had* to see her.

She was so tiny, sometimes it was difficult to glimpse her behind the piled bales of linen. The animal instinct in him knew she was interested... knew she waited to see him too. He had to contrive a way to see her on her own.

Foreign traders camped beyond Capernaum, mid-way between the fishing village and the town of Tiberias further down the lake. Their tents pitched in clumps on the gentle slopes above Magdala, at the entrance to the Valley of Doves. This strategic T junction meant they caught travellers coming down from Nazareth and Sepphoris as well as those passing between Tiberias and Capernaum on the main route to Jerusalem. A well-beaten track led from the Roman Garrison up through the grass and boulders to the traders' camp. Roman soldiers took a brazen delight in flaunting their capacity to buy sexual favours from the camp at any time of day or night.

Jared dreamed of the honeycomb of caves around the Valley of Doves. What was her name? He didn't even know her name! He scowled as his needle dug into the broken netting. The hired workers immersed themselves in idle chatter as they worked; mostly ritual boasts of men intent on winding up callow youths. Jared seethed with malicious anger against them and against his own inexperience.

"But," he swore under his breath, "t'wouldn't always be that way."

Chapter 4

"LEAH?" Leah turned her head with genuine pleasure to greet the familiar, lilting voice. Plump and generous Sarah was far more 'family' than neighbour. She was Leah's first friend when she and Jairus came to live in Capernaum a dozen years ago. Sarah's husband, Simon, was a fisherman, and with Kezia betrothed into the fishing community, it further sealed Sarah's feeling of kinship with Leah.

Sarah's enquiring eyes searched the room, "Where's Kezie?" she asked.

"Gone to the wash-pool with Joanna."

"Oh." Sarah couldn't disguise her disappointment. "Well, I brought over some dates… and almonds… I knows they're her favourite." Sarah settled herself by the table; Leah recognised the sign – this would not be a short visit.

Life in Simon's household ran on the orders of Sarah's mother, Esther. The widow Esther had lived in her son-in-law's house from the beginning of the marriage, and her viper's tongue all too often reduced her daughter to a trembling wreck. Leah's home was Sarah's precious refuge against regular mother-daughter eruptions. Sarah hugged the dish of dates and nuts on her knee.

"Simon said he couldn't believe his eyes when Kezie sat up like she did after being, well…" Sarah sifted a few words through her mind before she carried on "…after being so ill and that… an' everyone thinking she was *dead!*"

"God's miracle, Sarah," Leah's face beamed with unusual radiance. The spinning she had neglected since Kezia's illness was now tranquil therapy. "Kezie would be dead if it hadn't been for Jesus," she said. "I still can't take it in. But," a surge of emotion rose in her throat at the memory, "thanks to him we still have a daughter."

"And…" Sarah eyed the unmistakable bulge in Leah's tunic, "t'won't be long an' you'll be nursing a son!" She adjusted her skirts more comfortably on the three-legged stool. "I can tell, you know," she gave a confident nod, "it's the way you're carrying." She lifted her shoulders, correcting the tilt of the dish on her lap, "I'm always right!" she added with total confidence.

The spinning wheel gently whirred and clicked. Leah sighed.

"I pray you *are* right, Sarah." Her nimble fingers worked quickly and for a couple of minutes both women shared a comfortable silence.

Leah detected Sarah was churning inside. Guessing at 'mother trouble' again, she asked as casually as she could, "How long was Simon away this time?"

"Nine *weeks!*" Both words erupted an octave higher than normal. Sarah hung her head, embarrassed at her outburst of frustration and irritation. "Oh, Leah, my dear," she shook her head, " I don't mean to bring you all my worries but, I… well,… who else can I can turn to?"

Leah put out a hand to still the wheel. "What is it?" she decided it would be best to stop spinning and give Sarah undivided attention. Sarah looked down at the calloused hands fidgeting round the dish of fruit. She bit her bottom lip.

"It's Simon," she confided in another great sigh. "He says he's leaving the fishing." Leah couldn't disguise her shock. "Yes!" Sarah emphasised, "Leaving the fishing! Him *and* brother Andrew… and maybe Zebedee's sons too."

"You mean James and John?" Leah was incredulous. "Why?"

"Now don't get me wrong, Leah… I don't want to say nothing 'gainst Rabbi Jesus, seeing as how he made Kezie well an' all, an' I know he an' your Jairus go back a long ways, but… well, to *my* way of thinking, my Simon spends too much time with him and the other men." Unable to hold the dish still, Sarah laid it on the floor. "That Jesus has turned all their heads with his fine words."

Leah grappled with the totally improbable idea that Simon would ever leave fishing.

"Lots of people think Rabbi Jesus is a prophet," Leah reminded Sarah.

"Huh!" Sarah grunted. "Doubt if Mordecai would agree with that!" Mordecai the Pharisee was Jairus' uncle and had lived in Jairus' house since his own wife died. Leah was led to believe the arrangement would be 'temporary' but that was all of eight summers ago. Mordecai was of the old school, inflexible and dogmatic. Yet in the old man's eyes Kezia could do no wrong. Leah surmised Mordecai would forgive anyone who restored Kezia to health. But she could never be sure.

Sarah's hand was nervously making sure no strands of hair had escaped her scarf. "I heard Jesus caused a right rumpus last time he was in the Synagogue. Simon said Mordecai looked like he'd have a heart-attack he got so angry." Sarah let out a long sigh.

"Oh, yes…" she conceded, "Jesus does wonderful things, Leah, I don't deny that. He's kind and he tells them beautiful stories but…" her face crumpled as she fought to stem the tears. "He's taking my man away, Leah…" She buried her face in her shawl, "What'm I goin' to do?"

Leah got up and poured them both a cup of water from a small pitcher by the door. Passing a cup to Sarah she said, "Simon wouldn't leave you."

There was a pause. "I don't know." Sarah's face half emerged from the shawl. "Sometimes I feel like I don't know anything anymore." She sniffed in misery. "Brother Andrew keeps saying they've found the Messiah – an' I just don't know what to think. Oh, Leah, I'm worried to death. If Simon leaves the fishing what does he think we're going live on… *prayer*?" A sob juddered through her body. "It's caused us such arguments, you wouldn't believe!" Sarah shook her head in despair.

Leah turned the spinning wheel into action again unsure as to what comfort she could offer her neighbour. If anyone could make Simon change his mind, she thought, it would be Esther. Esther's stern face was stamped with the lines of poverty and toil. Leah often wondered how Sarah could possibly have come from Esther's womb; they were as different as milk and vinegar.

Leah's foot worked the treddle. "What does Esther say?" she ventured to ask.

Sarah threw back her head, emitting a strangled sound somewhere between a snort and a yell.

"Oh! Esther thinks the sun shines out of his backside… she'll defend *anything* Jesus does an' she'll take Simon's side against me every time. She says…" Sarah affected her mother's northern brogue, " 'better a meal of vegetables where there's luv than a fatten'd calf with 'atred'." She gulped her water. "She's no help at all!" Sarah moaned bitterly. She got to her feet and brushed her hands down over her outer coat.

18

"Well, there we are, this won't do. Must get back. Sorry to have missed Ke-" as she spoke Adah struggled through the door, her shoulders weighed down with pitchers in each hand. Sarah smiled kindly, she was a sweet girl. Leah was lucky to have such a willing servant-girl in the house, she wished she could pay for a servant – but not on Simon's wages!

Sarah waved a hand towards Leah's belly, "Remember now, you've got to take care of *both* of you."

Before Leah could make a suitable reply, Sarah's rounded, homely figure was gone.

Leah sighed: 'Oh for Sarah's child-bearing hips!' she smiled at the irony. Sarah had the right hips but her womb, like Joanna's, had not been blessed with life.

Adah sang to herself as she worked through her daily routine. Merrily, she piped tunes she had learnt from the threshing floor and snatches of folk-songs the women sang at the washing pool. Unlike previous servants, Leah had no need to supervise this girl. She fetched water, swept, washed, ground grain for their bread, carded wool for spinning and helped to prepare meals. She and Kezia worked together without rancour or rivalry and, for the moment, both girls were kept highly entertained by Joanna's breezy tales of city life in Sepphoris.

Sometimes Leah doubted her sister's more colourful accounts, but then, Joanna's glass was always half full whereas, Leah had to admit, her own natural tendency was to see her glass as half empty… and fast evaporating. The shuttle's rhythm lulled her thoughts back to Sarah's news… beyond belief! Her mind raced with the implication such a move would have on Sarah. 'How would they live?' The grey wool she was weaving into a tunic grew on the loom. 'What'll Jairus say about it?'

Suddenly, a sharp stab of pain caught Leah's breath. She winced and grinned in the same moment – the baby – he kicked! She had felt his first kick! Yes, she was certain of it, HIS first kick of life.

***

Three months later

Jairus refilled Mordecai's wine-cup and then his own. The meal over, the two men lounged on wide cushions beside the low table. Kezia nestled against Mordecai's chest in the way she had done since before she could remember. In her uncle's arms she had listened to stories of all Israel's great heroes. She clamoured for her favourites like the young boy Joseph and his fantastical dreams, his nail-biting dangers and his eventual governorship of all Egypt and saviour of his family. The vivid characters burned into her dreams. With imagination in over-drive, Kezia wove herself into the love story of Ruth and Boaz and fancied her Uncle Mordecai as the great prophet Elijah, all flowing white hair and beard.

A special bond had grown between uncle and neice, a closeness that made Leah prickle with resentment.

Jairus spoke towards his uncle, "Zebedee came to see me this morning," he muttered, ignoring the fact that Leah was seated nearest to him at the table. "He's concerned James and John might leave the fishing and go off with Jesus." He took a deep swig of sweet Cana wine. "If that happens, he wants to know Jared is settled… with a wife." Kezia's stomach knotted. Her gaze darted between her parents, to her uncle and back to her father.

"He's pressing me to set a date for the marriage." Jairus

20

jiggled the wine-skin to guage how much was left. He poured the contents into his cup.

Kezia's heart pounded against her ears. Mordecai's arm tighten around her as if he understood her fright. The old man coughed; no way was his dear girl ready to move into Zebedee's household as Jared's wife.

"I told him…" Jairus continued, unconcerned with Kezia's reaction one way or the other, "we couldn't have a wedding before Passover. I may be away in Jerusalem for several weeks before then," he finished the wine and dabbed his mouth with a cloth. " But, *after* Passover," he smiled at his daughter, "*after* Passover, we'll have the finest wedding Capernaum has ever seen!"

Kezia partially relaxed. Passover was ages away. Jared could drown by then, she told herself, her imagination willing to clutch at any improbable straw.

"It'll take all that time to get a wedding coat woven," Leah said, trying without success to find a comfortable position. She was due by the next full moon and, already her belly was stretched and swollen beyond any other of her pregnancies. The last couple of months she had withdrawn from all her chores, desperate to hold her son to full-term. She didn't know how she would have managed without her sister's competent presence. Joanna sat erect on the other side of the table looking from Kezia to Jairus to Leah, her expression as inscrutable as an owl.

"On my way back from Jerusalem, I'll buy you the finest tunic in Bethlehem." Jairus spoke as if wearing an expensive robe was all that was needed to seal a perfect union.

"You lucky thing," Joanna chipped in, realising Kezia would need buckets of coaxing if she was going to look forward to this wedding, "Bethlehem embroidery is *the* best…

bold designs… *very* stylish!" She gave an encouraging nod, "You'll look beautiful, chicken."

Kezia's stomach curdled. She swallowed hard. Her eyes concentrated on the floor, lips firmly closed.

Adah, for whom the opportunity of a wedding had never arisen, imagined it would be the most exciting day of her life. She grinned at the prospect as she busied herself in the corner, straining lemon peel, herbs and flowers out of a small flagon of olive oil. The scent was Leah's favourite to freshen the room from mealtime odours. Adah's biggest ambition was to become a servant in Kezia's household, but, for the moment, she was aware her current mistress' needs were paramount.

The Pharisee Mordecai released his arm from around Kezia and let his hand stroke down over her tunic from her shoulder to her thigh. He slapped the top of her leg as he stood up.

"We need to talk," he said to Jairus. He spoke with authority, as head of the household not as a family guest. "We'll walk down to the harbour." He directed in his curt fashion. Jairus respectfully followed his uncle out of the house.

Joanna seized the opportunity of time with Leah.

"Go on, you two," she pointed to Kezia and Adah, "Why don't you go down to Sarah's…? Find out what they'll need here to help this baby boy into the world." Adah placed her air-freshner on the shelf and Kezia pulled her cloak from the hook behind the door.

"That's right," Joanna encouraged, "learn all you can, chicken," she gave Kezia a knowing wink, "'twill be your turn soon enough!"

***

Light clouds scudded high across the sky, obliterating a fragile crescent moon. Autumn had brought her sharp nip to the night air, and as the wind gusted off the lake, the two men pulled their thick woolen cloaks tight around themselves.

All the boats were fishing out in deep water so their conversation by the harbour wall would not be overheard. Mordecai sat on one of several boulders in the shelter of the wall. After a moment or two Jairus joined him. The men sat peering out over the inky blackness of the lake to the shadowy hills in the distance. Behind them, up in the caves of Mount Arbel, Zealot torches flickered secret messages out across the water.

"You need to be very careful, my son," Mordecai began, his voice measured and grave. "I won't mince my words for you, and you must understand," he coughed, "what I have to say is for your own good."

***

"Soon be over!" Joanna soothed as her sister' face screwed up in discomfort. She delighted in time alone with her sister, they could relax together when the men were out of the way.

"You've done so well this time." Joanna's praise was heartfelt. "Just a couple more weeks, eh?"

Leah sank back on the fleece. "I think he's got four legs!" she tried a weak smile as her hands pushed against the place on her belly taking the full force of unborn legs. "He's as strong as an ox!" she complained.

"Well, that's exactly what you want, isn't it? A good strong man to take care of you in your old age." Joanna bent down and tenderly patted Leah's distention.

"You don't have to worry about a thing," she purred,

"We're all ready. Sarah and her mother have been on stand-by for the last six months! And you know Kezia can't wait. We've a pile of towels, swaddling bands…" she glanced at the items in the corner, "Oh… and I've scrubbed the cradle! Everyone's ready," she exclaimed theatrically, and pointing at her sister's belly, she mouthed to the baby, "We're just waiting for *you!*"

Leah shut her eyes. The life within her felt heavy. Pregnancy had sapped every ounce of her energy. She felt shattered. She breathed through her mouth, relieved that Sarah and Esther lived so close. Their experience gave her confidence. The mother and daughter team took their birthing duties with utmost seriousness and, though latterly Esther had left the actual hands on delivery part to Sarah, most of Capernaum called for both women when birth was imminent. Every household had stories of mothers who died in childbirth and each woman faced the stark reality that new life burst into the world through agony and danger. Leah's jaw jutted in determination, she wouldn't fail Jairus this time.

She opened her eyes and watched her sister trimming a new wick for the oil-lamp.

"I'm glad you could stay this long, Joanna," Leah said, watching her sister fondly. "It's thanks to you I've carried full-term." Joanna made a dismissive, snorting noise. Leah held her younger sister's gaze, "Yes, it *is*," she insisted. "But, when my son is born, then you must go home. You've been away from Seth long enough."

"He'll be fine. You know Seth… he'll have a stream of people taking pity on him." Joanna said lightly.

"You know what I mean," Leah cleared her throat in a manner that signalled she would not be deflected, "It's not good to let the marriage bed go cold." Joanna threw back her head in laugher.

"Oh, you worry too much, sister. But," she added, tongue-in-cheek, "if it makes you feel better, when I get back to Sepphoris, I promise you, our bed'll set the whole city on fire!" The raucus guffaw was louder than she intended. She caught disapproval in Leah's eyes. "It's all right," she assured in a more subdued tone, "Seth's a good man. He understands."

Joanna drew the woollen shawl across her shoulders. "Anyway, in two shakes I'll be back again for the wedding." She left a pause for Leah's reply. There was none.

Joanna decided both parents were to blame for Kezia's over-protected childhood. Having a servant-girl in the house had shielded the girl from much of the hard work Joanna remembered from her own growing-up. Leah had kept the girl far too young for her age. Too young for marriage that was for sure! Joanna wondered what her sister *really* thought of Jared. She offered her own opinion.

"I think Kezie's too young for marriage!" her dark eyes tried to decipher her sister's expression. Impatient for an answer she prompted, "What d'you think?"

Leah massaged the top of her aching thighs. Her lips pursed in thought, "Jairus says Zebedee's got a good household." Lines deepened on her forehead, her discomfort was becoming unbearable. "Salome's kind… we've always got on well." Her hands moved over her distended belly. "Then there's Zebedee's sister and her two girls," Leah paused as she thought of the widow, Anna. "I don't know…may be just me, but strikes me Anna's jealous of Salome."

"Salome's got three sons, that's why!" Joanna replied. Leah took off her head-scarf and flicked her long dark tresses free.

"Just so long as Salome takes care of our Kezie," she said wearily.

"Sure she will," returned Joanna, "but what I meant was, is Kezia ready to be a *wife*?"

Leah's eyes closed again as she sighed, "We've got a while yet…there's Passover before the wedding… and she'll have plenty of weaving to do to get herself ready for the celebration." Leah knew exactly what her sister meant but she was not going to be drawn on the subject. She merely added, "Being with me when the baby comes will be good experience for her."

Joanna sensed her sister had terminated that area of conversation. She changed tack.

"I look at Kezie and I think, 'was I ever that young and innocent?'" Joanna exhaled loudly in jovial disbelief.

Leah chuckled, "You certainly were that young," she giggled, "but *never* innocent!"

The two women sat embracing the silence, preoccupied with both memories and premonitions for the future. Leah couldn't admit it to Joanna, but she knew her sister was right. She and Jairus had over-protected their daughter, but, surely it was understandable – she was their only child to have survived. Each time Leah's womb had prematurely shed a foetus, so Kezia's life became the more precious.

Leah felt strength haemorrhage from her. Too soon Kezia would be gone from their home. She'd be a woman quick enough then!

Joanna feared the forced leap from child to woman could spell trouble. Kezia was far too dependent on her father and old Mordecai. Oh well, she thought, she wasn't going to dwell on it; after all, what did she know about bringing up daughters?

She got up. "Can't let Adah's fire go out," she said, moving round the spinning wheel to fetch an armful of logs from the basket behind the door. Leah winced in pain. Joanna stared quizzically at her sister.

"You starting, dear?" she asked. Leah arched her back in an attempt to get comfortable. She gasped and grabbed the towel beside her.

"My waters have broken." She bit her lip and flopped down against the pillows, one hand out-stretched for Joanna's.

Chapter 5

JAIRUS waited for his uncle to continue. The old man was getting slow. Jairus felt irritated.

"Pharisees in Jerusalem have a high opinion of you, Jairus." Mordecai picked at his teeth with his thumb-nail. "There's a *secure* future ahead of you, but…" he hesitated, coughed and spat onto the cobbled ground, "You've got to …how shall I say?… You must distance yourself from Jesus…"

"Uncle," Jairus broke in, "the man's my friend…from boys, we've been together from boys." Jairus' patience snapped, "And… and look… Against all the odds he *healed* our Kezia when you yourself had come to tell me she was dead!" His voice rose in frustration, "You should have seen him… he was amazing… he didn't give up on her…I can't just…just turn my back on him!"

Mordecai grabbed at his arm, "Keep your voice down," he murmured, peering round furtively. "People are getting restive… the Zealots are pushing for a leader, and we can't have that. The last time we had one of these so-called Messiahs… well, you remember…" he spat again. "Roman soldiers… *animals!*" Mordecai lowered his voice to a hoarse whisper, "If it happens again, they'll be worse than ever . Jesus is *dangerous*… Your friendship is in the past, it cannot continue!"

Jairus stood up, furious at his uncle's patronising tone. "Uncle," he protested, "don't dictate to me!" Mordecai sprang to his feet to face his nephew. He forced his shoulders to straighten and his rat-bright eyes sparked in retaliating anger.

"If you value your life, Jairus," he rasped, "you'll not be seen with him again."

"What do you mean, 'if I value my life'?" Jairus couldn't help a dismissive sneer in his reply. He had no time for his uncle's melodrama.

"There are plans, my son," Mordecai whispered secretively, "there are plans. But – think carefully. In five year's time..." he shrugged, "maybe less, *you* could be in the Sanhedrin in Jerusalem." His lips curled into a smile, "The last time I spoke to Caiaphas..."

"Oh, Caiaphas!" Jairus had never liked the man, " that bigoted old f–"

"Hold your tongue!" Mordecai jabbed his index finger vehemently into Jairus' chest, his whisper so emphatic, spittle flew beyond his beard. "I'm telling you, boy, you keep *away* from him or..."

"Or what?" Jairus demanded standing his ground.

"Or you'll *die* with him!" Mordecai's threat was delivered with deliberate, chilling menace. "What'll happen to your precious family then? Eh?" His whisper rose to a strangled sqeak, "*Eh?*"

***

"Stay calm... I'll go for Sarah and Esther." Joanna made for the door. "Don't go away!" she grinned at Leah over her shoulder. Joanna sped to Simon's house, her heart thumping every footfall in a breathless mixture of thrill and panic.

Esther gathered her cloak and the sharp knife kept exclusively for cutting umbilical cords. Sarah flushed with delight that her friend was on the point of delivering full-term and Joanna, a stranger to child-birth, was only too pleased to trust her sister to the mother and daughter expertise. The three women bustled up the road to Jairus' house. Kezia and Adah skipped ahead, eager to see and do and be part of this awesome event.

"You girls needn't think it'll all be over in five minutes," Esther gave a stern warning. "Could be hours yet before the baby comes." Even when she was pleased, Esther managed to sound gruff.

Clutching her abdomen Leah uttered spasmodic yelps as the contractions increased. Joanna poured water into a bowl and placed it over the fire, then squatted by her sister's side allowing the midwives ample room for what they had to do.

"Keep calm. Take deep breaths now…" Esther instructed. Joanna took her sister's hand, "Do you want Jairus to know you've started?" she asked.

Leah shook her head. For weeks she had rehearsed in her mind the moment she would present Jairus with their son. She wanted that precious and intimate moment to be free of her personal indignities and anyway, Leah knew Jairus had many Synagogue duties to attend to; he and Mordecai would not want to be disturbed. Her breath became fast and shallow as the sharp pains made her eyes water.

Now the actual moment of delivery was looming, Kezia was seized with trepidation. Hot tears stung and overflowed as her mother writhed and sweated in pain. This was not the joy of childbirth Kezia had imagined.

Adah, waiting for Esther's instructions, hovered around the room like a bee pitching from flower to flower.

Sarah manoeuvred Leah into the birthing position.

***

Jairus stared at the wall... at the ceiling... at the blue velvet curtain obscuring the Ark and the Holy Scrolls. He sat at his desk staring with unseeing eyes. He didn't know what to do. With Leah's time near, she had taken to sleeping with Joanna and, with his sister-in-law's continual presence becoming an irritation, he sought a haven in the Synagogue.

He got up and stared through the window at the night sky. He tried to concentrate his mind into orderly, reasonable arguments but thoughts raced from one thing to another, jangling into dead-ends, criss-crossing his brain until the ceiling swam in front of his smarting eyes. Never in his life had he confronted such a crisis of conscience.

How could he possibly betray his boyhood friend? Jairus pictured their home village of Nazareth, an impoverished straggle of homes, a Synagogue and a well. Few tradesmen worked in the village, the baker, a weaver and two carpenters. Jairus' father was the weaver and Jesus' father one of the carpenters. The fever epidemic had decimated the village, leaving it little more than a hamlet, relegated to just another satellite village for the prestigious hill-top city of Sepphoris.

Memories flooded back of how they used to play round the ancient well while their mothers drew water... in his mind's eye he could see the two small boys eavesdropping by workshop doors, fastening on the mens' bitter conversations. The voices raised in loathing against the occupying Roman army still rang in his head.

Jairus looked around the empty Synagogue, in darkness save for the beeswax candle burning in front of the Ark. How grand in comparison to the simple, rough-hewn building in Nazareth where he and Jesus first learned to read the sacred Scrolls. A sudden rush of nostalgia seized him and he longed for the uncomplicated, innocent life of his boyhood.

What if Jesus *was* the Messiah? Jairus hid his head between his hands. Kezia's healing was nothing short of an act of God, but... why had Mordecai turned against him? Jesus had healed many people – done such good things – he gave down-trodden people hope. Exilaration swept over him each time Jesus came to his Synagogue. He was...different...*so* different. Charismatic! Jairus watched people entranced by his teaching, cheering and calling for more. What he, Jairus, would give to teach like that... to hold the attention and admiration of the crowd...

His memory tossed up theoretical accusations. If Jesus had the power to heal now, how was it he couldn't save his own wife? It didn't make sense. Dinah was a sweet girl. Jairus would have married her himself if Jesus hadn't got in first! Jesus had changed after Dinah's death...

God of Abraham! Jairus banged his fists together. What was he to do?

He turned from the window, sat down again and faced the wall. He refused to think about Jesus any longer. He had Kezia's dowry to sort out... and wedding celebrations to plan... and there'd be his son to take to the Temple... to celebrate and make a sacrifice and... Jairus ran a despairing hand through hair that was as thick and chestnut as his daughter's. Lord God of Abraham, would this night never end?

***

"Give us some air!" Esther waved Joanna to move away. Kezia flew to Joanna's bosom. Esther lifted Leah's tunic.

"Oh, by all that's holy!" she gasped. Kezia felt her aunt's body tense. She had no idea what Esther meant, but by her tone, and the effect it had on Joanna, it was bad.

"Look, see?" Esther spoke to Sarah, "Oh my Lord, it's a footling!" Joanna and Kezia craned their necks to see but the midwives' bodies screened Leah from their view.

Sarah put a hand to support an emerging bloody leg. "Poor lamb!" she exclaimed. Leah yowled in pain. Sarah waited but, regardless of Leah's efforts to birth the infant, the single leg protruded on it's own.

"Tricky…" the older woman murmured. She dreaded 'footlings'. In all her years she had only attended two, and both had died. As she stared at the single leg, it became obvious that it was beginning to swell. Taking stock of the situation she commanded, "Sarah, you must get the other one out, fast!"

Kezia lifted her head to Joanna. 'The other one?' her eyes queried, 'was it twins?'

"I'm sorry, my love," Sarah said softly, "I've got to do this. Your baby's coming out the wrong way round and I've… I've got to get his other little leg out… quick as I can."

Years of experience gave the older woman an air of dependability as she directed Sarah in the technique of inserting two fingers into Leah's vagina in order to bring down the other leg.

With tenderest care Sarah hooked out the second leg. Leah was rigid in her position and hyperventilating in fear and agony.

"Hush, now, Leah," Esther knelt by her head, "deep breaths and try to push as you breathe out." Esther demonstrated what she wanted Leah to do.

Leah leant back into Esther's arms, perspiration running

33

down her face and neck. Sarah focussed on the protruding, wrinkled buttocks. This was no straightforward birth. Sarah's lips and eyebrows pursed in fierce concentration. Her mother had told her about 'footlings' – but this was Sarah's first. She knew it would be touch and go.

"Give me a hand here, Adah," Esther was finding it hard to hold Leah's writhing shoulders and, for all her wispy appearance, Adah was as strong as any woman twice her age and size.

Kezia hated watching her mother in such a state. Distraught, she whispered into the folds of Joanna's headscarf, "Will she be all right?" Joanna was silent.

It was several seconds before she replied, "We just have to pray, chicken."

Leah's agonised scream reduced Kezia to sobs.

"Don't push for a moment, Leah," Esther ordered, "we don't want baby in shock. Hold steady now… that's it… *gooood…*"

"Nearly there, dear," Sarah encouraged.

The door flew open. Zebedee's wife, Salome, and his widowed sister Anna, burst in to lend their support. Anna considered herself an experienced midwife, and as Kezia was to be their future kin, she took it that she had every right to be at this birth. Salome bent to wipe Leah's face. Kezia wanted to run away, away from her mother's screams, away from the blood and the revolting smells.

In a lucid moment Leah implored, "Is he all right?"

"Hush, dear," Sarah whispered, "just let's get this over."

The women coo-ed in a soothing chorus of encouragement.

Sarah held the buttocks as skinny, veined shoulders emerged. Cramped on the floor she gingerly turned the silent, bloodied baby so the back was uppermost before the head emerged.

"Steady," Anna intervened. She had to say something. Sarah, sweating almost as much as Leah, glared at the univited advice from the uninvited Anna.

"Right, now, *push* girl," Sarah urged. Still supporting the baby's body she waited for the head to come. Leah screamed.

"Praise the Lord!" Sarah uttered as the head slid into her grasp.

"Clean out the mouth," instructed Esther. Immediately, Sarah wrapped a tiny piece of cloth round her fore-finger to prize open the lips and clear the mucous from the new-born airways. Suddenly, mewling, juddering cries penetrated Leah's semi-conscious. Too exhausted to speak, she sank limp onto the waiting mattress.

"Bring us the bowl, Kezie," Sarah called as she tied the cord before Esther made the cut. Gently she cleaned the crinkled and now bawling infant as Anna grasped the swaddling bands to help bind them round the little body. Esther smoothed Leah's hair, wiped a cloth over her face and Salome covered her with a fresh blanket. Adah cleared away the bloodied cloths and cleaned the floor.

"What is it?" wailed Leah, struggling to see her child, frantic to be told her prayers had been answered.

"Here you are." Sarah handed the delicate new life into the fold of Leah's arms, "'Tis all done now, my dear." The women gathered round, wreathed in smiles of palpable relief. "Take a look for yourself," beamed Sarah, exhilarated with her triumph. " Isn't she perfect?"

Chapter 6

MORDECAI pushed at the Synagogue's main door at the precise moment four young boys on the inside pulled it, jostling to escape their weekly Torah lesson. The boys flattened themselves against the wall in respect for the old Pharisee, allowing him to enter. Mordecai blessed the boys with his public smile, a display that creased skin around his mouth and eyes but held neither warmth nor sincerity. He squinted at the boys and muttered disparaging noises as his musty robes brushed their young shoulders. Once clear of the old man, the boisterous lads bolted for home.

The Pharisee scowled. His own advancing age and mortality felt assaulted by the boys' speed and vigour. He despised the knowledge that one day he would be replaced in the Pharisaic brotherhood by their like. Bile rose in his throat. Like an old wolf eyeing aspiring, young cubs from a distance, Mordecai winced with an involuntary spasm of jealousy.

With heavy steps he crossed the main worship area and opened the door to the side teaching room. Jairus slouched at his desk, bearded chin resting on a fist. Mordecai lowered himself onto the stone bench against the wall. Jairus didn't look up. A butterfly alighted briefly on the desk, then fluttered up and out of the window, leaving the two men to their silence.

"My son," Mordecai said finally, "you mustn't take it to heart." His voice gravelly with concern. His nephew made no response. The old man tried again, "Be patient, there's always 'next time'." He reasoned.

Jairus' fist crashed on the desk. *"Fourteen years!"* he yelled bitterly. "I've waited fourteen *years*! What have I done that the Lord must punish me like this?"

Mordecai sat without reply while he tried to steady the pumping in his chest, shocked by Jairus' raw anger. Thoughts chased each other along the long corridors of his mind. From his personal standpoint he considered his nephew had everything for which to be thankful. Mordecai's only son had been born lame and died young; his wife had been dead some eight years and the horizon of his own demise drew ever closer. He wore the blue Pharisee's robes with pride, but he recognised his influence was dwindling – he belonged to the past whereas Jairus was a man with a future. Jairus was Ruler of a thriving Synagogue, held the respect of the Chief Priest in Jerusalem, had a loving wife , and now – two daughters.

Mordecai glared at the disconsolate figure behind the desk. His strict pharisaic mind judged self-pity a sin.

"Instead of anger, my son, wouldn't it be better to remember the many blessings the Lord God has bestowed on you?" Hunched on the bench, Mordecai fixed faded eyes straight ahead. When Jairus didn't reply, he spoke his mind.

"You're in no fit state to be here today. Go home." He paused before adding, "I'll stay here… and pray for you."

A pressing weight bore down on Jairus' eyebrows, throbbing across his forehead. Overwhelmed by dark waves of anger and disappointment, his brain and mouth refused to function. Rising to his feet, Jairus walked to the window facing Jerusalem and stared out over the cluster of flat rooves and up into the cloudless sky. He stood for what seemed an eternity, until the voice behind him repeated, "Jairus, my son… go *home*."

***

Lying on her fleece, Leah watched the women bustle and chirp around her. They flitted across the room from one place to another like twittering bull-bulls, fluttering from branch to branch. Jared's mother, Salome had woven a striped blanket for the baby's crib. Anna, with nothing precise in mind, nevertheless, had no intention of leaving Leah's house before Salome, Sarah and Esther. Her pin-prick eyes fastened on Kezia's every move. She wondered how Kezia would handle and care for the infant?

Anna assumed a peculiar, jealous ownership of her brother's household and was over keen to cultivate Zebedee's future grandchildren. If Kezia's was the womb to carry those grandchildren, she felt it her responsibility to make sure the girl was a suitable mother.

Her mother's screams of childbirth firmly dispatched to memory, Kezia's face glowed with sisterly pride. Rocking the baby in her arms, she crooned a lullaby over the litte swaddled body. Sarah tried to tempt Leah's appetite with her latest batch of sweat-meats in a vain effort to distract her from Esther's over-detailed explanation as to how footlings nearly always died.

Joanna, her mission accomplished, talked to the air as she packed belongings into her basket ready for her journey home. Against this background hubbub, Adah stoked the courtyard fire under a black cauldron of simmering pottage.

"You're clucking like a *real* chicken now!" laughed Joanna

turning to Kezia. "And," she continued, wagging her finger and feigning a mischievous scowl, "don't think that cuddling your baby sister is any excuse to get out of your chores."

Anna's lips fastened in a thin, straight line. She nodded agreement without a trace of humour. Anna had to grudgingly admit, the girl looked a natural mother.

Anna had worried Kezia was too fanciful and pampered to be practical. Of course, she mused, she had a lot to learn, but, Kezia could prove a hard worker. Anna's lizard-like neck rippled as she swallowed. She would make certain sure the girl *would* work hard.

Jairus hovered in the doorway. He eyed the room full of women with caution. He felt as if his home had been invaded. Their chatter stopped as soon as the women saw him. Except for Kezia, they all melted to the back of the room as Jairus strode to where Leah lay on her mattress.

The eyes that looked up at him brimmed with a terrible sadness, and as her husband towered above her in his best Synagogue robes, she saw his gaze fixed on the empty cradle.

Jairus touched his wife's shoulder and creased his face in an effort to smile.

"You carried full-term," he said, and immediately regretted the remark. A nervous cough and he spoke again. "You must be tired." The forced smile stung Leah's heart. She noticed her husband came to her without so much as a glance in the direction of their baby in Kezia's arms.

"What shall we call her?" Leah asked softly. Jairus had at least decided on a name. Without hesitation he replied, "She will be called Zipporah."

"Zipporah!" Kezia echoed with delight. "Zip-por-rah! Oh look, Father," she beamed, "look – she opened her eyes – she knows her name!" Kezia swung the baby round to face her father. Jairus stared at the crinkled, red face being thrust towards him. He looked into the unfocussed eyes of his own flesh and blood. But not the faintest spark of fondness stirred in his heart. It was like looking at the offspring of a complete stranger. 'Oh God of Abraham!' Jairus sighed inwardly… 'if only she *did* belong to someone else.'

"Zipporah was the mother of the great Moses," Jairus spoke to Kezia in a controlled, teaching voice, "and who knows – one day this Zipporah will give birth to a great man too." He found it impossible to say 'our' Zipporah, he could only bear to speak of the child as an item, 'this' Zipporah. He turned back to Leah. "Rest now." His gut twisted with guilt. It felt as though an iron fist had crushed the breath from his lungs. He hated the sight of all those women gloating over the little runt. Jairus turned on his heel and left for the male bastion, his Synagogue.

Leah sank back on the fleece. Her husband had not even tried to disguise disappointment. She knew what was in his heart. She had failed him again. A black depression weighed on her mind and body as if she had been buried beneath a ton of lead. She closed her eyes and turned her head to the wall. Would she have another chance to bare him a son?

***

The meal that night resembled a wake. Leah withdrew upstairs to her bed, Mordecai and Jairus mopped bread around their plates without a word between them. Kezia sat glum-faced at the prospect of saying goodbye to Joanna in the morning, and Joanna, knowing full well that Jairus couldn't wait to see the back of her, remained close to the cooking pot. Adah licked her lips, emptying her bowl with relish. Even so, her keen, nut-brown eyes anxiously studied the four living statues.

From under badger-shaggy eyebrows, Mordecai watched Kezia nursing Zipporah. Gone was the carefree child. She had changed overnight. She would be too busy with the baby now to take his hand, to walk through the fields with him, to gather wild flowers and recite his favourite Psalms, to nestle her lithe body to warm his aged bones in the closing dusk. His shoulders sagged with the sorrow of loneliness and the dread of growing old. Uttering inaudible grunts he disappeared to his room. As if Mordecai's exit had been some sort of male signal, Jairus also got up and left the room.

Kezia returned a sleeping Zipporah to the cradle. "I'm going to miss you so much," she looked across to Joanna.

Joanna shrugged her shoulders, "I'll miss you too, chick", she smiled, "but…time for me to get back to Sepphoris… see what my Seth's been up to!" She made a face at Adah who giggled as she gathered the dirty mugs and bowls.

"Anyway," Joanna continued, "you've got your hands full now. And not many months to Passover, it'll be here before you know it. Seth and I'll see you then. And," she offered as an after thought, "you never know… your father might let you come to Jerusalem with us this year."

Kezia's eyes lit with expectation, "D'you think so?"

"Can't see why not. If your mother's well enough to travel that far by then… well… they can't leave you behind, can they!"

Zipporah stirred. Her face contorted. Infant concentration tensed her whole body and, for a second, she stopped breathing before expelling a full-on, peircing yell. Kezia flew back to the cradle,

"Oh, Zippie, *don't*," Kezia cooed in horror.

"You used to make that noise!" Joanna announced, unperturbed by the screams. "That's the cry of a will-full child!"

"What can I do?" Kezia looked to her aunt for a solution. Joanna scooped two last dates into her mouth. She picked out the stones before offering her advice. "Best get her out in the air – take her for a walk. Babies like movement!" she said with a knowledgeable air. "Go on… walk down to the harbour with her," she smiled. "It's only wind – she'll soon fall asleep."

Kezia fastened the wailing infant in a sling over her shoulder, tying the ends around her waist, and walked out into the lane. Zipporah's lower lip trembled before a fresh wave of sobs rang into the air. Kezia looked round, fearful in case anyone should accuse her of causing the baby to cry. The lane was empty. She couldn't see anyone, but that didn't mean she could not be seen. Eyes that watched her at every opportunity were watching now.

"Come on, you howly-boo," she whispered into the sling as she trudged down the lane to the harbour.

Joanna was right. With each step Zipporah's sobs juddered down the scale as she relaxed to the rhythm of Kezia's body.

Two men turned into the lane out of a narrow alley. Kezia instantly recognised Jared's older brothers. Smiling to herself she reasoned that, if James and John were home, then the Rabbi Jesus would be around somewhere. The fishermen, her future brothers-in-law, looked at the bundle on her shoulder, gave a cursory nod of acknowledgement and hurried past. She longed to shout after them, 'Where's Jesus?' but she knew she could never do that. A warm flutter of excitement tingled in her stomach as she neared the water's edge. Jesus often sat under the clump of trees to the right of the harbour…

She took the path that curved away south towards

Magdala, the neighbouring village to Capernaum. If only she could see him…

That morning, a gale had whipped wavelets into white peaks of frenzy but now, as Kezia picked her way along the gritty shingle, the lake was mirror smooth. A sudden blaze of turquoise flashed into the water as a kingfisher dived on a fish. From a warm rock, a lizard, head cocked sideways, fastened a beady eye on the girl before it scuttled under a boulder.

Kezia pulled the edge of the sling over Zipporah's face to protect her from the ravenous midges.

Suddenly she stopped. What was she doing? There was no sign of Jesus. She should take the baby home…

She turned to retrace her steps and – there he was – sitting alone with his back against a date palm. He smiled. Dejection evaporated in an instant and Kezia quickened her stride over the grass to where he sat.

"What've you got there?" Jesus called.

"My new baby sister," Kezia replied, breathless with the joy of finding him. "She was crying, so Joanna told me to walk her," she explained in unnecessary detail. "And it's worked!" she grinned at her achievement.

"Come and sit down," Jesus said to the hovering nursemaid.

"When I saw the brothers, James and John, I… I hoped you'd be here." A blush crept up her neck as she realised the Rabbi would know she had been searching for him.

"Ah, yes, James and John," he pulled a blade of grass, and played it between his teeth. He gazed across the water, streaked blue and silver with afternoon reflections.

"Of course," he nodded, "you're betrothed to their young brother aren't you."

This was not a subject Kezia wanted to talk about, but she

seized an opportunity. "Father says the wedding will be after Passover, you will come, won't you, Jesus?" She looked at him, willing him to promise. Jesus sighed, folded his arms as his eyes followed a flock of egrets fly past, flapping white wings against the clear sky. He didn't speak until the birds disappeared into trees further down the shoreline.

"Kezie, you don't know what you're asking." His voice slow with sadness. "I'm sorry," he went on, seeing her expression, "I'd love to be at your wedding, and you know the last thing I want is to disappoint you, but, well... I'm sorry, but it won't be possible."

"Why not?" Kezia's question shot out before she could check her tongue. She knew she had over-stepped the mark, it was the height of discourtesy to question a Rabbi. However, there was no hint of irritation in his voice as he replied:

"I have to go away, Kezie."

Kezia stared at the man in desperation. "Why? When will you be back?"

Jesus picked up a handful of rough, grey sand and let it slip through his fingers. "I don't know," he said after a pause.

"Take me with you," she pleaded in the earnest tone, not of the child he knew, but of the woman she was fast becoming. Jesus was taken aback by the intensity of her request. He leaned forward, his hand reaching to touch the side of her face.

"Kezie, oh dear Kezie... you can't come with me. Look, in a few months you'll be Jared's wife... the start of a whole new life."

" It's because I'm a girl, isn't it!" she accused, "You won't take me with you because I'm a *girl*!" Unchecked tears of anger moistened her thick eyelashes. "Why did God make me a *girl?*" she ranted. "If I was a man I *know* you'd take me with you..."

"Hush!" Jesus shook her arm. "Stop, stop." For a few seconds he studied the swaddled child asleep in Kezia's arms. "Kezie," the deep voice was gentle, "being a woman is the Lord God's choice for you. Just think, you have been given the power to bring the miracle of new life into the world, like this little one here." He stroked the velvet top of Zipporah's head. "Giving birth to another life is the most wonderful of all blessings." His eyes smiled. "God's miracle. Never forget that."

Kezia oozed frustration from every pore.

Jesus felt for his belt. He unfastened the kid pouch. Slowly he emptied seven gemstones from the pouch into his left palm. Kezia stared, were these the 'stones' her mother had told her about? The ones that had been laid on her fever-ridden body?

"You see these stones, Kezie?" Jesus touched each one with his index finger, "I want you to have them." Kezia studied the coloured rocks. She felt a sudden and inexplicable magnetic pull towards them, the flecks and markings seeming to dance in the sunlight as they rested in the Rabbi's hand. Jesus saw her fascination. He held them for Kezia to take.

Kezia stared in awe. "They… they're beautiful." She held them, examined them, caressed them. Their shapes varied but each one was roughly the size of a date. Kezia loved her mother's turquoise necklace that she wore for special celebrations, but the stones she held felt tangibly holy. She examined their colour and markings, trying to figure out a favourite. She turned over the fluorescent, milky stone, pushing it against a stone as yellow as liquid sunshine. She touched a dark, honey-coloured stone, which shimmered like the eyes of a wild cat but then, her attention was caught by tiny flecks of gold in a stone of deepest blue. She gasped at the green stone which looked as if it had been painted with green waves in perfect symmetry. The last two stones were the colour of the first buds of an almond tree, a pale, pearly green.

"It's almost as if they are living," Kezia murmured. Then she looked up and, in a wave of panic, asked, "What do I do with them?"

"They are healing stones," Jesus told her, "used from ancient times in many places in the world. But the stones need a keeper with a God-given gift." She looked into his face as he continued, "When you use them, you must pray in the name of the Lord your God," he held open the kid pouch for Kezia to drop the gemstones inside, "and, believe me Kezie, you will bring comfort and healing to many people." He folded Kezia's hands over the pouch, "Think of me and you will know when and how to use them. But," his gentle eyes darkened with intensity, "this is our secret," he said, "don't tell anyone that I've given you this pouch and… keep it with you… always."

Zipporah squirmed in her sling, giving notice she was awake and about to extend her lusty vocal talent to claim attention for herself.

"Time to take the little one home," Jesus spoke softly. Kezia's mind suddenly went blank; she struggled to think what she should say. At last she managed a small whisper:

"I won't tell anyone."

A wild moment overwhelmed her. She longed to fall on his neck, to kiss him as she had seen young girls kiss soldiers in stolen passion behind the harbour wall. She wanted to scream her undying love across the water and vow to follow him wherever he went… A tidal-wave of burgeoning passion surged through her body taking breath and speech away. Kezia longed to stay by his side – for ever.

In silent resignation, she adjusted Zipporah's position, tightened the sling around herself, then turned from the man who had not only brought her back to life, but had kindled the fires of her nascent love and desire. She turned from the man she had placed at the centre of her universe. Slowly, her eyes downcast, she walked away.

Once more the baby settled to the movement as Kezia made her way back home. At least with Jesus at her wedding she could bear it, but without him… She wondered where he was going? Maybe, if Jared joined his brothers James and John as Jesus' disciples, then she'd be able to go with them too…
… perhaps…

"What're *you* doing?" The sharp question shook Kezia from her day-dream. Jared stood arms folded, blocking her way.

"Er… I… I was walking Zippie," she flustered. Her gaze had been on the ground as her thoughts spun in wistful circles; she hadn't seen Jared approach.

"Liar!" he snarled. "You've been with that Jesus. I *saw* you," he mouthed with a cold quietness. He moved closer so that he was almost standing over her, eyes glinting with menace. "You'd better not go having any of your secret meetings when you're my wife."

Kezia's voice rose in defense: "It wasn't a secret meeting. He was just…there."

Jared caught hold of her arm, rough fingers digging hard into her flesh, "You shouldn't be down here. Soldiers come here to swim… naked!" He forced his face against her cheek. "You keep away, d'you hear?" She twisted her head away reddening with the pain in her arm. "Just remember," Jared hissed, "you belongs to *me*." His lips barely moved. His words were a whisper but stung like hailstones in a winter gale. Satisfied with her intimidation, he threw her arm away from him in the way he would discard a bone. Kezia stumbled in her haste to escape.

Regaining her balance, she clutched Zipporah protectively and ran for home.

A shiver of foreboding swept across Kezia's mind. To what kind of life had her parents consigned her? Her arm throbbed from the pressure of Jared's rough fingers. She must speak to her father... surely he would understand...?

Never before had she doubted anything Joanna had said, but now, there was a hollow ring to her aunt's blythe assurance that 'everything will be alright'. Jared scared her.

How could everything be 'alright'?

Chapter 7

"NO!" he barked. "No, she can't!" Jairus was adamant. "You need her here. There'll be plenty of other years, but she's *not* going this time." His thick eyebrows knitted in the sullen glare which, since Zipporah's birth, had become his permanent expression.

Leah inwardly recoiled from the brusque, sombre man who snapped at all her attempts at family conversation. Where was the handsome husband with even teeth and Jerusalem manners? The man who sat at her table, wore the clothes she washed and whose babies she had carried, was a stranger. Even Adah, their bubbly servant-girl, had long since stopped her humming and singing whenever Jairus was in the house.

Mordecai downed the remains of his wine. A glance passed between him and Leah. The old man cleared his throat; "She's of an age to go…"

"I said 'No!'" thundered Jairus, "She stays with her mother and… and that's final."

The chair legs squealed on the flagstones as Jairus pushed himself away from the table, stood up and marched out of the room. Kezia sat by her mother not daring to utter a word. What had happened to her father? He never used to be this way; it was as if he had forgotten how to smile. How she missed Joanna's warm, flamboyant presence.

"I'm sorry, Kezie," Leah put an arm round her daughter. "You'll go with Jared next year." Kezia looked across at her uncle. He opened his arms.

"Come here, child," he invited; she gladly moved to his embrace and let herself be folded in his arms. "Leave it with me," Mordecai consoled her, "I'll talk to your father." He stroked her hair, responding to the warm contact with her strong young body. "It's a difficult time for him," he tried to mitigate Jairus' behaviour. "Try to understand, Kezie, there's a lot on his mind just now."

**

Two sparrows bobbed and pecked at the crumbs Kezia had sprinkled along the window-ledge. A third fluttered to join them and for a few hectic seconds they pecked in harmony till the ledge was clean. Once they had cleared the last speck of bread, the birds flew off.

Kezia lay on her mattress staring up at the square window in her room. A lone sparrow, in the hope of left-overs, hopped onto the ledge. He fixed Kezia with the bright, black bead of his eye, clearly pleading a crumb for himself. "Sorry little bird," she said quietly, "I haven't got any more." The sparrow cocked it's head, hesitated for a brief, disbelieving moment, and was gone. Wistfully she gazed beyond the empty ledge into the grey sky. Clouds scudded up from the south and the humid air felt storm-heavy. "Lucky birds," she sighed, "you can fly away. I wish…" She turned on her side and shut her eyes in defeat.

Since Zippie's birth, everything had gone wrong. Never before had Kezia been conscious of sadness or tension in the home, but, watching the way her mother daily ignored her adorable little sister, Kezia felt deeply disturbed. She loved Zippie so much, and she loved her mother, but the way her mother treated the new baby was unnatural.

Leah sat for hours carding, spinning, or working the wooden shuttle across the low loom or she would be hidden away in her room, 'resting'. To all intents and purposes Adah ran the household. As for her father... Kezia sighed. Her laughing, gentle father had vanished. He seemed to spend all his time in the Synagogue, and when he came home he only growled and slammed doors.

Jesus had gone away too. James and John had gone with him, making the final break with their father's fishing business. The village women whispered about the Rabbi Jesus, his diciples and the group of women that attended them; it was hot gossip on street corners, the washing pool and the threshing floor. Kezia longed for Jesus to come back and stay with them like he used to when she was younger.

Despondency weighed on her shoulders... she had no idea when she'd see him again.

'After Passover,' she told herself, rolling back to stare up at the window once more, 'after Passover...it would be the wedding. *Her* wedding.' Kezia's face contorted in tearless horror. She wanted to scream at her father, 'I *won't* marry Jared', but, she knew it was useless to demur. It was all arranged. There was no escape – her fate was sealed.

She pictured Jared's ferocious-looking father, Zebedee. A towering figure of a man whose booming voice frightened many a child away from the harbour. She'd be living under his roof... he would be her father-in-law. Jared's mother was different – soft-spoken and thoughtful with kind eyes... A flock of egrets flew past the window, sharp white silhouettes against the leaden clouds. Kezia liked egrets, such delicate, graceful birds. She decided Jared's aunt, Anna, was more like a heron – thin and still and always silently watching – waiting to pounce on her least mistake.

Twisting a strand of hair between her fingers, absent-mindedly she put the hair into her mouth. She sucked on it at the thought of Jared's cousins. Her heart sank further.

Miriam, Anna's eldest, had a withered arm. No-one would marry her. She was destined to stay at home and care for her mother, or at least, that was the rumour Kezia heard at the washing pool. The village women pitied poor Miriam and with a twitch of their eyebrow, a nod and grimace, they gave heavy hints that Miriam was not the sharpest knife in the box. Anna's second daughter, Debra, younger than Kezia by a couple of years, was raucous, immature and generally irritating. She was betrothed to some boy over at Bethsaida…

Kezia yawned.

Neither of Anna's girls would be any company… not like Adah. Hard-working, faithful little Adah – she was her best friend.

Kezia wriggled under the blanket as distant thunder broke over the Syrian hills beyond the lake. To the young girl on the cusp of womanhood, the crashing and banging in the sky sounded like the overture of doom. She fancied her whole world was hurtling beyond her control. The thought of going to live with Jared in Zebedee's house felt like preparing for prison. Her last confrontation with Jared, when he accused her of meeting Jesus in secret, had truly unnerved her. Fear welled in her chest at the thought of Jared coming to her bed. She wasn't quite sure what he would do to her.

Once, she'd caught a glimpse of a ram mounting a ewe. She had watched until her mother pulled her away. Kezia tried to be logical. The ewe hadn't run away so, maybe it wasn't bad.

Idly she imagined herself on all fours as Jared mounted her, but, in the growing gloom of the room, Jared quickly faded out of her thoughts. She let her dreams fly to another man. The man she knew she would always love.

Her fingers felt under the mattress for the warm softness of the kid-pouch. She pulled it out and tipped the stones onto the blanket. In the darkness, the stones gave a luminous quality as though they contained some mysterious energy. She fingered them, marvelling that Jesus should entrust them to her. She remembered him telling her to pray to the Lord God. Kezia touched each stone with tender reverence – she had never come across such flawless stones. Touching them gave her a sense of being close to him.

Thunder crashed again. Lines of poetry her Uncle Mordecai recited from one of the great prophets fell into her mind; 'I looked at the earth – it was a barren waste: at the sky – there was no light.'

I looked at the mountains – they were shaking, and the hills were rocking to and fro. I saw there were no people, even the birds had flown away."

Lightning seared the sky followed almost simultaneously by a tremendous and prolonged crack of thunder, as if the sky was being torn apart in agony. The sparrows fell silent. Rain fell from the clouds in rods.

Kezia packed the stones away and hid them back under her bed. She realised she hadn't said her prayers to the Lord God. Her thoughts were interrupted as Adah crept into the room. Thinking Kezia was already asleep, the little servant-girl padded noiselessly to her mattress. The storm raged directly overhead. Kezia sat up and whispered over to Adah, "Do you believe in the Lord God?"

Startled by Kezia's voice, Adah wheeled round. "Oh Kes!

I thought you were 'sleep," Adah pulled her blanket up to her chin. "What a thing to ask!" she groaned. That kind of question was beyond her.

"*Do* you?" persisted Kezia. Adah was tired out; it was no time to be thinking such thoughts; she was only a servant-girl, she believed what she was told.

"Do *you*?" Adah batted the question back to Kezia as she turned her back to the window.

Lightning lit the room for a split second like the light of a thousand candles.

"No," Kezia replied. And speaking slowly and deliberately into the darkness she said: "No, I don't think I do… not any more."

Chapter 8

"TELL me all about it, won't you?" Handing Kezia a basket packed with bread, olives and dates, Adah did her best to mask her disappointment. "I shall want to know *everything* mind," she said, the corner of her mouth tilting upwards in an impish smile.

Kezia adjusted the blanket roll on her back. Her cup and water bottle hung suspended from the leather strap over her shoulder. She hooked the basket into the crook of her arm and stood grinning, intoxicated with the thought of going to Jerusalem. In one way she hated leaving Adah behind, but on the other hand, she couldn't wait to be on the road.

Leah, still far too weak for such an arduous journey, sat in the courtyard beneath the vined pergola. Adah gathered Zippie in her arms.

"Come on, no dawdling!" Joanna rounded up her niece to join the gathered huddle of women burdened with all the necessities for their journey. Like a shepherd leading his flock to new pasture, Mordecai, in his blue Pharisee's robes, moved to the front, the women following dutifully in his wake. Jairus had gone up to Jerusalem the previous week but the men of Capernaum had only just left. It was their custom to travel on ahead of the women in order to find a suitable place along the Jordan valley for the overnight camps.

A delicious thrill of adventure flushed in Kezia's cheeks. She walked along, eyeing her companions, relieved that she knew most of them. Over the years she had grown very fond of Simon's wife Sarah but was wary of Sarah's mother, the forthright Esther. Sarah and Joanna revisited the drama of Zippie's 'footling birth' and repeated their astonishment that Leah had survived such an ordeal.

Jared's aunt, Anna and her daughters Miriam and Debra, the trio she would be living with once she married, minced along, keeping themselves to themselves. Kezia wondered if she would ever be accepted under Zebedee's roof. Looking round she counted half a dozen of the women she met regularly at the washing pool. All of them had been to Jerusalem for Passover before, except Kezia and Debra. But, now she had reached the age of thirteen, Kezia told herself, this was her rite of passage to womanhood.

The topic of Zippie's birth and growth exhausted, Joanna linked her arm in Kezia's.

"However did your father agree for you to come to Passover this year?" Joanna was intrigued as to Jairus' change of heart.

"'Twas Uncle Mordecai," Kezia replied. "He said next year I'd be married and…" Kezia giggled, "I could be pregnant and not able to travel." Joanna's lips pursed. She nodded in agreement. Kezia continued, "He also told Father *he* wanted to show me Jerusalem while he could still look after me." Anticipation of their journey convulsed her with nervous giggles, "Uncle said *he* might be dead by next year!"

"Your Uncle Mordecai's a wily old fox!" Joanna laughed her infectious laugh. The women moved along in a hum of easy chatter and Kezia, who had never been out of Capernaum before, glowed with the frisson of adventure.

***

From the slope below Mount Arbel, Jared had been watching the travellers' camp that sprawled over the other side of the narrow valley. Wedged behind a craggy, limestone pillar he had a natural vantage point from which to see where the girl went when she came back from the market. Women from the camp collected their water from a spring that bubbled fast and pure out of the hillside. A well-worn path was visible between the camp and the spring, and, guessing the seductive foreign girl would go to the spring, he decided that was the best place to meet her.

Hunger gnawed in his gut, he'd been up on the hill for hours. In the fading light, he moved to where it was easier to scramble down the slope. With his mother , aunt and cousins gone to Jerusalem for Passover, Jared took advantage of his freedom. It was good without the women fussing him, even his father treated him more like a man. Without female prattle, endless questions and pointed looks, he could do what he liked.

Making his way towards the spring, Jared flexed his developing muscles. Dark hair covered his arms and each day he felt his beard thickening. He fantasied about himself, likening his body to the handsome King David – the young king about whose prowess women sang their songs. Jared smirked as he imagined women admiring his physique, desiring him, throwing themselves wantonly at his feet.

Cooking smells drifted towards him on the breeze, dogs barked in warning, but, keeping to the path, he was well clear of the travellers' tents. Above the spring he found a redundant termite mound which gave him just enough concealment from the camp. He sat and waited.

But not for long.

The girl had seen him leaping and sliding down the slope, and she knew what he wanted. Pert and excited, she left her father's tent and took a pitcher to the spring. Pretending surprise at meeting him, her cheekbones lifted so high as she smiled that her eyes disappeared behind slits below her thin eyebrows. Jared watched her bend to fill the pitcher wondering what to say. When she stood up, the pitcher filled, he pointed to his chest, *"Jared,"* he said, feeling somewhat foolish. Then pointing at her he lifted his eyebrows waiting for her response.

The girl giggled, "Pei Qi," she piped. For a few moments they stood smiling awkwardly at each other, unable to do anything but repeat, 'Jay-red' and 'Pye Chee'. Glancing over her shoulder to make sure no one else from the camp was in sight, still smiling, Pie Qi held out her hand.

Jared fumbled in the purse on his belt. He offered her one denari, at which Pei Qi shook her head, chortled with disbelief and held up three fingers. Jared swallowed hard. His heart pumped wildly at the prospect of what three denarii would buy. Her silk tunic clung lightly to the curves of her petite body, and at that precise moment his pulsating lust would have lavished three hundred denarii to possess her.

Securing her pitcher against a rock, the girl pocketed his coins. Then, with an irrisistable little noise, half chuckle, half gulp of delight, she grasped his hand. Nimble as a young gazelle, she skipped further up the hillside, and lead him into the mouth of a shallow cave.

***

Open green pasture and small, stone-hedged fields stretched in a fertile ribbon down the Jordan River valley as far as Kezia could see. Far over to her left the lofty mountains of Moab rose in a range of russet hills and deep ravines. On her right, the familiar gentle slopes of Galilee had long since given way to loftier, sculpted crags, intimidating in their starkness. Kezia marvelled at the contrast of the endless, open hills and lush valley with the tightly packed, black stone houses and maze of lanes she had left behind in the fishing village of Capernaum.

The Capernaum pilgrims had been on the road for three days when the new sandals rubbed a sore on Kezia's big toe. Joanna made her a wad of greased sheep's wool to wrap round her toe to ease walking. Kezia was too embarrassed to mention how her shoulders and shins ached with the unaccustomed distance.

"Where will we camp tonight?" she asked Joanna. Her aunt strode along as if every day she walked twenty odd miles before breakfast. Joanna squinted ahead, searching for a landmark.

"We can't be far from Jericho," she said, vaguely. "I seem to remember…" she shaded her eyes, "we, er… we camp by a little stream. And that means," she slung an arm across Kezia's shoulders, "that means my dear chicken, tomorrow… you'll have your first sight of Jerusalem!"

Kezia mirrored Joanna's wide grin and, as she looked to the others, they too were smiling and nodding, each thrilled with personal anticipation. Even Anna. Kezia looked to her Uncle Mordecai who responded with a wink of encouragement. He knew how proud Kezia would be when she saw her father sitting with the Teachers of the Law in the Temple. It was an unusual honour for a Synagogue Ruler from a lowly village to be invited to stay with the High Priest in Jerusalem. Mordecai's hopes for Jairus' elevation to the Sanhedrin rode high.

Esther leaned wearily on her stick, grateful that Sarah was able to carry both their bundles. Her skin stretched tight round her swollen legs, making each step a painful effort.

"Thanks be to the God of my Fathers I've made it another year," she struggled to talk and walk at the same time. "Don't think my poor old feet will er… will make this journey again." Esther summoned up a determined spurt to which the younger women gladly responded; each one eager to end the day's trek, pitch camp and eat.

Dust billowed in the road behind them. Mordecai spat phlegm onto the road with deep-seated hatred. "Huh!" he snarled, "I thought we hadn't seen the 'dogs' in a while."

Horses hooves vibrated on the compacted earth, felt before they could be seen. In moments a detachment of soldiers came pounding down the road towards the tired group of women. Realising they were a mile adrift from Seth and the rest of the men, Mordecai marshalled the women off the road. They cowered on the verge waiting for the cavalry to pass. The soldiers thundered past, swords pointed in horizontal menace. Deep-throated cries of "Aaargh!" were calculated to induce maximum fear in the women.

But as soon as the horses had thundered passed, the soldiers pulled them to a hoof-juddering halt. The Commander trotted back to the huddled group, playing his whip between his fingers.

"You!" he shouted at Mordecai. "You… you stinking old goat! What're you doing with all these bitches? Any spare for us?" he sneered over his shoulder to his men.

Mordecai drew himself to his full height, "We have the right to celebrate Passover in *our* Holy City," he adopted an imperious voice. He glowered at the young man astride the sweating mare, a quintessential picture of arrogance in brass helmet and scarlet tunic. The soldier manoeuvred the horse in front of Mordecai. He jabbed his whip into the Pharisee's face. He leant over the saddle; *"Right!* You don't have any *rights* old man," he drawled, "You've been granted *permission* that's all. The great Caesar graciously grants you permission to recite your mumbo jumbo in that god-forsaken slum-on-a-hill you call a 'city'. Huh!" He reared the mare at the women who fell back in terror. "You should go to *Rome* ," he bawled at the Pharisee, "Now, that *is* a city! *Peasant!"*

He snatched at the reigns, pulling the horse almost on top of the old Pharisee. The Commander cracked his whip against Mordecai's staff with such force, the staff clattered from the old Pharisee's grasp.

The mare snorted, nostrils flared, agitated hooves pawing the beaten earth of the roadway.

"Take your whores," the soldier barked. Then he noticed Kezia. She was the only one in the group worth looking at, glorious chestnut hair, waving down on her shoulders, slim figure and eyes that looked straight through him in naive defiance. He looked her up and down. Her defiance ignited a challenge in his loins. 'Oh yes,' his imagination took flight, 'that one is ripe for the taking.'

Diverting his gaze from Kezia to the Pharisee, he smirked at the venom in the old man's eyes. The soldier reverted his gaze back to the fledgling woman. He lingered on her breasts as his tongue wiped slowly over his lips.

He imagined ripping away her cloak… tearing down her tunic. He longed to grapple her naked body to the ground… feel her defenseless arms beat against his shoulders as he overpowered her…

Inhaling deeply, he shifted uncomfortably in his saddle. He weighed his immediate lust against his prospects of promotion. His orders were strict: 'Keep the peace!' Raping a Jewish girl at Passover could incite an uncontrollable mob. He sniffed, tugged once more at the reigns, wheeling the mare away from the group. Ambition won. But he would take her some other time... she was worth waiting for.

"Bloody festivals!" the Commander bellowed, whipping at his mare as he rode off at the head of his battalion. Twice a year he had to make the tiresome journey – sometimes more, depending on the degree of unrest the Governor ordered to be quashed. All along the road through the Jordan valley he passed travellers, pilgrims and traders, religious men and civil servants, all of them making their way to Jerusalem. What did they see in the place? It was nothing compared with the city of his birth. The Commander took perverse pleasure in his power to make carts swerve off the road and sweep people into the gutters as his detachment cantered past.

'Cursed people,' he breathed, 'why couldn't they be trusted to celebrate in a civilised manner?' He dug his spurs into the mare. Their festivals always ended in riots and bloodshed. Oh, how he hated Jerusalem... cramped, dusty place... full of belligerent peasants and those arrogant, self-serving Priests – he despised them all! Their meat was tough and Jerusalem prices were higher even than Corinth! He counted the days to when he would be relocated back to the army's coastal headquarters at Caesarea.

As soon as the soldiers had galloped away, Kezia, pale and shaken, dashed to her uncle. Soldiers had not frightened her before. The ones based in Capernaum never harassed local people; in fact the Garrison Commander there had even been to their house to speak with her father. Her mother said one of the Centurions had donated a small fortune to enlarge her father's Synagogue.

"Dogs!" spluttered Mordecai holding Kezia close. "He'd have to kill me before he touched you, my lovely." She quivered in his arms. Something in the Commander's eyes unnerved her. She didn't need to be told what he wanted. A door slammed shut on her carefree life. Kezia knew childhood was gone for ever.

Seth ran to Joanna. "We saw the soldiers...did they...? Are you alright?"

"We're fine," Joanna breezed, "we had Mordecai to fend off the army and, as if he wasn't fearsome enough, Esther threatened to run them through with her fish knife!" Everyone laughed loud guffaws of relief at Joanna's description.

Kezia loved the way Joanna could turn anything into a joke. Laughter lifted their tension and she watched Seth's lips tenderly brush against his wife's cheek, concern written all over his clean-shaven face. Kezia liked Seth, he was fun – and his bizarre purple headdress! No-one else but Seth could wear such an outlandish turban.

The men had joined another group of pilgrims from Nazareth, Cana and Sepphoris, and within half an hour, the women found an encampment of tents pitched beside the stream Joanna had remembered. Kezia took her turn with the rest of the women in the nightly task of baking bread and preparing the potage. All turned to and shared chores as naturally as if they were one family by their own fires at home.

Mordecai, being the only Pharisee present, prayed the blessing over the food and wine before they ate.

"Tomorrow," he intoned, " as we approach Jerusalem, we shall sing Psalms of Ascent, just as our fore-fathers have sung every year for hundreds of years. We will make camp on the outskirts of Bethany where, I think several of you have cousins. Then," Mordecai cleared his throat and looked into the sky as if he wanted to make sure God himself was listening, "we'll celebrate Passover in Jerusalem no matter how many foreign dogs foul our Holy City." He raised his wine cup and sang:

"O give thanks to the Lord, his love is eternal." The people, their weary faces flushed in the camp-fire glow, stood to raise their wine cups, suddenly envigorated by the word 'Jerusalem'. They shouted their response in a burst of confident energy:

"His love is eternal!"

***

Sleep eluded Kezia that night. She gazed up at the stars wondering how Adah and her mother were coping back at home with Zippie. Then, when she finally shut her eyes, rearing hooves smashed so vividly into her face, her heart raced in re-lived panic. She tossed her head from side to side in an effort to blot out the memory of the baying horse and its leering rider. Somehow, something cruel and intimidating in the Commander's eyes, reminded her of Jared.

No! No! She wanted Jared out of her brain too.

Kezia reached for the kid pouch secured on her belt. She caressed the soft leather. By now she knew each stone by it's shape. Just to feel them between her fingers brought a sense of calm. The Rabbi's stones meant more to Kezia than all the diamonds and precious gems she'd been told adorned the High Priest's breastplate. She wore them each day hidden beneath her tunic, and at night she stowed them under the mattress. A secret that only Adah shared.

The darkness was warm and the tent, even with the flaps open, felt airless. Kezia used her blanket for a pillow. She lay awake between Joanna and Miriam, both of whom had long been breathing the measured rhythm of deep sleep. Kezia stared out at the myriad pin-pricks of light sprinkling the endless heavens. The longer she stared the more of distant clusters she could make out. Was Jesus watching these same stars? Surely he would be in Jerusalem already. If only she could see him...

Tomorrow they would reach the Holy City... and... maybe...?

***

Well before sunrise, the men had the camp dismantled and everyone assembled, eager to begin the final few miles of their journey. Jericho, a sprawling town of sand-coloured, flat roofed dwellings, clustered in a green oasis at the very edge of the Judean wilderness. The town sat at a main cross-roads for travellers coming up from the Salt Sea to the south, across from Moab in the east, the Galilee to the north and Jerusalem to the west. Esther instructed Sarah to take the women into Jericho's market to stock up on fresh fruit and vegetables for the evening meal when they pitched camp in Bethany. Esther wagged her head from side to side.

"You'll be too tired to go foraging when we get to Bethany," she scolded. "And they won't have anything worth buying by the time *we* get there." She stabbed her stick in the dust for emphasis. "I've seen the poor benighted things they try to sell in Bethany!" She sat heavily on a convenient boulder. "Go on... get the things now, and be quick about it!"

Sarah's mother, swathed in a shawl, bent and tired with age yet still the dominating matriach, dispensed her orders with undiminished force. Kezia's heart went out to Sarah.

Mordecai strutted over to the women, "We'll meet you the other side of the market, by the Jerusalem Gate," he informed them. Turning to Kezia he added, "It's a dangerous road from Jericho up to Jerusalem. We must keep together, and the Lord God will watch over us." He touched the side of her head, his fingers lost in the thick waves, "Hurry on with the women and maybe you'll find some pomegranates for me, eh?" He winked.

Anna was delegated to remain with Esther and give her an arm over the uneven road. Meanwhile Joanna and Sarah forged ahead at such a pace, Kezia and the others were obliged to trot in order to keep up. The market stalls appeared identical to stalls in Capernaum, except there was no fresh fish and Jericho's fruit was so plentiful, it piled in haphazard, colourful pyramids.

Purchases complete, but no pomegranates for Mordecai, the company regrouped by the Jerusalem Gate, then struck out on the road taking them westwards away from the town, across the narrow plain and on up into the Wilderness. The road to Jerusalem meandered up the wadi floor and, with barren mountains rising steeply on either side, Kezia felt she was entering a roofless tunnel. Seth and the men from Sepphoris walked in front leading four laden donkeys. Mordecai followed with Kezia and the women.

For about five miles the sheer height of the cliffs along the ravine shaded them from the sun's direct heat, and the men led the pilgrim group in songs and prayers. A collective excitement lifted their spirits as they climbed, onwards and upwards, out of the wadi into the piercingly bright wilderness sun. Their cloaks billowed in the desert wind and the donkeys dropped their heads to shield their eyes against the swirling grit.

"What d'you think of the wilderness, Kezie dear?" Sarah asked when they stopped for water and to give older women in the group time to catch their breath. Kezia felt over-awed by the vast scale of the unfolding landscape. If she was truthful, it was a shock. She found it ugly and scary. She expected robbers to burst out from behind a rock at any moment and bludgeon them all to death. No! The wilderness was not her favourite place.

Clusters of Bedouin tents blended into remote valley shadows and, way ahead on the horizon, shepherds guarded flocks dotted over distant slopes. Every hillside was rutted with the ribbon paths the sheep and goats had made over the years. Apart from those few signs of life, the wilderness seemed just mile upon mile of vast, desolate, baking... nothing.

Sarah guessed, by the girl's uncharacteristic silence, that the hostile surroundings had come as a major culture shock. Kezia had, after all, spent her entire young life in the lush crescent on which Capernaum had been built, an area dappled with shady oaks, poplars, and terebinth, groves of date palms, olive trees and small fields of flax and barley. She was used to gentle, rolling hills and the distant, mysterious heights of Syria above the lake. Sarah tried again to engage her:

"Expect we'll all be glad to get to Bethany?" she prompted. "There's a house where Jesus stays..." she had Kezia's full attention. "They're friends of my cousins, so, we might all meet up." Sarah beamed encouragement. She herself couldn't wait to find her husband, Simon, and the prospect of meeting up with Jesus brought a wide smile back to Kezia's face.

Suddenly a warning roar came from the men ahead. Sarah glanced up to see them gesturing to the women to get away from the road. She wondered what on earth was the matter, but then she saw it.

"Don't look, Kezie," she breathed, yanking the girl off the track.

"What is it?" Kezia caught Sarah's alarm.

"Oh, *look*!" screamed Debra running to Sarah. Joanna, who had been walking with Seth, was at Kezia's side in a flash; with one hand she folded part of her cloak round Kezia's shoulders and with the other hand she grabbed Debra's scrawny arm.

"Stop staring, child!" she commanded. "*This* way and mind you don't fall." Joanna led the women on a hasty detour away from the road. They scrambled over the scree to where the men waited for them.

No-one spoke.

What Kezia saw that day in the Judean desert would remain etched on her memory for ever. At the side of the road a disembowelled figure hung like strips of blackened leather flapping against a rough, Roman cross. Eight to ten weeks exposure to the desert sun and wind, had dried the flesh and shrivelled every human feature. The Roman Emporor had passed a law that crucified victims could not be taken down and buried but had to hang as a deterrent to anyone else who dared challenge the authority of mighty Rome.

Kezia's stomach heaved. She wretched in revulsion. She had heard the word crucifixion but this was the first time she'd witnessed what it meant. She trembled at the appalling and terrifying sight.

Mordecai pushed through the men to find Kezia, and leaving Joanna, she ran to him, throwing herself on her uncle in distress.

"How can they do such a thing?" she sobbed into his chest.

"Foreign scum!" the old man spat. "Romans trample on us as if we were ants under their feet. Oh, Kezia," he stroked her hair, "you had to know sometime. These evil scum have crucified thousands of our people, *thousands* of them, I tell you. They want to stamp us out, but one day… *one* day the blood of our brothers will be avenged!"

Mordecai raised tear-filled eyes to the sky, "'God will surely *break* the heads of his enemies!'" he thundered a phrase from his beloved book of Psalms. The men from Sepphoris exchanged uneasy glances at the Pharisee's outburst, but said nothing. The incident acted as a spur for the whole group as they hurried from the scene of death in order to reach Bethany as soon as possible.

Kezia vowed she would for ever hate the Romans and anything to do with Rome.

Chapter 9

SARAH was relieved to have Anna walk with her mother and hold on to Esther's arm. Esther had stumbled too many times since the site of crucifixion. It made Sarah realise her mother's health had deteriorated far more in the last twelve months than she had noticed. The way her mother leant so heavily on her, had made her lower back ache. Sarah felt desperate to get her mother to Bethany for a proper rest at their cousin Rachel's home.

Any suggestion that the doughty matriarch should 'rest' in Bethany while everyone else went to celebrate Passover in Jerusalem was bound to cause another row, but, Sarah rationalised – she'd just have to meet that when it happened. She'd get Simon to talk to her, he was the only one she ever listened to… Simon or Jesus. That's if she could find either of them! Passover attracted thousands of pilgrims to Jerusalem but she knew most people from the Galilee would camp near Bethany.

Sarah paused briefly to drink from her leather water bottle. 'Oh well,' she thought, 'I can't bother the others with my problems.' She clutched her head-scarf tight against the desert wind: 'Stubborn old woman,' she sighed with exasperation, 'should've stayed home!'

"Not long now!" shouted Mordecai, eyes alight with

exhileration as he neared the Holy City. Kezia looked round for Joanna but she had linked with Seth again and was deep in conversation. Debra and Miriam had also joined the Sepphoris group and now Sarah and Anna walked each side of the struggling Esther. Kezia was glad not to be walking with Anna. She couldn't get on with her somehow, at least Salome was more like her own mother.

The Galileans concentrated on banishing the memory of the roadside crucifixion and regain some semblance of normality. Walking with Mordecai as he reminisced helped take Kezia's mind off the man on the cross.

"You know, Kezia," her uncle spoke as if he was about to recount an epic from scripture, "you know, I've made this journey nearly every Passover for fifty years." Kezia gasped. "Yes," the old Pharisee continued, "before your father was born, I walked this route with my father and his father." He breathed deeply as if the very air was holy. "The Passover meal is the same and the words we say are the same, but… the *joy* is always fresh." Memories envigorated him. "Do you understand?" He studied her fresh, unsullied face. "Every year we look back to God's hand in our history when Moses led our people out of slavery in Egypt." He paused, "… And every year we long for his Messiah." He squeezed Kezia's hand, "One day … one day he *will* come, my dear. We…" Mordecai's words were drowned by a shout from Seth:

"There! Over there!" All eyes strained to the far hill, visible at the head of the valley. Kezia could make out a vast rampart on the horizon.

"Is that the Holy City?" she whispered. Mordecai's sight was fading but his memory was chrystal clear as to the image before them. "Yes, my child." His sonorous tone echoing against the desert rocks, "The Holy City and the Temple of

71

Jerusalem!" The whole group halted to gaze in wonder. Kezia was not the only one whose eyes became unexpectedly moist.

Re-energised by the sight of Jerusalem, their spirits rose and the rest of their uphill trek to Bethany passed in a babble of anticipation. The wind died away and even the donkeys sensed the end of their journey and food.

To Kezia's huge disappointment, from where the men pitched their camp, Jerusalem, even though it was barely two miles away, was obscured by the hill range they called the Mount of Olives. The slopes around the little village of Bethany had spawned a temporary tent city, tucked down between the bushy olive groves and cypress trees. The ground transformed into a close patchwork of tents, animals, children, cooking fires and washing lines. Plumes of whispy smoke spiralled into the sky above the evening fires and the air filled with thick fumes and smells from a hundred cooking pots. Kezia stood by the women's tent soaking up the scene. So many people – so much *noise!*

"Tomorrow," Joanna said, grasping Kezia's hands and dancing her in a circle, "we'll walk over the Mount of Olives and then you will see *all* of the city." Joanna hugged her tightly, praying the experience of the dried cadaver on the cross earlier in the day hadn't shattered her niece's excitement for the city. "But," she smiled, "as my dear Seth will always tell you, 'first things first' – we must *eat* and then… a good night's sleep!"

Meal preparation became bonding time amongst the women and girls, a time when they could talk back over the day's events and set them in manageable context. They had just finished eating when the rain started. Darkness draped the hillside as the heavy shower drove the women into their tents. They listened to the songs from surrounding tents, as people burst into spontaneous singing of psalms and folk songs. Some tunes Kezia recognised, but most were totally new to her and many in strange languages.

High up in the Judean hills, the air was degrees colder than the previous night in the Jericho valley. Kezia snuggled into the thick cacoon of her blanket. She lay wide awake long after the chatter in the tent had subsided and the other women were asleep. She heard a relay of good-natured shouts as friends parted for the night. Despite the rain, it was obvious many were determined to make the most of their partying. Lulled by the insistent drum beats, the rhythmic clapping and carolling, she pictured couples dancing and whirling by damp camp fire embers.

Every so often the human sounds were interspersed with bleating sheep or the breying of a donkey. It seemed to Kezia as though the whole world had converged on Jerusalem for Passover.

In the gloom of the tent the emaciated, blackened corpse returned to her mind. Haunted by the surreal image, she began to wonder who it was… what crime had he committed to deserve that brutal death… why were Romans so cruel, so sadistic? They must be the most vile people on earth to carry out such despicable savagery.

She shuddered; what would she see tomorrow?

***

"Can't believe it!" declared Sarah, linking her arm in Joanna's, "Mother's quite happy to stay in Bethany… no fuss, no argument… not like her at all!" Joanna looked back to make sure Kezia was following before murmuring, "She must've been worn out by the time we got here last night."

The women approached the brow of the Mount of Olives, traditionally the favourite place from which to see the panorama of Jerusalem. The immense Holy Temple never failed to cause a gasp of wonder. Mordecai declared King Herod's flamboyant, imposing creation was the most staggeringly beautiful building in all the world. Since conquering the land of Israel, the Roman Emporor had stripped the Jews of all political power. Nevertheless, under rigorous supervision, they were allowed to retain their religious leaders and customs. So long as the High Priest kept his side of the bargain and crushed the merest whisper of insurgence against Rome, then he and his entourage were extended the privilege of religious autonomy. This invidious arrangement well suited both Roman authorities and the High Priest.

However, to the taciturn individual soldier of the occupying troops, the expanse of stone, marble and gold was nothing but a blatant gesture of arrogant rebellion.

Anna's sharp eyes scoured every road junction lest there be the remains of more horrendous crucifixions. Debra's chilling fascination with the murdered corpse, a fascination that bordered dangerously on delight, had been a shock. Towns and villages in Galilee were mercifully sheltered from the full impact of Roman occupation but the capital city was another matter. Miriam dutifully towed behind her mother but Debra's eyes were out on stalks for anything macabre.

"Busy today!" Joanna observed. Below them in the Kidron valley, the roads choked with pilgrim traffic. All along the road coming in from Bethlehem, the road through the valley immediately below them and the road winding up the other side of the city wall leading to the Damascus Gate, a continuous tide of humanity threaded their way towards the gates in the fortified city walls.

Intermingled with people Kezia watched the camel trains, flocks of sheep and goats, dozens of donkeys and ox-drawn carts piled with everything from cooking pots to cages of live chickens and doves. A constant drone from people and animals echoed up the hillside to where the women stood.

"Look!" yelled Debra pointing towards the city ramparts. Kezia's eyes glazed in awe at the great marble edifice dominating the city.

"Soldiers!" shrieked Debra, "Will they kill us?"

"They're on guard in case there's trouble," rebuffed Joanna who, having seen it all before, was increasingly irritated by Anna's youngest. "There's always some sort of disturbance around Passover. Hot-heads with no brain pretend they can fight against the imperial power of Rome." Joanna tried to make light of the military presence, "You won't even notice soldiers by the time we leave Jerusalem."

Anna delivered a smart swipe across Debra's head, "And keep your voice down!" she hissed, "How many times have I told you?" Anna's lips disappeared inside her mouth in disapproval.

"Have you seen anything quite so wonderful? ", Sarah whispered reverently.

Wide-eyed at the magnificent building, Kezia queried: "Is that real *gold*?" The sun glinted off the ornate capitols that topped the great white marble pillars and the carved edgings to the gigantic wooden doors.

"Only the best for the Lord our God," was Joanna's laconic reply.

"*Love* the stone," sighed Sarah, a remark which made Kezia suddenly realise that, apart from the white marble of the Temple, all the buildings in and around the city walls were built in the same warm, honey-coloured lime stone. Such a total contrast with the dull black, volcanic stone of Capernaum.

"Let's wait here a while." Joanna settled herself on a low wall beside the road. "Seth and Mordecai won't be long." She turned a smiling face towards her neice who stood mesmerised by the streams of people pouring in and out of the city gate.

"What's that?" Kezia pointed to a square structure to the right of the Temple, "The one with a flag."

"That?" Joanna yawned, "That's the Antonia Fortress. It's where the Roman Governor keeps his men and horses. He stays there too when he comes up from Caesarea." She wiped the back of her hand across her forehead. "The flag means he's there now." She spoke with a finality of expression that defied more questions. Sarah tried to move the subject away from the fortress as she said to Kezia:

"See that grand house over there, Kezie?" Kezia nodded as she spied the palacial dwelling abutting the city walls, "Well, that's where your father's staying." Kezia gaped. "That's where Caiaphas, the High Priest, lives." Sarah finished.

Kezia was speechless. Fancy, her father staying in a mansion like that!

Seth came up on the end of Sarah's statement, playfully he slipped a blindfold over Kezia's eyes, "And if you misbehave," he said in a theatrical whisper, "you'll find yourself locked in the High Priest's dungeon for ever and *ever*!"

"Oh, take no notice of him, chicken," Joanna confiscated the blindfold and threw it back at Seth, who ducked behind the wall laughing.

Mordecai began the steep descent through the area of huddled graves where he'd been to place a stone on his wife's grave. Alarmed by a wild crowd of people making their way along the path to where the women were waiting for him, he quickened his pace. The shouting and ululating grew louder – there was no way he would be able to reach the women before the mob.

"What are they shouting?" Debra enjoyed unsavoury things from a safe distance, but was clearly disconcerteded by the rowdy tide of men, women and children fast bearing down on her. The women strained to decipher the chanting.

Seth rejoined them, adjusting his turban.

"Sounds like 'Hosanna'… something…" he offered. He jumped on the wall to see better. "Looks like they've got someone on a donkey… not sure… can't see til they're past that wall." He waited "…Yes, they're leading someone but… too many people to see properly."

Seth pulled the women into the verge against the wall, "It's a happy crowd," he assured them, "they won't harm you." Kezia watched a sea of palm branches waving to the rhythm of the peoples' chant, surging ever closer. Apprehension fused into a thrilled fascination at the unusual procession; she only wished her father could be standing with her, he'd explain it all to her.

Suddenly, through a forest of arms and branches she recognised the figure on the donkey.

"Jesus!" she yelled in delight and turned to Joanna, "It's Rabbi *Jesus!*" At that moment, Sarah caught sight of Simon, her husband, and behind him his brother Andrew with Jared's brothers James and John. All the disciples were there… and more. Propelled by the atmosphere, the women joined the shouts of "Hosanna! Blessed is he who comes in the name of the Lord." Whoops and whistles and singing escalated into a hysterical mantra as Jesus rode level with Seth and the women. Kezia stood on tip toe waving and yelling out her

'Hosanna' at the top of her voice, willing Jesus to see her. For a split second Jesus' eyes locked into hers – her heart exploded with joy. Before she could breathe, the moment was passed. Jesus was gone – submerged in the ecstatic crowd. It happened so quickly Kezia couldn't even remember if he had smiled. All she knew was that she had looked once more into the deep-set, velvet eyes she adored. Her whole body and soul sang with elation.

"*Blasphemy!*" spluttered Mordecai, hauling himself over the wall. "What does he think he's *doing?*" The Pharisee stood in the middle of the track flailing his stick at the retreating crowd.

"But, Uncle," Kezia began to explain, "didn't you see? It was Rabbi Jesus – wasn't it wonderful?"

The women read Mordecai's face and remained silent. The old man stood recovering his breath. "That man," he growled, "that man will bring us *trouble*. He had no right to… to…" he pointed after the crowd snaking up toward the city gate. "The city's crawling with soldiers, any hint of a rebellion and they'll make us pay, you mark my words!" The old man boiled with rage.

"But…" Kezia began.

"You don't understand, child," Mordecai cut her off. "What that Jesus has done is reckless beyond words. He's… he's a… a *fool* to incite the crowds like that…and if he's not a fool, then the very devil himself is in him!"

Kezia had never seen her uncle rage before, but, having vented his anger, he quickly subsided. "Come now," he said reclaiming his dignity, "I'll take you to the Temple."

Mordecai straightened his prayer shawl. "Follow me, but…" he stared each one in the eye, "I warn all of you, keep away from that Nazareth man."

The clouds which had been lightly powdered across the blue sky now fused together in a dark blanket; a keen wind blew locks of Kezia's hair across her face. Her uncle was wrong! Jesus was the last person to cause trouble.

Sarah bowed her head against the wind as they walked down to the Kidron valley. She felt all flummoxed and worried. What was her Simon doing carrying on like that? Waving bits of palm, chanting an' all? She didn't understand. She wouldn't relax til she got him home.

Crossing the Kidron valley, Mordecai pointed out the grave of the prophet Zechariah and the tomb of King David's son, Absolam. She knew he was inordinately proud of these ancestors in the faith, but Kezia neither knew, nor cared about ancient prophets or princes, her thoughts were centred on catching another glimpse of Rabbi Jesus. He was the reason she had begged to make this pilgrimage.

Sliding her hand beneath the warm cloak, her fingers clung to the kid pouch. When she had the chance, she would show Jesus how she kept the pouch with her… always.

Chapter 10

'IT'LL be a surprise.' Leah ran her finger over the finest green silk under–tunic she'd ever seen in Capernaum's market. Her finger traced the embroidered white butterfly decoration and imagined Kezia wearing the garment for her wedding night. It was a perfect surprise gift.

She and Jairus would have to seriously plan the wedding once he returned from Jerusalem. 'Where, oh where,' she wondered, 'had the years gone?' The memory of Kezia's first step seemed like last year, and now, here she was, buying clothes for her wedding! She picked up the tunic and smiled at the fine-boned, foreign girl behind the stall.

"Hun'red sheekel!" the girl sang at her in a metallic, foreign accent. Leah frowned. She dropped the tunic.

"Thirty!" Leah replied. The girl with almond eyes kept smiling. She picked up the garment and purred, "Beautiful, no? For you, lady, aytee sheekel."

"No, no," Leah shook her head from side to side. "Fifty," she tried.

The girl's straight, black hair bobbed as she nodded. She pressed the tunic into Leah's hands, *"Beauteef'l'"* she coaxed, "Please lady… fifee fi sheekel… I take *beeg* loss! Yours?" she urged. "Last one." Pei Qi pleaded, her eyes enlarged in emphasis, every inch the professional saleswoman.

Leah looked longingly at the tunic. She had to buy it. 'Beaten down by a child,' she sighed to herself, but she knew the delicate fabric was worth far more than fifty five shekels. She had a bargain. Before the price went up, Leah counted the coins into the girl's outstretched palm.

With most of the soldiers deployed to keep order in Jerusalem over the Passover season, Capernaum's market had halved in size. Traders had seized their advantage to follow where thousands of pilgrims flocked into the Holy City. Festivals guaranteed good profits. However, Leah's domestic arrangements were relatively unaffected by the annual exodus of families to Jerusalem, with plenty of local fish and fruit for Adah to collect.

Leah made her solitary way through the market stalls, lingering to compare other tunics. Several would have been suitable for a young bride, but none were as dainty or as exquisitely embroidered as the one she had bought. She allowed herself a warm glow of satisfaction. It was a good buy.

Walking home, the pleasure of her purchase faded and a hollow emptiness opened within her. With Jairus and Kezia, and most of her friends gone to Jerusalem, the days dragged. She longed to share the Passover meal with her husband and daughter. The enforced separation pulled her down with a despondency which told her it was all her fault… childbirth had left her too weak to travel, yet again. Anxious thoughts criss-crossed her mind – would Jairus take another woman to bear him a son? Would he make Jerusalem his permanent home? Life without him would be unbearable but deep inside something told her distance was not their only separation.

Leah was consumed by thoughts of what Jairus would be doing in the Holy City. Of course she was proud of her husband seeking to be part of the Sanhedrin, but, she worried that such promotion would make her company seem drab and uninteresting. She blamed Mordecai. Filling his head with ideas – she frowned – the old man was living his own thwarted ambitions through his nephew…making sure he stayed with the High Priest, licking boots, introducing him to members of the Sanhedrin… Capernaum wouldn't be fine enough for him soon. Her body shivered.

Drops of rain spotted the dust. Leah looked up at the darkening clouds, she would have to hurry or be caught in the spring downpour.

In the middle of scrubbing the floor, Adah welcomed her mistress as she came through the door. The servant-girl was in action every waking minute.

"Zippie's been asleep since you went out," she relayed cheerfully, but just on cue, Zippie opened large, accusing eyes and began to whimper. She was at the stage when she liked being propped in a sitting position and, if put outside the confines of her pen, could manipulate herself across the floor at startling speed.

Leah's heart sank at the sound of Zippie's whimper. She sat down at the loom, Kezia's surprise package in the basket by her side. For a few moments she stared unseeing at the loom. Pulling herself together, she threaded the shuttle and began to work it from side to side, the automatic rhythm of weaving. Leah blanked out Adah's chatter. She was deaf to Zippie's cries. She adjusted her thoughts from Jairus' absence to the forthcoming preparations for Kezia's wedding.

She intended Kezia's wedding to be an event Capernaum people would talk about for years. Back when Kezia and Jared were small children, Zebedee had negotiated a generous bride-price for Kezia. Now the wedding was on the horizon, Leah began to think of the dowry her daughter would have to take to Jared.

She changed the wools over from red to black.

Leah's mind wandered back to her own wedding; she had been so full of life, so much in awe of Jairus, tall and athletic with humourous eyes. Her parents looked on the handsome, ambitious young man from Nazareth as a gift from heaven. A smile flickered across her face as she remembered how she and Joanna had sat on their mattress the night before her wedding, helpless with laughter. Both sisters swore they would have servants and many, many sons…

The shuttle stopped. Tears distorted her vision. 'Life never turns out as planned,' she pursed her lips in resignation. Life had changed so much over those fifteen years. Her beloved parents both long dead. She only had one servant – and worse, no sons.

Jairus' ambition was driving him away; she could not compete with the Temple. Would she lose him? Had she already lost him?

If only she could bear a son…

She thought of Joanna and Seth. They had no servants and Joanna's womb was stubbornly barren, yet they seemed close and happy together. Leah had never understood her sister's lack of concern over this blight to her life… but, then… that was Joanna… frivolous and flighty yet, at the same time, inscrutable even to a sister.

Leah flexed her back. Her hands felt stiff and her exhausted limbs numb. She stood wearily and glanced into the cradle, "Maybe she'll be a beautiful woman," she sighed, "she certainly isn't a beautiful baby." With that comment she disappeared upstairs to hide Kezia's surprise wedding present.

Adah's gentle heart stung from Leah's waspish remark.

Hurriedly she wiped her hands and went over to Zippie making the little cooing sounds the baby loved. As she bent over the cradle all whimpering stopped and Zippie shone a toothless grin at her nursemaid.

"There, there…" Adah propped the baby so that she was able to see all that went on in the room. "You're just nosey, you are," she murmured. 'If only' she thought as she smiled down at Zippie, "fonly your mother would take proper notice of you. 'Tis'n't right," she sighed.

Adah's skinny finger had not reached Zippie's tummy before the baby convulsed in a ripple of throaty chuckles. A warm love passed between them. The little slave-girl loved the baby as if she were her own. Zippie knew and responded. Adah's finger changed from tickling the tummy to run along Zippie's hot gums. She let out a thrilled squeek.

"Oh! I do believe you've got a tooth coming," she trilled with as much delight as if she had found a gold nugget in the recesses of the child's mouth. "You'll have such a big smile for your big sister when she comes home, you will."

With the wedding present safely tucked away, Leah came down the stairs and returned to her position at the loom. She hadn't fed or held her daughter for days, being quite content to leave Adah to care for the child. Each time she looked at Zippie, a knife turned in her heart. She was a girl. She was the cause of Jairus' coolness.

The loom was her comfort, the only place she felt secure. Methodically she took up the weaving again, absorbed in the fabric's slow but regular growth.

Leah worked a pattern her mother had taught her. Complicated enough to look intricate, the design repetition in contrasting red, black and sand, was surprisingly straightforward. Leah missed her mother. She missed Sarah too. Sarah's weaving was so even – she was a gifted weaver who understood the requisite tensions for different wools. Time passed quickly when Sarah sat with her at the loom. Leah missed the homely routine of Kezia spinning while she and Sarah worked the loom, gossiping for hours on end. Leah paused and looked at the floor. The house felt so empty.

***

Kezia's head felt fit to burst with every new sight, sound and smell of the historic city. Everybody shouted – either in greeting, to clinch a purchase, to clear a path for mules and carts or to avoid being run down by wagons or animals. The military presence was inescapable. Soldiers were everywhere, on the ramparts, watching the traders in the market, standing in clusters of threes and fours on street corners, clutching their spears, facing the Temple. People pressed past giving Kezia the feeling that, at any moment, she would be caught up in a crowd of strangers and lost for ever from Mordecai and her family, down one of the score of darkly narrow and mysterious alleys.

Her imagination thrived on watching the different faces and costumes of pilgrims from far-off countries. She couldn't wait to describe it all to Adah and her mother when she got home. Whichever way she turned something new and exciting filled her eyes and heart. The whole world was in Jerusalem!

And, suddenly she was standing in front of the Temple itself.

King Herod's masterpiece of awe-inspiring, imposing opulence. Building work was still in progress with men high up on scaffolding and a steady background beat of hammer on stone. Mordecai's hand guided her past tall Temple guards who squinted and frowned into the morning sun. They entered the main precinct where everyone, even gentiles, were allowed to gather.

Money-changers haggled at their tables and hundreds of lambs bleated pitifully in wicker pens. It had never before occurred to Kezia that Passover meant the mass slaughter of lambs and doves. As she walked with her uncle she couldn't help feeling sorry for the doves, squashed in their cages, stacked higgledy-piggledy on top of one another, huddled in gasping fear, waiting to die. The louder the humans shouted at each other, so the birds and lambs responded with their own crescendo of terror. Only the sparrows were free to fly and perch and chitter and cheep above the milling crowds.

Mordecai left the group and disappeared through the high doors to the Court of Israel to find Jairus and tell him his daughter was outside, waiting to greet him. It was the part of the Temple for men alone.

After a few minutes Jairus swept out, beaming his welcome. This was the father Kezia had always loved, she glowed in his embrace and prayed he was 'back' for good. Just then Jairus caught sight of the High Priest, Caiaphas, entering the Temple Gate with his retinue of priests, Sadducees and teachers of the law. Chest jutting in pride, Jairus led his daughter to be presented to the most important man in Jerusalem.

Caiaphas, his bulk as wide as a house, glided passed. He wore the ceremonial ephod of sumptuous brocade in purple, scarlet, blue and gold thread. His robes and swagger was more regal than King Herod and the twelve jewels sparkling on his breast plate had the desired impact on the dazzled spectators from the country. Tiny golden bells tinkled from the hem of his under robe as he processed across the Temple forecourt with measured holiness. The High Priest contrived a condescending smile, which almost reached Kezia, before he turned abruptly into his private rooms in the inner Temple. The door slammed behind him.

Embarrassed by the High Priest's public rebuff, Jairus pulled Kezia back to the others, "I'll take you to Abner's house," he said as if the encounter with the Caiaphas had never happened, "we'll celebrate Passover with his family." He gave his daughter a reassuring smile. Taking her arm he continued, "We can eat there today and you can tell me all your news."

Kezia was glad they weren't eating anywhere near the High Priest, however opulent his robes, ornate his jewel-encrusted rings and exalted his position. She had taken an instant dislike to his wet eyed, supercilious manner. Jairus led his daughter and uncle to the house of his friend Abner, while Seth and Joanna opted to take the rest to Jerusalem's market.

***

"This has been the best day of my life!" Kezia gushed to Joanna as they began the climb back over the Mount of Olives to Bethany later that day.

"Mine too," echoed Debra dancing round an olive tree at the entrance to the cemetery. Modecai and Seth led the way while the women trailed behind loaded with provisions. Despite their weariness, all were eager for another day in Jerusalem before Passover. Tomorrow they would have time to buy souvenirs to take home, time to meet Sarah's cousins and time to pray in the Holy Temple. Sarah had found Simon in the market and made him promise to come over to Bethany to talk some sense into his mother-in-law. Secretly, Kezia was convinced Rabbi Jesus would come with him.

The sun, which had shone for most of the afternoon, now hid behind thickening clouds, allowing a strong wind to depress the early spring temperature. However, the steep climb to Bethany and their tents kept them all warm, even Anna's pallid cheeks flushed with exertion. Approaching their camp, they found two dozen or more new camps had sprung up on the slope since they had left in the morning.

"Good for Bethany traders." Seth remarked, and ruefully wished he had brought some of his own pots and mugs to sell.

"Oh dear!" said Sarah on hearing the unmistakable wail of mourners, "Sad time for somebody." She kissed Kezia and left the group to walk over to her cousin's home. She had not gone many paces before it dawned on her that she was walking directly towards the wailing. Sarah gathered her skirt and ran the rest of the way to Rachel's house. The wailing grew louder. Sarah knew – she just knew – it was for Esther.

Rachel met her at the door.

"I'm so sorry, Sarah." Rachel spoke through tears as she held out her arms to comfort her cousin. "But it was peaceful. Peaceful and quick." Sarah went into shock. The first thought that flashed into her mind was – 'Good! At last I'm free'. Then guilt flooded over her that she should ever think such a terrible, selfish thought.

She stood rooted in Rachel's arms, dry-eyed and numb. Suddenly, sweat broke on her brow as she felt her stomach churn. She rushed outside to vomit in the yard.

Before sun-rise next morning, Rachel's husband Joel set off for Jerusalem in search of Simon. Rachel helped Sarah perform the intimate ritual duty of laying out her mother's body. Rachel organised two flute players and two wailing women to lead the body from the house to the graveside. Most funerals in Bethany relied on the services of the familiar quartette.

Throughout the day Sarah sat by her mother's embalmed corpse, rocking to and fro, weeping and moaning into her shawl.

As Kezia helped Joanna gather kindling for the fire, she ventured to ask, "Why's Sarah so upset? She never got on with her mother."

"Love's a funny thing, chicken," Joanna replied. "Maybe Sarah's crying for the mother she wished Esther had been." She gave Kezia a meaningful look. "D'you understand?" Kezia shrugged. She was not at all sure she understood what Joanna meant.

At sun-set, Simon and Joel bore Esther's wrapped body on a light stretcher to the sloping cemetery on the Mount of Olives overlooking Jerusalem. Seth stood with the men at the open grave as Mordecai donned his prayer shawl and intoned the special liturgy for the dead.

As custom dictated, Sarah and the rest of the women watched from a distance. In deference to Sarah's bereavement, she was excused the normal chores of the day. Rachel and Joanna swiftly delegated jobs amongst the other women. Following the burial, the mourners returned to freshly baked bread and a small cauldron of vegetable pottage. Neighbours had spread a sheet with cheese, eggs, olives, fruit and a selection of nuts, enough for everyone who squeezed into Rachel and Joel's courtyard to offer sympathy and share memories of Esther.

Kezia sat beside Joanna. Her appetite was gone. Esther's

death cast a sombre hush over the Galilean pilgrims. But, more important to Kezia's mind, it had scuppered her precious day in Jerusalem her father had promised. Time was slipping away. Already, tomorrow was Passover.

Chapter 11

HIGH above the noise and bustle of the street below, Jairus sat on Abner's wide flat roof. He sucked at the hookah, deep in thought. Water bubbled through the ornamental bowl, cooling the sweet, mint-flavoured smoke. Jairus watched his wisps of smoke rise, float and dissolve on the afternoon breeze. Each puff of smoke evolved it's own unique shape, poised in the air for a few ethereal seconds…and was gone. Abner's roof was a haven on which to think and make decisions. A potent mix of anger, jealousy and guilt throbbed in Jairus' mind.

A silver-smith by trade, Abner had met Jairus a couple of years before on one of Jairus' regular visits to the Temple. Artistic and thoughtful, Abner had no wish to intrude on Jairus' inner conflicts. He rested beside his friend in patient silence, taking his turn with the hookah.

Since the humiliation of the High Priest's public snub, Jairus realised his future in Jerusalem teetered on a knife-edge. All he had worked for was in danger of crumbling to ashes. The thought that he'd never be more than just ruler of a back-water Synagogue stabbed him with acute depression. Gold embellishments on the Temple caught the evening sun so that Jairus had to shield his eyes from the glare. It felt as if the building itself was taunting him. The great stones stood so close to Abner's roof, yet Caiaphas was wrenching the Temple opportunities out of his grasp. All his dreams… all the connections he had built up over the years… were they destined to crash to nothing? Smoke escaped down his nostrils. He coughed.

"You're very quiet, Jairus," Abner ventured, not wishing to pry but recognising his friend was wrestling an inner demon. Jairus appeared deaf to the remark. After a pause Abner tried again. "It's good to have you and your family here for Passover." It was his way of offering a change of subject if Jairus was unwilling to unload his problem.

"We had a meeting, you know," Jairus said finally. He watched another swirl of smoke evaporate into the sky.

"Yes… I know," Abner replied in a level voice, keeping his eyes on the slate-grey clouds creeping up from the wilderness.

Jairus' hands moved in agitation and his words tumbled out. "D'you know what they want to do?" He stared unblinking at the silver-smith. "They're going to *arrest* him! They've paid a few oiks to slander him…it's… it's a set up. They're determined… absolutely determined to get rid of him." He pulled hard on the pipe and dropped his gaze to the tiled floor.

"I stood up," he continued in an effort to justify himself. "I said I didn't think he'd done anything to warrant a trial… "

"And old Caiaphas wasn't impressed?" Abner guessed. Rumours of the High Priest's ruthless deals were common knowledge. He would allow nothing to stand in his way or jeopardise his own and his family's tenacious grip on power.

"He cut me dead today," Jairus admitted, incensed by the flash-back. "I swear he's as fat as an Egyptian toad!" he spat.

"Talk like that'll get *you* arrested, too." Abner remained calm.

"If they *do* arrest him…" Jairus shifted uncomfortably. "I'll have to attend the trial."

Silence fell between the men. Abner considered Jairus' options.

"Will you support your friend Jesus against Caiaphas?" Abner's voice was low. Jairus stared over the Temple, to the city walls and beyond into the wilderness. A violet-blue haze hung across the distant horizon like a symbolic haze over his own future.

Abner repeated his question, "Will you?"

"If I do… I'm finished." Jairus finally articulated his predicament.

"You could always warn him to leave the city before Caiaphas' men get to him." Abner suggested in his soft, reasonable voice. "He'd be safe down at the coast – he could take a ship from Joppa – stay away till Caiaphas gets it in for some other poor sod." He reached for a handful of pistachios from the basket between them.

Jairus couldn't reply. Getting Jesus away from the city would do nothing to heal the rift between himself and the High Priest. If he was to have any hope of securing Caiaphas' blessing and gain promotion into the Sanhedrin, there was no alternative. He would have to support Caiaphas against Jesus – in public. Sweat broke out under his armpits at the stark implication of such a betrayal.

***

For people whose daily lives rarely lifted above routine drudgery, the celebration of Passover was their glorious annual highlight. Sarah opted to stay in Bethany with her cousin's family while Anna and her girls boasted their privileged invitation to help James and John prepare Passover for Jesus and the disciples. Kezia was incensed to think Debra would be serving at Jesus' Passover table while she was at Abner's house on the other side of the city.

Mordecai led Kezia, Joanna and Seth back to Jerusalem and Abner's house to celebrate with Jairus. The narrow streets were even more crammed than before with much jostling around the market stalls, shouting and high spirits. Seth bought eggs, dates and wine and a wooden toy top for each of Abner's boys. Jairus promised the paschal lamb.

Abner's house was tall and narrow with a courtyard at the back. Entrance was directly into his ground floor workshop and only a thin curtain divided that area from where vegetables were prepared and pots, pans and utensils hung on the wall. When Seth met chickens scratching in the yard, he laughed at his carefully chosen gift to the family of a basket of eggs! However, Abner's wife Judith explained her chickens had gone off lay and she had been worried she would have to buy.

She ushered her guests upstairs where cushions were arranged around a low table. Mordecai took a swift count and was relieved there was, after all, enough room for ten people. Judith lavished generous hospitality on her visitors; their servant brought bowls of water to wash the men's feet while Judith herself offered Joanna and Kezia perfumed flannels for their face and hands. Kezia sniffed deeply into her flannel. The stink in some of the city streets had been nauseating.

Three sons clattered down the stone stairs from the roof to greet the strangers; the painted tops causing whoops of delight. The youngest, Dan, who Kezia estimated must be about six, was going to ask the special question at their Passover meal. An intense, puny child, he blinked at the world from behind long, dark lashes, with the same doleful eyes as his father.

"It's an honour to welcome you to my home for Passover, my friends," Abner said. "Please feel this house is yours." He bowed respectfully towards Mordecai. "And for the young lady who is soon to be married," he smiled at Kezia, who blushed at being singled out, "I have a small, a very *small* wedding gift." Turning round to a shelf he lifted down a copper dish on which lay a leather purse. He handed it to Kezia, "I hope you will like it," he said, "and when you wear it, please… remember your friends in Jerusalem." Real warmth glowed in his smile.

Carefully Kezia prized open the neck of the purse and drew out a delicate silver brooch.

"Oh, Abner, it's *perfect!*" she gasped at the intricate work, "look! A pomegranate… in a cushion of tiny leaves," she cried, holding the brooch for Joanna to see. "Oh, thank you Abner, thank you a thousand times." She held it against her cloak, "I promise, I'll remember you all," she looked fondly at each of them, "Everything's wonderful…how can I ever forget today?"

Gratified by the genuine pleasure his gift had given, Abner took Mordecai, Seth and his boys up the stairs to the flat roof while Judith prized Joanna and Kezia away from the brooch and down to tackle the task of preparing and cooking the Passover meal.

"Anyone home?" Jairus' voice rang into the workshop. He brushed aside the curtain and slammed the dead lamb on the scrubbed table by the window. Kezia gave an involuntary shudder, the animal was so young – head lolling, its gentle mouth open above where crimson blood trickled into the warm fleece where the throat had been slit.

The women worked relentlessly. Judith skinned and gutted the lamb and prepared it for the spit. Joanna undertook baking the unleavened bread. Kezia's jobs included boiling eggs, chopping herbs and filling dishes with salt, haroseth, almonds, raisins and pistachios. Judith also asked her to trim the lamps, make sure the honey pots were full and wine cups ready to go on the table. The table centrepiece, Abner's own design and pride and joy, was the special silver candlestick, the family reserved for use at Passover.

Soon the unmistakable, sweet, rich aroma of roasting lamb permeated the house.

After long hours of preparation, the meal was ready. Abner arranged his family and guests around the table, making sure Dan sat between himself and Mordecai. With the lamb served, Dan clambered on to his stool and, in a well-practised treble, asked the annual question: "Why is this night different from all other nights?"

Mordecai smiled indulgently, regretting as he did each year, that his own son had not lived long enough to be able to ask the Passover question. The Pharisee launched into the ancient prayers of Passover with all the pomp and drama he could muster. The evening passed in eating, drinking, listening to the famous story of Israel's deliverance, and singing and dancing to the traditional Passover songs.

***

"I had to pinch myself," Kezia told Joanna on the walk back to Bethany, "To think we were celebrating Passover here – in *Jerusalem!* I don't think any other Passover will ever be quite so special."

"You could be right," said Seth linking Joanna and Kezia

on each arm. "I'll never forget when I was old enough to ask the question. I was almost too scared to speak. And," he gave a jaunty skip, "I've been like that ever since!"

"Our Kezie doesn't believe a word you say!" Joanna quipped brightly. Even Mordecai joined in the laughter as they climbed the steep slope over the Mount of Olives to their Bethany camp.

For the first time Kezia felt stirred by the full impact of the ritual meal and the story of her ancestors' suffering. It reignited her faith in the Lord God of Abraham, Isaac and Jacob. Undoubtedly the cups of wine added to her elation, but she swung along the path feeling included at last in the adult world. Her father had promised they would spend all the next day together and her heart was bursting with happiness and hope. Kezia couldn't wait.

There was still a chance she would see Jesus again…

Chapter 12

KEZIA woke with a jolt. Joanna's hand clamped on her arm.

"C'mon chicken," her whisper was urgent, "get up. Quick! We must go."

"Why?" Dulled by sleep, Kezia was slow to react. Joanna was rolling her bed-mat while Anna pecked at her girls to hurry themselves. Kezia rubbed her eyes. She peered out of the open side to their tent. "It's still dark," she yawned.

"Never mind that," bustled Joanna, "get a move-on. We're off in two minutes flat."

Kezia reached to grab her cloak as the men began taking down the tent around her. What was happening? Something terrible must have happened – Kezia sensed it in the silent intensity in everyone around. Automatically she rolled her mat and snatched up her belongings.

"Don't ask, just do as you're *told*!" snapped Anna hustling her girls into the night air. Kezia joined them, craning her neck for sight of Sarah.

"Where's Sarah?" she whispered.

"She's staying," Joanna replied crisply, cushioning cooking pots with her rug as she stuffed then into the bag.

"Are we ready?" asked Mordecai. He pointed his stick at Seth who, with the other men from Sepphoris, had saddled the donkeys and strapped on the tents. Seth nodded.

"No noise... from anyone," Mordecai commanded. "We should make Jericho before dawn. Follow me."

In haste the women shouldered their baggage and moved behind the old Pharisee as he led them to where the donkeys waited. Mordecai stretched out his hand to Kezia. Her heart pounded with dread. Too frightened to ask her uncle the reason for the sudden evacuation, she clasped his hand as if it were a rope thrown to save her from drowning.

The little group of Galileans scrambled down the hillside and into the desert shadows. Rain clouds made the sky feel oppressively close. There was no moon to guide them, but the innate instinct for survival, swiftly adjusted their eyes to the darkness. The sure-footed donkeys led them down and down, every hurried step distancing them further from Bethany... and Jerusalem.

Disappointment welled in Kezia's throat. Tears pricked her eyes. In her emotion she didn't realise how tightly she was gripping her uncle's hand. What could have happened that was so terrible? Why wasn't her father with them? Was Sarah alright? Each question became a dart into her brain, tensing her body with the pain of unknowing. Her wonderful Passover was ruined. Why? Sandal-leather scraped on the scree path and the donkey hooves clipped an eerie rhythm in the barren landscape. Kezia felt she was descending into Sheol.

No-one spoke til they reached the first spring. Finally, Mordecai decided it was safe to stop, replenish their water bottles and rest a few moments. It was time to tell the women what had happened.

"They've arrested the Nazareth man." He stated in brutal clarity. The women gasped. "The Temple guards have orders to arrest *any* of his followers. The Romans too – they'll imprison anyone connected to him."

"But why?" Kezia wailed. Mordecai's hand smoothed her hair as he answered her gently,

"You saw for yourself how the mob behaved on the Mount of Olives. I told you there'd be trouble!" He rested heavily on his staff, his eyes searching back up the inky hillside in case they had been followed. "We wouldn't have known but Zebedee's boy James ran over to Bethany to tell Lazarus. Sarah heard and sent him down to the camp to warn the rest of us." He gazed up into the sky in despair, "I tell you, *no-one* from Galilee is safe until this... this so-called Messiah is silenced!"

Kezia panicked: "What about Father?" she cried. Mordecai tried to sound convincing, "Your father's a friend of the High Priest, my dear, don't worry about him."

Kezia was desperate to know what had happened to Jesus but instead she asked, "But, Sarah?" she turned to Joanna who was shouldering her load ready to be on the move once more.

"Seth says Sarah won't come home without Simon." Joanna, visibly upset, nevertheless made a brave attempt to sound normal. "Come on," she chivvied, "several miles to Jericho yet!"

Kezia's mind whirled in agony. 'What would they do to Jesus?' The cadaver leapt back into her mind and her legs lost their strength. Silently, she prayed. She prayed with a fervour that hurt and made her head pound with each footfall. Then, she remembered what her uncle had said, her father was a 'friend of the High Priest'.

Immediately her anxiety lifted. 'Father won't let anything happen to his friend Jesus,' she told herself. She relaxed. Jesus would be released – she was *positive* he would be released.

Darkness slowed their flight as they retreated along the stony, undulating desert paths until, at last, they reached the narrow wadi. Black silhouettes of acacia bushes framed the steep slopes. Kezia startled at the sound of footsteps running up behind her. She looked round but it was only some small children.

A scream echoed in the still air, then a sickening thud. Anna hit the ground. Another scream went up further back from another group of Galileans who had joined the escape from Bethany.

"Seth!" Joanna shouted for her husband. Debra howled and Mordecai beat the air with his stick, roaring at the children to get out of his way. Anna clutched her head and moaned as her fingers came in contact with hot, sticky wetness. Joanna and Kezia bent over Anna to help her to her feet.

"Vermin!" she wailed as she struggled to her feet hanging heavily on Joanna. "Vermin! The little urchins've robbed us!" Seeing her mother had lost her bundles, Miriam began to weep.

As suddenly as they appeared, the children were gone.

A classic ambush. Surprise and speed being the prime weapons of bandits who knew every cave and boulder of the Judean wilderness, day or night. Anna slumped to the ground again. Seth took off his turban, ripped a length of the purple cotton and gently bound Anna's head wound. She drank weakly from his water bottle. Eventually, he managed to calm Anna and her girls.

Kezia had never seen Seth without his turban. He used to say all Sepphoris knew the potter by his turban. Now, with his hair loose to his shoulders, he looked quite different; he was far more handsome without the turban, his fine bone structure made him almost beautiful. He looked much younger than Joanna.

"Hellish place!" rasped Mordecai, humiliated at being outwitted by mere children. Realising his shoulder-bag was gone, he cursed himself that he'd been too old and weak to prevent the attack.

From that moment Seth quietly took command. One of the other men reported two of their women had suffered the same fate as Anna. Each one knew the children had been set on them at the bidding of adults; adults who would still be lurking close by in the darkness. Another attack was highly probable.

Mordecai's bowels curdled in rage. He looked at the shaken group. Men, women and children who had trusted him. And his own darling Kezia. He could not have born it if she had been attacked. And all because of that… that *madman* from Nazareth. Fury sapped the old Pharisee's strength. He held Kezia's hand not so much to lead her but to support his own weary legs. He was so angry his thoughts were incoherent. How dare that Jesus spoil their time in Jerusalem through his arrogant and misguided teaching. He'd always been too holy for his own good – now look where it had got him! Causing uproar! Time he was put away! Mordecai glanced at Kezia's ashen profile. He'd murder Jesus if any harm came to her.

Seth held the lead donkey's reign. Joanna walked close at his side. A desert owl hooted from an acacia bush. Immediately all eyes strained in the direction of the bird's call, suspicious in case it was a robber's signal. Joanna edged closer to Seth.

"What d'you think they'll do to him?" she whispered. Seth sniffed in the cool air before answering.

"I'm afraid he hasn't helped himself, my love," he sighed.

"What d'you mean?" Joanna was perplexed.

"Well, you can't undermine authority… you've heard him taunting religious high-ups… well, you just can't get away with that sort of thing." Seth felt genuine concern. Joanna cast a quick look over towards Kezia before whispering at her husband's neck. "Kezie'll be inconsolable if anything happens to her Jesus." They walked on, their pace slackened by fatigue. "What crime is he supposed to have committed? He's a *good* man!" Joanna spoke her mind but Seth only shrugged.

"Yeah," he agreed after a while, "he's a good man but, well… being 'good' doesn't exempt men from having enemies." He clicked his tongue to encourage the laden donkey. "At best they'll flog him." He seemed reticent to say more. "Even if the worst happens," he paused, "…Kezie's young. She'll get over it." He gave Joanna a resigned smile and put his arm round her shoulders. "Life goes on, Jo," he said simply.

At last the first shimmer of dawn broke above the Moabite hills in front of them. Pale tendrils of gold and grey streaked the indigo sky and the outline of Jericho's flat rooftops came into view. The sky lightened by the minute. The wilderness was behind them. Hot and exhausted from their flight, the Galilean pilgrims reached Jericho – and safety.

"Let the women buy food," Seth said, his voice strong and decisive. " Then, once we get to the other side of Jericho, we'll camp by the river and *rest*!" The men nodded agreement. Capernaum was still three day's walk.

Chapter 13

"TOO many boats!" boomed Zebedee helping his hired men sort the night's catch. "Not enough fish to go round." He scowled at the meagre catch, mentally totting up his likely earnings.

"Nets should have twice this number," he groused. Since his older sons, James and John, left to follow the Rabbi Jesus, fishing had run into the doldrums. Two of his hired men had also left, taken themselves off to Sepphoris to join the building trade.

'Builders!' Zebedee scoffed and spat. 'What do fishermen know 'bout *building!* He shot a glare at his youngest son. "And when you come back from wherever your little mind has been," he said sarcastically, "you can jump out, boy, and fix the ropes."

Jared was gazing into the flat, grey water, unaware the boat had come so close to land. Too much wine at their Passover meal the previous evening combined with a long night out fishing had numbed his concentration. He bristled at his father's jibe as he leapt into the soft coldness of the lake. The sun had not yet risen above the Syrian hills. There was no wind and the water, hills and sky merged in misty, pearlescent grey.

"When's 'e gettin' wed?" called one of the hired men. Crude, guttural laughter carried through the dawn air. "Ee'll be back down t'earth soon 'nough then!" Jared's temper rose but he covered his anger with a shrug and rueful grin. He secured the ropes round the harbour posts without comment.

"Don't blame you, boy," said the older of the men, "I'd be thinking of 'er too, if I'd a bride like 'er." The boat moored against the harbour wall with a violent jolt. Women lined the wall, clutching baskets, eager to buy fish fresh, straight from the boat. Their expressions mirrored the small catch. Zebedee had worked the lake all his life but couldn't remember such a lean time. He scowled at the women inspecting his night's catch. 'Women!' he turned his back on the them. 'Never satisfied! Perhaps *they*'d like to spend all night out on the lake…'

Jared helped the hired-men tip fish into three baskets, and sort fish to sell immediately from fish that would be put to dry on the wracks. He glanced briefly in the direction of the traveller's camp… The memory of his last visit to Pei Qi caused his blood to pulse hot through his veins. The morning sun rose into view and, as he bent over the fish baskets, a welcome warmth seeped into his bones.

He cursed his brothers. All very well for them to swan off with that Rabbi, but it meant his jobs had doubled. He was slogging his guts out and still he could never win his father's approval. John was the favourite. Jared knew that. He'd always known that. He spat into the fish basket. The thought of spending the rest of his life on a fishing boat engulfed him in a black depression.

He turned his mind to Pei Qi. He wondered what kind of country she came from… idly he dreamed of seeing more of the world… of making money…of being his own boss.

***

Adah hunched on the end of her mattress, her arms wrapped around herself for comfort. She sniffed back the last of the copious tears that left her red-eyed and drained. "'Tis awful," she whimpered into the darkness of the room she shared with Kezia. "'Tis awful."

Kezia sat bolt upright against the wall. It felt as though an iron band constricted her chest so that she could neither move nor speak. Her longed for visit to Jerusalem had given her the most exciting days of her life and now plunged her into a pit of utter despair.

That afternoon her father had come home with shattering news. News that, at first Kezia could not believe – had never thought possible in a million years – news that Jesus was dead. Her hero… dead. Crucified! Hung up to die in agony like that terrible cadaver that haunted her from the cross-roads outside of Jerusalem. Kezia froze in tearless shock. No longer a little girl who could run to her father and sob hot tears into his shoulder, she had become a woman. And she was learning the hard lesson that generations of women before her had learnt – how to bear pain silently and within. She sat motionless and dry-eyed, as detached from her previous existence as the marble statues she had so recently admired in Jerusalem.

Kezia swore she would never have feelings again. Never… ever. The total trust she had placed in her father had proved pathetically naive. Brutal realisation dawned that he was not all powerful, he couldn't always make things better. He was just a man from the little fishing village of Capernaum. He had no influence whatsoever in Jerusalem. Flung into her new-found adult world, Kezia's eyes had been opened to adult barbarism. It was an alien world from which she longed to run away.

Adah gently rocked Zippie's cradle with her foot. "'Tis *awful*," she repeated.

Through the adjoining wall Mordecai snored the laboured snore of age.

***

The hinge creaked. Leah's heart missed a beat. Jairus came into the bedroom. He had not shared her bed for months and though she didn't feel strong enough to bear his weight, her heart leapt at the chance to conceive a son. Jairus slid in beside her on the mattress. Tears leaked from the corners of her closed eyes as she yielded to the urgent thrusting of his need. Her greatest dread had become reality. Now she knew beyond doubt – he no longer loved her.

Without a word he rolled off her fragile body and fell asleep. Leah lay still. She listened to his breathing. She could feel the warmth from his body. She had adored him, thought that she knew him, but, lying side by side in the darkness, the truth was hard to bare, they had become strangers. Was it possible new life could spring from such a perfunctory coupling? A tidal wave of loneliness swept over her.

'Lord God… King of all the earth…' she began, then her words trailed off. They stuck in her throat, hollow and meaningless. Leah tried to remember one of the Sabbath Psalms Jairus read in the Synagogue. Subconsciously her right hand covered her heart with the effort to dredge holy phrases into focus.

'May the Lord answer you when you are in distress…' she squeazed her eyes shut as her lips moved in silent concentration. 'May he give you the desire of your heart… may the Lord grant all your requests." As the words came back to her she mouthed them with the emphasis and confidence she had heard Jairus use. Leah could no longer share such conviction.

Her thoughts crept back to the prayers her paternal grandfather had taught her. Prayers to the ancient gods of Canaan, prayers which Jairus had strictly forbidden. She pictured herself and Joanna as little children, standing earnestly on either side of their frail grandfather's knees. It all seemed so long ago yet her childhood awe and reverence for those ancestral gods had never faded. Leah decided to add weight to her previous prayers with prayers to Baal and Astarte, the traditional Canaanite gods of love and fertility. She would willingly, she told herself, pray to any god, she didn't care which god it was just so long as… just as long as she could bear a *son*.

She turned her face to the window. A star flickered brightly from another world. Her grandfather used to say a bright star signalled an imminent birth. Leah stared into the sky willing to grasp at the flimsiest straw of hope. Surely, Astarte had given her a sign?

Chapter 14

IT WAS stifling. Bodies that had jammed themselves into the Synagogue overheated with ill-temper and too close a proximity to each other. Flies, attracted by the delicious proliferation of sweat, buzzed excitedly through the congregation. Men squashed round the bimah while their women and children craned their necks from behind pillars. Some smaller children were lifted to stand on the windowsills. An overflow hovered outside the door, all straining to hear an official take on the momentous rumours that had agitated the whole community.

In all his long years Mordecai had never witnessed such a clamouring throng. The entire Capernaum village seemed to be crammed into the building. He finished reading from the Scroll of the prophet Ezekiel. He rolled it up and passed it to Jairus to return behind the doors of the Ark. The old Pharisee sat down to instruct the people.

A tangible scent of menace percolated through the men as they jossled for position infront of him. Mordecai cleared his throat…avoiding eye contact, he directed his gaze across their heads to the top of the window-frames.

"Brothers," he began in the voice he kept for his Sabbath sermons, "the Sovereign Lord says, 'The people will be secure in their land. They will live in safety and *no-one* will make them afraid…'"

"What about Jesus of Nazareth?" A front-row heckler jabbed a work-worn forefinger in Mordecai's face. The Synagogue erupted. The question opened the flood-gates to pandemonium.

"Where is he?" shouted another.

"He's *alive!*" came a reply from the side.

"Can't be!" a murmur wafted round.

"We've *seen* him!" declared the weaver.

"He's the Christ!" yelled another.

"*Blasphemers!*" Mordecai almost choked with rage. The crescendo of wonder, anger and utter disbelief grew increasingly volatile. Jairus stood up.

"Brothers, *please!*" Jairus struggled to be heard. "Listen. The Rabbi Jesus was crucified." His words drowned in roars from the floor.

"As God is my witness," Jairus shouted, "I watched from the city walls. I saw a soldier drive his sword into the man's side." Roars of horror vied against howls of approval in equal measure.

"Believe me, brothers," Jairus persisted, "Jesus of Nazareth is *dead* and *buried!*"

"You saying my sons are liars?" Zebedee thundered from the side. Jairus blanched.

"I'm saying," he spluttered against an upsurge of shouts and hissing, "I'm saying they've been... mislead... deceived..."

"My sons stake their life Jesus is the Messiah!" Zebedee would not be silenced. At the word 'Messiah' total uproar broke out. A stick, hurled at Zebedee, clipped the shoulder of the man next to him. Women at the back screamed and ran from the Synagogue with the younger children. Men's fists flew. Youths gawped, mesmerised at seeing their elders and betters brawling in an undignified melee. Never had they found the Synagogue so exciting!

Mordecai rose to his feet. Holding up his staff to the people he cried, "Peace, brothers. *Peace*, I beg you." His hands splayed in an attempt to shape a reasoned argument. "Let's see this through the eyes of scripture," he tried a conciliatory tone. "How can this Jesus possibly have been the Messiah? Why! The book of Moses categorically says 'a man hanged on a tree is cursed by God'." Mordecai battled against jeers and strident cat-calls. "Men of Capernaum, can't you see," he implored, "Jesus hung from a tree – a wooden cross! Would our Sovereign God curse his own Messiah? "

Zebedee roared back: "The prophet Isaiah said, 'then shall the eyes of the blind be opened, and the ears of the deaf unstopped'. Well, Pharisee," he taunted, squaring angular shoulders at Mordecai, " we've been witness to these things – you can't deny it!" Men brayed in agreement. Mordecai endeavoured an explanation but Zebedee had no time for his arguments. He knew what he had seen and he believed what his sons had told him. He turned on his heel and elbowed his way through the congregation to the Synagogue door. A third of the men walked out behind him. The enormity of what had just taken place stunned the remaining people into silence.

Mordecai mustered his authority. He glared at the men, his eyes dilated with shock and mistrust.

"This is no way to behave before the presence of Almighty God," he barked. "Go to your homes!"

Without Zebedee, the people's anger defused. They left, chuntering and shuffling their way through the great cedar doors.

In the empty Synagogue, Jairus turned to his uncle in despair.

"What is happening?" He walked to the window and rested an arm against the cool stone frame. The outburst had unnerved him; he was the Synagogue ruler, but he had totally lost control. The congregation's mood had shaken both men. Mordecai sat in the seat reserved for Pharisees, his shoulders stiff with anger.

"Oi," Mordecai sneered, "there'll be another Messiah come next Passover."

"But… they say Jesus is alive!"

"Take no notice," Mordecai snapped. "*You* saw him die. It's all a lot of Jerusalem jiggory-pokery, that's what it is." He sniffed and rubbed his hand around his white beard. "Leave them be, my boy. Don't worry yourself."

Jairus stared out of the window. The distant hills above the lake shimmered blue and tranquil in the morning sunlight as if mocking the storm raging in his chest. He felt sick.

***

"Mother! Do y'know what they're saying?" Keziah burst into the house, her face animated with anticipation, hair tousled in her rush to get home. The market was ablaze with rumour. Across the fish and vegetable stalls, over the spices and at street corners the word was the same:

"Rabbi Jesus is alive!"

'The fishermen have *seen* him,' declared others, fuelling momentum to the sensational news. Kezia flew home with only half a basket of provisions. She left Adah, with Zippie strapped on her back, to buy the olives, cheese, spices and honeycomb her mother wanted.

"Is it true?" Kezia demanded, her heart soaring in wild hope. Leah was flummoxed. Salome had called earlier, babbling some great tale from James and John. Salome said they'd had a meal with Jesus, but… Leah was confused…Jairus hadn't said anything. She needed to wait and ask her husband what it was all about. Oh, how she missed dear Sarah. Sarah was so down to earth. She would know what had happened.

"Could it *possibly* be true?" Kezia asked, practically jumping from foot to foot when the tall figure of her father in his Synagogue robes came through the door.

"Don't listen to wicked gossip!" Jairus was curt.

"But, Father, *everyone's* saying it."

"Then everyone's *wrong!*" he snapped. Leah wanted to tell him what Salome had told her but she realised, the mood he was in, it wouldn't make any difference. She stirred the stew in silence. Kezia took advantage of the fact that, now she had been to Jerusalem, she was an adult. She refused to be sidelined like a child.

"Wouldn't it be wonderful if he *is* alive." Her eyes shone as she watched her father sit on the stool by the window and slip off his sandals. A sandal still in his hand, he pointed it threateningly towards his daughter.

"Don't talk like a little fool," he exploded. "Jesus is *dead*. I was there remember. A whole group of us, Pharisees, Sadducees, scribes, elders – we all watched from the city wall. And I tell you *Jesus is dead!*" He stood up and spoke emphatically. "That's an end to it. I forbid his name to be mentioned in my house!" He swung round and took the stone stairs to the roof two at a time.

Alone on the flat roof, Jairus stared back at the roof of the Synagogue reliving the ugly division in the congregation. How could the people be so deluded? Suddenly, as he looked out over Capernaum, he realised how much he wanted to go back to Jerusalem. But as he tried to think logically, he knew that was impossible until after Kezia's wedding. Kezia's wedding into Zebedee's household…

Merciful Heaven! He had better make peace with Zebedee or the marriage could be cancelled. That would be a devastating humiliation. Jairus stretched his shoulders and sighed aloud as though a great pain had seared up his spine.

***

"Stay *still*, Kezie." Leah tried to place the bridal headdress so that the dowry coins sat level and didn't fall over Kezia's eyes. "That's better," she said with satisfaction. "Now, let's look at you." Leah sat back on her heels and smiled up at her daughter with delight. "Oh, Kezie, you'll be the toast of Capernaum!" Leah laughed and the years fell away. Momentarily, it seemed their roles had reversed as, behind the embroidered head-covering, rich with coins and decorative beadwork, Kezia's expression held a world of care.

"Mother…" she began, embarrassed and flustered and desperately wishing she could talk to Joanna or Sarah rather than her mother. Leah dropped her eyes. She knew by the intonation exactly what was coming next.

"When I get married…" Kezia tried again.

"And that won't be long now," Leah interrupted.

"Well, when I get married… you know… that night… well," her nose wrinkled with the effort of finding the right words, "… what will it be like?" Leah avoided her gaze by standing up and removing the bridal headdress, folding it meticulously and packing it away safely in the cedar wood box.

"It'll be alright, Kezie," Leah reassured her with a bright tone she would have used in encouraging her daughter to try a new fruit. "It might hurt a bit the first time but, as you get to know each other more… understand each other, then, well… it's *natural*. It's what happens."

Kezia blinked. *What* happens? Her mother's words left her no wiser and even more apprehensive. Leah feared another question was on it's way. She killed it by hastily adding, "Of course, the Lord God ordained it for the creation of children. Just think, Kezie, your very own children."

As if coming to Leah's rescue, Zipporah pulled herself up by the bars of her wicker pen. Displaying two bottom teeth and a dimple, she burbled for attention.

"Oh! Where's Adah got to?" Leah turned, grateful for the distraction. The moment for intimate conversation had passed. Kezia went to lift her sister out of the pen.

"I'll take her," she said. "Expect she's wet."

***

The slam reverberated off the black stone walls of the empty Synagogue. Mordecai let the door swing and it had crashed heavily behind him. He walked purposefully to the side room where Jairus taught boys to read the scriptures. Alarmed by the crashing door, Jairus leapt up. He relaxed to see it was only his uncle.

"What now?" he sighed, resigned for Mordecai to regale him with news of more unrest. It was as if he had been plunged into the middle of a religious civil war. The Synagogue congregation had halved in three days. Men argued in the street, outside their homes and down on the quayside. Men he had known for years shunned him. His whole comfortable, predictable world had fractured in a few short hours. So many conflicting stories were flying around he wasn't sure what he believed any more. One thing was certain, it was crucial word of this unrest in Capernaum did not reach the ears of Caiaphas.

"I've been talking to Zebedee." Mordecai sat on the front stone bench nearest the Ark. "He says his boys won't be coming back. Nor any of the others. Even Levi... you know, the one who used to take our taxes. All the men that blasphemer took from round here are staying in Jerusalem."

Jairus' thick eyebrows rose. "Even Simon?" he asked.

"The whole cursed bunch of them!" the old Pharisee spluttered. "And *Simon*," he added in exasperation, "I hear Simon's the worst one! Standing up *preaching*...hectoring any mad-brains who'll listen... claiming this has all been prophesied. *Prophesied!*" he crowed in derision. "I ask you! Simon's an ignorant fisherman from the backwater of Bethsaida. What does he know about prophecy?" Mordecai sneered. He scratched in his beard under his chin. "What's got into the man?"

"What happens now?" Jairus slumped opposite his uncle.

"You need to get on with Kezia's wedding, my boy. Take the peoples' minds off all this. Give them something to celebrate, bring them together... fill them with good wine... and please God, they'll soon forget all this nonsense." He looked hard at Jairus' gaunt face.

"Believe me, my son, I've lived through these things before. The Messiah won't come from *Nazareth*, that's for sure!"

Chapter 15

"ADAH'S sick" Kezia announced as Leah brought the bread basket to the table. "I'll take her some bread but she won't want any pickled fish."

Jairus tore a piece of bread and dipped it in the basin of olive oil. He looked across at Mordecai as if for approval, then at Kezia before staring at the plate of olives on the table.

"Your wedding day is fixed, Kezia." Kezia's knuckles turned white around the bowl she held for Adah. Her mouth wouldn't open. She stood still by the table.

"On the next full moon, we've chosen the third day after Sabbath." Jairus glanced at Leah and smiled his satisfaction. "The third day brings a three-fold blessing. It's all arranged," he continued, " Your mother tells me all your clothes are made and you have everything ready."

Kezia's mind was trying to work out how long since the last full moon. She waited for her mother to say something but it was Mordecai who spoke:

"Ah, that's good news!" he rubbed his hands together and winked at her. "Everyone loves a wedding. You'll do us proud, my dear."

"You won't recognise her in her bridal finery," glowed Leah. She put her hand on her daughter's arm, "I don't think you realise, Kezie, but you've grown into a beautiful young woman."

Colour rose in Kezia's cheeks, more from fear than pleasure at her mother's compliment. She clutched Adah's bowl in one hand, picked up a cup of water in the other and disappeared upstairs without a word.

Adah lay on her mattress. She opened weary eyes as Kezia dropped down beside her.

"My wedding day is fixed," she blurted out in a resigned voice.

"Wonderful!" Adah responded with a weak smile. "I'm so looking forward to it."

Kezia banged the cup of water on the floor causing drops to spill over the side.

"Means I shall have to go and live in Zebedee's house," she sighed.

"Yes, but... we'll still see each other... at the washing pool... and in the market," Adah ran out of strength to speak for a moment. With effort she added, "I'll miss you."

"I'll miss you too," Kezia replied. She noticed the servant-girl's hair was wet with perspiration. "Is there anything else you want?" Adah closed her eyes. She shook her head. Kezia looked intently at the frail body on the mattress. Adah wasn't just unwell, she was ill and illness was unpredictable and frightening. Zippie sat gripping the lattice of her pen, huge eyes watching them both.

Silently, Kezia left the room and crept down to her mother's side.

"I think Adah's got a fever," she said. Leah frowned but said nothing. Kezia tried again, "Should I bring Zippie down here to you?" Leah refilled her husband's wine-cup before replying.

118

"Oh, she'll be alright with you and Adah." She sounded casual.

"But what if Zippie catches the fever?" Kezia asked. Jairus glanced up at his daughter.

"Your mother's right, Kezie. Zippie'll be fine. Don't worry." He and Mordecai carried on eating.

"Adah's really ill, though." Kezia couldn't believe her parents weren't bothered. "She needs a doctor," she added solemnly, knowing it was not her place to suggest such a thing. She lowered her eyes as the atmosphere around the table changed. It was on the tip of her tongue to say… 'if only Jesus was here he would make her well' but the expression on both her father's and her uncle's face precluded any mention of Jesus. It was best she didn't say anything more.

Finally Jairus pushed his empty bowl away, "We'll see how she is in the morning," he said.

**

Zippie opened her mouth like a ravenous baby bird. Each morsel was anticipated and demolished in rapid succession. For a baby who entered the world in such trauma, she was growing into a placid, smiling child.

"What a *heavy* girl you are!" Kezia cooed as she balanced her sister on her knee. Zippie gurgled back without a care in the world. Kezia looked over at the inert figure on the mattress. The bowl of fresh bread and olives lay untouched on the floor, as did the cup of water.

With Zippie fed and settled for the night, Kezia sat in the gathering gloom, her anxiety increasing with every moan and toss that Adah made. Never before had she been with anyone suffering from the fever, but even with her lack of experience, it was obvious Adah was fast deteriorating.

It wasn't until getting ready for bed and hiding her pouch under the mattress that it occurred to her... she wondered...
... would it help? Dare she try?

Nervously she fumbled with the stones Jesus had given her. With a fluttering heart she tipped them out onto her blanket. Gingerly she moved them into patterns as she considered what to do. Her favourite was the deep blue with the flecks of gold. It reminded her of sunlight dancing on the lake. Kezia picked that one first and placed it at the base of Adah's throat. Instantly Adah thrashed in spasm and the stone fell on the mattress. Kezia retrieved it and studied the rest of the stones.

She gazed in bewilderment. Suddenly, she was aware her palms and fingertips began to tingle. She wiped them down her tunic. In desperation she placed all seven stones with trembling fingers. The milky stone and the shimmering honey-coloured one she placed each side of Adah's neck, and the rest she positioned from Adah's breast-bone to her stomach. She leaned over her friend putting her hands each side of Adah's head to still the writhing. Adah's breathing was erratic and her skin felt damp and clammy.

"It's alright, Adah," Kezia whispered. "Jesus will heal you. These are his stones."

Kezia felt her own temperature soar as she looked intently at the bird-like body on the mattress. Adah's taut expression began to relax. She no longer writhed and tossed. Quietly she drifted into a calm sleep.

Taking a chance that Adah would lie still, Kezia moved the blue stone back to the base of Adah's neck and put the milky chrystal on her moist forehead. "Stay still, Adah," she urged softly. "Stay still and sleep. Jesus will heal you." She sat back on her heels exhausted and unsure what else she should do. Her fingers and palms itched and burned inexplicably. She lifted one of Adah's lifeless hands in hers. Using a little almond oil, she began to massage first the hand and then the arm before repeating the same action with the other hand and arm. Adah made no response.

At last, disconsolate and tearfull, Kezia gathered the precious stones, returned them to the pouch and hid them under her mattress. Slipping into her bed, she pulled the sheet up to her chin and stretched out till her toes peeped from under the blanket. If Jesus was alive, she reasoned, why, oh *why* didn't he come to Capernaum? There was so much she needed to ask him about the stones. In the stillness she was aware of her pumping heart. If Adah was no better in the morning; Kezia thought to herself, she might as well throw the stones away.

***

"Come on, 's not like you t' over-sleep!" The familiar voice drifted into Kezia's head but her eyes felt too heavy to open. Until she realised who was speaking! The scales of sleep dropped away and she sat bolt upright on her mattress. Adah had Zippie in her arms and had obviously been up for some time. Kezia stared. There was no trace of fever – not even of weakness.

"That Anna's downstairs." Adah offered her news with her usual air of passing on a deep confidence.

"What does she want?" Kezia asked as she dressed.

"She's looking at your wedding coat and things." Adah's eyes twinkled with anticipation.

"You'll look so lovely, Kezie, you really will. Won't be long now."

'No,' thought Kezia, 'from the next full moon, the third day after Sabbath. Not long enough.'

"I heard them say," Adah chirped merrily, "one of the visitors here from Nazareth is taking the message back to the mistress' sister in Sepphoris. So many people will be coming, Kezie, it'll be the biggest party." Zippie fidgeted and grabbed a handful of Adah's thin hair. "An' you'll be having babies of your own." Adah extricated her hair from Zippie's tight grasp, "Oh, you little kitten! I'll have no hair left in a minute." With that she disappeared down the stairs, the child slung on her back. Kezia flopped back on her mattress – stunned.

'She doesn't know,' Kezia said to herself, 'she's no idea how ill she's been,' Her palms and fingertips tingled once more as she recalled the stones she'd placed on Adah's body the previous night. Was Jesus right after all? Would she be able to help people? She wouldn't tell Adah what she'd done. Not yet anyway. And she certainly wouldn't be throwing the healing stones away now.

"There you are!" Leah greeted the late appearance of her daughter. Anna's eyes narrowed as she realised Kezia had only just woken but her lips made an effort to curl in greeting. The girl would have to be up and about earlier than this when she was under Zebedee's roof, that was for sure!

"We were just looking to see about your jewellery," purred Leah fingering her own fine set of silver filigree earrings and necklace inlaid with the lapis lasuli. "These were my mother's and I wore them on my wedding day," Leah said with nostalgic pride, "they're family treasures Kezie." Kezia smiled as she peered over her mother's shoulder at the box full of beads, bracelets and earrings. She loved jewellery and she knew her wedding day was the one chance in her life to wear glamorous and extravagant things. It would be a day she would look back on for the rest of her life. Leah displayed Kezia's headdress to the inquisitive Anna, who ran her fingers over the two rows of dowry coins and the shell and bead decorations.

"Jairus brought the coat back from Bethlehem." Leah determined that Anna should relay to Salome that Kezia would have nothing but the best when she joined Zebedee's household. Anna, equally determined not to be impressed, gave the wedding clothes her closest scrutiny.

"I must wear the pomegranate brooch Abner made for me," said Kezia.

"Pomegranate?" quizzed Anna.

"Yes, it's beautiful. A dear little pomegranate in leaves… all silver," Kezia replied.

"Fine *Jerusalem* silver," Leah added. "And look, Kezie, you've not seen this…" she went to the cedar chest by the wall and took out a roll of linen. Unwrapping the linen she held up the green and white silk tunic she had purchased from the foreign girl in the market. Kezia took a sharp intake of breath.

"Oh Mother… it's silk!" Leah nodded, thrilled by her daughter's reaction. "I've never worn silk." Kezia took the garment from her mother's hands. She put it to her cheek in delight. "It's as light as a cobweb and soft as…" she had to think, " as soft as the top of Zippie's head," she said and burst out laughing.

"It's for your wedding night," Leah told her. Kezia buried her reddening cheeks in the cool silk folds.

Anna had no wish to be drawn about her own wedding. She didn't want Leah to know that she'd been a servant-girl, just like Adah when the young firebrand fisherman first met her at the southern shore of the lake. At that first meeting he'd taken her for his wife, then brought her back to Capernaum, several years before Jairus and Leah came to the village. Deciding to make a quick retreat before questions were asked, Anna picked up her basket of vegetables and muttered, "Well, it'll be nice to have some more help about place. My girls could do with some sensible company." Then, her sharp little eyes on Kezia, she added. "Jared will be a good man to you. Mind, his father relies heavily on him now his brothers have left."

"But they won't be away too long, will they?" asked Leah as she carefully wrapped the jewellery ready to be tucked away until the wedding day. Anna's thin frame had moved to the door, she turned her head but there was no smile as she spoke.

"Can't see as those boys will ever come back. Salome says they've more important work to do than fishing." And with her parting shot, Anna was gone.

Leah's mood turned serious. She sat down and took both Kezia's hands in hers.

"Kezie, my dear," she began in a halting tone. "When you're in Zebedee's house you'll find they think differently about… certain things. You see…they don't agree with your father." Leah wondered how to continue.

"You mean about Jesus being alive?" A weak smile broke on Leah's face with relief that Kezia understood what she meant.

"Yes, yes dear. It is about the Rabbi Jesus. But you see, you will be in *their* house so you mustn't speak against Zebedee."

"But you've always encouraged me to think for myself." Kezia was mystified by her mother's change in attitude. Leah held firmly to her daughter's hands.

"I'm just saying, Kezie… don't argue. Whatever you think or… or want to believe, and I know you thought the world of Jesus, so did I, but you must never speak against your husband or your husband's family." Leah wasn't sure what expression she read in her daughter's eyes.

"You do understand, Kezie, don't you?"

"I will be a good wife," Kezia replied in a dutifull whisper, devoid of her usual enthusiasm.

As Leah stood up, Kezia threw her arms round her, clinging tightly to her mother's slender body. For several moments they stood in a wordless embrace, each fighting a locked-in fear for what the future would bring.

Chapter 16

Seventeen days later

"THERE now, you'll rival the Queen of Sheba herself!" Joanna stood behind her niece, struggling to fasten the silver and lapis lasuli necklace round the flawless skin of Kezia's neck. It matched perfectly with her silver pomegranate brooch that Abner had given her for a wedding present from Jerusalem. Leah fussed with last adjustments to the bridal headdress. These were just finishing touches to elaborate preparations that had begun at first light. Kezia had been bathed, her hair washed and braided and her body massaged with scented oils. With the necklace in place, Joanna swung back to inspect the eye make-up and lip rouge she had expertly painted on the young bride.

"Mmmm," she murmured, suddenly aware of Kezia's maturing beauty, "shame to cover my handiwork with a veil!" Playfully she jabbed her forefinger on the tip of Kezia's nose. "Cheer up, chicken," she joked, "it's not a funeral." Kezia broke into a broad smile. Joanna exuded a warmth and laughter which encouraged Kezia to regard her presence like a good omen, a guarantee that her wedding would be a happy celebration after all.

Joanna picked up the lace veil. "I remember your mother's wedding day!" she crowed.

"You've never *seen* such rain!" she cast a glance to her sister for confirmation. Leah laughed. Kezia had noticed her mother seemed happier in the last few weeks than she could remember.

"Rain!" Leah giggled, "Thunder and lightning! We had one of the worst storms for years. It wasn't many steps from the wedding bower to Jairus' family home but we got *soaked*."

"Well, the Lord's blessing you today with blue sky and sunshine." Joanna squinted out of the small window. "And it sounds like the whole village is out there waiting for you!"

Musicians had been playing their instruments outside the house for the best part of an hour. Flutes and lyres, trumpets and cymbals – all contrived to heighten the villagers' anticipation as they waited for the bride to emerge.

"Where's Adah?" Kezia, adorned and beautiful, looked round for her friend.

"She's gone with Anna and the girls," said Leah, " they've gone to dress the bower. There's been no holding Adah this morning, she couldn't be more excited if it was her own wedding day."

"I expect she's tied Zippie to the bower," Joanna made a straight-faced comment looking at the empty pen.

Leah's defense was in place; "How could I manage to get Kezie ready with Zippie round my feet?" she whined. Joanna changed the subject.

"So Bride…" she took Kezia's hands in hers, "you're all ready but, are *we*?"

Elegant as always, Joanna's coat was a plain, light pinkish dyed linen and in her headscarf a small gold clasp held three exquisite peacock feathers in place. Leah wore her best embroidered cloak over a fine cotton tunic with mother-of-pearl necklace and armlets. Genuine warmth and happiness engulfed Kezia as she returned the smiles from her mother and aunt. For a few precious moments she forgot the nerves that had kept her awake the previous night. Taking a deep breath, she steadied herself for the momentous leap she was about to make into a new life.

Outside, cheers and applause rippled through the crowd. "Ah," said Leah, "he's on his way!"

Joanna fixed Kezia's veil in place just as the door opened. Jared stood tall and lean, silhouetted against the midday sun pouring in from the courtyard. His beard was thickening and he too had washed the dark hair which hung to his collar.

"Here she is, Jared." Leah smiled at the young man to be her son-in-law. "We're all ready."

Jared stared at his bride and grimaced with unexpected pleasure. She looked radiant and he knew every man in Capernaum would envy him today. His older brothers, James and John were still in Jerusalem but their absence gave him a sense of freedom; he enjoyed being the second man in the family after his father. He'd had enough of being the young boy, he'd had enough of being in his brothers' shadow. He was a man now in his own right; soon to be a married man at that, then he'd be shown some respect. He moved closer to take Kezia's arm. To her relief there was no strong fish odour. Instead he smelt of sweet cedar wood and his tunic was fresh and unstained beneath a long sleeveless cloak his mother had woven in red and blue stripes. Kezia smiled shyly through the veil as she reached out to take his calloused hand.

A jamboree of musicians, family, neighbours and friends surrounded the bridegroom and bride as they paraded to the wedding bower. The cymbals didn't always clash in time with the drummers but no one seemed to mind or even notice. Children scampered in and around the crowd taking it in turns to dart up to Kezia with handfuls of wild flowers. As they passed Simon's house, Kezia's eyes searched in vain for any sign of Sarah. The shutters were tight closed and the door barred.

'Dear Sarah,' thought Kezia, 'she always said she'd be at my wedding… but then, how could she know…'

Nearing the Synagogue the singing, ululating, flutes and trumpets fell silent. Then two lute players from Tiberias began to play a gentle love song as the couple took their last steps up to the great door.

Inside the Synagogue the wedding bower erected for the ceremony in front of the bimah, hung with garlands of flowers, olive branches and swathes of coloured materials. Jared led Kezia by the hand until they both stood beneath the decorated awning. Jairus, Zebedee and Mordecai watched with obvious approval. Jairus and Zebedee had agreed to bury their differences for the sake of Jared and Kezia's marriage. The two men accepted that the normal closeness that would have grown between the two families would not be nurtured. However, they agreed to civil pleasantries on the understanding their social involvement would be infrequent. Jairus had decided to return to Jerusalem without further delay, before another Sabbath. There would be few occasions where his presence would be necessary.

Mordecai's heart missed a beat as Kezia walked towards him, her headdress coins faintly jingling above her veil-covered face. It was hard for him to reconcile the poised beauty, clothed in bridal finery, as his little Kezia, the adoring child he'd watched grow to womanhood. It was Kezia who had lifted his pangs of loneliness following the death of his wife and son, she who had curled in his arms to listen to his stories, Kezia, the one he had come to desire for himself.

He coughed in an attempt to check tears welling in his eyes. He looked at the young bridegroom standing awkwardly under the bower. Distant kin he may be, but, Mordecai's eyes narrowed. He wasn't good enough for his Kezia. Jared's heavy lids and full mouth gave the impression of a selfish, sullen insolence – no mistaking he was Zebedee's boy. The final chords of the love song faded and the assembled congregation waited for the promises and blessing.

With supreme effort to control his emotions, Mordecai stepped forward to conduct the wedding ceremony.

"The sacred Scroll of the prophet Malachi tells us the Sovereign God's purpose for marriage. The Eternal and Sovereign God will make you one body and one flesh in the Covenant of marriage. Your children will be called the children of the Most High." Mordecai looked in turn between Jared and Kezia. He took a deep breath:

"Jared, son of Zebedee, I charge you before the Lord your God to make this solemn vow." Sweat broke out on Jared's hair strewn lip. His mouth went dry.

Mordecai continued gravely, "Repeat after me… Kezia, I will make you my wife."

Jared's voice went husky with nerves as he repeated the words after the Pharisee…

"I will be true and faithful… I will show you constant love and mercy… and make you mine for ever… I will keep my vow and make you mine… you will acknowledge me as your Master."

Mordecai looked down on the bride. "Kezia, daughter of Jairus, before Almighty God will you make your solemn vow to be faithful to this man and to acknowledge him as your Master?" From behind the veil Kezia consented in a firm voice.

On the old Pharisee's direction, Jared took off his outer coat and symbolically placed it round Kezia's shoulders. Mordecai nodded and said; "She is covered by your garment, she is yours. So may the Lord bless you and keep you. May the Lord pour out happiness upon you that you may be fruitful and multiply. Peace be upon your house!"

Wild applause broke out the moment the blessing was complete. The dancers stamped and twirled as Jared led his bride out of the Synagogue accompanied by the combined chords from every musician in the area. Adah ran to the newly-weds to place myrtle crowns on their heads.

"I'm so happy," she squealed, "you look perfect, Kezie."

Jairus made sure nothing was stinted for his daughter's wedding breakfast. In a field at the edge of town, recently harvested of barley, tables groaned with fresh fish, a roasted kid, sweetmeats and delicacies, eggs, fruits, nuts and olives and flagons of wine. Everyone entered into the joyous celebration in high spirits. Musicians took it in turns to eat and drink so that some kind of music played the entire time. After the feasting came the dancing.

"I must be first to dance with the most beautiful bride in all Galilee," Seth whisked Kezia into the middle of the field which had been cleared for dancing.

"Oh, the buffoon!" chuckled Joanna to Leah as they watched. "Seth dances like a camel with its legs tied together!" The sisters creased with laughter. The fact that Seth had little skill at dancing only served to put others with similar drawbacks at their ease. In moments a dozen couples were whooping and skipping round the field, shouting, laughing and teasing each other.

"You've got another one, Seth." Kezia grinned up at the new purple turban.

Seth jumped and clapped to his own particular rhythm as he relpied, "King Herod decreed that the finest potter in the land shall always wear *purple*! How else, my dear, are the good people of Sepphoris to find me?" He whisked her back to Jared who stood mawkishly with his fourth cup of wine.

"Your wife, man," Seth told him, "has the feet of an angel." Jared couldn't think how to reply to the potter's compliment; he nodded self-consciously and downed his wine.

Mordecai sidled up, "Can you spare a dance with your old uncle then?" Still in his flowing, blue Pharisee's robes, he took Kezia's arm as other couples joined them to form a circle. The musicians stepped up both tempo and volume as the dancers swayed and stamped, jigged and wove in and out of the circle. As the afternoon wore on a breeze sprung up from the lake, reviving the revellers who returned their appetites to the restocked table.

Leah took hold of Joanna's arm. "There's something I want to tell you," she whispered drawing her sister aside from the other women. Joanna looked concerned.

"What is it? Are you ill?"

"No, no, nothing like that!" Leah rested against the stone hedge and put a hand on her belly. Her eyes conveyed her news.

"Leah, that's *marvellous* – but, why so secretive?" Joanna gushed a spontaneous hug.

"For one thing, this is Kezie's day," Leah said softly, " my news will wait. And for another, I've had too many false hopes in the past... I need to be sure everything is alright before Jairus knows. Joanna," she dropped her gaze to the earth, "this is my last chance to bear a son."

Joanna's response was bluff. "What are you talking about! Of course it's not your last chance…" Leah raised her hand to Joanna's arm,

"Oh yes, it is. I know it in my heart… I have no more strength. If the Lord grants me a son. I can die happy…"

"Leah, don't say such a thing!" Joanna was shocked.

"I must say it, Joanna, for I want to know that if… if I should die, then you will look on Kezie as your own and help her care for my son."

"What about Zipporah?" Joanna asked. Leah shrugged.

"Poor Zippie," she sighed. "She belongs to Adah more than me. Zippie will always have a mother."

Joanna recovered her composure, gave her sister another brief, tight hug and said, "Don't you worry, sister, you know how precious Kezie is to me. But, she's married now and it'll be Salome and Anna who'll be her help."

Leah stood up from the hedge, seeing Seth making his way towards them. "No," she said firmly. "Kezie will look to *you*." She paused, "I think we both know that," she smiled, "and I'm glad."

***

It had been a long day. Months of nervous anticipation, the tense solemnity of the wedding blessing together with hours of dancing, singing and talking to the scores of guests conspired to make Kezia feel exhausted. By the time the musicians gathered themselves to accompany the bridal party down to Zebedee's house, Jared was none too steady on his feet. The good-humour of the day continued as the sun dropped below the Galilee hills. The unseasonally warm air carried sounds of celebration way into the night. Jairus soaked up the villagers' congratulations on how everything had worked according to plan.

"You'll be well satisfied with today." Mordecai surveyed the exuberant crowd. Jairus nodded.

"Yes! A good day." He stifled a yawn, "Couldn't have gone better!" He smiled and took his uncle's arm. They walked away from the raucous young men and girls who surrounded his daughter and new son waiting to tow them to their nuptial tent. Zebedee had erected the tent on the side of his house. Cramped but adequate for the time being. Plenty of time for Jared to build an extension to his father's house or perhaps build his own. Time would tell.

Zebedee had given a good bride price and Kezia was taking a considerable dowry as Jared's wife. The field was emptying fast. Leah had already gone home with Joanna, Seth and Adah.

"You're a fine host," Mordecai offered by way of congratulation. "You can rest easy, my son, Zebedee can have no complaint at today." He sniffed and belched from over-indulgence. "I told you, they'd soon forget all that talk of Jesus being alive. Five minute wonder, that's all!"

Arriving home, Jairus took himself up to the roof to reflect on the day and enjoy the quiet dusk. Like most wedding celebrations, he knew the party for Kezia and Jared would continue in the morning and last for several more days yet. He looked to the far end of the lake, up in the hills where pin-pricks of light were appearing in the deepening darkness like dropped stars.

But Jairus' mind was far away. He couldn't wait to get back to Jerusalem.

***

Boisterous whoops and ululating remained outside the nuptial tent long after Jared and Kezia had been ceremoniously pushed inside. A mattress sprinkled with poppy petals and sprigs of rosemary was the only furnishing. Kezia had brought her belongings in a basket which she placed to one side of the mattress. She looked at Jared. This was the moment she had dreaded. She intended to be a good wife, she wanted to please her husband… but she wasn't sure how.

Jared slumped down on the mattress pulling roughly at her coat so that she fell on top of him with an embarrassed squeal. The proximity of her perfumed neck and the expression in her direct gaze caused him to roll away from her. He wasn't ready. "You'd better light the lamp," he said gruffly. Kezia got to her feet and busied herself about the oil lamp,

Jared sat up, leaned forward and held his head between his hands. Images of Pei Qi throbbed in front of his closed eyes. It was so quick and easy with her…he knew what to do with Pei Qi… but Kezia… this was serious. She was his wife. Suddenly the weight of expectation bore down on him crushing the energy out of him like the grinding stone in the olive press. He knew his mother would be round in the morning for the ritual examination of the sheet, proof of Kezia's virginity. His stomach wasn't used to the spiced goat meat and he'd eaten two many of his mother's sweetmeats.

Nausea made him sweat. His head pounded.

Kezia removed her bridal headdress and began to undress. She folded her Bethlehem coat and placed it over the leather pouch and stones she had hidden in the bottom of the basket. Removing her tunic, she fumbled, self-conscious of her nakedness in front of this man; someone she hardly knew and of whom she was more than a little afraid. This man who was now her husband and master for life.

Lamp-light flickered over her firm, upturned breasts casting a warm amber glow across the rest of her nubile body. Silently, she combed her hair. From now on she would only be able to wear her hair loose indoors; anywhere else she would need to cover her hair like every other wife. Joanna had impressed on her that she must always perfume her body and comb her hair before lying with her husband.

The shimmering silk tunic her mother had given her slipped over her head clinging to her ripening contours. Finally, when she could think of nothing else to do to prolong her absence from her husband's side, Kezia perched tentatively on the side of the mattress. She gazed demurely at the oil lamp. Her shallow breathing caused her heart to race. She bit her bottom lip.

Only then did the sounds register. Looking closely at the figure sprawled across the mattress, she realised Jared was fast asleep.

***

Kezia woke with the sensation of drowning. She gasped as Jared's full weight expelled all the air from her lungs. The pain made her shreak in terror as he lunged inside her. It felt as if with the next thrust she would be split in two. Jared cupped a hand over her mouth, swearing and cursing at her to keep quiet. He wouldn't put it past sneaky little Debra to be listening outside their tent.

Just as she thought she was dying in agony and asphyxia, he stopped. He fell back on the mattress panting. Kezia curled away from him, shaking and sobbing into her pillow, legs pulled up in foetal position against the pain. She could never get used to this. Her bruised body went into shock. She shivered in the silk tunic but, until Jared was asleep, she was too afraid to move and reach for the blanket.

***

Anna was round at first light. Her lips simpered as she took in the scene. Miriam brought a bowl of fruit but Debra began at once ferreting in Kezia's basket. "I want to try on your wedding headdress " she said lifting it out.

"Put that back, my lady! " Anna ordered. Kezia crouched motionless on the mattress, blanket pulled up over her knees. Jared had crept out while she slept in order to avoid his mother's visit, but Anna was not expected. Anna was the *last* person Kezia wanted to see.

"Get up, my dear," Anna made a poor attempt at sweetness but Kezia heard the underlying command. She complied. Excruciating pain between her legs made walking a torture, but she would *never* confide in Anna. With Kezia off the mattress, Anna enacted the mother-in-law's role, pulled back the blanket and inspected the sheet. An involuntary gasp signalled her surprise at the amount of blood on the sheet, but she made no comment. Her curiosity was satisfied. She could report back to Salome; Jared had wed a virgin.

Miriam stood in the middle of the tent, the bowl of fruit in her hands.

"My dear soul, girl," Anna tugged impatiently at Miriam's arm, "put the bowl *down*. Do I have to tell you everything?" Miriam blushed and placed the fruit bowl on the floor. Kezia felt sympathy for the crest-fallen girl, "Thank you Miriam," she managed, her voice a mere whisper, even a whisper hurt.

Anna's older daughter responded with pitiful gratitude for

that small recognition. In a circular motion Debra flounced in and out of the tent.

"Jared can make you a table soon," Anna said. "Now, I'll need you to grind some more corn…we ran out yesterday. Put on your normal clothes first, then you can always come and change to go back to the party." With that she turned on her skeletal heels and pulled Miriam out of the tent. Kezia swallowed the lump that burnt her throat. This was it. She was a married woman now – and there was work to be done.

"Kezia?" Anna's voice trilled from the courtyard.

"Coming!" A desperate longing overwhelmed her, an impetuous craving to beg Joanna and Seth to take her back with them to Sepphoris… Was this how her life would be? No longer Jairus' daughter but Jared's wife… or Anna's slave.

Chapter 17

WEEKS ground into joyless months. Kezia faced her new routine in Zebedee's household with resignation. Daily, she and Miriam made yogurt, fetched water with the servants, and baked bread. Debra gathered kindling wood, generally messed around and took every opportunity to poke fun at Miriam or snipe bitchy comments behind Kezia's back. Anna's skill at manipulating the women for her own advantage made the Roman Emporor look like a novice. She went to the market, and spent hours, like Leah, with the spindle and the loom. Easy-going Salome avoided confrontation with her sister-in-law, preferring the option of a quiet life.

Jared proved erratic with his marital demands. Most nights he went out with the fishing boats, but, on the nights he slept with his wife, his needs were quickly sated. Leah had been right in one aspect, it was never as bad as the first time, nor did he attack her in her sleep again. The discomfort was bearable so long as it was short-lived. Kezia considered it a most unnatural and unpleasant way to make babies.

Jared never spoke during their coupling nor did he offer any kind words, or attempt to kiss her then, or at any other time. Her days passed working alongside Miriam, who, though retiring and monosyllabic, blossomed in the company of her new and encouraging kinswoman.

Kezia's weekly highlight was the visit to the washing pool to meet Adah and Zippie. As Leah's pregnancy progressed, Salome suggested Kezia should visit her mother most days to monitor her condition.

Jairus left for Jerusalem two days after the wedding and before the celebrations concluded. He left without knowing Leah was carrying another child. Kezia worried for her mother who, although radiant with the prospect of a son, nevertheless looked pale and ethereal, as if an evening breeze could pass right through her.

Two and sometimes three times a week, when the day's work was done and before the fishermen went down to their boats, men crowded into Zebedee's courtyard. These gatherings reminded Kezia of the days when her father had received travelling Rabbis and Pharisees around their table. But the overriding reason for her interest centred on the stories the men told about Jesus. Squeezed behind Salome, bits of stone wall jutting into her back, the hours spent listening to the men discuss Jesus became bright lights in her dull weeks. There was always a visitor who brought fresh news from Jerusalem, news of Simon, and the brothers James and John. Zebedee had taken to calling Simon, 'Peter', and voiced, with considerable pride, that James was now 'Leader' of the Jerusalem disciples.

Zebedee gloated over each chance to boast about his elder sons. Jared boycotted the gatherings.

"Sick of hearing 'bout them!" Jared fumed whenever Kezia attempted to tell him about his brothers. "What're they doin t'earn their keep?" was his only comment.

Although she missed Sarah being around, and she knew how much her mother missed Sarah too, Kezia was glad she was safe with Simon in Jerusalem. No wonder she hadn't been able get back for her wedding. Listening to the men's animated conversations, they made it sound as if Jesus was alive. Kezia didn't understand. They never actually said where he was, but they laughed a lot, prayed a lot, passed round bread and shared a wine cup together.

Kezia knew her Uncle Mordecai would fly into a purple fury if he heard half the things she heard in Zebedee's courtyard. To her, the men's enthusiasm became a real tonic. She longed to hear more. Their good-humour was so different from the droning formality of worship in the Synagogue. Each man seemed convinced that Jesus had given them some miraculous new way of life: a life of freedom and blessing. Kezia listened... and wondered... and held tightly to the pouch hanging from her belt...

With Esther dead and Sarah away in Jerusalem, Anna took upon herself the role of Capernaum's midwife. Kezia prayed Joanna would come back to help with her mother's labour. Anna wasn't 'family' and it didn't seem right she should wheedle her way to sharing her mother's intimate moments.

Some nights, lying alone on the hard mattress, Kezia fantasised about what it would be like to have her own baby. Every time she thought about it she prayed it wouldn't be a girl. Her own, limited experience had taught her life was infinitely better for men than women. She thought of all the girls and women she knew and decided they were like caterpillars confined for ever in the chrysalis of home and drudgery while men clould fly free as butterflies.

In the secret depths of her being, Kezia longed to fly.

***

Since the marriage, Jared found it increasingly difficult to see Pei Qi. But see her he must. She became a compulsion, an addiction he could not live without. On the rare night his father didn't need him, he would take a small boat and row down towards Magdala. From there it was less than a mile's walk to the traveller's camp. Once in the cave he would make three convincing owl calls… and wait. So far his secret hadn't been found out.

The fishing boats had brought in better catches recently and Jared had not been able to get away for nearly three weeks. Finally, he told the hired men he would take out his own boat:

"Get a good catch from further down the shore." They looked at him in disbelief. "Nearer side of Tiberias," Jared bluffed. "You don't need me tonight." The men said nothing. Jared was no great help anyway, let him go down to Tiberias… or wherever! The older men had their suspicions about his motives but it was none of their business.

Jared pushed the boat out into the black water of the lake. Thoughts of Pei Qi excited him fit to burst. A late summer squall whipped waves high against the side of the boat but nothing could cool his ardour for the smiling, foreign girl who had bewitched his senses.

He pulled the boat onto the beach at Magdala. He walked toward the travellers' camp, the sacking over his shoulders clinging damp and heavy as he climbed to their usual cave. The air inside the cave carried the fetid odour of a disused latrine. Jared stood in the entrance sweating from anticipation and exersion from his hasty scramble up the hillside. Cupping his hands to his mouth, he imitated an owl's hoot. He smirked. No-one would know his calls from a real owl; his impersonation was the best he'd heard.

Biting at his nails, he leaned on the wall to wait.

Time passed.

Pei Qi did not appear.

Jared repeated the calls. Maybe she hadn't heard him the first time.

Again he waited.

Jared's acute hearing picked up a rustle of undergrowth. He stood, flat against the cave wall, in the shadows lest it wasn't Pei Qi. A high-pitched giggle preceded her into the cave. Jared leapt forward and grabbed her to him, tasting spice on her tongue, aroused beyond control by her wriggling body. When she drew away he reached into his pouch for the required denarii and Pei Qi looked up into his face smiling as ever. She held up an extended hand to indicate her fee had gone up to five denarii.

Jared didn't have five denarii on him, but he wasn't going to be denied his pleasure for want of a couple of coins. Growing accustomed to the near darkness of the cave, he shook his head and grinned down on her. It was then she touched her belly. She made a cradle of her arms and rocked them to and fro. Jared swallowed. Pei Qi pointed at him then to her belly and nodded enthusiastically. Jared took an involuntary step back and shook his head. His mind went into melt-down. What was she on about? She couldn't be having his child – how many other men paid for her? He shook his head vigorously, he wasn't going to be caught like that!

Pei Qi snatched at his hand to place it on her stomach still nodding – still smiling. He wrenched his hand away as she tried to nestle against him. His rough response provoked a stream of garbled invective. All smiles were gone. He startled as her voice rose higher. Pei Qi began to scream at him. Terrified someone might hear them, instinctively he covered her mouth with his hand. Squirming, with the reflex of a wounded jackall, she sank needle sharp teeth into his flesh. Jared yelped and jumped back.

Pain ignited the touch-paper of his fury. He lunged at the girl clamping both hands tight around her throat. Pei Qi fought back, writhing and beating tiny clenched fists against his bare arms. Jared's grip tightened round her neck as he shook her. All he could think of was that he had to stop the foreign whore from shouting. He squeezed with all his might. She must *stop*. she must...she *must*... he would *make* her stop...

He felt her relax and fall limp in his arms. The sensation of her soft, warm body, yielding in silent submission, defused his anger. In manic lust he ripped up her tunic and forced himself hard and deep inside her. His violent stabs induced the ecstasy of release he'd craved too long. He panted and grunted as if he was hauling a whole night's catch ashore on his own, then slumped against her, crushing her slight frame like a rag doll against the cave wall.

Suddenly the sweet satisfaction that rippled through his body turned to stark horror. He opened his arms – Pei Qi's body slithered to the ground. Even in the darkness, he knew...

She was dead.

Seized with panic, he peered out from the cave, scanning the dark hillside for any sign of movement. A few fires smouldered in the distance but, except for the occasional barking dog, he could detect no sound or movement from the tents. All at once his head swam. The suffocating night air closed down on him in thick, ominous waves. His impulse was to run, but shock rendered his legs to jelly.

He sank to the cave floor, his back to the girl's body. Whore! Why had she done this to him? His fingers clawed at his hair in desperation to sort out a solution. But the more he tried to think the more wild and scrambled his thoughts became. He must get rid of the body... *fast*... but... how?

"Is something wrong?" Kezia feared her cooking wasn't good enough. Jared stared into his bowl of lentil soup pushing the spoon round and round without tasting it. Salome hovered, making a pretence of not listening to their conversation but, every now and then, darting concerned glances between the couple.

"Aren't you hungry?" Kezia tried to coax a response. Jared sulked into the bowl. At last he broke the silence.

"There's no money in fishing anymore," he slurred. Salome promptly sat down at the table opposite her son.

"Don't go saying such things to your father!" she said quickly. Debra and Miriam wiped bread around their empty bowls, eyes fixed on their cousin.

"You can't leave the fishing, too!" Anna chimed. She pinched her lips together and folded her hands in her thin lap. Jared gave a dismissive snort.

"Well," he drawled, " it's true! S'not enough fish for all the boats that's on the lake now." He dug a crust into the soup and slurped it into his mouth.

"Your father says the fishing's better now than it's been for years!" Salome accused. Jared ignored her. Debra couldn't contain herself,

"Are you going to Jerusalem?" she quizzed.

"Nope!" he replied, his answer thick with bread.

"What then?" Anna demanded in high-pitched pique.

"Goin' to Sepphoris." Jared's announcement met with silence as the five females round the table digested the statement, none of them quite sure whether the news was good or bad. Precocious as ever, Debra leapt in with another question:

"What'll you do?" she badgered. Now that he'd plucked up the courage to speak of his intentions, Jared devoured the contents of his bowl and looked to Kezia for more. Dutifully she refilled her husband's bowl and fetched more bread to the table. Debra grew bored waiting for her answer. Gleefully, she offered her own news:

"I heard one of the foreign traders is missing." Debra looked round for impact. "One of the girls…"

Anna tut-tutted with her tongue, "We're not interested in foreign girls," she snapped.

Debra, who never knew when to keep quiet, blurted: "*I* think she's been murdered!"

Anna swung round on her youngest. "I'll murder *you* in a minute if you don't hold your tongue!"

Kezia tried to make sense of what Jared had said. Sepphoris! The weariness from her day's chores fell away and a smiled played at the corner of her lips. She liked the idea of going to Sepphoris. She would be near Joanna and Seth. She liked the idea very much indeed. She waited for Jared to finish his second bowl.

"Men are saying," he said finally, "there's *real* money in the building trade." Salome's heart sank at the thought of Zebedee's reaction. "They say," Jared went on, avoiding his mother's eyes, "they say there's not enough men for quarry work nor on the building sites…and pay's good!" He began to talk with conviction, "It's a whole new city up there. Markets and a bank, grand houses and…"

"What d'*you* know about building?" Anna demanded. She knew her brother's boy; he was no builder, he hadn't the muscle for heavy manual work in a quarry. Salome could feel her stomach knotting.

"They want more men," Jared slouched, sullen and

defiant. "And we're going." If he had bothered to look in Kezia's direction, he would have seen a glint of pleasure and support. Anna got up from the table and went to the spindle. Her fingers tweaked and tugged nervously at the wool.

"Well," Salome said at last, "*you'll* have to tell your father then. But, he won't like it!" She turned to Kezia, "And when's your mother due? This is no time for you to be leaving her." In the shock of Jared's announcement, Kezia had forgotten her mother's condition. She thought for a moment before making any comment.

"Her time isn't yet. And she's got you," she said in an effort to soften Anna's glare, "And there's Joanna. She'll be with mother for the birth." The young wife tried to sound confident as realisation hit her that birthing was ever more precarious for her mother. The girls looked at one another in dismay. In just a few months Kezia had brought a sparkle into their lives and they couldn't imagine her not being around. Debra considered bursting into tears but checked herself in case an outburst banished her from the room and denied her first-hand knowledge of what was going on. Salome said no more. Jared chewed some olives and spat the stones noisily into the soup bowl.

Chapter 18

KEZIA seized on the idea of going to Sepphoris as a great adventure, a welcome blessing to escape from Zebedee's repressive and joyless household.

The glow from the single oil-lamp cast gentle shadows on the otherwise stark interior of the tent. Kezia sat on the edge of the mattress drawing the tortoiseshell comb slowly through her hair. She looked at Jared who already lay across the blanket. For days she had felt his tension and tried to understand the pressure he must be under, as the remaining son, to tell his father he intended to leave. Ever since his brothers James and John had left, Zebedee never missed an opportunity to tell people how Jared would carry on the family fishing business… and now…well! It took a brave man to defy Zebedee's legendary, volcanic temper. Brave – or desperate. Jared's eyes were closed but Kezia wasn't fooled, she knew he was awake.

"Didn't know how you felt about the fishing," she said quietly.

"Why should you?" Jared replied without opening his eyes.

"We could stay with Joanna and Seth while you find work."

"Didn't think you'd want to leave Capernaum."

"I'm your wife," Kezia reminded him. "Wives go with their husbands."

"May as well go tomorrow, then." He sat up and studied her. She was so calm, she didn't make a fuss like the other women. His wife was so accepting…so beautiful. Why was it so impossible to love her? He must be mad, he told himself.

"Better get some sleep," he muttered at her, then lay down again and turned his face towards the wall.

***

With her arms around Leah and the protrusion of her unborn sibling, Kezia fought back her tears. The reality of saying goodbye to her mother, to Zippie, Uncle Mordecai and Adah poured a cold shower on her initial excitement at the Sepphoris plans.

"I feel I'm losing you for the second time," sighed Leah, kissing Kezia's damp cheeks. "But you'll come and see your baby brother, won't you?" Zippie, her head a mass of darker chestnut bubbles than Kezia's had been, lodged on Adah's back, securely strapped in place. Sensing the emotion of the moment, the child began to wimper.

"Of course, I'll come," Kezia promised. She extricated herself from her mother and moved to bid farewell to her uncle.

"Oh, my Kezia! My sweet child." The old Pharisee shut his eyes as he held her close. "I cannot smile until you return to Capernaum." He kissed the top of her headscarf prolonging the embrace. "Promise me you won't forget your old Uncle Mordecai." He broke the embrace and placed his hand on her shoulder, "Don't forget to say the prayers I taught you and… and the Lord God bless you with *many* sons."

Kezia turned to Adah. It was even harder to say goodbye to Adah; she was like a sister and they shared so much. Kezia threw her arms round the slender servant girl and felt the tremble of her sorrow. She went to speak but the words stuck as her throat tensed in a sharp pain. Instead, they exchanged quivering smiles as Kezia picked up the bundle of all her worldly goods and walked away down the lane to where Jared waited for her. Her sandaled feet made a dull thud on the compacted earth of the roadway; each thud taking her into another life. She just wished she could take her family, mother, Zippie, Uncle Mordecai, Adah – she wished all of them could go with her to Sepphoris.

***

At the corner of the lane, Kezia turned to look back. Her family stood waving. They waved her out of their sight. A dart of panic caught her breath. Walking into this next phase of life, suddenly felt very lonely. It was an entirely new sensation to be removed from her family's close support. Jared strode out in front of her as she committed to memory each familiar black-stoned dwelling, each date palm and glimpse over the short, ploughed fields below the hills.

They walked in silence, south along the shore road towards Tiberias. Kezia relived in her mind the last time she had set out from Capernaum – that fateful pilgrimage to Jerusalem. So much had happened since then. The couple trudged through Tiberias and, after about three and a half hours they reached the end of the lake and the wide plain at the beginning of the Jordan valley. From now on they had to take the main road west that climbed into the hills, the main trade route to Nazareth, Sepphoris and on to the Great Sea ports.

The intense heat of summer was long past making the climb into the Galilee hills much easier to cope with. At the top of the first rise, Kezia stopped and turned to savour her last glimpses of the lake. Clouds and currents carved swathes of varying blues and greys across the water. The higher they climbed, the brown Syrian hills reflected in the water on the far side. Kezia gazed down on the lake for the last time. It was strange looking down, she thought the water looked more serene and beautiful from the high road in the hills than from the water's edge.

"Can't stop yet." Jared's pace was unrelenting. "Couple more hours before dark. When we find a stream, we'll bed down." Kezia was curious as to why they had walked all along the lake and through Tiberias before striking out to the west. She was sure Joanna never came through Tiberias. Joanna came down through the Valley of the Doves below Mount Arbel, a far more direct road and closer to Capernaum. However, Kezia had learnt not to question her husband. His mood was reasonable at the moment so it certainly wasn't worth upsetting him.

Thoughts of Joanna and Seth helped to dull the ache of leaving Capernaum. After all the things Joanna had told her about where she lived, an almost mystic assurance welled up in her heart – it felt like a moment of destiny and gave her a new confidence. Kezia was positive she would find happiness in the new city.

The back of Jared's black, wavy hair glistened in his neck. But it wasn't only the uphill climb that made him sweat. As he forged ahead of his wife, his mind fought with the nightmare images of his terrible secret. Every cave mouth in the limestone escarpment, every boulder, every step he took, he saw the crumpled figure of Pei Qi. The possessions slung on his back taunted him with the same weight as his lifeless burden had been on that dark night.

He walked in a daze, churning over and over his every action… of using his fish knife to hack off the child-like limbs… of filling the sacks they had previously used on the cave floor…weighting them with stones… the effort of rowing his small boat almost to the middle of the lake… heaving the sacks over the side… washing himself… scrubbing the blood from his fingernails… sluicing the boat… then finally, exhausted, rowing back to Capernaum's harbour to face the scorn of his father's hired men. They had laughed at his empty net.

"No good going to sleep on the job!"

"You've got a lot to learn yet, boy."

"Try a bit o' bait next time!"

They'd sneered at his ability. It rankled that they never treated his brothers James and John like they treated him. He cursed them all over again as the road levelled out onto a plateau. They paused, surveying the open countryside spread out before them. A cluster of flat-roofed houses and black goat-hair tents made a welcome sight. Jared looked round at Kezia who was, by this time, struggling to match his pace and stride. Beneath a threatening black cloud, the setting sun dazzled in a brilliant gold stripe. Kezia squinted at her husband.

"This'll do." His voice sounded relieved. "We'll make Sepphoris early tomorrow."

As they approached the jumble of dwellings, ragged children ran to greet them. One small girl slipped her grubby hand into Kezia's and danced along beside her. Kezia smiled down at the child's exuberance but had no energy left to join in. Sheep and goats roamed nearby and a work-worn donkey stood tethered outside the first house. A charcoal fire glowed in the courtyard tended by a plump woman. She looked up as the young couple stopped in the road. The child clung to Kezia's hand.

"Peace be on your house." Jared eyed the woman with a winning smile before asking, "Where's your spring?"

"Over here!" replied the small girl tugging Kezia across the yard, by-passing the woman, who was, in all probability, her mother.

"Where're you heading?" the plump woman called after them.

"Sepphoris!" Jared's tone gave the impression he was engaged on very important business. The woman returned the stranger's smile and her years fell away. She held his gaze and tilted her head. Kezia, in her tiredness, was more resigned than irritated by the way Jared was so much more pleasant to strangers than to those he was supposed to love.

"We've hay in the barn if you need to spend the night." She then turned her gaze to Kezia. "You must eat with us," she added with unexpected, genuine warmth.

Dusk fell swiftly as the woman and her shepherd husband lingered round the spluttering embers talking with Jared. Kezia played with the girl and sang her some folk songs she and Adah had sung to Zippie. At last Jared led her over to the low-slung, ramshackle barn. A dozen or so chickens had already taken up their night-time positions and clucked with sleepy curiosity at the human disturbance. The sweet scent of hay in the barn was blissfully soporific and Kezia lay back against a rick, thankful to close her eyes. For once she was oblivious to the stars twinkling through great gaps in the roof. Jared lay down heavily beside her. She braced herself to accept her wifely duty, but he made no attempt to touch her. Too weary even to register relief, she lost consciousness and sank into that inner dimension of sleep.

The lure of just a few more miles to their destination was the incentive Kezia needed to be up and away from the farm as soon as possible. The dawn air was fresh and crisp and degrees cooler than back home in Capernaum. The gradient of the road was steady but nothing as steep as leaving Galilee. More people and carts appeared on the road the nearer they got to Sepphoris. When they came to the cross-roads where the Beth Shean road met the road to the Great Sea, suddenly the whole world seemed on the move in each direction. Traders on their camel caravans, farmers with laden donkey-carts, artisans and peasants, shepherds and Roman cavalry, clusters of men like Jared obviously seeking work and travelling rabbis with their disciples. A continual flow of travellers picked their way along the newly laid Roman road.

"It's like going to Jerusalem!" Kezia said as she walked behind her husband's shoulder. Jared's determined stride belied the fact that he'd never been on that road before and, as they walked by all the other people, he was having major qualms about leaving the security of the fishing boats. Fishing was all he knew. Leaving Capernaum was a desperate reaction. He dared not risk any stall-holders linking him to the missing girl…

"D'you know where Seth lives?" he asked. A wagon rattled past as he spoke, it's driver cursing and whacking the wayward oxen's bony rump with a stick.

"What d' you say?" Kezia hadn't heard for noise of the wagon.

"I said, d'you know where Seth lives?" he repeated, his voice raised in impatience.

"Joanna said the pottery's just inside the Nazareth gate… you only have to ask for the potter in the purple turban!"

Kezia smiled at the thought of Seth's unconventional head wear. "Everyone will know where he lives." Optimism and confidence rang in her reply.

"Look! That must be it!" Jared moved to the side of the road and stopped. They neared the wide valley that divided the village of Nazareth from the imposing range of hills on top of which stood the shining city of Sepphoris. The highest hill that had just come into their vision. A vast aqueduct followed the ridge until it disappeared into the city wall. Kezia snatched the opportunity of their pause to drink from her leather water carrier. The first site of Sepphoris inspired very different emotions from her first view of Jerusalem. Kezia was only visiting the Holy City for the few days of Passover, but as she looked across the valley towards the walled city, she knew she was looking at a place she was going to call home.

The road led straight across the lowland patchwork of pasture and crops. Soon the towering ramparts grew out from the boulder strewn hill, dominating the entire landscape. It was all so much bigger, cleaner and more modern than Jerusalem. Kezia noticed a jutting outline with what looked from a distance like rock circles facing out across the valley.

"What's that?" she asked Jared. He looked up, blinking at the sun-baked stones.

"Don' know," he muttered, irritated at his ignorance of city buildings. "Maybe some place they have races." He threw a guess as an afterthought. As they approached the gate, the village of Nazareth was just visible behind them. "Must be Nazareth Gate," Jared declared.

The guards at the gate scrutinised each traveller as they entered and the sudden slow progress caused an impatient bottleneck. Men in fine-woven garments with a purposeful air pushed in front of an old woman, her cart piled with vegetables.

A donkey weighed down with wicker baskets received a kick from its driver as it paused to snatch a clump of dried grass. Kezia watched in amazement as a small detachment of soldiers came out of the city gate laughing and joking. She'd not seen soldiers behave like that before – what a difference to the soldiers who had harried the pilgrim party on the way to Jerusalem. The soldiers ignored the passing travellers and instead of their notorious march, they ambled down the road.

There was no point in waiting for space to walk in through the Nazareth Gate. It was every man, woman and donkey for themselves. Immediately the city bustle and noise swept the young couple from Capernaum into its hold.

They stopped, creating a human island amid a constant steam of assorted traffic. They stared down the length of what had to be the widest street in the world. Hundreds of people meandered round the shops and stalls for as far as the eye could see. Silently they both wondered how they would ever find the potter's house in this hectic swirl of strangers.

"Perhaps we should try that way," suggested Kezia pointing to a street running to their right, parallel to the city walls. After a few paces Jared stopped beside an old man guarding sacks of fragrant spices.

"We're looking for the potter with the purple turban," he said self-consciously. The old man clapped his hands, flashing Kezia a gap-toothed smile.

"You mean Seth? Seth the potter?" Jared nodded. "Well, you've not far to go." The old man stood up. "Pottery's just round the corner there," he waved his arm as if they would be going round several corners, "Can't miss it…all his pots're outside."

"Thank you, sir," Jared bowed his head in deference. Kezia's eyes smiled at the old man, a smile that lifted his whole day.

"Am I *seeing* things?" Joanna looked up from her kneading, astonishment and delight sparkling in her eyes. She flew out from behind the table to fold Kezia in her strong embrace. "Is it really you, chicken?" she stroked Kezia's cheek with a floury hand. "Oh, this *is* a surprise. I'm so pleased to see you...both." She hastened to add the word 'both' remembering her niece was now wed.

In a trice her expression changed from joy to concern. She held Kezia at arm's length as she asked; "Your mother? What's happened? Is she alright?"

Kezia nodded, "She's fine," she assured her aunt. "Tired but she's fine... and Zippie's walking now!"

"When's the baby due?" Joanna tossed in her mind how long before she should go to her sister to be with her for the birth.

"Another month yet."

Joanna beamed at the reassurance. She turned to Jared. "You couldn't have come at a better time, young Jared – Seth's a man short today. Go through," she pointed at the door in the wall across the courtyard, "he's just across the yard." Jared hesitated. "Go on – we've got women's things to catch up on!" She dismissed him with a good-natured shove and Jared took himself out across the yard. Joanna poured two cups of water, gave one to Kezia and returned to her dough.

"Put your things in the corner and take your coat off, child." She checked herself as she studied the young woman removing her outer cloak. "Oh, but you're not a child are you, chicken... no... you're a... stunningly lovely, married woman."

In Joanna's company, the rigours of their journey fell away. Kezia felt instantly at home. Within hours it was as though she had been in Sepphoris for months. Arm in arm they toured the lower market to buy meat, figs, small honey cakes and, to Kezia's amusement, bread. She could never remember Leah *buying* bread – this was a real city novelty. Joanna said that, as soon as Kezia was happy to look after all her men, she would go down to Capernaum until the baby was safely delivered.

"How many men do you have?" teased Kezia.

Joanna laughed into the sunshine, "You'll have to wait and see!"

Chapter 19

MORDECAI was aghast. The visiting Pharisees monopolised the entire evening recounting the latest scandal in Jerusalem. The old man's white eyebrows knitted together in an unruly hedge of disapproval. Long after the men retired to the guest-room, Mordecai remained on the roof, trying to digest what he had been told. Had the world gone mad?

His mind turned back to the days when the brothers Simon and Andrew, and Zebedee's boys James and John had been in the Synagogue school as his pupils. Good boys, they were. Keen, bright... eager to learn. He'd watched them mature into men of integrity...it was beyond belief to hear what they were doing now. The Pharisees said Simon, or Peter, the name he insisted on using, led groups of men and women to pray in the same room together... praying *together*! It sounded as if Simon was setting himself in opposition to the High Priest, praying and healing and telling deluded crowds that the Nazareth man was the Messiah. Mordecai shook his head in disgust. His frown clenched into a black scowl. Wicked, *wicked* blasphemy! There'd be civil war next.

At least the Pharisees brought good reports of Jairus. On the High Priest's orders, Jairus had accompanied a group of Sadducees and Temple guards to Bethany to issue decrees against any Jesus followers in the village meeting together. Any man who dared defy Caiaphas risked imprisonment. Mordecai sighed deeply. Jesus was causing more trouble dead than alive!

Oi! He spat and lifted his eyes in despair. What was the world coming to! His anger boiled against Simon and the other men. Their behaviour risked destablising his beloved Holy City. If Caiaphas didn't clamp down soon and *hard,* the Romans would smell insurgence. Then where would they be?

***

Leah twisted on the mattress. Sleep eluded her. Now that her belly was so distended, it had become impossible to find a comfortable position for anything, let alone sleep. She missed Kezia. Missed her help, that cheery smile, her optimistic manner… dear Kezie… Leah wondered what her daughter thought of Sepphoris. Their village of Capernaum was more or less an extended family – city life would be very different, but then, Leah reassured herself, Joanna was there to take care of her. Harder for Jared though… Leah pursed her lips… she doubted he would take to building work easily. Carefully she shifted her body on the mattress. She thought about her son-in-law. The boy had been unsettled ever since his brothers left to follow Jesus.

She thought about Jesus too. She missed his visits. Oh, how had everything gone so wrong? He had saved Kezie's life – he should have been a welcome friend – Leah's face crumpled at the thought of crucifixion. Jesus didn't deserve to die like that… hung up like a common criminal. No man should be put to death that way. The gods had been cruel. Leah longed for things to be as they were before Kezia's illness. Life had been stable and predictable.

She massaged her taut belly. A boy this time, she knew it!

She had prayed to every god she could think of; her parents' gods of Canaan, a strange four-armed idol an old woman had given her as a good-luck charm, as well as Jairus' god. She touched her bulge lovingly – soon she would hold him – soon she would see Jairus' face as he lifted up his son. Soon…

***

It had never crossed Adah's mind Kezia might leave Capernaum. The house was so empty without her. Empty and… and somehow lifeless, even though Zippie was a chuckling handful, nevertheless it just wasn't the same without Kez. No-one to joke with, help her gather dates or race back home from the market. Adah curled up under her blanket and listened to the night sounds; barking dogs, distant fishermen calling to each other on their way to the harbour, horses' hooves as soldiers rode by. This was the time, when, with all their work done, she and Kezia would whisper and giggle and dream. Suddenly, deep inside her soul, Adah felt the cold depth of loneliness.

***

"I'll take you down to the quarry," Seth informed Jared the next morning. "I'll tell them you'll work non-stop…all day… and you're not interested in a wage…"

"Seth!" Joanna scolded. "Don't tease!" She turned to Jared. "Don't take any notice of my man – I don't." And she threw a towel at Seth in playful irritation.

"Quick!" gasped Seth, "Retreat! My wife attacks me!" Disappearing out of the door he called over his shoulder, "I've asked Ben to take the top shelf out of the kiln before he takes the order down to the bank."

"Is Nico coming today?" Joanna asked, trying to be serious. Her husband retraced his steps to poke his head round the door.

"Don't think so," he said. " He's in the courthouse." Seth caught Kezia's expression. He gave her an eggagerated wink. "This is a *godless* city, my dear." Kezia was never sure when he was joking. "Gone!" he sang from the courtyard.

"Now you see what I have to put up with!" Joanna grinned as she cleared the table. Kezia wanted to ask 'who is Nico?' and 'what's he doing in the courthouse?'. Guessing her curiosity, Joanna answered the queries.

"Don't worry, chicken. Nico's not been arrested. He's working in the courthouse on some big mosaic." She busied herself picking up water pots and handing one to her niece. "He's an *artist*." She spoke with obvious admiration. "Seth says 'one of the best', so, we're blessed to have him help here now and again."

'Nico'. That was a new name to Kezia, she didn't know anyone called Nicodemus in Capernaum. "Where does Nicodemus live?" she asked innocently. Joanna picked up the sweeping brush.

"It's not Nicodemus, Kezie, it's Nicolaus. He lodges wherever he is working." Kezia was intrigued but also wary. Nicolaus sounded foreign.

Shouldering the water pot, Kezia wondered if Seth, his assistant Ben and the mysterious part-time helper Nicolaus was the extent of Joanna's 'men'.

***

Jared followed in Seth's flamboyant wake as they made their way down the main street. He was amazed how many people waved or spoke to the potter. Consequently, progress was slow but quickened once outside the Lion's Gate. The quarry, a good mile from Sepphoris, was a deep scar gouged out of the hillside. As they drew closer and saw the extent and depth of the quarry, Jared guessed there had to be hundreds of men working in it. He'd never seen a quarry like it – so deep – noisy – crawling with men; men with pulley-ropes, men with picks, men guiding donkey wagons – stacking, shouting, a ceaseless rhythm of dust-choking grind.

Seth spotted the foremen leaning on a cart, his eagle eye on a group of stone cutters. He glanced up at Seth's shout.

"Don't come down here Potter!" he balled. "You'll get your fancy hat dirty!" Taking the comment as his invitation, Seth led Jared down the steep quarry path to where the foreman stood.

"Got a fresh set of muscles for you!" declared Seth slithering on the last few uneven rubble. "A good, strong worker from Capernaum – reliable – needs a job!" The potter came straight to the point. The foreman weighed Jared up and down like a farmer scrutinising an ox before committing to the purchase.

"'Spose you're another of those fishermen," he growled wiping the back of his hand under his nose. Jared's cheeks flushed behind his beard.

"I'll work hard, sir," he said. Seth looked from one to the other with a hopeful smile.

"Week's trial then." The foreman was gruff. "We'll see if your worth a wage at the end of it."

Seth clapped Jared on the back, "There! It's a start. We all have to start somewhere." With that he turned and hurried up the steep slope back to the roadway. "See you tonight," he called without turning round.

The foreman directed Jared to a group of stone cutters in the bottom of the quarry. His first job being to stack stone ready for the wagons to haul up out of the quarry and away to the building sites. Back-breaking, heavy work, demanding more stamina than concentration. At last all the heaving and sweating of the quarry took his mind off Pei Qi.

This was a fresh start.

***

Years rolled off Joanna as she escorted Kezia to all the essential areas of the city. She delighted in taking her to the well, the site of the weekly lower market and the daily higher market. She led her niece along the city's central street with the broad pavements, colonnade and varied shops and stalls. Kezia was captivated by the dazzling array of wares as they passed shelves of delicate glass bowls and bottles, coopers and coppersmiths side by side with money-changers and a cobbler, as well as stalls stacked high with vine leaves, sheep and goat's cheese. The sounds and intoxicating smells of the street, from sweet incense and exotic perfumes, mingled with pickled fish and the soft timber smells from the carpenter's work shop.

Even the people seemed different to those she was used to in Capernaum. The women's tunics and cloaks were of a far superior quality than Kezia was used to, and many cloaks were tied with ornately twisted material belts or gold buckles. Joanna showed her how to identify Roman servants by their distinctive tunics.

Massive new buildings reflected the wealth and burgeoning importance of Sepphoris. Joanna pointed out the magistrate's house, the bank, council offices, Synagogue, bath-house and the theatre and that was only down one street.

When they returned home, Kezia's mind buzzed with city sights. Her cheeks glowed with sheer excitement. On her first venture away from home, she had been overawed by Jerusalem, but here in Sepphoris, big, brash and noisy though it was, she wasn't over-awed but happy. In a curious way, despite her sadness at having left all those she loved in Capernaum, the vibrant pulse of this modern city awakened her inner spirit. Kezia had come to life.

***

Clouds that had earlier threatened rain lifted by the evening so Joanna laid out their meal under the vine canopy in the courtyard. Ben, Seth's young assistant, slept in a tent attached to the back of the pottery and always ate at Joanna's table. He sat cross-legged on the ground, his tunic splattered in slip and smears and smudges of clay. Kezia noticed his thick, long lashes as they lowered in shy greeting.

Jared leaned against the upright of the canopy in an attempt to ease his aching back. Creamy grey quarry dust clung to his black hair and in the streaks of sweat down his neck. He could hardly feel the bread between his blistered fingers and hungrily waited for his bowl of stew.

"My wife…" Seth began, "My Joanna is the finest cook in all Sepphoris!" He lifted his cup of wine, drank, put the cup down and savoured the taste.

"You mean 'in all the Galilee'!" Joanna prompted. Kezia ladled stew into the five bowls as Joanna sat next to her husband. The way husband and wife interacted left Jared bemused. His mother never spoke on equal terms with his father and hardly ever sat next to him to eat. Somehow it didn't seem proper, but, he decided, it must be the modern, city way. He didn't think much of it. He wasn't going to accept cheek like that from Kezia.

In a mix of affection and satisfaction, Joanna watched Kezia filling their bowls. The young wife had adapted naturally to their rather unorthodox household. Joanna tore off a piece of warm, stone-baked bread as she spoke;

"Well, here's the second finest cook because I shall be teaching her *everything* she needs to know to keep you men well-fed." Kezia smiled but kept her eyes on the stew bowls.

Joanna turned directly to Seth, "After Sabbath I need to go to my sister. But, you needn't worry, that gives me a few days to get Kezie into our routine. She's perfectly capable of running the house for me 'til I get back from Capernaum."

The men ate, content to know their meals would be unaffected by Joanna's absence. Apart from Seth, so long as there was food on the table they didn't much bother who put it there.

Psychologically, Kezia had grown several inches taller. She had a cause, a purpose, a role of her own to fulfil.

That night, in the corner of the pottery where Joanna had put down a mattress for them, Jared was snoring before Kezia joined him. As she lay beside him she was aware of his spasmodic tics and rapid breathing. For a long time she had imagined he suffered from nightmares. She lay calmly holding the pouch of stones that she so carefully kept out of his sight. The stones had become her comfort, a source of warm peace. Beneath the shelves of plates and jugs, Kezia settled to the best night's sleep she had managed since becoming Jared's wife.

Chapter 20

JAIRUS' brisk pace was hampered by the many people still pushing their way into the Temple precincts. Squeezing past and behind knots of people, Elders, pilgrims, Temple guards and money-changers, Jairus hurried toward the great gates. Once out of the Temple he turned left, taking the road down towards the High Priest's house. The summons had come from Caiaphas himself, and with each stride Jairus tried to decide whether it meant praise or reprimand. He couldn't recall anything he had done to merit either. Since his return to Jerusalem he had played the dutiful servant, adopting a low profile around the Temple, observing every ritual and prayer time, cataloguing scrolls and welcoming visitors.

Caiaphas' extensive house wedged itself into the hillside below Mount Zion. The balconies, halls and dungeons covered a greater area than any other Jewish house in the city. Built in the style of a lavish palace, it mirrored its owner's self importance and jealously guarded status. Jairus shared one of the many guest rooms with three brothers from the coastal town of Joppa. He wondered if they too had been summoned to the august presence. He arrived at the roof level and ran down the outer stairs, down to the room where Caiaphas held audience.

"Come!" the familiar, high voice answered Jairus' knock.

Jairus straightened his robes before he walked in. Caiaphas sat on a dias surrounded by a group of attentive Pharisees and various teachers of the law. Silence fell as the men turned to inspect the Synagogue Ruler. Jairus felt vulnerable under the penetrating stares of the Temple professionals.

The brothers from Joppa were nowhere to be seen.

"Ah! My dear Jairus," the High Priest greeted him with smooth bonhommie. "I want you to meet our honoured guest." Gaining confidence that such a greeting was unlikely to precede a reprimand, Jairus bowed and walked forward. Caiaphas waved a flabby hand at one of the Pharisees standing to his right; "This is one of Rabbi Gamaliel's *finest* disciples." Jairus nodded to the honoured guest, a short, swarthy individual, clean-shaven in the Roman fashion, exuding an air of intellectual superiority. The High Priest addressed his guest Pharisee with honeyed confidentiality.

" This is our man from Capernaum…the one I was telling you about." Caiaphas lifted his massive figure from his seat with a gentle tinkling as the golden bells danced on the fringe of his robe. Protruding eyes peered down at Jairus from the dias.

"Jairus, this is Saul of Tarsus." Caiaphas introduced the men taking a callous delight in the fact they would take an instant dislike to each other. "I've told Saul about your… er… your *trouble* in Capernaum." Jairus attempted to diffuse such talk but Caiaphas would not be deflected. "It may not be much at present," there was steel behind his smile, "but these are volatile times, Jairus." As the High Priest inhaled his bejewelled breastplate rose in regal fashion. "An unattended canker is a dangerous poison." He relished Jairus' unease. "We can't have your Synagogue in factions now, can we?" His voice lifted with a hint of laughter, but there was a cold menace in his stare.

"I have decided Saul will return to Capernaum with you. It's time we made an example of these *blasphemers*." Spittle sprinkled his greying beard as he accentuated the word in disgust. "Anyone caught spreading heresies about that Nazareth man, you will bring here to Jerusalem… in chains." His eyes glinted with satisfaction. "A spell in my dungeon will soon settle where their loyalties lie!" The Temple retinue sniggered.

Jairus and Saul regarded each other warily, like two mountain bears sizing up their opponent's strength. Jairus felt Saul's gaze penetrate his soul. His first thought was Zebedee's house group. He swallowed hard. What havoc was this Saul going to cause?

Caiaphas cleared his throat. "You will leave at first light tomorrow," he ordered. Then, nodding round the circle of men gathered to discuss the Capernaum problem, he sneered, "Well now, I'm sure we can leave this matter in brother Saul's capable hands."

Jairus realised he was trapped. Caiaphas was not only dismissing him from the Temple but sending him home with a spy. If Saul arrested Zebedee then, as ruler of Capernaum's Synagogue, *he,* Jairus, would be labelled the traitor.

"Let's eat!" The Chief Priest's words hardly registered with Jairus. His mind whirled with thoughts of Kezia – she was in danger in Zebedee's household. He didn't trust this Pharisee, Saul. Somehow… he must get word to Zebedee.

***

The day after Sabbath:

Very early in the morning, on the first day of the week, Seth walked with Joanna to the Nazareth Gate. He had arranged for her to travel down to Capernaum with a group of basket weavers, a blacksmith and some women dye-sellers.

"I need to know you've company for the journey, my love," he said gently.

Joanna touched his arm, "Don't work Kezie too hard, mind. And let your Ben go with her a few times until the shopkeepers know where she lives." Seth nodded.

"I'll be home as soon as Leah is on her feet," she promised, moving her cheek towards her husband to be kissed. Seth obliged.

"Here they are!" he turned to greet the basket-weavers. Joanna knew the women from the lower market and was glad to travel with them. They led two old donkeys, laden with willow baskets, suspended from each side of their saddles. The blacksmith drove a mule-cart while the dye-sellers carried their goods on their backs in the same fashion as Joanna carried her belongings. The troupe trudged laboriously out of the city gate. Seth waved.

"Safe journey!" he called. Joanna blew a kiss before disappearing out of sight. Seth walked back to the pottery, whistling. There was a large order to complete... he really could do with Nico for a few days...

***

The quarry foreman sat at a long table. A scribe perched beside him scratching marks on a papyrus sheet as the foreman handed out the allotted pile of coins to each man in line. Jared looked enviously at the coins. Living in his father's house, he had never been given a proper wage like the hired hands on the boat. He had scrimped his money together by selling baskets of fish and making sure he pocketed most of the profit. He waited in file to receive his own pile of coins.

When Jared's turn came, the foreman glowered up at him.

"The new fisherman," he snorted dismissively to the scribe. "What's your name?" he barked.

"Jared, sir. Jared, son of Zebedee," he said, his gaze fixed on the coins.

"You'll do," the foreman grunted handing up the wage. "Next!"

Jared moved along pushing the money deep in his tunic pocket. Despite aching muscles, cut hands and exhaustion, a certain elation swept over him. He'd earned money; his *own* money. Finally he was independent of his father.

***

"You're very kind to us, Seth," Kezia murmured as she carried the shopping back to the pottery. He had insisted on accompanying her on her first solo visit to the city's main street. Whenever she made a purchase, Seth was at her shoulder telling the shopkeeper, "She's my wife's kin. Make sure you look after her." At first Kezia was embarrassed by Seth's continual intervention thinking it meant he didn't trust her to buy what he wanted. But she soon realised that, as a stranger in the city, she was fair game to be over-charged, sold tired vegetables or sub-standard goods. She memorised the shops she would be using regularly, and smiled gratefully.

"My dear Kezia," Seth said affably, "you are a long way from home... my wife's gone off and left you to fend for us all..." he shrugged, "the least I can do is make sure you get fair treatment on your daily excursions." He carried a bag of olives which he happily depleted as they walked. Kezia became aware of someone following them. She swung round into the face of a peasant woman, bent with age, heaving herself along the pavement on a stick.

"Just a minute, dearie," the woman called. For a moment Kezia thought she had underpaid for some item but, as she was trying to think, the old woman came close, so close Kezia could smell her bad breath. She dressed like one of the bedouin women from the stalls; hoop earrings, jangling necklace and rows of gold bracelets on both arms. Seth turned round to see the peasant brandish her stick at the young wife.

"*You*! Where do you live?" she demanded.

"What's that to you, old woman?" Seth calmly took Kezia's arm and moved her to one side as he deflected the question. Kezia flinched as the old woman reached out and grabbed her by the arm. "*You*!" she repeated earnestly, "I've been watching you..." Kezia instinctively recoiled but the woman was determined to have her say.

"You're a *healer!*" she declared. Seth blanched and steered Kezia away down the street, but the old woman was not to be silenced.

"Don't you keep it to yourself, girl!" she called after them. "It's a *gift*. Do you hear? The Lord God has blessed you with a great gift." Seth bundled Kezia across the road and into an alley as the shouting followed them. "I know you're a healer... I see it in your hands... it's a gift... don't..." and they were out of earshot.

Heads turned as the potter escorted his new woman away from the outburst. Scarlet with confusion, Kezia fought to get her breath. Seth wanted her back inside the pottery before people took notice of the old crone. He was out of his depth... he knew all kinds of people would turn up at his door if they thought Kezia was a healer. He had enough to do being a potter without any 'extras' thrown in. He said nothing until they were safely back in the house. He decided not to mention the subject of healing. He put the near empty bag of olives on the table.

"I'm afraid one or *two* may have gone missing!" he stared into the bag affecting surprise. The relief that Seth was not questioning her over what had been said brought back a measure of composure.

The potter became serious. "Kez, I've got jugs and cups to deliver over to the theatre this afternoon. It's a two-handed job and… well, I haven't the time to spare, so I need you to help Ben with that." He looked at her closely. "Is that alright?"

"Yes, of course," she gave a half smile. She had heard about theatres but never seen one. She felt a bit apprehensive.

"Aren't they gentile places?" she asked suddenly diffident of the unfamiliar, cosmopolitan nature of the city as well as being fearful she would bump into the old woman again on the way.

"Kezia." Seth sat on the end of the table. Kezia stopped from emptying her shopping baskets, realising Seth had something serious to say. He looked at her with kind eyes the colour of hazelnuts. "You're not in Capernaum now, Kez," he said. "Things… attitudes are…how shall we say? Well, we're less rigid here. The Romans are not *all* bad people. They just happen to be born in a different country from us… that's all. Sepphoris is a peaceful city – we've learned to live together… side by side." He paused not wanting to make his explanation seem like a lecture.

"Now, I don't want you to be shocked when Nico joins us for a meal." He saw a hesitant cloud in her eyes. "Yes, our artist friend is a Roman… a gentile. But… first and foremost he is a welcome friend in my house." Without another word he smiled and left Kezia to prepare the meal.

When he had gone Kezia clutched the pouch attached to her belt. She looked down at it in wonder. The memory of Adah's recovery from fever blazed in her mind. She leaned against the table to steady the tremble in her legs. What was it Jesus had said to her when he gave her the gemstones? 'When you use them... you will be a source of comfort and healing.' Kezia bit her lip. *How* did that old woman know? Could it be true? Did she really have the gift of healing?

It was all too much. She had work to do, jugs and things to go to this theatre... a meal to prepare. She shook her head as if the shaking would banish the thoughts. She picked up her knife and began to dice the vegetables and chop herbs ready for the cooking pot.

***

"It's good to know Jared has found work," Leah said as she and Joanna sat staring into the fading embers of their evening fire. The courtyard was quiet. Adah had taken Zippie to her room leaving the sisters to catch up with recent happenings. Miriam, who had taken to making daily visits to enquire after Leah's health, had also returned home.

"I hope he knows what a good wife he's got," Joanna said with feeling. Leah closed her eyes and relaxed in the comfort of her sister's company.

"Yes," she said, "she's turned out a capable girl – despite all our spoiling!" she acknowledged with a rueful smile. Joanna yawned.

"You know," she said, stretching, "one thing I must say for those Romans, they've transformed the road down from Sepphoris. Some places I didn't even recognise where we were! But every improvement only seems to bring more travellers…"

"Sometimes," Leah mused, "it seems as if the whole world is on the move."

Darkness draped around them like a warm, velvet cloak.

"When do you expect Jairus home?" Joanna was always direct. Leah sighed.

"Not until after Passover." There was silence between them. "I'd rather he wasn't here until after the birth now." Silence fell again as both women considered the prospect of another difficult birth.

Leah began again: "Mordecai left for Jerusalem last week." She moved sideways to shift the swollen belly into a more tolerable position. "There's not many going to Jerusalem this year," she added.

"Not surprised," Joanna said quietly. "Doubt if I'll ever go back – not after last year! Anyway, Seth can't spare the time just now." She yawned again and rubbed the soles of her bare feet.

"Let's go to bed." Leah suggested. She lifted herself up and bent over her sister, cradling Joanna's head against the unborn child. "We've been waiting for you," she whispered. "I need you, Joanna." Caught unawares by her sister's tender embrace, Joanna found she had no characteristic, flippant reply. Such proximity to the baby left her speechless and wet-eyed.

Chapter 21

TIRESOME! Saul's company was as palatable as chewing chaff. His conversation, when he deigned to engage in any, erupted in tense bursts, peppered with self-righteous indignation. Any man whose views dared to differ from his own received short shrift. Jairus listened and said little. That suited them both.

Arriving in Jericho, the two men headed for the Synagogue. Jairus knew Rabbi Jonathan well; he was another friend from student days in Jerusalem. Rabbi Jonathan, generous with his hospitality, made both visitors immediately welcome in the Synagogue guest rooms.

That night, Jairus doubled up with a violent attack of stomach cramps. Jonathan's wife boiled a potion of ra leaves which she assured Jonathan would ease Jairus' abdominal spasms. The acrid mixture caused him to vomit and, for several days, Jairus remained in his room, too fearful to venture far from bed and bucket.

During this unscheduled and inconvenient delay, Saul took himself across the River Jordan, to the nearby village of Bethany-beyond-the-Jordan, hunting for any shred of evidence against 'Jesus followers'. The zealous Pharisee determined to eliminate the merest whiff of dangerous heresy.

Saul stood in Bethany's ancient Synagogue and roared dire

warnings against anyone found worshipping the man Jesus. The sparse congregation absorbed the tirade in stony silence. The Pharisee strode back to Jericho across the scorching, arid plain, convinced such gatherings occurred in Bethany, but unable to coerce anyone into giving him names. Back in Jericho, he found Jairus washed-out, but insisting he was fit for the next leg of their journey to Capernaum.

***

A week later.

Leah hovered attentively as her husband ate. He had been away so many months. She studied his features intently. She noted flecks of grey in his beard and one of his bottom teeth was missing. Deep lines scored his forehead and he looked tired. He had aged. She loved him so much.

Mordecai was much taken with Saul of Tarsus. The two of them engaged in deep and detailed conversation which gave Jairus a chance to eat his meal uninterrupted. Adah attended to their empty bowls and bobbed to and fro with extra bread, sweatmeats and wine. Leah sat away from the table as was fitting for a woman in such an advanced stage of pregnancy. Joanna sat with her, her fingers deftly working the spindle. Miriam and Debra had taken Zippie so that the esteemed visitor would not be disturbed. Leah's mind was far away from the men's talk. Her thoughts focussed on the imminent birth… if only Kezia was with her.

For a brief second, Jairus looked over and met Leah's gaze. She sensed his impatience for the bulge in her tunic to hurry into the world. She hoped he realised that it was also her dearest wish. Since he had come home and seen her condition, she had felt a new warmth from him. He had shown a tender interest in her health, had insisted she rest. To Leah's relief the visiting Pharisee was sleeping in the Synagogue guest room and not in their house. She had the impression that Saul of Tarsus considered himself far too important to stay with a mere Synagogue ruler. She hoped he would soon leave. She didn't want strangers around when she gave birth to her son.

Suddenly, Leah roused from her day-dream at the name 'Jesus'. Both she and Joanna paid attention to the men's conversation.

"No, no," Mordecai shook his head. "A few addled-headed fishermen tried to say he was the Messiah… but…well, you know how it is…a five-day wonder…" he petered out with a self-effacing chortle.

"But Caiaphas was told half the men in your congregation had been stirring up the people with lies and blasphemy!" Saul stared unblinking across the table at Jairus. Jairus wiped his mouth.

"Oh, I think you'll find Capernaum is a God-fearing community," Jairus returned softly.

Saul's accusing eyes bore into Jairus as if he could see the fracas that had taken place in the Synagogue etched in Jairus' pupils. With forced joviality, Mordecai refilled Saul's wine cup.

"Well, my friend," he simpered, "you'll have a chance to judge for yourself tomorrow." He put the wine jug down. "We all observe the Sabbath."

"All?" Saul asked, obvious disbelief in his cultured voice.

"Brother Saul, reserve your judgement for tomorrow." Mordecai's benign smile returned the visitor's stare.

***

Four days later.

Jairus stood on the harbour wall, his grey cloak billowing in the gusting breeze. Zebedee's hired men were mending nets and clearing up after gutting their night's catch.

Zebedee sidled up to Jairus. "'As'ee gone?" The fisherman's whisper came out of the side of his mouth. His men made no pause in their work, crude needles strung with thick netting rope, passing in and out of the broken fishing nets to close the gaping holes.

"Yes," Jairus sighed. "He's gone." He breathed deeply. Then, turning to face Zebedee. "I came to thank you, Zebedee." He stalled for a moment, wondering what more to say.

Zebedee shrugged, "No thanks needed," his reply was curt. "I've no wish to taste Caiaphas' dungeon! Nor have any of us." He looked up sharply into Jairus face. "Doesn't change the truth mind! We know it *here*," he beat a fish-bloodied hand on his bare chest, " We'll carry on with the house group but we're not fool enough to jeopardise the brothers." He turned back to his men leaving Jairus standing forlorn amongst the empty fish baskets.

Zebedee threw a final sentence into the air, "It'll take more than a strutting crow from Tarsus to stop the *truth*." The tone of his last remark signalled time for Jairus to leave. Jairus walked the short distance from the harbour back to the Synagogue.

"Well done, my boy!" Mordecai was waiting for him. They went together into the side room soon to be filled with youths. "I think we can safely say Saul was impressed by the size of our Sabbath congregation." He laughed down his nose. Jairus was distracted.

"I didn't know Kezia had gone to Sepphoris," he said.

"I… I couldn't risk her being in any danger. And, well…" he sucked on his teeth.

"I know… I know," Mordecai muttered.

"And old Zebedee. He's a loose tongue! He'd be sure to boast about his boys… bragging about them being Jesus' *chief* disciples." Jairus wiped his forehead. "The whole household would be seen as Jesus people."

"Capernaum's a tight community," Mordecai said wisely. "They'll stand together 'gainst a stranger – Pharisee or no Pharisee," he gave a deep sniff, "no matter whose star pupil he is." The old man eased himself down on the stone bench. He lowered his voice, "I told your friend Abner to go back by the high road… through Samaria." He looked around making sure they were alone before he whispered over to Jairus. "Your delay in Jericho gave him just long enough to alert us." He removed his headdress and ran his fingers through the shock of white hair. He nodded with satisfaction: "Well done, my boy. The whole congregation is grateful to you."

***

It had been a long day. The delivery of mugs and jugs to the theatre that afternoon had created much-needed shelf space for Jared and Kezia. Jared fixed a pole across their corner from which he draped one of Joanna's old curtains. The home-spun material gave a degree of privacy from any casual customers into the pottery. He leaned against the wall admiring his handiwork. Kezia wiped the shelf with a rag before arranging their few possessions in the new space; their combs, a tablet of soap, the couple of towels she'd brought from Capernaum and a lamp. She spoke happily without turning round.

"I went to the Theatre today."

"You *what?*" Petulance in his voice brought colour flooding into Kezia's cheeks.

"Well, I didn't exactly go *in,*" she tried to explain, "I helped Ben deliver Seth's order." She turned to face her husband's sullen expression. "That's all." She ended brightly. His aggressive reaction alarmed her. For the past few days her husband had seemed almost friendly, prepared to chat with Seth and Ben about the quarry, but explosive anger always lurked just beneath the surface.

"Don't want you going near any place like that." His eyebrows fused into a dangerous caterpillar above his eyes. Kezia stared at him for a few seconds before gathering up the courage to reply.

"Seth has given us a roof, Jared. I can't refuse to help in his business, now – can I?" she tried to sound reasonable. Jared scowled, reminding her all too clearly of his over-bearing hulk of a father, Zebedee.

"What would your father say if he knew you'd been to a *theatre?*" He knew he could hurt her with the mention of her father. Kezia knew her father's opinion on the way Romans spent their leisure time. As a strict Jew and Ruler of the Synagogue, Jairus branded all gentile activities indecent and immoral. Countless times he'd fumed about their race tracks, their wrestling and gambling, he and Mordecai denounced everything Roman, not least play-acting.

Kezia felt torn, but her obligation to Seth was uppermost. She couldn't see anything wrong in delivering pots wherever they were needed.

"I told you, I didn't go in or... or *see* anything." She shrugged. Jared took three steps to where she was standing.

"So now you cheek me!" he stood breathing down on her,

smelling her fear. He pushed her up against the wall, her shoulder just missing the sharp corner of the shelf.

"You're my wife. You don't go near those sort of places, d'you *hear*?" his breath blew against her cheek as he spoke. He looked down her slender neck. Her vulnerability excited him, "You're my wife… you'll do as I say." His body pinned her against the hard, uneven wall as he fumbled breathlessly with her clothing. Kezia submitted to the brute force of his passion, believing it was something wives had to endure.

With the curtain in place, no chink of light permeated their corner in the pottery. Jared lay restless on the mattress, rattled by the continual noise of the city. It was as though Sepphoris never slept. Never a quiet night like in Capernaum with just an occasional dog bark, the rustle of the wind or croaking toads and cicadas. No, this city banged and rumbled and shouted its way towards the dawn. Donkeys brayed, chariots scraped and clattered past at all hours of the night, soldiers balled orders, horses' hooves clopped on the new stone roads and men shouted to each other or at their wives… noise, noise, never ending noise.

The window was on the other side of the curtain which, Jared complained, made him feel he was in a cell. He wiped a hand over his bare chest, sweating in the oppressive humidity of Seth's pottery. How he longed for the sweet, cool night air of the lake. Every muscle ached and his eyelids drooped in fatigue but sleep was impossible. Jared tossed on the bed and sighed. Before he knew it he'd have to drag himself off to that dammed quarry again and the continual hammering that split his head.

Kezia curled herself on the edge of the bed. Unable to sleep with her husband's loud sighs and ill-tempered twisiting and turning, she lay still in the hope he would not guess she was awake.

Kezia's mind was engaged in its own twists and turns as she tried to untangle her emotions. Already she loved living in Sepphoris but she missed her mother, Adah and Zippie. She had embraced the freedom of running the house for Joanna, the shopping, cooking and all her new responsibilities, only bedroom duties crushed her spirit. Confidence in her growing maturity was countered by the loss of protection she had known as a child and intuition told her that the more she enjoyed city life, the more Jared would rebel against it. It seemed so bitterly unfair that every positive aspect of her life was clouded with the sting of disappointment.

Her thoughts went to her mother. Silently Kezia put her hand under the mattress to the kid pouch. Her fingers closed round the familiar contours of the gemstones. In the sultry darkness, Kezia prayed for her mother. She prayed for safe delivery of a son.

Chapter 22

ADAH leapt to her feet at Joanna's call. Sleep fell away in an automatic flurry as she threw a cloak over her tunic and dashed into the darkness for Anna. The middle of the night was not the most convenient time to give birth but Joanna swiftly relit the oil lamps and resurrected the courtyard fire to heat a pan of water. Adah sped down the earthen road to Zebedee's house.

Much to Adah's surprise, Anna made no complaint at being woken. On the contrary, she appeared genuinely excited to be called for Leah's birthing. Scuttling to Jairus' house, Anna was met by Leah's cries coming from the upstairs room. She bustled up the stone staircase, shooting orders at Adah to fetch a bowl of hot water and as many towels as she could find.

Leah squatted on the floor, a flustered Joanna supporting her shoulders.

"It's coming!" Joanna announced as Anna reached the bedroom door. Leah screamed.

"Here," Anna instructed Leah, "drink this." She opened a small skin of foul-smelling fennel root juice. Leah turned her head from the skin but Anna held her head and poured some of the liquid into her mouth.

"This one'll be quick, my dear," Anna declared with

authority, "Oh, what a mercy! You're nearly there!" Adah dabbed towels into the pool of blood and water on the floor.

"Where's Jairus?" Anna shot a glance at Joanna.

"On the roof," Joanna replied, struggling to keep her sister in one position as she writhed with the painful contractions. Anna knelt on the floor ready to catch the infant. The head was through

"One more push!" Anna encouraged. Leah uttered an almighty yell and pushed. The rest of the torso and tiny legs flopped into Anna's waiting grasp.

"Praise be!" she chirped in delight. "Oh, my dear, that was perfect!" Deftly she cut the umbilical chord at which the baby's tiny mouth opened and the first reedy cry resounded round the room. Anna took charge of the child and swiftly wiped the bloodied body, gently cleaning the navel with myrrh oil. Leah sank to the ground semi-conscious. Joanna bathed her face and ran a comb through her damp hair, to tidy it back off her face. Suddenly, Leah lifted her head towards Anna, her eyes yearning to know:

"Yes! Yes!" Anna answered the unspoken question, "It's a boy! You have a *son*!" As she bound swaddling cloths around the tiny bundle, Anna's face cracked into unfamiliar smiles. She positively beamed as though the success was entirely her own.

Tears of joy filled Joanna's eyes as she helped Leah on to the fleece. Adah twirled from wiping the floor, to carrying – to fetching, to cooing at the baby – all of a tremble at the sheer, intense wonder of it all.

"The God of Abraham… be praised!" Leah gasped in a near inaudible whisper, a weak smile of relief spread across her face. Joanna crouched by her side and held her hand. At that moment Jairus, who had heard his wife's labour cries, appeared in the doorway. He stood, hopeful but unwilling to enter such a woman's domain. He looked at Leah, as worn and washed-out as the sheet covering her fleece.

Anna presented him with the mewling bundle. "The Lord has blessed you with a son!" she said with aplomb, for all the world as if the boy were her own gift. For an instant, weak as she was, Leah wished Anna would drop dead. It was *her* place to give the child into her husband's arms. It was the precious moment she had dreamed of, lived for, rehearsed for so many months… how *dare* Anna steal her one moment of intimate achievement. But joy and exhaustion quickly drained her anger and she lay back content in the knowledge that, at last, at long, long last, she had borne her husband a son. She had not failed this time.

Jairus gazed incredulous at the crumpled red face protruding from the swaddling bands. A face topped with a mop of spikey, black hair. Tenderly he placed his little finger in the baby's open mouth. The new-born boy squinted in unfocussed bewilderment.

"My son!" Jairus murmured. "My *son*!" The women watched him in the unique rapture of fatherhood. Recovering his authority he shouted to the women, "He shall be called Jabez," he grinned. "Jabez… after my father." The tears would not be denied. "Jabez…son of Jairus!" He handed the bundle back to Anna, turned on his heel and left the room before emotion overtook him. It was no place for a man to linger, he told himself as he made his way back to his refuge on the roof. Joanna kissed Leah's cheek before tucking a blanket warmly round her sister's inert form. Adah hurried in from the courtyard with a cup of hot water fused with dried camomile flowers and honey.

"This'll help the mistress sleep," she nodded to endorse her golden brew.

"We could all do with a cup of this, Adah," Joanna smiled at the conscientious servant-girl with warm affection.

Mordecai heard the commotion. He knew what it meant but decided the morning would be soon enough to hear the news. Give the women time to clear up. Leah's screams had brought back uncomfortable memories of his own wife's labour. The old Pharisee made a clicking noise as he yawned. Women's business. But why did they have to make such a row? They should go away and give birth some place where they couldn't be heard. He turned over in his bed, pulled the blanket up over his bony shoulder to cover his ears, and, breathing heavily, lapsed back into a deep, snoring sleep.

***

"Jabez... Jabez son of Jairus!" Jairus repeated the phrase over and over, intoxicated by the mantra. He looked into the dark sky, his hands thrust deep into the pockets of his robe. Thick clouds masked the stars. The Synagogue and surrounding buildings rose out of the earth in sombre silhouette. Jairus wanted the dawn to break and the sky to blaze with the glory of his son's birth. A desperate impulse made him want to shout to all his sleeping neighbours, to wake all Capernaum to his news. An explosion of joy poured out of his heart the like of which he had never imagined possible. Jabez...son of Jairus!

Eventually, he sat down, facing south in the direction of Jerusalem, and pulled his prayer shawl over his head. He must make thanksgiving prayers to the Lord God of Israel for this blessing above all blessings – the birth of his son.

***

The infant's lips clung ferociously to Leah's swollen nipple. Adah was out at the washing pool with Zippie. Leah held her son as he fed, tenderly stroking the silk skin of his legs. She looked up as Joanna came into the room, cup in one hand and a broom in the other.

"Such a *strong* boy!" Leah murmured in a mixture of pride and surprise. Joanna stood for a few seconds gazing fondly at the dark hair hiding her sister's breast.

"I think you've smuggled in a little Egyptian!" Joanna teased. "All that *hair* – are you sure it's not a wig?" Both women laughed, entranced by the new life which already demanded their complete attention.

"Jairus is so happy," Leah basked in her achievement and the hope that it would rekindle her husband's love.

"Yes, I know," replied Joanna. "But… this won't do. Can't stop watching you and your baby all morning. Adah will be back any minute and she'll wonder what I've been doing."

Leah gazed down at the little parcel cuddled in to her breast. She was mesmerised by the miracle in her arms. Joanna felt overwhelming relief at Leah's safe delivery. It had been a serious worry; if she had lost blood to the extent of previous occasions, her life could have ebbed away. Leah had said it would be her last and Joanna was moved to pray her sister wouldn't have to go through another pregnancy. Indeed, it would be madness to expect such a fragile woman to conceive again, to say nothing of the fact that she was now passed the age of thirty.

Joanna squared her shoulders and went out into the courtyard. She had always been the strong one of the two sisters. Her hips were wide and her feet long… hers was the body to bear a dozen sons. She sighed as she unhooked the cooking pot from the iron frame over the fire. Why was life so capricious?

***

"I hear…" Mordecai drawled, scraping food from between his teeth with a splinter of willow, "I hear Saul of Tarsus caused a pretty panic in Jericho." He paused like a fisherman waiting for his fish to clamp on the bait. Jairus stared at his uncle willing the old man to spill the rest of the gossip. Mordecai reached out for more bread before saying, "Rabbi Jonathan's been arrested!" Concern darkened Jairus' face. That was the last thing he had expected.

"In fact," Mordecai continued, savouring his hold on the latest news, "Saul arrested the whole dammed household! Women and *children*! Marched them all back to Jerusalem." He cleared his throat of phlegm.

"Why bother with women and children?" Jairus was bemused.

"Ah!" Mordecai wagged his forefinger in the air. "Wise move on Caiaphas' part. Wise move indeed. Crack down *hard* from the beginning." He banged his fist symbolically on the table making the pistachios jump like crickets. "Make an example of these blasphemers. It's the only way to stop such wickedness." He downed the rest of his wine.

Jairus ran a hand around his chin. Lost in thought, he massaged his beard. He thought of the torment his friend Jonathan must be going through. What kind of man *was* this Saul? Why drag women and children to Jerusalem? The man must be mad. Too much learning!

"Jesus was popular in Jericho," he said with careful neutrality. " Caiaphas can't have *all* the followers arrested."

"Caiaphas knows what he's doing, my boy," Mordecai snapped. He dug his bread into the last of the olive oil. "He knows what he's doing."

The random pile of date stones on Jairus' plate captivated his attention. He stared at them as if they held the power to solve the Jesus dilemma. He had stayed in Caiaphas' house. He'd watched the obsequious behaviour of Levites and various teachers of the law, he'd witnessed ambitious manoeuvrings between Sadducees and Pharisees. If he were able to be honest, the High Priest's house was nothing but a viper's den of intrigue! 'Yes,' Jairus thought, 'Caiaphas knew exactly what he was doing!'

He glanced around the table, unwilling to catch his uncle's eye. He would not return to Jerusalem as long as Jonathan was in prison. Jonathan was worth ten of that stiff-necked Saul. Jairus poured more wine.

"Remember," Mordecai broke in on his thoughts, "Jabez must be circumcised after Sabbath." Jairus's whole face changed at the thought of his baby boy. Mordecai continued, "No need to go to Jerusalem. We'll do it here in the Synagogue. You'll have plenty of years to take him to the Temple when he's older."

Jairus nodded. With all the rumours and unrest, Jerusalem was no place to take his precious son.

Chapter 23

EACH day brought a new experience. Kezia embraced city life with unaffected eagerness. The general buz of Sepphoris energised and stimulated her enquiring mind. Every morning Jared was gone to the quarry just after daybreak, and, with Seth and Ben in the pottery, Kezia had the house to herself. The daily household chores were her priority before she went out to forage among the street stalls and marvel at the covered shops in the magnificent colonnade. The bread stall was her favourite. Whether the warm loaves were glazed with honey, or plaited and sprinkled with herbs and sesame seeds, she loved the sheer novelty of *buying* bread! She broke into a spontaneous smile every time she imagined what Adah would say to such a luxury. However, running the household as Joanna would expect, Kezia didn't miss the tedium of baking her own.

Each afternoon she helped in the pottery, stacking, cleaning, clearing, checking pots for damage and fetching water. Some days she helped Ben with deliveries. Winter had come to the hills and, though most days were crisp and bright, chill winds blew along the city streets.

From some of the streets, breath-taking views were visible between the fine, sand-stone houses. From the high hill to which Sepphoris clung, Kezia fancied that, on clear days, she could see as far as the Sea of Galilee, only the distant hills hid any sight of the water. On those clear days the horizon seemed just a couple of miles away, but, when clouds and mist draped lazily over the countryside, she felt the ghostly curtain became a symbolic wall of separation between herself and everyone in Capernaum.

In those first days, Kezia took every opportunity to look east in the direction of 'home', but gradually, she came to accept that it would never be home again. This bustling place of constant noise, exotic aromas, grand buildings and wide streets, this place where people of different races went about their business in an atmosphere of tolerance and peace… Kezia was content to call this place her 'home'.

Cooking for three men turned out to be less daunting than she expected. Jared was gradually breaking from his monosyllabic grunts and had even begun to initiate conversation with Ben. Although she longed for Joanna to return with news of her mother, there were times when Kezia felt she had always lived at the pottery.

"Mmm!" Seth hung his purple turban behind the door. "Smells good, Kez." He came to sniff the pot of stew Kezia had carried in from the fire. "Did I tell you? I'm thinking of sending word to Capernaum…" Kezia knew by his tone this was another tease. "No need for my wife to come home," he timed his remark as Jared came through the door. "Jared, my dear man, you don't mind if we all share your wife, do you?" Jared looked startled. What was the stupid potter waffling on about now?

Seth continued, "Every home should have a 'Kezia'… food ready for hungry men, smiling face, house swept…" his list of compliments was abruptly halted by someone pounding on the door.

Seth made a pained expression. "Now who has come to disturb our perfect life?" He opened the door on a waif of a boy, barely clothed, his hair matted and unkempt.

"Please sir," the boy piped, "can you send the healer-girl?" Seth was immediately serious.

"Who do you mean, boy?" he asked.

The boy pointed a dirt-ingrained finger at Kezia. "That one," he said. Then with renewed urgency he cried, "*Please* sir, can she come?"

"Now hang… hang on. Why do you need a healer, young man?" Seth was clearly suspicious of the boy standing barefoot in the doorway.

"'S'my father. He's done his back. Can't walk. Gran said she's…" he pointed again, "she's a healer-girl." The boy sniffed, at a loss to know what more he could say to explain his emergency. "*Please* sir…?" he whined.

Seth turned back to Kezia who stood rooted to the ground. Jared and Ben gawped at her in disbelief. Seth spoke gently; "Is this right, Kez? Are you a healer-girl?" he asked cautiously.

"I don't know," Kezia replied, flustered and awkward. "I really don't know."

Seth looked back at the anxious little boy before he asked Kezia, "Are you willing to see this young lad's father?"

"If I can… I'm willing to… if I can. But…" she turned to Jared, "Only if my husband gives his permission," she said. Jared's chapped lips lifted towards his nose.

"Please yourself!" he said dismissively, more interested in the pot of stew on the table than any little boy's plight. "Just don't be too long," he added in after thought. Kezia glanced at the table.

"Everything's ready for you, Seth." The kid pouch with

the stones always hung from her belt, and she quickly lifted her cloak from the peg behind the door .

"I think," Seth decided, "it would be best if I came with you." He took hold of the boy's shoulder, "I want to know where this young scallywag is taking you." Rough shanty-towns clustered on the slopes outside the city gates and, judging by the state of the boy, that's where he would take them. No place for a young wife to venture unaccompanied. Jared began to ladle out the piping hot stew, thick with lentils, herbs and vegetables. He and Ben attacked their steaming bowls.

Kezia felt safe with Seth. She had no idea what she was walking in to. In her struggle to stay calm it helped to feel she was offering to use the gift Jesus had given her. He meant her to be a 'comfort and a blessing', wasn't that what he'd said? But as she and Seth followed the boy, nagging doubts crowded in on her. What if there was nothing she could do?

Seth walked in silence, his thoughts embroiled with the implications of Kezia being a true healer. A terrible weight of expectation would fall on her young shoulders. If Kez had a true gift from the Lord God, then nothing could prevent its use. On the other hand, if the old crone in the market was mistaken… there would be ill-feeling and swift recriminations. Seth wondered to himself what Joanna would say. He missed her. He needed her back home.

"In here!" chimed the boy. They had passed through the Nazareth Gate and walked down the slope to where the poor lived among the hillside caves. A woman rushed from one of the cave openings, grabbed Kezia's arm and gabbled into her face. Seth didn't catch her exact words but gathered it was all about the man. He hovered making sure he could watch what Kezia was getting in to.

Coarse and filthy sacking hung across the interior behind which a man in his thirties lay on a mattress against the curve of the cave wall. In deference to their visitor, he was covered with a patched sheet. The boy and his mother stood with expressions of absolute faith as they watched Kezia kneel beside the man. He acknowledged her, tried to shift his position but cried out with the effort, rolled his eyes and whined like a wounded dog.

"Lie still," Kezia spoke as a woman cool in the crisis and in complete control. "Close your eyes and don't try to move." The wife clutched the end of her shawl across her face. In a hushed voice she tried to explain:

"Accident in the quarry." She pulled the boy in front of her where he fidgeted with the rag that passed as his tunic. "Brought him home on a stretcher they did," she confided. "He's been in agonies."

Kezia held the kid pouch in her hands and closed her eyes in prayer. Her lips moved but she made no sound. Her prayer finished, she took out the stones. Seth watched as she placed the deep blue, gold-flecked stone on the man's throat. Next she put the milky gemstone and the stone with green ripples on his breast bone, the yellow and the two glass-like green stones she placed on his stomach before finally balancing the brown and honey striped stone on his creased forehead. The man under the sheet hardly dared breathe.

"Lie still and the Lord will heal you." Kezia repeated her words slowly and deliberately until she could sense the man relaxing. Her hands burned with fierce heat. She spread her hands a few inches above the man's chest and, without touching the sheet, moved her hands as though she were massaging away the pain. She repeated the movement above his legs. All the time her lips moved in prayer.

Seth had never witnessed anything like it. He found it intensely moving, yet, at the same time, deeply, deeply disturbing. Kezia's hands became still above the man's head and then moved gradually down to his feet. She repeated the movements several times as though pulling something out of the way. Finally she collected the stones and replaced them in the pouch. By this time the injured man was fast asleep.

Kezia stood up, trembling from concentration. She gave the wife a smile of encouragement.

"Is he healed?" the woman asked. The enormity of a crippled husband dawning on her.

"I don't know." Kezia was honest. "Keep praying. And tomorrow," she suggested, "massage his lower back with olive oil."

Seth guided Kezia out of the meagre hovel and back up the uneven stone path to the city gate. Only then did she realise there was no distinctive purple turban.

***

"You never said you were a healer," Jared said in a tone more accusing than interested.

"I don't know that I am," Kezia replied quietly as she undressed in their corner of the pottery.

"How much d'you charge them?" he asked.

"I… er…" Kezia was baffled by the question. It hadn't entered her mind to ask for money. "… I…I couldn't ask for money!" she stammered.

Jared grunted in disgust.

"Anyway," she added, "I don't know if the man *will* be healed." She lay down beside him. The air smelt of quarry dust and sweat.

196

"Should've charged." Came the surly retort.

Kezia felt her eyelids close under a great weight of tiredness. "Jesus is the Healer, not me." She said, extinguishing the lamp.

Jared swore under his breath and pulled the blanket up to his beard.

"No point in letting you do it if they don't pay," He snarled. The remark was so utterly contemptible, Kezia pretended she hadn't heard him. She turned away from him and almost immediately sank into the oblivion of sleep.

***

"…and your father's called him Jabez!" Joyful words tumbled out as Joanna responded to the barrage of Kezia's questions. It was wonderful to have Joanna home – and with such exciting news! A little brother! Kezia's brown eyes glowed with pride as she heard how the baby boy had arrived with speed and, for her mother, so easily. It couldn't be better news. She longed to dance with Adah in celebration, inspect the baby's fingers and toes and rock him to sleep, just as they had done with Zippie.

"… but you should see his *hair*!" Joanna declared. "I've never seen a new-born with that amount of hair!" They chuckled together. "Adah will be able to weave it into a blanket for Zippie!" Joanna threw back her head in laughter. She felt happy to have left her sister well cared for in Adah's capable hands, even if she had to endure the dubious assistance of the all-seeing and interfering Anna plus docile shadow, Miriam. Joanna peeled off her cloak and poked stray traces of her dark hair back under her headscarf. She beamed – it was good to be home.

Looking round she noticed ingredients for their evening meal already prepared and covered with a cloth against the flies. Joanna approved. It was obvious Kezia had done a good job!

"Right!" she breezed, "That's all your news from Capernaum. Now," she folded her arms with a flourish and raised an eyebrow, "*What* have you done with my men? I called in at the pottery, expecting a hive of industry, and nothing… not a soul in sight! "

"Seth's gone to find Nico," Kezia replied over her shoulder as she fetched her aunt a cup of water.

"Oh, he'll have gone to the bath-house on his way home, then." The way she spoke made it sound to Kezia as though going to the bath-house was a regular happening. A bath-house was something else they didn't have in Capernaum.

Joanna pulled up a stool, sat down and slipped off her sandals. "Oh! My *poor* feet!" she exclaimed. "I've been on the road since first light and we didn't stop." She took the cup gratefully and downed the contents in one.

"So!" Joanna sat stretching her toes, "What's been happening while I've been away?"

Kezia regaled her aunt with her new experiences; getting lost in the lower market, helping Ben deliver Seth's products to big houses and making new friends by the washing stream. She was just about to tell Joanna about the old woman in the market and her visit to the injured man when Seth walked through the door.

***

Later that night:

Joanna knelt behind Seth on the mattress as she massaged his neck and shoulders with sweet almond oil laced with a drop of spikenard. Seth described how the old woman had accosted Kezia in the street and how the little urchin had come to the door for help.

"Did you know she was a healer?" he asked.

"No idea." Joanna was thoughtful; her hands worked along his shoulders digging in to tight knots of muscle.

"Has anyone in your family had that sort of gift?" Seth persisted.

"Not as far I know." Joanna was mystified. "Maybe something to do with her own healing. You know… when Leah was convinced she was dead and the Rabbi Jesus cured her." Silence between them was easy but they both wrestled to make sense of the inexplicable. After a while Seth reached up and caught Joanna's hands, holding them still on his shoulders,

"Ah, my love," he whispered, "you have healing hands." He leaned back against her. "So glad you're home," he sighed. She pressed her head on his shoulder, her hair falling seductively down over his arm.

"Oh, by the way," he said, "got a new design for my jugs!" His voice lifted in anticipation of a new range. "Something Nico's been working on…" Joanna sensed her husband's imagination was racing. "He'll be round in the morning," Seth enthused. Bringing her hands forward, he pressed his lips to her knuckles.

Joanna listened to the rhythmic puffing. Seth was fast asleep but Joanna's mind continued to whirl. In her tiredness each thought dove-tailed into another, jumbled, unfinished images… healing hands, Leah contorted in childbirth, her journey back to Sepphoris, Jabez' shock of hair, Zippie running rings around diligent little Adah, Jairus elated and proud, the pottery, Kezia as a healer, Jabez sucking at Leah's breast, her own empty womb... round and round the images taunted her. It was all too much! She raised a hand to her pounding forehead then threw back the blanket and turned over for the umpteenth time.

She faced the sleeping mound beside her. Seth was a good man, she reminded herself. She loved him; he was kind, respected, worked so hard – she inhaled deeply. If only he could... Oh, it was no use! She crept out of bed and went to stand by the window. The sound of horses' hooves on the cobbled street drifted through the open frame. A detachment of cavalry leaving? Arriving perhaps? Impossible to tell which. A cock crowed in the distance, way over the valley. Joanna rubbed her eyes in disbelief. Was it possible? Was Kezie a healer?

Chapter 24

SETH heard the two women clatter back from the market.

"Kez!" his voice called from the pottery. "Need your help."

"Boys!" Joanna smiled. "They can't manage a moment without us!" Kezia took her basket of vegetables into the house. Her aunt still looked tired after her journey home and Kezia imagined she could detect the faintest air of sadness.

"Will you be alright?" she looked at Joanna in case she needed to fetch more water.

"Go on with you," Joanna came to life and gave her a fond push, "I may have been away a few weeks, but I think I remember what to do in my own house!" she said. The familiar Joanna took command once more. Kezia laughed and disappeared over to the pottery.

Seth aimed a dollop of clay at the rotating wheel. With skill acquired from his life's work, the clay landed *splat!* – dead centre. Kezia watched fascinated as Seth's bare feet hit against the lower wheel which in turn spun the higher wheel on which he worked. His long, steady fingers worked up and down, sloshing water to smooth and transform the featureless clay into an elegant pot or everyday jug or mug. He didn't look up as she came in but focussed on his creation.

"Make us some more slip, will you Kez?" he asked. Ben

was out in the courtyard stacking pots into the kiln and a batch of dry pots sat on the table, lined up and ready for decorating.

Stooping for the slip bucket under the table she didn't notice another person was in the pottery. Turning, she bumped straight into him. Startled that, unawares she had touched against a strange man, she jumped back. Confused and embarrassed, she stared at the floor willing him to go away. Tentatively she raised her eyes to find the young man had not gone away. He stood looking down at her, smiling gently, his eyes, the rich mahogany of ripe dates. Taller than both Seth and Jared, his tunic was splattered and daubed with clay in the same messy way as Seth's and Ben's. 'Nico', she thought, 'this must be the Roman.'

"I want you…" he floundered for vocabulary, " this er, new slip…I want to make er.. slip." He carried on without introduction as if they'd been chatting all morning. He spoke softly with a thick, foreign accent. Kezia's mind blanked. She had never spoken to a foreign man before… or a gentile. Colour flooded her cheeks as she stood mute.

"Don't be afraid!" Seth called over, "Nico doesn't escape from the courthouse *every* day!" he chuckled over the wheel. A lop-sided grin broke across the stranger's serious face. The clean-shaven features, wide forehead, straight nose and square chin, made his face look as though it had been chiselled. His short hair was as dark as Jared's but it was oiled and, curled close to his skull, it accentuated his ears. Jared wore his hair long so she had never noticed his ears. Suddenly, in a fluster, Kezia realised she was staring.

"I show you," Nico turned to pick up a chunk of rock with a distinct, green seam. "See! This.…" he ran a finger along the seam, "Green… is copper. When is um, is ground and mix in slip…" he stuck the rock onto the table and picked up a chisel. "The fired pot," he puckered full lips to indicate pleasure, "beautiful blue glaze."

'Blue?' Kezia questioned in her mind. She tried to imagine it. 'But the seam was green! How could the glaze be blue?' She longed to see his lips pucker again. Her heart beat faster. Seth broke in on her thoughts:

"Blue as the sky!" he crowed from the spinning wheel. "The first *blue* pottery in Sepphoris. I tell you, Kez, we're going to be rich and famous!" Kezia smiled at the thought. Blue would certainly be different from all the usual reds, ochres and yellow glazes of the Galilee. She moved to lift the bucket onto the table at the same time as Nico reached to lift it for her. His fingers brushed her hand as he took it from her. A tingle seared through the centre of her body. In a supreme effort to breathe normally... she pulled herself together. What had come over her?

Legs that had turned to jelly wobbled unsteadily to the far side of the pottery so that she could fetch more water and the lighter coloured clay for mixing the slip.

Nico picked up a sharp flint chisel and began to dig the ore out from the rock onto the table.

"Most time," he said, scraping fast with short, firm strokes, "copper come from rock... er... like eezy." Kezia listened intently, riveted by his faltering accent. When he'd extracted as much copper as possible, he turned his face towards Kezia. "Now you do," his eyes smiled. "You grind these er, small... to fine... see... like powder." He lifted the copper granules into a stone mortar and pounded them with a short pestle. "Simple... just like er, you womens grind wheat."

He scrutinised the powder for impurities. "Then," he said collecting the powder on a spoon, "mix in bucket. Like er, thees." He looked at her with dark, earnest eyes, " Eef you mix bad... glaze bad." He frowned. "Our work be... spoil."

Seth joined in; "Don't worry, Kez'll mix it well. She's not slap-dash." Nico wanted to say more – anything just so long as he could stand and gaze at this beautiful young woman. Her eyes drew him, the tentative, haunting look of a deer about to take flight. But all he could manage was to murmur "Thenk you." Before returning to the line of jugs waiting for his decoration.

Kezia experienced a strange fluttering. Her fingers became clumsy and fire burned up her neck as her every fibre concentrated on grinding the grey-green chips into an ash-like powder. She waited for him to walk over and check her grinding. But he didn't. While the men worked Kezia turned over in her mind how amazingly different men were.

She'd never understood Jared. Brusque and unsmiling, he didn't know how to be gentle. He made her feel like his furniture. Growing up, she remembered how children in Capernaum were afraid of him. She had prayed countless prayers that she would not have to marry him, but her prayers had not been answered. Now she was his wife, she had to do things that wives did and... get on with it.

Her mind turned to her father; ever since she was a small girl she had adored her father, and, until the past year, he had always been so loving and understanding. She used to dream she would always live with her parents but, since that fateful Passover in Jerusalem, her father had changed. He had become aloof, almost as though his family was no longer important. She tried so hard not to irritate him but she felt his mind was always elsewhere.

A merchant stamped into the pottery and began to bargain with Seth over a basket of plates.

Kezia smiled to herself as she continued pounding the grit

and thinking about the men she knew. Uncle Mordecai! Old as the hills! Over the years her uncle had spent far more time with her than her father. All those stories he told about Moses, and Noah and King David – he was such a dramatic raconteur. She could see his eyebrows now, rising and falling in rotation to emphasise the tension of his tales… Yet he too had changed; he too was preoccupied and quickly disgruntled. All since their visit to Jerusalem.

The grinding stone worked better as her rhythm developed. Kezia realised both her father and uncle were furious with Jesus. But how could they be? To her, he was the perfect man. She remembered his calm, deep voice and the way he would laugh and sing. In girlish fantasy, Jesus was the man she longed to marry.

His crucifixion broke her heart.

But this foreigner… she glanced up. This clean-shaven artist with intense eyes and intriguing accent… she fumbled and lost the grinding rhythm. All the Jewish men she knew, her father, uncle, Jesus, the Rabbis, fishermen and farmers, they *all* had beards. To see a man's smooth cheeks, his exposed lips and chin, held a peculiar fascination. Kezia felt an uncontrollable magnetism to this stranger. For the first time in her life, her mind and body was beyond her control. Why this warmth inside, this quickened heartbeat and irrational desire to dance?

***

Jared glared. Suspicious of all strangers, he slouched in the doorway, debating whether to sit down at the table or walk out. What would his father say to him eating with a *gentile?* Seth sensed the charged atmosphere. He sat down so that Nico was buttressed between himself and Ben.

"Jared, my boy. Come… sit down." He motioned amiably. "Meet Nicolaus, our friend, the famous artist." He pushed a bowl towards Jared. "He's going to make us rich!"

Jared's eyebrows lifted in a manner somewhere between curiosity and scorn. Seth ignored Jared's peevish expression. Nevertheless, his fatherly tone rang with the authority of the head of his household.

"Living in Sepphoris is a great privilege." He spoke gravely. "Since the 'troubles' of our past, we have learned the terrible consequences of hatred. Today, we all enjoy the fruits of peace." He poured water into his mug. "As citizens of this beautiful city, we have *chosen* to live in peace with every member of the human race." Seth paused. "Hatred gets us nowhere." He stared directly at Jared until Jared dropped his gaze. "As I say, we have c*hos*en to live in peace." Recognising the fact he was under Seth's roof, Jared reluctantly took the seat next to Ben.

**

"Rich indeed!" Jared snorted, chucking his tunic on the floor. He felt contaminated – filthy – the meal stuck in his gullet. Eating with a gentile – whatever next!

"He's got a new slip to…" Kezia began.

"I don't want to hear!" Jared barked. "Don't care what he's got. He could have the pox for all I care. I don't want to eat with a *gentile*." He wheeled round on Kezia, "And I don't want you having anything to do with him, either." He stood in front of her naked and obdurate. "You're my wife!"

"I know how you feel," Kezia sought to be consilliatory. "But, Jared, this is Seth's home, we don't have a choice." She busied with a new wick for the lamp. "Seth and Joanna have been good to us." She paused. "Living here in the city…it's not like Capernaum. Try and think of him as an artist rather than a gentile?" she suggested.

"Artist! Playing round with prissy bits of stone and a paintbrush." He made a noise as though spitting a mosquito out of his mouth. "Child's play! Then," he added with a contemptuous sneer, "just what you'd expect from the potter's type!"

Kezia accepted it was pointless to say more. She picked up his discarded tunic and laid a clean one over the back of the stool. In the oil-lamp's glow she noticed a tare in the soiled tunic. Wistfully she remembered Sarah – dear Sarah, *she* was the one for mending! Oh well, better do it in the morning before she took it to the washing stream.

Jared came up behind her. Clumsily he ripped off her head-scarf.

"Get in bed," he ordered. Kezia hadn't finished undressing.

"Just a…" she began, but Jared grabbed at her and threw her down on the mattress with such force her shoulder cracked against the rough stone of the wall. Pain brought tears stinging to her eyes.

"*Now!*" he hissed, "You're my wife. You do as I say."

***

"What's this?" Seth's eyes widened at the sight. "Jo… here a minute!" he called over his shoulder. "What d'you make of this?" Joanna came to the door, vegetable knife still in her hand.

"Well!" she gasped in amazement. "What's it doing *here*?"

Two nervous eyes under a thatch of matted hair peered over the courtyard wall. Seth mouthed under his breath. "It's the boy who came for Kez." He called over to the boy, "Here, boy! Did *you* bring this animal in here?" The boy jumped down from the wall and slunk in through the open door. Joanna's heart went out to the waif in bare feet.

"Please, sir," the boy mumbled, "Father said it's for the healer-girl. He c'n walk now. He's back to work, but he said… *she's* to have it." Joanna saw the way the boy looked at the donkey, a creature as much skin and bone as the boy himself. "Father said he's no money so she must have… have the donkey." His voice tailed off as he fixed his gaze on the floor.

"He's your friend, isn't he." The warmth in Joanna's observation moved the boy to drag a hand over his eyes.

"Father says she's got to have it." He sniffed dolefully.

Seth stood in the doorway, inspecting the animal at a safe distance. He wasn't familiar with donkeys.

"He'll need hay." Joanna was being practical. She came out and scooped an arm round the boy's thin shoulders, "You come in here with me. You'd best mop up some pottage before you go home."

"Yes…" Seth began, "Yes, have some breakfast. And… um… and thank your father for his…" The donkey's mournful eyes lifted to the potter, "… his gift."

"He wants a drink," the boy said as he disappeared inside with Joanna.

"Right!" Seth stared at the animal while he tried to get things straight in his mind. A couple of days ago the boy's father lay immobile… now he was back to work? Was Kezia a healer after all? "Extraordinary!" he exclaimed to the drooping animal.

"Where did *that* come from?" Ben walked in to the courtyard to the unlikely sight of Seth leaning forward, engaged in eye contact with the most mournful looking donkey imaginable.

"He needs water and hay," Seth replied. "And you, my dearest Ben, are just the man to deal with it." That said, Seth whistled his way across to the pottery.

When Kezia returned, basket of washing on her head, she found Ben adding cabbage leaves into a bucket, most of which was taken up by a donkey's head. When Joanna told her the man with the back injury had recovered enough to go back to work, she became subdued and lost in thought.

"He's got no money, so he gives you his donkey," Joanna told her. "That's gratitude!"

"But I don't want to be paid," moaned Kezia. Joanna took both her hands in her own and looked deep into her innocent face, "Well, chicken, I think it's a bit out of your control." She kissed her forehead. "Today, a donkey has been added to our family." A hearty chuckle echoed round the room, as she voiced, "I dread to think what tomorrow will bring!" She took her niece in a reassuring hug, "Come on, now, up to the Cardo – we need food for our men tonight."

"How many tonight?" Kezia tried too hard to sound casual.

"Our faithful three – Seth, Ben and Jared." Joanna slipped a sleeveless cloak over her tunic and tucked her purse into the deep tunic pocket as she spoke.

Kezia matched Joanna's brisk stride as they made their way to the Cardo. She stifled her secret turmoil. Fierce tentacles of disappointment threatened to choke the fun of shopping in the Cardo. If only they were shopping for *four* men…

***

Jairus cradled his son as if the infant would disintegrate with

209

the slightest pressure. He tucked the shawl under the baby's chin as he sat on the roof, soaking in the calm beauty of dusk.

"There!" he whispered, pointing into the sky, "That's the Evening Star. The first star you see in the night sky." Jabez' quizzical gaze focussed on the hole in Jairus' beard which emitted strange sounds. Mordecai sat alongside the father and son. He too searched the deepening indigo sky.

"When I look at the sky," Mordecai began to intone a psalm, both men relaxed with the poetry of ancient liturgies, "at the moon and the stars, which you set in their courses – what is man that you care for him?"

"The Lord God promised our Father Abraham his descendants would be as many as the stars in the sky," Jairus added. Quoting scripture with his uncle was their private theological game.

"…and grains of sand along the seashore!" Mordecai completed the verse with a triumphant relish. "Ay!" he mused, "We have a great God of miracles." He turned to look at Jairus, "And you, my son, hold the greatest miracle in your arms."

"Indeed. The Lord has blessed me." Jairus considered all the generations of fathers who had held sons under the velvet blanket of the endless, dome of sky. "I pray Jabez will grow to manhood in a land free from Rome's tyranny."

"Pity Kezia ever went to Sepphoris." Mordecai yawned. "You must miss her." Little did he realise that since Jabez had come into the world, Jairus had not given his daughter a thought.

"Of course," Jairus insisted. A wave of guilt flickered across his mind. Now that he held his son, nothing and, sadly, nobody, meant as much. He had gained immortality. His own flesh and blood would procreate… he would live on in future generations. He had achieved the ultimate that a man could achieve.

"I was thinking," Mordecai began. "Leah should have her daughter with her at this time." He paused. "Women after childbirth can often be… how shall I say… well, *melancholy*." Jairus let his uncle burble on. "I think Leah could do with having Kezia around."

"She has a husband now. She can't come running home just when she wants to," Jairus replied.

"Oh, don't tell me Joanna can't take care of that Jared for a while." Mordecai had been scheming how to bring Kezia back to Capernaum and now he seized his chance.

"I'll go up to Sepphoris and bring her back for a week or so?"

Jairus continued to rock his son. "You don't want to do that, Uncle," he responded. "Leah's got plenty of help. Sometimes, my house…why, it's so full of women, it ceases to feel like *my* house. It's worse than when Sarah was always round here." Mordecai had decided on his plan; he would not be denied.

"But, I've nothing else to do, my boy. I'll take my time… go easy. I'll bring her down to see her little brother. She'll love that." Jairus lost interest.

"Ye-es," he agreed. "She'll be longing to see him. But… wait a while before you make the journey. It'll give Leah time to recover some strength. She'll be able to enjoy Kezie's company all the more then."

The old Pharisee leaned back. He had won. He would go to Sepphoris and bring Kezia back home – home where she belonged.

The two men stayed on the flat-roof, refreshed by the cool

air blowing off the lake. Below them, Adah bit into the bread and olives she had not had time to eat earlier. Zippie lay curled asleep on Adah's bed, thumb between her open lips. Enough light filtered through the window that Adah didn't need to light the lamp. She loved the darkness when, the day's work over, everything was still.

It seemed ages since she and Kezia had shared their room. The space felt hollow. Adah chewed slowly, lost in thought. She wondered what Kezie was doing in Sepphoris. Whether she had time to remember her. She had hoped Kezie would come home to see the new baby, but she supposed it wasn't that easy for her, what with being married and all… and no servant girl, so she'd likely not have a minute to herself.

Adah finished her supper and snuggled in beside Zippie. At first Adah had been upset that her mistress hadn't wanted the little mite, but now, as her arm enfolded the child, she was glad. Very glad. Maybe it was nice to be married, to have a man give you a home and love you. But, from all she had heard down at the washing pool, it didn't always turn out like that! She nestled close in to the toddler. Zippie reacted in her sleep, kicked her legs and turned over. Adah smiled. She didn't need to go through all that rigmarole of birthing, it was enough for her that she and Zippie had each other to love.

Leah lay quietly, resting but not asleep. Jairus often came in to take Jabez from his basket, walk round with him, sing to him or take him up to the flat roof. Up there he'd sit for hours talking as though the infant was already one of his pupils in the Synagogue. She couldn't believe the change that had come over her husband. To have a son was more than happiness to him, it had fulfilled him; it was his public statement of his manhood. Sixteen long years they had waited and prayed for a son, now Leah felt she had completed her duty.

But at what cost? Every sinew in her body dragged, she felt like a leaden weight and as desirable as a bundle of wet washing. Her strength was gone.

Chapter 25

A month later:

THE magistrate had ordered a consignment of pottery dipped in the new glaze, and to complete this prestigious order, Nico had given Seth many hours at the pottery. Once fired, the cups and plates turned a striking blue, deeper than the bluest cornflowers. Seth held up a plate for Joanna and Kezia to inspect.

"See," his eyes alight with the thrill of success, "fit for a King's table!"

Joanna nodded approval. "Suppose, I will make do with your rejects… as usual."

"Of course!" Seth laid the plate reverently on the table. He put a hand to his wife's cheek, "I'm afraid, my love, I'm the only *perfect* vessel you possess!" Joanna clicked her tongue and rolled her eyes in despair before they all collapsed in laughter.

Nico worked on three designs. The most expensive was the completely blue pottery, next in price were items where he had painted a band of blue slip around the centre, and finally, the utilitarian models in the indigenous red clay of the Galilee, varied decoration incised with a fine bone marker. The blue colouration was so innovative that orders already came in from the theatre, the bank and even the Governor.

The magistrate's order was Seth's vital commercial boost. Some days he was at his wheel for hours on end producing over a hundred cups a day. On the days he made jugs, Ben's job was to attach the handles. Kezia helped pack orders but the days she most enjoyed were when she went out delivering with Seth and Nico. Seth soaked up the recognition the blue pottery had created and glided along the streets dispensing hearty greetings to friends and customers. The purple turban nodded so much, Kezia waited for it to fall off. Heads turned as the unlikely trio passed by; flamboyant potter, handsome Roman artist and the stunning, nubile woman in a dusky pink cloak.

The contrast between the fishing village of Capernaum and the modern city of Sepphoris excited Kezia each day. She could cross the stone roadways in the rain without getting the hem of her cloak and her feet filthy, and walking the wide pavements was safe compared to the continual evasion of carts, donkeys, soldiers and everything else on wheels, two or four legs that trafficked along the rutted, earthen roads of Capernaum.

All her life she had watched clouds scud across the lake, constantly changing the colour of the water and hills beyond. Now, from between the new, limestone buildings of Sepphoris, she watched clouds scud over the towering hills causing shadows to sweep over the countryside as if engaged in some mysterious game of chase. It felt like living in a city on the top of the world with all Galilee spread out below.

Sometimes actors and mime artists performed in the market square. Their gaudy costumes, exaggerated gestures and exotically painted faces instantly drew knots of spectators. People stood rocking in time to the songs or heckling and goading the bawdy sketches. It occurred to Kezia how perfectly Seth would fit into an actor's life.

Back in the pottery, the men took little notice of Kezia as she ground, mixed, fetched water, stacked wet pots, counted dry ones and generally busied herself with the routine chores. All the time she listened avidly for Nico's voice. For hours afterwards she would turn a phrase over in her mind, recapturing the inflection of his accent. He was nothing like her impression of a 'Roman' at all. In fact he wasn't like anyone she had met before.

***

Jared's change of occupation from fisherman on his father's boats to the pounding, hand-ripping work in breaking and lifting stone, had wrought a radical change to his physique. Weight fell off as he sweated in the back-breaking and unrelenting labour at the quarry, which, on hot days, became a furnace and on cold days caused his feet and hands to turn numb. Muscle had built in his legs and shoulders, yet the rest of his body appeared scrawny and slightly stooped. Kezia couldn't help but notice that in his pinched and constantly disapproving expression he had become, in these short months, a mirror image of his Aunt Anna.

It was worse, of course, on the occasions when Nico joined them for the evening meal. Her husband's jealousy burnt into her with every move she made as she placed food on the table or carried away dishes. He bristled whenever he caught Nico looking at her or speaking to her. She dared not look at or answer the artist when Jared was present.

Kezia noticed the way Nico smelt when he'd been to the bath-house. Not the sweet smell of incense that hung on her father's clothes but a hint of musky perfume that she found dangerously addictive. She contrived every chance to pass behind him as he sat for the evening meal. Surrepticiously she breathed in his scent, holding it inside herself. Even after he had left the room, she would pass his empty cushion and fancy she could still detect a faint waft of his scent.

Joanna's 'men' to feed had grown from three to five: Seth, Ben, Jared, Nico and now little Josh, the boy with the donkey.

"Best he eats with us," Joanna declared. "His father can't afford to feed all his brood." She abhorred any whiff of charity, "Anyway," she breezed, "Little Josh has the belly of a mouse!" She scraped the wooden paddle firmly round the bottom of the pan, added more stock, then sipped at a spoonful to taste her soup. The boy trailed at Joanna's heels and she, in turn, bandied a natural rapport with him, sending him on errands and occupying him with 'jobs'. His chief responsibility, to everyone's relief, remained the donkey.

Two, and sometimes three times a week, new faces began to appear at the pottery asking for the healer-girl. Seth had told her she must never go on these visits alone, either he would escort her, or Ben or Joanna. Approaching the poor, dismal hovels outside the city wall, Kezia was truly grateful for their support. Many lived in black goat-hair tents, reminiscent of the tents that camped outside Bethany at Passover. Some homes were little more than caves, while other families, with older sons, managed to build small dwellings from the rough stone littered over the hillside. Her reputation as a Healer spread like wild-fire among those unable to afford a doctor's fees.

She tended to the bruised, the feint, those with stomach disorders, fevers and skin diseases. Calmly, she laid her stones on each anxious body, invoked the name of the Lord God to heal them, prayed over them and gently anointed them with olive oil, infused with rosemary. She and Adah had learnt to infuse herbs in the oil back in Capernaum. The expression in the people's eyes affected her deeply. They treated her with hushed deference and touching gratitude. If Joanna was her companion, the family could be sure a pot of lentil soup would be left behind.

"A good meal'll do them as much good as anything," was Joanna's forthright motto.

To Jared's intense irritation, Kezia never brought home any money, but 'gifts' were regularly left by the pottery door. Pots of wild honey, pickles, olives, a baskets of eggs, goats' cheese and mounds of green vegetables made a regular appearance. One day Joanna even found a battered cushion that had obviously served as a pillow through several winters. She sighed. What did they sleep on now?

***

"Oh, there you are!" Joanna prodded the embers into a final burst of heat beneath the cooking pot. "Trust Ben to get you home for meal-time." Kezia trailed into the courtyard behind Ben. The 'men', Seth, Jared, Nico and Little Josh were already at the table tucking in to bread, a spicy sesame paste, cheese and olives. Kezia looked at the pot as Joanna lifted the lid to fill the extra bowls. The thick, cloying smell of lentils, onions and cumin churned her stomach. Sweat broke out on her neck and forehead and an involuntary urge made her gasp for air. Leaving Joanna and Ben standing by the fire, Kezia bolted for the latrine.

Ben tried not to notice Kezia's speedy exit. Maybe she had caught something from the old woman they'd just visited. But, he was hungry, so he decided not to say anything.

" Go on with you…" Joanna ordered Ben with motherly bustle, "take this in with you."

218

Joanna pushed a steaming bowl into his hand and followed him inside carrying two more. The widest smile spread across her face – a knowing, satisfied smile of immense pleasure.

***

"How do you know?" Seth scratched the back of his neck. He watched his wife remove her headscarf and flick her hair loose onto her shoulders.

"I just *do!*" Joanna replied, her face radiant. "Women *always* know these things… it's instinct."

Seth turned his attention to his toes. He sat cross-legged on the mattress and rubbed each one in turn.

"Has she said anything?" he asked, digging at a lump of hard skin.

"Not yet." Joanna slipped out of her tunic.

"Just like you to know before she does!" Seth quipped. "When do you think you ought to tell her?" Joanna picked up a blanket off the stool and threw it at him.

Seth lay asleep, his face to the wall. Joanna lay thinking… planning… imagining. She wanted to rush down to Capernaum and tell Leah there and then. Eventually, she pulled the blanket up, turned on her side and, with a deep breath, shut her eyes. They'd need a bigger table…

***

In the morning Kezia's cheeks were unnaturally flushed. Dark circles beneath her eyes indicated a restless night. Joanna studied her closely.

"How do you feel, chicken?" she asked. " Well enough to go washing?"

"Yes… yes, of course." Kezia murmured avoiding her aunt's gaze.

"Hmmmm." Joanna made a decision . "Well, I don't think so. You look washed out – you won't have strength to walk there and back. And you're a big girl now, I can't *carry* you like I used to years ago!" she joked.

"Oh, but I…" Kezia protested.

"Oh but..nothing!" Joanna broke in. "You have to take care now. I want this baby to be strong and…"

"What baby?" Kezia stared at her aunt in disbelief. Joanna wrapped her arms around her neice and held her close.

"My dear, dear chicken," she purred, "*your* baby!"

Chapter 26

"HOW did we live before donkey-power?" Seth posed his smiling question to Little Josh before dispatching him with panniers strapped on each side of the animal and instructions to collect as much brushwood and dry dung as the baskets would hold. There had been times in the past when pots had to wait for firing because Seth didn't have enough fuel for the kiln. The advent of Little Josh and the angular transport meant plenty of fuel was now stacked in the courtyard and the kiln could work full tilt.

Seth threw an arm round Ben's shoulders as they studied the squat, brick kiln.

"Think it's had it," Ben moaned, fingering a wide fissure along the top.

"Time to build a 'proper' kiln." Seth declared. Ben's eyebrows raised, waiting to hear more. He was fed up with the continual repairs to Seth's existing model which was months past its optimum efficiency. Seth stood back to inspect the courtyard and guage the best position for a new kiln.

"We'll build a walk-in kiln… you know… like the ones in Tiberias." He adjusted his turban.

Ben looked around. "Where will you put the donkey?" he asked. The courtyard shrank daily with various household necessities. Seth turned, waved a dismissive hand and disappeared inside the pottery.

"Oh… Joanna'll take care of that," was his parting comment. "Plenty of room inside." Ben shrugged. Seth was a lucky man to have such a tolerant and accommodating wife, but, Ben wondered, how she would take to the donkey inside was another matter.

Kezia was packing a box with the new, blue plates, ready to take to the banker's house. Between each plate she laid a sprinkling of straw to make sure no damage could happen in transit. Seth saw her run an admiring finger over the leaf decoration. He smiled. "Nothing like that in all Galilee," he said with pride. Then, with a grin he added, "Pity we can only keep the ones that go wrong." He sat down at his wheel. "Jugs today," he continued happily, "rows and rows of *jugs*!"

With the box filled, Kezia set about shifting the previous day's bowls out in the sun to dry. But concentration was a problem. A voice inside her head kept whispering, 'you're having a baby… having a baby… a baby!' Out of her own body… *her* baby! It was thrilling but, remembering her mother's screams when she gave birth to Zippie, spasmodic waves of panic dampened her joy. Perhaps her pregnancy would lift Jared's spirits and make him feel more settled. At least, that was her hope and prayer.

Suddenly, a compulsion seized her. An overwhelming need to run home to her mother. She stood, oblivious of Seth, a pile of bowls in her hand, as though she had completely forgotten what she was supposed to be doing. She longed for her mother's calm reassurance, for Adah's bright, sisterly company… for her father to be proud of her. She felt sick… frightened… she wanted to cry… she was having a baby!

"Kezie!" Joanna's voice rang across the courtyard. "Look

whose here!" Kezia put down the bowls and emerged, blinking into the sunlight. She let out a squeal of joy:

"Uncle Mordecai!" The Pharisee stood with Joanna in the doorway across the courtyard. Mordecai opened his arms and his eyes creased in pleasure. Kezia flew into the familiar folds of his Pharisee's robes and the nostalgic comfort of his firm embrace.

***

The magistrate grew impatient for his formal dining room mosaic to be completed. It meant Nico hadn't been to the pottery for several days, a fact for which, in the light of her uncle's unexpected arrival, Kezia was profoundly relieved. The old Pharisee was too set in his ways to be able to sit at table with a gentile but, the Pottery seemed strangely forlorn without the artist's skewed, infectious grin. However, his absence averted a scene with Mordecai, something which Kezia was desperate to avoid.

Everyone applauded the news of her pregnancy and Joanna prized out of Mordecai every last detail about Jabez, Leah and Zippie. Kezia laughed at the thought of her little brother with so much hair – how she longed to see and hold him. Mordecai suggested she return with him to Capernaum for a few weeks to spend time with her parents and Jabez. Seth clapped his hand on Mordecai's back.

"My dear Mordecai, I'm sure the Synagogue Elders will expect you to stay for a few days first." Seth filled the Pharisee's cup of wine, "And, please, I beg you, Capernaum must not keep her long." He put on a pleading expression as he addressed Kezia.

"Kez, you're totally indispensable to our production line.

How can you leave us on the brink of fame and fortune?" Joanna set down a bowl of fresh yoghurt and a plate of dates and almonds.

"Don't make the poor girl feel sorry for you!" she scolded. "It'll be a perfect tonic for Leah to see Kezie and know she's carrying a child." She sat herself next to Kezia and gave her arm a fond squeeze.

Never one to miss a business opportunity, Seth immediately suggested Kezia could take the donkey loaded with blue pottery for sale in Capernaum's market.

"I'll send down the army to fetch home the donkey with all my profits!" he quipped though Mordecai failed to be amused at his mention of the 'army'.

Always the convivial host, the potter kept conversation and laughter going throughout the evening. The fact that Jared was getting through a few too many cups of wine did not escape Joanna's eagle eye. Not a good sign.

***

"You didn't tell *me* you were with child," Jared accused when he was alone with his wife in their corner.

"I didn't know myself this morning – not when you went to the quarry." Kezia defended herself, disturbed by his attitude. Jared hunched on the stool while he took time to process the situation. His body tensed in anger.

"Whose is it?" he demanded. Kezia stared, lips parted in fear.

"Y*our*s!" she declared, appalled that he should doubt her.

"Strange it's only happened since that…that so-called artist's been sniffing round you." He didn't meet her gaze. Kezia was distraught. How could her husband think such a thing?

224

"I've not been with another man," reduced to tears she sank fully clothed on the mattress. Jared bit at the nail round his thumb.

"How do I know?" he pouted. "Can't see what you're doing when I'm not here, can I?" He stood up and peered out of the door, making sure no one was in the yard to overhear their conversation.

"Going out to all these places," he snapped, "mixing with strangers… that Joanna's a bad influence." He drew his wrist under his nose, "You behave more like a whore than a wife."

"Jared… listen…"

"No! *You* listen! We're not staying here. I'm taking you back where I can keep my eye on you. We're going back with Mordecai. For good."

"What about the quarry?" Kezia gulped through the tears.

"Curse the quarry. I *hate* it!" he swung round his temper rising. "And I hate this debauched city, too." He pointed his finger at her, "And *you*…" his eyes shrank into slits of malice, "you're getting ideas above yourself – thinking you're some wonderful healer! It's not… not decent." He paused, breathing heavily, anger stifling his ability to express himself in words. He moved away from the door,

"Jared… please… I…"

"I'm telling you – it's got to *stop*!" The threat was no less vindictive for it's muted delivery. Kezia's heart pounded in fear.

"But I'm…"

Before she could utter another word, his right hand lashed across her face. Her head went sideways with the impact and she caught her breath in pain. He caught hold of her wrist and held her to him in a vice-like grip, twisting her arm up behind her back. His face pushed into hers.

"Don't answer back!" He spoke in a sinister whisper that seemed to come from way down in his throat. Kezia's eyes shut against the throbbing welt rising on her cheek. "There'll be no more of your 'healing'." He gave an extra wrench to her arm making her gasp. "D'you hear?" Kezia quivered in shock, fear and pain. Eventually, Jared threw down her wrist and she shrank away from him down onto the mattress. He stared at her with the eyes of a crazed polecat.

Any second she expected him to lunge down on top of her, ripping her tunic as often happened in his frenzy to possess her, but, this time, he straightened his back, turned and melted into the night. Kezia buried her face, sobbing into the mattress.

She lay listening, waiting, terrified of what he would do when he came back.

***

At first light, Kezia was up to tidy away their corner behind the curtain before Seth and Ben came in to work. Jared had not returned.

Joanna took one look at Kezia's face. She ordered Little Josh to feed his animal and hurried Seth out of the house. With the men gone, she pulled up a stool and sat opposite her niece.

"Look," she began, her gentle face bending forward in concern, "are you going to tell me what's wrong, chicken?" Kezia fought against a further surge of tears. She couldn't possibly tell Joanna how Jared had accused her of being a whore. Joanna waited.

"Jared's…" she began at last. "He's um… he says we're going home to Capernaum – for good." The statement took

226

Joanna from the ground up. She blew through pursed lips but otherwise sat impassive without comment, allowing Kezia to continue in her own time.

"…says he hates quarry work." She knew it was a lame excuse and was sure Joanna took it as such, but she couldn't say any more. Joanna tussled with her own emotions. She loved Kezia as her own daughter – enjoyed her company – was thrilled at the thought of a baby at the pottery – but the red marks on the girl's cheek… that was a danger signal. A bleak mist crept across her heart, chilling the recent happiness.

"Well," Joanna finally spoke, "when you're married, you… can't always do what you want." She sat back on the stool, folded her arms and looked out through the open door. "If your husband says you're going back to Capernaum, then you have to go." She had a nagging feeling there was far more to Jared's decision than she was being told.

Kezia was desperate to steer the conversation away from herself and Jared. She asked Joanna the direct question she had often wondered, "Are you sad you've not had children?"

Joanna, though caught off guard, was quick witted enough to respond with a characteristic, flippant retort: "Children!" she trilled. "Do I need to remind you I'm married to *Seth*? Then there's Ben…and Nico…and now Little Josh… how many *more* children do you think I can cope with?" As Kezia smiled the bruising on her cheek ached. Joanna flowed on.

"Let me tell you what my mother – your grandmother – used to say. She said, 'little girls grow into women, wives and mothers, but little boys will only ever be little boys!'" Joanna sat chewing the truth of her mother's wisdom. She knew her mask of fun had nearly slipped. For a while she and Kezia sat in silence.

"To be sure," Joanna said at last, "at the beginning it never crossed my mind my womb would stay shut." She fiddled with a wooden spoon. "But... I'm blessed. Seth's a good man." She paused, obviously choosing her words carefully before she spoke. "He loves me, and... he *needs* me." The women were emotionally so close but as they sat together, neither was prepared to be honest about their marriage.

Joanna picked up speed once more, "I'd give the world to see your mother's face when you tell her your news!" she breezed, getting up from the stool. A look of abject despair clouded Kezia's face.

"But I won't be back *home*. It'll be Zebedee's house again... and..." Kezia trailed off.

"...and the dreadful Debra?" Joanna forced a smile.

"Anna's worse!" Kezia said. The name fell out of her mouth like a heavy brick. "I can never please her."

"Oh, but she'll be pleased enough when you give Zebedee a grandson, and Salome will be there to take your side." Joanna assumed a positive air. "Cheer up, chicken. It's not the end of the world!" In a bid to stave off her own tears, she began a ferocious bout of activity.

***

Two days later:

Kezia heard whistling in the pottery. Nico was back. She put three cups of water on a tray and made her way across the yard. Joanna had gone to buy new baskets, Mordecai had found a second home in the Synagogue and Little Josh was on an errand, so it would only be Seth and Nico. Stepping inside the pottery, Kezia saw no-one sat at the wheel. Nico

228

was alone. Disconcerted by this intimacy, she put the tray down and made a dash for the door.

"Don't go," he called, "please... don't fear." His entreaty brought palpitations to the base of her neck.

"I must go," the strangled voice seemed to come from the ceiling.

"I miss you when er... when you leave."

"No, you won't," Kezia replied too quickly. She hadn't meant to sound sharp.

Nico moved towards her to pick up the cup of water. Their eyes met. Time suspended as a lightning flash of desire blazed between them. But, in the blink of their eyelids, the moment was stifled and relegated to the realms of impossibility.

"Thank you... for... the drink." His hair had grown since their first meeting so that his ears didn't seem big any more. She tried to smile but the corners of her mouth trembled. Nico downed the contents of the cup

"How long you away?" he asked. Kezia avoided his gaze. Her eyes flitted round the pottery shelves in an effort to store every shelf and pot in her memory.

"Jared's going back to the fishing boats." Disappointment drew furrows across his forehead.

"So," he brightened, "I bring er, I bring pottery to you... sell... er in Cep'num?"

"No, *no*... you can't do that!" Kezia turned on her heels and sped across the yard to the house.

Half-way down her throat a hot pain, like a rock that had become stuck, threatened to choke her. She swallowed repeatedly in an attempt to regain control. She felt dizzy. A wave of heat flooded her body chased by a wave of nausea. She clutched the end of the table in a bid to steady herself. She felt wretched – drained – useless. Maybe Capernaum was

229

the best place to be. In this condition she was no help here to Joanna or Seth… or… or anyone.

Nico stared at the row of plates waiting for decoration. He sighed. He had no heart to work on them now – not now. His enthusiasm for blue pottery had evaporated. From the first moment of their meeting he had carried her face into his dreams. He watched her move around the pottery with a quiet serenity, unruffled and smiling even at the busiest times. He memorised the folds in her tunic and imagined the feel of her hair she kept banished and secret beneath the headscarf all married women had to wear.

Without her brute of a husband around their shared delivery journeys had become the highlight of his life. He didn't care that some people stared to see him walking the streets with a Jewess. A Jewess and another man's wife. Kezia was more striking than any of the girls in his home village outside Rome. She had brought colour and sparkle into his days – since knowing Kezia, his mind had overflowed with ideas and designs. It was inexplicable but she made him feel alive. She was the most beautiful woman he had ever met… the woman he wanted for his wife… but, reality depressed his spirit – she was leaving – walking out of his life as suddenly as she had entered it. She could never be his. Never.

Snatching his bag of tools, Nico left the pottery and meandered up the main street to the magistrate's house. The owner of this modern, palatial property had commissioned the young Roman artist to design a mosaic floor in the room where he would entertain rich and influential guests. The template for the border pattern and corner motifs of vines, birds and animals had been authorised, and small piles of the coloured tesserae waited on site. Work on the floor was well underway.

Suddenly, as he neared the house, inspiration struck. A picture formed in his mind's eye for a central feature, one which would make the magistrate's floor the envy of every patrician in the city. Nico's pace quickened over the last few yards and he leapt up the wide steps to the imposing double doors. Once inside the main room he took his charcoal stick and sketched his fresh inspiration into his design.

Chapter 27

"LEAH?" The warm familiar voice roused Leah from fitful sleep. Her eyes shone in recognition and she lifted her arms for her friend's embrace.

"Oh, Sarah!" Leah murmured. "Oh, I thought I'd never see you again." Sarah stooped to enfold the frail body on the couch.

"You silly goose!" Sarah chided. "Why, I haven't even been to my own home but I had to stop by here first." She straightened up, then immediately sat down by Leah's side. "I heard your news," she beamed, "where is he?" She looked in the empty basket beside the couch.

"Jairus has taken him while I rest." Leah's voice was strained and weak.

"And where's Kezie?" Sarah had missed Leah's bright daughter as much as Leah.

"Kezie and Jared are married now. They're living in Sepphoris with Joanna."

"Oh *dear*! I've missed the little maid's wedding an' all." She sighed in genuine disappointment. "We heard Jairus had a son but we... well, we didn't get news of any wedding." She wiped her nose. "So where's Adah and... and that dear little Zipporah?"

"They're around somewhere," Leah said vaguely. "But tell

me all your news, Sarah." She reached out and took Sarah's hand. "Oh, it's so good to see you. You don't know how much I've missed you."

"I've missed you too," Sarah nodded. "So much has happened. Oh, I hardly know where to start…"

"Is Simon with you?"

Sarah's smile faded as she replied, "No, not this time, dear. I've come back with the brothers James and John."

"They've come *home*! That's wonderful."

"Well, no. Not exactly." Sarah rearranged herself on the couch. "They're not *staying* as such. They're on their way to Damascus."

"Damascus? What on earth are they going there for?" Leah couldn't see why anyone should want to go to Damascus. Sarah was equally confused.

"I don't rightly know, my love. It's all to do with that nasty bit of work Saul from.. where was it… oh, it's tip of my tongue… *Tar*sus!" she remembered. "Well, he's boasting about how he's met the Lord Jesus!" Leah gasped.

"I *know*," Sarah agreed, "Simon says it's a clever trap to get Jesus followers arrested." For a moment she became quite agitated, but then her shoulders relaxed and she beamed an apology at Leah:

"Oh, my dear Leah, here's me going on and on but you don't want to know all this." She settled herself like a hen fluffing herself down on her eggs, "Now, tell me about *you*."

Leah averted her eyes from Sarah's concerned gaze. "My days are numbered, Sarah," she said quietly.

"You mustn't talk like that!" Sarah protested but she was shocked to see her friend lying on the couch so thin and frail. Leah looked a very sick woman indeed, nevertheless Sarah determined to be encouraging. "What you need is some of

233

my nice hot milk with fennel seed. You remember, I used to bring it over before when you'd…" she checked herself from blurting out 'when you'd lost another baby', and changed it to, "When you needed a bit of a boost, like." Leah shook her head.

"The bleeding won't stop." Leah confided. "Since Jabez came… it hasn't stopped." She gave a rueful smile, " Not even your hot milk can save me now." Sarah was choked – she couldn't reply.

***

Little Josh stroked the donkey's earth-brown ears, whispering an earnest explanation to the animal as to why the panniers were so heavy. The donkey scuffed a hind leg in the dirt, impatient to be moving. A nose-bag with barley and wilting green leaves from the past couple of meals rested over it's balding spine; his doleful expression was plain, 'I can smell it, why can't I eat it?'

Mordecai walked tall across the courtyard, the hilltop breeze flurrying round his blue robes. Seeing the old man, the boy slunk round the other side of the donkey's head. He felt the old Pharisee's eyes pierce him with disapproval.

"Have you made your prayers, boy?" Mordecai's inquiry was intimidating.

"Yes, sir," he lied.

"Do you know the Commandments of Moses?" the Pharisee probed further. Little Josh squirmed. What were they? He gave the white-haired old man a blank stare. Undeterred, Mordecai stuck his staff under the boy's chin.

"You'll know them by the time we get to Capernaum, boy." The donkey's lip curled back over rotten teeth as he brayed. Little Josh interpreted his friend's voice – they were in for a deadly dull journey.

Jared emerged from the pottery, belongings slung across his shoulder. Seth and Ben followed him, Seth in uncharacteristic silence. At the same time Joanna and Kezia came out of the house, Kezia, draped with hessian bags across her back. Joanna eyed the donkey for space to hang a bag of food and some material she had woven for Leah to make into a first tunic for Jabez.

"Come along, then," bustled Joanna, anxious to be rid of them whilst she could still smile. She squeezed Kezia in a brisk farewell hug, "Mind how you go, chicken. No falling over. And make sure they don't walk you too fast!" She directed her last remark over Keziah's head to the brooding Jared.

"Travel safely, my dear," Seth embraced her with a flourish. Jared, failing to offer any thanks for Seth's hospitality, led the group out of the courtyard. Little Josh pulled on the donkey's reign with Mordecai pursuing his shoulder. Kezia walked away from the pottery her gaze fixed on the donkey's back feet. She knew if she looked back, she would turn and run and fling herself into Joanna's arms. From the first moment the city of Sepphoris came into view, Kezia knew... some sixth sense informed her that she would find happiness. Why was that happiness to be wrenched away? Each step throbbed through her breaking heart. That same intuitive sense told her there would be no happiness with Jared in Capernaum.

Once out in the street, she kept her eyes on the road ahead, afraid to look up in case Jared accused her of looking for Nico. If only she could have seen him one last time. She frowned as she walked. She belonged to Jared. Nico was a foreigner. She must forget him. She must never think of him again. Putting her hand in the pocket of her cloak, her fingers closed around the kid pouch and the seven stones Jesus had given her. They had to be hidden at all times now for fear Jared would throw them away.

Each leaden footstep took her further and further away from Joanna and Seth's loving home and laughter. They passed through the Nazareth Gate and down the sloping road towards the junction with the great highway. Against all the passing distractions of human and animal traffic, groups of helmeted Roman soldiers in their scarlet tunics, flocks of sheep straggling behind young shepherds, merchants and rotund civic clerks, Kezia's head pounded to the repetitive beat of The Commandments. Mordecai spoke each Commandment and Little Josh repeated the edict three times. Mordecai settled into the rhythm, determined his pupil would not only learn the Holy Law of Moses, but that once learnt, it would never be forgotten.

Jared lumbered way out in front. He couldn't wait to get back to Capernaum; to plunge his aching muscles into the sweet, cool water of the lake… to wash away the vile, choking dust of the quarry… to hear the creak of the old wooden fishing boats to hoist the mast… and to make certain his wife kept away from gentile contamination. No one would remember the missing foreign girl now… it was all in the past.

When they reached the crossroads, they didn't take the road on which Jared and Kezia had first come to Sepphoris, but the downward path towards Magdala. Kezia knew Jared was too proud to admit it, but she was positive he had brought her along the wrong road. The hills were covered in a patchwork of freshly ploughed fields and swathes of wild flowers. But their beauty was lost to Kezia's unseeing gaze.

The front dining hall in the magistrate's house

commanded sweeping views over the city wall, and eastward down the valley. The great highway to Capernaum was visible until it dropped behind the lower hills of the Galilee on the horizon. Nico watched the dusky pink figure until she disappeared into the distant heat haze. The gods were cruel! All he had left was a burning image in his mind's eye. That tentative, sideways glance, the flawless skin and tantalising neck… Nico turned from the window, leaned back against the wall and closed his eyes in despair.

The morning wore on and breeze gathered strength. Leaves and market detritus swirled along gutters and into corners. Nico sat and stared at his unfinished floor. Men worked around him plastering the walls and, in another room, painters busied themselves painting dramatic frescos. Nico had no heart for work. All he could think about was how Kezia's retiscent gaze could turn so easily into an entrancing smile that took his breath away. Aimlessly he fiddled with the tessera, rippling his fingers through the tiny pieces of stone, he tried to recapture the sound of her laughter.

***

Debra shrieked. Anna spilt the milk she was decanting from jug to dish and swung round to admonish the girl. Then she saw the figure in the doorway. Salome ran to greet her son.

"Jared!" she gasped, "Oh, *Jared*!" Anna rested the jug on the table and smoothed her rough hands over her apron. Her arms ached to be thrown round his neck as she could have done only a few short years before. But Jared was not her son, nor was he any longer Zebedee's little boy. He was a married man. Jared grinned self-consciously into the room, taking in the familiar scene and cooking smells.

"Come inside! Come inside!" Salome insisted. Flung into confusion by the surprise arrival, Anna lifted the lid from the pitcher to see how much water was left. Debra propelled herself across the room and stood tugging at Jared's tunic, waiting for a present from the big city.

"Don't stand there," hissed Anna, "get the man a cup." It was then Salome saw Kezia hesitating in the evening shadows.

"Come in, my dear," she motioned with her hand. Anna gazed admiringly at Jared's manly bearing, he was so much like she remembered her brother when they were growing up. Salome brought her youngest son a chair.

"Oh my, but your father will be *so* pleased to see you. This is the Lord's doing... your brothers are home too!" Jared registered surprise more than pleasure as his mother continued, "They've gone with your father to the Synagogue. Gone to pray for a good night's catch. You'll see them in the morning."

"How long you staying?" Debra wasted no time. Jared rested his elbows on the table while Kezia, exhausted from the journey, sank down on the floor beside him.

"Go and get your sister. Hurry!" Anna ordered. Debra flounced passed Kezia and out of the house. Anna followed to refill the water pitcher. Kezia lowered her head at the deliberate rebuff.

"You'll be famished," Salome was saying, retrieving the cooking pot and giving the left-over contents a stir. "Here, it'll be cold by now, but it's tasty." She bustled to give both weary travellers a bowl of pottage and the bread she had kept for the morning. She studied the pair as they ate, her eyes darting from one to the other. Suddenly, Salome crouched beside Kezia, and put a hand on Kezia's arm that was lifting the spoon to her mouth.

"Why!" she exclaimed, "You're with child, aren't you!" Salome trilled. Kezia smiled and nodded. Salome looked over at Jared, "And what were you thinking of… making this poor girl walk down from Sepphoris? You know what trouble Leah's had to keep a child in her womb." She shook her head in disbelief. Jared devoured his supper, disinclined to explain his actions. Salome turned back to Kezia. "Does your mother know about the baby?"

Kezia pushed her cloak off her shoulders to the floor. "Uncle Mordecai will have told her by now," she said wistfully. "We walked back together." She omitted to tell her mother-in-law about Little Josh and the donkey laden with pottery. Salome's eyes were bright with excitement.

"You best get yourself over to your mother before dark," she said. Then in an effort to prepare her she added, "She's not picked up as she should after the boy's birth, you know. It'll be a good thing if you stay with her a few days." Jared ignored his wife's glance to him for permission. Nothing could have pleased Kezia more than to escape back to her father's house and stay with her mother and Adah.

Anna returned with the pitcher. Kezia likened her presence to a roving mosquito; humming and hovering, waiting to bite and infect. She felt a new sympathy for Salome, it couldn't be easy for her to share her home with Anna and her girls.

"You go," Jared's words came muffled from somewhere inside a mouth full of pottage. Kezia got up and hurried out into the closing gloom. Cicadas replaced the bird song as she made her way from the harbour to her father's house. Despite her aching feet and legs, once out of Zebedee's oppressive household, her energy returned.

Footsteps clattered round the corner. Debra and Miriam

dashed past her. Miriam waved but, propelled along by Debra, couldn't stop. In that moment Kezia realised the gulf that had opened up between the young girls and herself as a pregnant wife. Expectations weighed upon her shoulders. What if she *was* like her mother and couldn't hold a child in her womb? Fear tightened her throat. How would Jared react if she delivered a girl? Would she be welcome in their house?

Nearing home, the thought occurred to her that if James and John were back, they would have news from Jerusalem and Jesus. Rounding the corner an oil lamp glimmered in the window of Simon's house. A smile immediately curled on her lips. Sarah must be home.

Little Josh squatted on the doorstep beside the tethered donkey. Kezia looked at the house she had once proudly thought so large and imposing. Her months in Sepphoris, surrounded by tall Roman mansions and extravagant civic buildings, all framed in mellow sandstone against the open sky, made the second largest house in Capernaum look positively modest. The rough-hewn, black stones of her father's house and of the cramped little houses nestled together along the road, wore a joyless face in the deepening evening shadows.

She smiled at the boy munching happily alongside with his docile companion. She ruffled his hair as she passed by into the courtyard where a fire was still burning.

"Kezie!" Adah yelled her greeting, leaping up from the embers and rushing to hug her dearest friend. Their embrace was long and tight as both realised how much they had missed each other. "Oh, Kezie, you're *home,*" Adah sighed. "But, c'mon… your mother's in here." She took Kezia's hand and they almost skipped into the room where Leah lay on the couch, a willow crib by her side.

Kezia's spontaneous laugh released her crazed emotions. All she could see poking from a blanket in the crib was the thick, spikes of hair just as Joanna had described. Her mother lay pale and emaciated. Kezia hardly dared to hold her in case she broke in two. In so short a time, Leah had become an old woman.

"I knew you'd come." Leah's voice was weak but her smile rolled away the years and Kezia caught a glimpse of the mother she loved. "At last, Kezie," Leah glowed with pride and acheivement, "you have a brother!" Kezia picked up the mop-haired bundle and rocked him in her arms.

"Hello Jabez," she whispered, "hello wee one." Tenderly she pulled away the shawl to expose a sleeping face. Looking up she saw Zippie standing in the doorway at the bottom of the stairs. Big, wondering eyes stared at the visitor, the corner hem of her tunic hung chewed and wet from her mouth. Kezia's face broke in the widest smile for her little sister. "Zippie!" she cried, "What a big girl you are!" She crouched down to Zippie's level, "Come and give me a kiss."

Zippie stood sucking her tunic. Kezia returned Jabez to his crib and held out her arms to the uncertain toddler.

"Come along, my bird," she said, "come to your big sister."

"Go on," Adah urged. Confident in Adah's permission, Zippie flung herself towards Kezia and settled happily in her arms. Adah draped a blanket over Jabez in his crib.

"Where's Father?" Kezia asked, with Zippie wiping her cheek with chewed tunic. Leah roused herself to a sitting position.

"He and your uncle are over at the Synagogue," she grimaced. "Where else!" They shared a smile of understanding. Leah looked puzzled, "Is it true Jared's come back to the fishing?"

Kezia nodded. Leah visibly relaxed. "I'm so pleased. You'll be home to have the child." She took a drink from the cup beside her. "I've prayed…" she took a deep breath, she wanted no tears in front of her daughter, "I've prayed so hard that the Lord God will… will spare me to see my grandson." She looked at the young woman cradling Zippie. "You're strong, Kezie," Leah said, "you won't have my troubles."

Adah relieved Kezia of her wriggling sister and took the toddler upstairs to bed.

Kezia sat by her mother's side and took her hand. They both had so much to say to each other but, as the light from the oil lamps flickered gentle shadows on the wall, neither spoke a word.

Chapter 28

"TOLD 'ee t'wouldn' last!" The older of Zebedee's hired men twitched his nose and raised his eyebrows at his mate as their boss's youngest son appeared round the end of the houses. He walked erratically round the harbour towards his father's mooring.

"T'was madness to think 'e could go quarrying." He spoke his mind unconcerned who may be listening. The two men had worked for Zebedee since before Jared was born and, having watched him grow to manhood, they had no time for him. "Always the same…" the older man growled under his breath, "the last born's never no good!" He picked up the folded net and packed it into the two-man boat he and his mate were taking out.

Zebedee was on board his new boat, bigger by far than his other four boats and good for the deep water. Small, two-man boats stayed close to shore with lighter nets. Jared's move to Sepphoris had left the old fisherman short-handed, and he had been forced to hire and train another man. Demand for salted fish far exceeded what the boats could catch and business was better than Zebedee could remember.

The previous day had been one long celebration. In honour of his three sons being home at the same time, Zebedee made the extravagant gesture of buying a calf. Half the men in Capernaum had either stayed to share the generous roast or dropped by to greet James and John. Jared soon realised that the entire conversation centred on his brothers and the miracles that were happening in Jerusalem. He adopted a pretence of interest but was irked by the endless accounts of people his brothers called 'Believers'. Because of their leadership responsibilities in Jerusalem, James and John were held in the highest esteem by the village men.

Jared, however, wasn't in the slightest interested to hear how they ate or how many times they prayed in the Temple. He scoffed inwardly to hear that some men, obviously soft in the head, had sold property and handed over their money to the group. He couldn't believe their stupidity! The name Jesus cropped up all the time; so much so, he half expected the Rabbi to walk in and join them. Bored by the pious prattle, Jared skulked away to a corner of the yard where Debra consoled him with choice cuts of meat and cups of beer and new wine. He had no love for his cousin, but it pleased him to be waited on.

***

The jacket that had hung loose against his angular shoulders when he left for Sepphoris, now clung tight over muscles developed by the quarry work. It was only for decency's sake that he wore it during the walk from Zebedee's house to the harbour. Once aboard, he would work, as he had always done, in his loin-cloth. James and John had already left Capernaum. They set out for Damascus at first light. The journey would take them five, maybe six days or more; Jared was glad to see them go.

As his son neared the boat, Zebedee's weathered face

beamed with the transparent joy of answered prayer. Jared stepped off the harbour wall, one foot on the sturdy wooden boat. Suddenly his limbs froze. Blood drained from his face and hairs on the back of his neck pricked like nettle rash.

"Ged on board!" Zebedee boomed. "What's the matter with you? Didn't expect me to work single-handed did you?" Zebedee's bulk lumbered down to the prow. "And this one's cheap!" He jerked his head in the direction of the new hired hand. "Never can catch these foreign names," he snorted, "but I've told him, on my boats, his name's Levi!"

Jared stared in horror at the undersized young man with straight black hair scragged back into a tight plait. Levi's slanting eyes squinted at his master's son. He bobbed his head and smiled profusely with oriental deference. Jared broke out in a flood of sweat at his resemblance to Pei Qi. He swallowed hard as his bowels churned.

Recovering his composure he jumped down into the boat. Just coincidence, he told himself. Capernaum was a market for traders – foreigners were always looking for work. It didn't mean anything. Coincidence.

In a deliberate statement of superiority, Jared removed his jacket, revealing muscles twice the size of the new hired hand. Zebedee hoisted the sail while Levi untied the rope fastening the boat to the harbour. Jared stacked baskets ready to separate the catch, all the time keeping a wary watch on the little foreigner. Gradually the southern breeze caught the sail and the heavy boat eased away from the harbour wall, past the small boats and out into deep water.

"We'll take her nor-east!" Zebedee shouted. "Watch the birds. They knows where fish is." Jared looked over the water to Bethsaida. Fishermen rarely went out during the daytime, but this day was overcast and grey and the hills of distant Syria loomed dark and foreboding. Some three miles out, Jared lowered the sail. Levi went about his work with a permanent, ingratiating smile. Irritated and unnerved, Jared resolved never to turn his back on this… this 'Levi', whoever he was.

***

"… and Seth sent this specially for you, Mother." Kezia peeled back the swathes of faded material in which the precious bowl had been cushioned. With a proud flourish she presented it to her mother. Leah and Sarah gasped in admiration.

"Oh!" Leah took hold of the bowl, looking at it as if it were covered in gold. "What a colour!"

"My! That's some handsome bowl," agreed Sarah running her fingers over the glaze. "I've not come across a colouring like that before."

"It's Ni…" Kezia checked herself, "It's Seth's new line." She enthused. "He's sells to all the rich people in Sepphoris."

"No, no! Mustn't touch," Adah pulled Zippie's grasping tentacles away and anchored the child firmly on her knee.

"I've brought a whole batch of pottery like this to sell in the market," Kezia informed them. Leah's delighted expression stalled and somehow, with the merest switch of a facial muscle, she registered displeasure at the idea of her daughter trading in the market.

"You've not done anything like that before, have you dear?" she enquired.

Kezia looked over at Adah. She coloured, "No," she admitted, "but I've been in the pottery when Seth has been selling and… well, I thought you'd let Adah help me."

"Oh yes!" Sarah wasn't going to be left out. "An' I'll help

too. Better than selling ol' salted fish any day, eh?" Her stomach wobbled as she laughed to Leah. Zippie chuckled and bounced on Adah's knee. Leah relaxed at the thought of Sarah overseeing such a stall.

"Well," Leah agreed, "those baskets are taking up a deal of room. And I suppose the sooner you sell it all, the sooner we can send back Seth's donkey." Leah hadn't been entirely happy about Little Josh and the donkey but, in the excitement of Kezia's homecoming, they had been somewhat sidelined. Sarah got up to leave.

"Good timing, Kezie, dear," she said, "it's the *big* market tomorrow. Wouldn't be surprised if we shift the lot by noon!" she beamed. "I'll be round first light then we can go get a good pitch."

Kezia looked round at the panniers pushed up against the wall. "Dear Sarah," she smiled in gratitude and relief, "you're wonderful!" Kezia held out her arms for Zippie who, infected by smiles and laughter, transferred happily to her sister's embrace. The feel of the toddler's warm little body, wriggling into position, filled Kezia with unexpected feelings of protection and contentment. In reality, Zebedee's house, her husband and her marital bed was just down the lane, but, with Zippie snuggled close into her bosom, that part of her life seemed a million miles away.

***

Sarah mopped away perspiration from round her nose and neck with the bottom corner of her apron. The last customer left. Their stall was bare.

"Oh my!" Sarah grinned at Kezia and Adah, "If that wasn't a whirlwind!"

"If I was rich," said Adah dismantling the tresle, "my house would be filled with blue pottery."

"Get that Seth to send down some more and we'll all be rich!" Sarah chuckled as she firmly tied the tops of the leather purses. "Good job we've finished before the storm blows up." She looked up at the gathering clouds, heavy as charcoal ash.

"We'll go back to my place to count this." She tapped her nose with a fore-finger and whispered, "Your place has too many ears these days." Kezia knew exactly what she meant. Miriam was looking after Zippie and Anna was likely to drop by at the least convenient time. The presence of Anna and Miriam guaranteed the ears, eyes and mouth of 'the dreadful Debra', as Joanna had called her. The thought of Sarah's house was sanctuary indeed. Kezia turned to Little Josh. He had spent the morning holding the donkey's reins, taking in the cut and thrust of Capernaum's market. He'd watched wide-eyed as four burly merchants vied with each other over two platters and more than doubled the price Seth charged from the pottery.

"Josh, you've been a good man," Kezia told him. "If you put these empty panniers on your donkey, then on your way back you can help Adah collect sticks and things for the fire. I'll go with Sarah." Adah nodded. What an amazing morning it had been! Wrapping the beautiful jugs, plates and mugs for the customers was a novel experience which had passed too quickly. She hoped they'd soon have opportunity to sell more of Seth's wares.

Kezia jumped at the chance to talk to Sarah alone.

"Didn't think we'd take half this much…" Sarah looked at the coins piled on the table in front of her. "Oh dear!" she sounded wistful, "Can't tell you the last time coins sat on my table like this." Kezia began filling the purses again.

"Sarah…" suddenly a serious expression on her face. "Where's Jesus?" Sarah slumped on the stool and sighed.

"My dear Kezie… I don't know!"

"But James and John talk about him like he was in Jerusalem with you all. I'm confused! What's going on, Sarah?" Kezia reached out and put her hand on Sarah's arm. "Please tell me, I'm not a child any more. Father says Jesus was crucified by the Roman soldiers. He *saw* him die." When Sarah was silent, Kezia pursued another tack; "What does Simon say?" she asked.

Sarah cleared her throat, "Simon says… he says 'Jesus of Nazareth is God's Messiah'. Sarah spoke slowly, being careful to report her husband's exact words. "An' he says, 'the Lord God brought him back from the dead'… um, but now, 'he's been raised to God's right hand'." She gave the last three words equal weight. Her recitation concluded, she looked at Kezia.

"What does that mean?" Kezia didn't understand any better.

"Oh, Kezie dear, I don't rightly know," Sarah wailed. "All I do know is that Simon – oh, an' since the Master gave him the name 'Peter', that's what he calls himself these days! Well, he and the others are going about healing and doing all sorts and saying it's 'all in the power of the Holy Spirit'." She looked crestfallen as she continued, "But, I'm afraid… to my mind, what they're doing is *dangerous*." A long sigh shuddered through her body.

"All the disciples – and there's hundreds of them now – they're getting threats and some of them get beaten up. The other day," Sarah lowered her voice, "one of them, a lovely young man he was, well…" she swallowed before telling Kezia the terrible truth, "he got took outside the city gate and… stoned to death." Kezia drew back in horror. Tears stood ready to spill from Sarah's kind eyes.

"They're convinced that Jesus was… *is* the Messiah," she went on, "an' they're all prepared to die for their belief. I worry so for my man." The light-hearted banter of the morning was a distant memory. Sarah's round, motherly face that had been all smiles in the market, was now tense and haggard as she considered the implications of her husband's new life.

"What do *you* believe, Sarah?" Kezia's question was asked with mature gentleness.

Sarah screwed up her face as she shrugged, "To tell you the truth, Kezie, I don't know what I believe. But," she squared her shoulders in an effort to make the best of things, "it's like this… if I'm going to hang on to my man, I've got to go 'long with what he says. So long as I'm there to cook and do for him, it doesn't really matter what I believe." She sniffed hard.

Kezia stared round the room. It seemed a lifetime since she had been in Sarah's house. Esther was still alive the last time she'd sat at this table. She visualised Sarah's mother arguing over the cooking pot, wagging her finger at Sarah through the smoke… and gruff, affable Simon, inviting friends to come and listen to the Rabbi Jesus. Kezia shut her eyes in dismay. Life was so different then.

Chapter 29

"WHAT'S the matter with Seth?" Jairus sat by Jabez in the rush basket, his voice level but Kezia knew he was irritated. "He should sell his own pots."

Leah spoke from her couch, "Sarah and the girls had a rare time. They came back full of it!" It had made a change for Leah to hear how merchants haggled and bartered over the new pottery from Sepphoris. Her eyes held renewed interest in life. Her family association with the modern pottery was better than a tonic for her spirits. Jairus jiggled the basket, impatient for his son's eyes to open and return his gaze. Mordecai sat in the corner stroking his beard, his eyes darting between each member of the family.

"It appears," Mordecai felt Kezia's efforts warranted support, "the stall was a roaring success!" Kezia flashed him the radiant smile of triumph.

"And such fun, Uncle!" she said as she wound a skein of wool with Adah.

"Fun!" Jairus was distainful. "Is that how you entertained yourself in Sepphoris?" Kezia didn't reply. "And what does Jared think of your new trading skills?" Her father's sarcastic tone failed to intimidate her.

Her reply was cool as she continued to wind the wool; "My husband is only too keen for me to make money."

Jairus poked his finger into Jabez' clenched fist. Leah's head tilted on one side, glowing with pleasure to see how totally besotted Jairus had become with the baby. He didn't lift his eyes away from the basket as he said; "Don't make it a habit, that's all."

"The two scribes from Beth She'an are on their way to Tyre. They'll take the road to Sepphoris." Mordecai informed Jairus. "They can see the boy back… see Seth gets his money safely." He coughed. "In fact," he went on, "they'll be glad to have use of a donkey to carry things."

"Hmm," Jairus grunted. "Perhaps after Sabbath we can get back to normal." Jabez had woken but instead of adoring his father's face, mewled for his mother's milk. Jairus turned to his daughter, "And you must return to your husband's home then. Come and see your mother when you can be spared." With that he left for the Synagogue. Mordecai saw Kezia's face drop.

"When *your* time comes, dear," Leah said, "then you can stay here with me." Disappointment turned to panic as Kezia registered the fact that one day, a child would burst out between her legs into the waiting hands of Sarah and Anna. The skein dropped from Kezia's grasp. Adah grabbed it before it fell to the ground and, without a word, laid it aside on the window shelf. She had only had Kezia home for a few short days and now she had to go to Zebedee's house. Adah swallowed. She couldn't let her mistress know her feelings.

"C'mon Kezie," Adah chirped, "let's get on with the baking. Miriam'll be back with Zippie any minute… the baking stone should be hot enough by now…" Kezia followed Adah into the courtyard diverting her thoughts from childbirth to their market success. Seth would be pleased, very pleased. Surely he would send down more wares… she began to wonder who might bring them…

***

Two months later:

"How's Leah today?" Anna looked up as Kezia came in, water pitcher balanced on her headscarf. Anna was trying to teach Debra to weave, but Debra proved a severe challenge to her mother. Kezia lowered the pitcher and secured it on the table by the waiting mugs.

"Sarah's found a wet-nurse," she confided, "Mother's milk's dried up." Aware this wasn't enough information for Anna she added sadly, "I don't know how much weaker she can get…I really don't."

"She could die!" blurted Debra weilding the shuttle. Anna's face pinched white with fury at her daughter's tactless outburst.

"No-one's asking you," she snapped. " Get on with your work!" In Anna's opinion Leah was sinking fast and couldn't possibly last for the birth of Kezia's child. "Here," she pushed a small plate of dates into Kezia's hands. "Jared's asleep, but put these by his pillow for when he wakes."

"I'll take them!" Debra sprung up from the loom and pushed between her mother and Kezia.

"Let her," Kezia said. "I need to catch the vegetable seller. I'd better go now otherwise all the best will be gone." Her heart was heavy. Her mother was fading before her eyes. She had no desire to put dates beside her husband's pillow.

"Mind you don't wake him," Anna warned as Debra scampered off to Jared's tent clutching the plate of dates. Kezia made her way to the market in the hope she might meet Sarah.

"Mother sent these!" Debra shouted, loudly. She knelt by her cousin waiting for a response. He rolled over to face her

253

– yawned and stretched, then yawned again. He rubbed his eyes and glared at the girl.

"Why d'you wake me up?" he growled. "You're nothing but a pest!" Debra sat back on her heels giving a coquettish smirk.

"Your wife should be here to give you dates," she said tartly. "She's not looking after you, is she?"

"Shut up!" Jared raised himself on an elbow. "Pass the water bottle." He snatched it from her and took deep gulps to wake himself. He splashed some water over his hair. Debra watched his movements, her small eyes bright and penetrating.

"Clear off!" slurred Jared slumping back on the pillow. He closed his eyes.

Unperturbed, Debra retorted, "One day you'll want me to look after you." He grunted in derision.

"One day," she persisted as she flounced out of the tent, "*one* day… you'll see."

***

"Did you know…?" Sarah's question left no time for an answer, "there's a whole load more of that blue pottery on sale in the market…" She had hurried to catch Kezia and was quite out of breath with excitement. "But it's not Seth selling it," she burbled on, "I don't know who he is… he looks, well,… he looks like a *Roman*!" Sarah couldn't help but say the word as if it were slightly indecent. Kezia's face lit up as if fifty candles reflected their glow onto her cheeks. Sarah tugged her arm towards the pottery stall she had seen.

Nico spotted the dusky pink cloak at the same moment Kezia saw him. A bolt of lightning rooted her in the ground. Sarah caught the smile that passed between them and her own heart fluttered in confusion.

"It's Nico, Sarah. He's the artist I told you about… Seth's friend. These are his designs and his blue glaze…" Kezia's voice rose in line with the colour in her cheeks.

"I see." Sarah spoke quietly but with the effect of cutting Kezia short as they came to the stall.

"Joanna asked of me to say, er, how you are." Nico's accent fell on her ears like sensual notes from a harp. They stood smiling at each other.

Sarah looked at the other young man serving, " An' who's that?" she asked.

"That's Ben, Seth's assistant potter," Kezia replied as Little Josh ran towards her. "Oh, and Little *Josh*!" He flung his arms round her apron in joy. "Not so 'little' now, eh?" she tugged his ear in affection. " You've grown, Josh!" Looking at him, it was hard to remember how matted his hair had been on their first meeting, the benefits of Joanna's cooking had certainly filled out the puny limbs. Josh stood as tall as he could in front of Sarah and Kezia, basking in Kezia's praise, every bit the reliable little market 'runner'.

Kezia could feel herself being pummelled and pushed on all sides by people pressing near Nico's stall. The blue pottery was fast becoming the market's star attraction.

"I must go," she called to Nico as the crowd carried her further away like a boat drifting uncontrolably out to sea, "give my best greetings to Joanna and Seth." She hesitated, pulse racing. She ought to send Joanna news of her mother, beg her to come down to Capernaum, but she knew Joanna had much to do in her own life. There was nothing she could do for Leah that Sarah and Adah couldn't do. Her chance to tell Nico was gone; the pressing crowd elbowed the women away and in moments, the artist was out of sight.

Sarah decided not to mention the 'foreigner'. The palpable

chemistry she had just witnessed between the two had been a total shock. 'Oh dear,' she told herself, 'what a good thing Kezie was home from up in the city… whatever would happen if Jared suspected?'

"Dear, oh dear!" Sarah murmured, her thoughts escaped out loud before she could check herself. Kezia shot her an anxious glance.

"What's wrong, Sarah?"

Sarah shook her head, "No, no…nothing dear." A short, nervous noise left her lips, a sharp exhaling that should have been a laugh. "Silly me!" she exclaimed and quickened her pace.

Nico craned his neck for sight of the dusky pink cloak but a human tide of wives, servants, traders, soldiers and merchants with slow-moving camel trains obliterated his view in seconds. In comparison with Sepphoris, Capernaum's market was cramped and ramshackle; fish stalls squeezed between spices one side and fine linens on the other. Children raucously banged into tables piled with fruit in order to run off with any item that toppled into the road.

The lower end of the market stank. That was where farm wives sat to pluck and draw chickens, discarding feathers in one sack and intestines into the gutter. Around their bare feet, flies gorged themselves on blood and excrement.

Standing behind the pottery stall, between baskets and vegetables, Nico had an overwhelming desire to abandon his table, chase after her and beg her to return with him to Sepphoris. The thought of not seeing her again was unbearable…

"Watch it!" Ben warned, "Don't drop it. That's my wages for the day!" Although he grinned, he was deadly serious. Nico realised the ewer he was holding was about to crack it's lip against a stack of platters. The purchaser, one of the local tax-collectors, handed over his denari, clutched the blue ewer protectively under his cloak and hurried away.

"Another satisfied customer!" Ben watched with approval. Nico shrugged. His mind was torn – on one hand it was thrilling to see the blue pottery selling faster than Seth could make them. On the other hand, the euphoria of their success was hollow without Kezia.

***

Three days later:

The service ended. The great wooden doors were open throughout the time of worship. The men filed out into the early summer heat-wave, muttering to each other in low, reverent tones. The old Pharisee had preached with narrowed eyes, thundering his emphasis and waving his arms expansively as he urged the congregation to put their faith in the God of Abraham.

"…our father, Abraham left his family, his home and his country!" He milked the drama to the enth degree. " 'Go!' the Lord Almighty told him. 'I will bless you and make you famous! And you will be a blessing.'" Heat and exertion caused Mordecai to sway momentarily and his eyes rolled to the Synagogue roof. He recovered and breathed heavily.

"Ah, yes!' he affected a pause, swallowed his saliva and pointed his forefinger at each man before him, "Our father Abraham is your example. Men of Capernaum…" he pulled his shoulders back and uttered his challenge. " Go and do likewise!"

The men's sweating bodies had turned the Synagogue air thick and sultry. As the last few straggled out of the doorway,

Jairus got up and walked to where his uncle still stood, savouring the effect of his oratory.

"Thank you, Uncle." He put his arm on the old man's shoulder. "That message was for me… I know." Jairus looked into his uncle's moist eyes. "I do appreciate all you've done for me over the years… and I know you want me to…" Mordecai didn't wait for his nephew to finish.

"You will go, then?"

Jairus nodded.

"My son, Caiaphas won't ask you again…and the letter was signed in his own hand… I recognised it." Mordecai moved towards the bench along the far wall talking as he went. "And you won't be the only one he's written to, but, it will be to your advantage if you are the *first* to arrive in Jerusalem." He gave Jairus a knowing nod.

"But what about Leah?" Guilt tugged at his conscience.

"Oi! Women!" Mordecai sniffed and sat down. "Your Leah's never been strong. But she'll be alright. She's got a wet nurse now, she'll soon pick up, you'll see. There are enough women to take care of her and the boy while you're away. Have faith, my son, have *faith*!"

"Like our father Abraham?" Jairus grinned.

"It's your *time*, Jairus. Don't delay… it won't come again." Mordecai removed his prayer shawl from his flowing white hair which seemed more wispy than Jairus remembered. He folded the striped shawl across his lap. "Will you stay with the silversmith?"

Jairus nodded. "For a few days at least." He glanced round the empty Synagogue. It was a place he had loved and served for sixteen years – but now, he studied the black stone walls and small windows – it was a place he couldn't wait to leave behind. Too many members of the congregation he could no longer trust. Like an old cloak that had once been treasured, he had outgrown the Synagogue, he longed to move on. He longed to be in Jerusalem. This was his chance.

His uncle, obviously tired, shut his eyes as he murmured, almost to himself.

"Hold fast to the truth! These are turbulent times... Caiaphas needs men like you." He leant against the wall easing his aching spine against the cool stone. "We'll soon appoint a Ruler in your place. There's an eager young man in Beth She'an... he'd be very suitable." He studied his nephew's profile. The full head of hair was dark even though the beard was liberally flecked with grey. Jairus carried himself with the dignity of authority. Mordecai's long-held ambition for his nephew was on the brink of fruition. He offered his advice in a low whisper.

"Hold fast to the truth, my boy, and the Lord will be with you."

***

Five weeks later:

The noise was unbearable. Paid mourners wept and wailed their respect. The hideous, high-pitched laments bore into her forehead until Kezia felt her head would burst. Upstairs, Anna and Salome instructed Miriam in the ritual washing of Leah's body and the proper way to anoint it with myrrh and spices.

Kezia clung to a hysterical Zippie. The pervading atmosphere of adult sorrow unhinged the child who reacted with flailing arms and legs and heart-wrenching sobs. Kezia had planned that Sarah would perform those last, intimate rites, not Anna, but Sarah had returned to her Simon in

Jerusalem a month since. Angry and betrayed, Kezia felt like a bystander, an outcaste in the middle of her own household. The stones had betrayed her. They had healed people she didn't know… why didn't they heal her mother? Weak and defeated, she vowed never to use them again. Her eyes, hot and sore from crying, closed in despair… If only Joanna had been there…

"Hush Zippie… don't cry… hush…" Kezia tried her best to soothe the child.

Kezia's first instinct was to vent her anguish in screams and tears but she was just too exhausted. Four nights she had sat with her mother. Had held Leah's hand as she called out in vain for her husband to come to her. Had watched her mother drift in and out of consciousness, struggle in the grip of halucinations until finally, she lay comatose, unseeing, unknowing. Her breathing became so shallow, several times Kezia thought she had died. In the end it was Ruth, the wet-nurse, who gently pulled the sheet over Leah's face and Kezia realised her mother had gone for ever.

"I tried…" she confided to Adah. "I… I laid the stones on her…" she sobbed, "but… they were no good." Adah sat, tears streaming, listening in silence.

"I prayed to God…" Kezia's voice trembled, "but that didn't work either." Adah sat on the bed beside her friend and rocked her gently until both Kezia's and Zippie's convulsive spasms of grief subsided.

***

Mordecai organised the men for the funeral. There was no way word could reach Jairus before Leah's burial that afternoon. No time either for Joanna to reach Capernaum

260

for her sister's hasty committal into the ground. The old Pharisee swung into professional mode, enlisting the resident grave digger, and marshalling Zebedee, Jared and two of Zebedee's hired men to stretcher the body to the grave.

Capernaum's cemetery lay on higher ground, a mile to the west of the town, an area at the base of the hills, free from flooding by the winter rains. Mordecai raised his hands to heaven and intoned the ritual prayers for the dead. Kezia stood with the women, grieving at a distance. Her hand rested on her protruding belly, feeling the movement of a child her mother would never hold. In those solemn moments, her physical distance from her mother's burial seemed to encapsulate her emotional distance from the funeral.

Surrounded by neighbours, friends and relatives living in Capernaum, she nevertheless, felt on the outside of all that was happening. Some of these women had known Leah all her life, others ever since she and Jairus had moved to Capernaum. Over the years they had shared their stories, their laughter and their tears down at the washing pool or while they shared the task of grinding flour. Not so long ago, they had all laughed and sung at Kezia's wedding; now they stood together in sorrow, mournful effigies, huddled against the rocks in the fading daylight.

Kindness and sympathy could not alleviate the sense of utter emptiness. It had been obvious to all that Leah was dying, but the shock of her actual death was unexpected and overwhelming. Kezia gazed across to where the cluster of men obscured her view of the pitiful linen-wrapped shape on the stretcher. Adah stood beside her mopping her eyes on the sleeve of her tunic, her fragile tear-cup already full to overflowing.

Prayers concluded, Leah's corpse was lowered into the earth. Mordecai led the men back to the Synagogue allowing the women to move to the graveside and pay their own last respects.

A terrible pain tore at Adah's heart. She'd loved her mistress dearly. Leah had taught Adah and Kezia side by side, taught her all the things a woman has to learn – how to skin a goat, how to prepare a lamb for Passover, how to grind corn and cook bread on the baking stone without burning it. Leah had been her teacher for how to spin wool, and how to wash, dye and weave it. Even Adah's tiny patch of herbs in the courtyard was due to Leah's encouragement. Since coming to Leah, the little servant-girl had never been beaten and every skill she possessed she owed directly to her kind and patient mistress.

Salome watched Kezia with concern. She looked heavy with child now. She turned over in her mind the fact that two children had been left without a mother. Kezia would have to take her mother's place and that meant she and Jared would need to live in Jairus' house.

Anna pursed her lips in disapproval over Jairus returning to Jerusalem. Wrinkles deepened round her tight mouth as she whispered to Salome, "Goodness only knows how long he'll stay there." Her snort was dismissive, "… No business to leave his wife, weak like she was."

Salome knew Zebedee's messenger had gone to Rabbi Jonathan in Jericho and they expected he would take the news to Jairus in Jerusalem. 'Yes', her thoughts returned to her youngest son, 'Jared would have to live in his wife's home – for a while, at least.' She sighed. Life just wasn't the same without her James and John. She tried to gauge the shape of Kezia's protrusion. Quite high… very likely a boy! Salome's knuckles whitened as she clutched her hands together under her cloak. The memory of Leah's many miscarriages spurred her to earnest prayer. 'Merciful God, let Kezia carry this child to full time.' She repeated the prayer with an earnestness that bordered desperation.

Anna's mind had moved beyond the funeral. With Leah gone, she and Salome would take equal share of Jared's son. She bent to place a stone on Leah's freshly covered grave.

Chapter 30

"SO sorry…" Nico's eyes were dark pools of genuine sympathy. He stood behind the pottery stall gazing at Kezia's solemn face. "I will tell to Joanna. She come to you?"

Kezia shook her head. "No, there's nothing she can do." A weak smile passed for thanks. "She has far too much work with the pottery." Nico nodded. Her protruding belly was noticeable.

"Yes, always she is er… busy." His expression brightened. "Seth he built *two* new Kiln…" Kezia's face flickered with interest as Nico continued, *"Beeg,"* he used his hands to describe the kilns' height and width, "Beeg… so a man walk inside!" Kezia's features broke in laughter at the idea of Seth walking inside a kiln. Nico's heart soared at her nearness. He wanted desperately to pour out all the things that had happened since she returned to Capernaum but her demure, grieving presence, standing at the stall, tied his tongue.

"Another potter work now." Was all he could say.

"And Little Josh?" Kezia asked, suddenly feeling lighter.

Nico laughed, "Oh, he *eat!*" They laughed in unison. "And he… er… he and donkey take orders all over the city." A silence fell between them. As Kezia looked into his eyes her body tensed in sudden inexplicable excitement. A blush rose from her neck.

"Here," Nico was saying as if he feared, any second, she

would turn and run from him. He picked up a blue dish and offered it into her hand, "Please take. For your home."

"But…"

"No, *please* take." An involuntary sigh left his lips as she put the dish in her basket.

"To er… remember me?" he whispered. Tears welled in Kezia's eyes. She turned and hurried away as fast as her heavy belly would allow. Adah and Zippie were waiting for her at the end of the stalls.

Nico had no time to watch her. Two Egyptian men from a camel-train haggled between themselves over the one remaining blue jug. Nico served them but his sale gave him none of the usual delight. He was spell-bound by her unselfconscious beauty. She was even more beautiful and dignified in her sorrow than he remembered. Pregnancy had given her cheeks lustre and serenity. His scrambled thoughts swirled on a cloud of tenderness towards her. Why, oh why did Jewish wives cover their hair? He tried to imagine…

***

Jonathan stood in the doorway, head bowed. Jairus read the body language. He knew the news before Jonathan uttered a word. He laid down his quill, got up from the desk and walked to the window overlooking the Temple court of the gentiles. Jairus breathed deeply to steady himself. Below him the dove-sellers were in demand from folk in from the country, seeking to purchase their sacrifice. Raucous shouts of money-changers along with general Temple hubbub clattered into the room. Jonathan stood silent.

Finally, Jairus addressed the window-frame, "What about the boy?" he murmured.

"He's fine. A bonny fellow." Jonathan assured him. "No worries there. Kezia and half of Capernaum are mothering him." Jairus continued to stare out of the window, his back to his friend. Jonathan guessed Jairus had no intention of returning home immediately. He broke their silence:

"Old Mordecai'll be teaching him prayers before he can walk!"

Jairus shrugged in reply. "I think…" he said, containing his emotions, "… think I need a walk."

***

After their meal, Jairus sat up on the roof with Abner, a routine they had established since Jairus had come back to stay in the silversmith's house. Abner sucked on the mouthpiece of his pipe, deep in thought. He cleared his throat, "You can bring your boy here, you know." Before Jairus could protest, he continued speaking in his soft, calm southern voice. "You can trust Judith," he blew smoke in the air with a half laugh, "she's had enough practice with our boys!" His gaze followed two birds, black silhouettes against the evening sky, circle the Temple ramparts looking to roost.

Abner's next comment put a seal on the conversation, he looked over at Jairus as he murmured, "The boy needs his father." Such spontaneous generosity had Jairus floundering for words.

"My friend… that's more than… you're a *true* brother. How can I thank you?"

Abner drew deeply on the pipe lifting his hand in a casual gesture.

"Perhaps it's not the right time to say this my friend,

but…" he pushed his tongue hard against his front teeth as he tried to formulate his request tactfully. Jairus waited.

"Say what you must, brother," he encouraged. After a few moments Abner said what had long been on his mind.

"Well, it's like this," he began. "I feel you are the only one I can turn to for this favour." Jairus raised an eyebrow.

"You see… well… as you know, I have no brothers… and… if I should die, there is no-one to care for my boys and Judith." Abner lapsed into silence while Jairus caught up with where the 'favour' was leading. "It would be a great comfort to me if… well, if I knew that you would take them for me. You know… raise my boys as brothers with your Jabez. And," he gave a wry smile, "Judith is not past child-bearing."

"But you're a fit man, Abner. You –"

Abner cut him off, "Yeah! Yeah. I'm not thinking of dying *tonight!* But, seriously Jairus, none of us knows what the future holds. We make our plans but we both know what can happen to plans." He blew a slow, thin stream of smoke above their heads. "It would make me a happy man to know I could count on you."

"The Lord God of Abraham be my witness… if you die, then – yes, I will treat your boys as my own…and… and take Judith for my wife."

Abner felt weary. He reached out his right hand which Jairus clasped warmly in his own.

***

"Maybe two weeks, my dear." Mordecai was not exactly sure how long he would be at the Pharisaic Council in Beth She'an. He kissed Kezia's cheek, "But it will give you and Jared time to grow accustomed to living here. It's not easy for a man to live in his wife's home, remember that. He is a good boy to honour his father-in-law's house." The old man scratched the side of his beard, unsure what to say next: "The Lord bless you, Kezie," he said fondly, picked up his staff and walked out of the courtyard, robes billowing behind him. Ruth, the wet-nurse, came down the stairs, Jabez clinging on her hip.

"Not long now and he'll be weaned." Her voice held more than a tinge of regret. She had become as attached to Jabez as Adah was to Zippie.

"That boy'll be twice the size of Zippie in no time," grinned Adah busily chopping onions and garlic for the chicken broth. "An' soon," she chirped, "they'll be having a little play-mate!"

Adah's dream had come true. Kezia was her mistress now. For the rest of her life she would be secure, part of the household she loved. Adah's face wreathed in smiles of contentment.

Zippie clapped and bounced in her pen, engrossed in sunny, indecipherable conversation.

Panic knotted in Kezia's chest. She realised she might only have a month to six weeks before giving birth. Thoughts of Anna catching her first-born and being the first to hold him filled her with foreboding. She picked up wood to take out to the fire.

"If only Joanna could be with me for the birth," she sighed. The weight of her child seemed a constant pressure on her bladder.

"My husband'll go for her, dearie, if that's what you'd like." Ruth was ever willing.

"But she's so busy," protested Kezia. Ruth sat down adjusting Jabez into a suitable position to be clamped to her breast.

"Now look, my lovely," Ruth said in a motherly way, "'Tis

not five minutes since you've had to cope with your dear mother passing. Next best person for you is your mother's sister and don't have any doubts, mind, she would *want* to be here for you." Ruth spoke with conviction. Kezia glanced at Adah who nodded vigorously. Ruth smelt victory.

"Well, then. That's settled!" she declared with satisfaction. Ruth had many of Sarah's homely ways. "He can go up to Sepphoris after Sabbath. They should've finished the barley harvest the end of this week." Kezia's shoulders visibly relaxed. A great wave of relief washed over her at the thought of Joanna helping to birth her baby. She could cope with Anna's acid presence, and even the dreadful Debra, just so long as Joanna was there. The whole idea gave a much needed boost to her confidence. Perhaps things would be alright after all.

***

Next morning dawned overcast and windy. Jared came home surly. The boats had been out all night but had barely caught enough fish for themselves let alone for market. Ruth was still taking Jabez home with her each night and Adah had gone to the washing pool. Apart from Zippie, burbling merrily in her pen, Kezia was alone. Jared slouched against the wall glaring as Kezia rustled up a plate of bread and olives. In an effort to please him and lift his mood, she put some ripe figs on the table and fresh yogurt in the blue dish Nico had given her. Jared tore hungrily at the bread. It had been a long, frustrating night and the unseasonal wind-chill gnawed into his bones.

Olive stones hit the floor. Zippie squealed with delight thinking it was some kind of new game. Kezia retreated to the corner of the room and picked up his old tunic she was patching. Jared grabbed the new blue plate.

"What's this?" he demanded, his voice brittle with spite.

"Seth's famous blue pottery," Kezia replied softly.

"Where d'you get it?" his face behind the beard reddened in rage.

"From the market. He's got an outlet…"

Jared jumped up from the table, "You've been seeing that Roman dog again, haven't you?"

Kezia was flustered, she began, "He comes down to the…"

"So you don't deny it!" Jared spluttered. "People have seen you, you know. They tell me how you smile at him… how you sidle up to his stall…you…you *whore*!" He screamed the last word in her face, picked up the dish and dashed it to the floor. The dish smashed in smithereens flinging yogurt in all directions. Zippie stopped bouncing, eyes wide with fear. Kezia sat motionless, her heart pounding so violently against her chest she could hardly breathe.

"…and you think I'm going to bring up that dog's bastard?" He pulled her up by her shoulders and began to shake her. She raised her arms to push him away.

"Stop it! Please, Jared… stop…" But Jared, oblivious to her cries, in frenzied fury, slammed his fist across her head.

"Ahhh!" Kezia screamed out in pain. "Stop… please… stop!" but Jared hurled her aside watching as she fell heavily on the stone floor. He stood over her, a menacing hatred in his eyes.

"I never wanted to marry you in the first place… Miss High and Mighty… but you're nothing more than a dirty little *whore*…" between screams he lashed out with his foot, mercilessly kicking into her writhing body. Zippie's whimpers rose to hysteria. Suddenly Jared stopped kicking and leant back against the wall. Kezia clutched her belly, moaning and twisting in agony, blood seeped from where the pottery shards had scored across her legs and hands.

"If I hear you've seen him again," he panted, "I swear… I swear I'll *kill* you!"

Kezia quivered on the floor, waiting each second to receive a further violent blow. After what seemed an eternity, a final kick landed square into her belly. Kezia screamed like a ewe caught in a trap. She curled over in her agony. Jared stood over her, his hand lifted, threatening to lash at her head. Then, his pleasure suddenly dissipated. He spat on her and stormed out.

As soon as she dared, Kezia cried out for Adah.

But Adah didn't come.

She tried again. This time, fear shot through her cries as the pain of contractions took her breath away. In terror she realised her waters had broken.

Still no one came.

Kezia was alone.

Chapter 31

JARED stamped into his father's house confident his mother would have a meal for him. But the house was empty. He stared around – where was everyone? His father would be down with the boats and his mother, Anna and girls either in the market, or down at Job's pool with their washing. He looked for the servants – no-one in sight. He turned on his heel and made for the tent adjacent to the stone house, erected for the newly-weds but now sagging and in need of attention. Since his last outburst against his wife, Jared had taken to sleeping in the tent again.

He bent to lift the flap.

"Clear off!" he growled. The diminutive shape on the mattress struck a provocative pose. Debra ignored her cousin's command to leave, which infuriated him further. She smirked at his expletives.

"Little witch! What d'you think you're doing?"

"My cousin's wife doesn't please him any more." Debra met his stare with an expression both brazen and childish. Jared slumped on the stool, his back to the girl.

"So what d'you think you can do about that, then? You're a *child*," he spat the remaining words over his shoulder, "nothing but a waste of space!" Debra considered for a moment.

"You could show me how to help..." she used her little girl voice to diffuse his anger.

"Get out! Evil little cow!" Debra took no notice. She sat tight.

"I may be a girl-child, but that makes me a *safe*-child."

Jared swung round, "Where d'you hear talk like that?" he demanded. Debra gave an insolent shrug.

"Fishermen talk... they don't notice me... but I hear what they say... and I know what they do!" She boasted with a precocious toss of unruly, raven hair. Jared jumped up and lurched towards her. He wanted her off his bed and out of his sight.

"Don't talk disgusting," he snapped. He knew very well what the fishermen meant. Yet, when the words came from his own kin, acting like a common market-place whore, he found it profoundly shocking. He grabbed at her arm and pulled her up. She stood defiant and close, making no attempt to move away from him. The smell of his mother's scent wafted from her hair.

"No-one would know." Debra was accomplished at the fertive whisper, she found a new excitement in the realisation of her feminine power. Jared's resolve was quick to crumble. She was willing, he told himself, and... it was true, she *was* safe.

"I won't tell anyone," she coaxed, moving her hand up his thigh.

***

Joanna sat on the bed cradling Kezia's head and shoulders in her arms. Kezia's thick, chestnut hair fell nearly to her waist. Joanna stroked it tenderly.

"My dear, sweet chicken. I'm so sorry... so sorry..." she

murmured. Adah sat on the other side of the room grinding sesame seeds. Zippie sucked on a length of old blanket in silence, dark, fearful eyes glued to the women. Ever since Adah had come back with the washing to find Kezia on the floor, Zippie was a changed child. The bubbly, chuckling, outgoing little girl was now withdrawn, nervous and pouting. Adah said it must've been the shock of Kezia collapsing,

"She'd have known something was terrible wrong, poor little mite," Adah explained to Joanna. "Couldn't've happened at a worser time, what with me out and Jabez over at Ruth's." She shook her head like an old woman, " Oh, t'was a dretful day t'was, and no mistake!"

Joanna tightened her arms round Kezia. "I should've been here for you, chicken." She sighed, "I've let you down," she pressed her cheek on the top of Kezia's head. "But you'll be alright now. Just rest a few more days. And don't worry, you're young, you'll give Jared more sons." Kezia's lips tightened. As Adah looked across the room at Kezia with her eyes closed, she was struck by the resemblance to the way Leah used to lie, wan and listless, after Zippie's birth.

They heard Ruth's voice singing as she crossed the courtyard. "Jabez is a-comin…Jabez is a-comin…" She appeared in the doorway, the boy strapped to her back. An ideal wet-nurse, Ruth was happy to sit around all day and play and laugh at anything. She possessed little sense but more than made up for her short-comings with a generous and loving heart.

"Here we are!" she announced. "I brought some honeycomb." She laid her basket by the loom. "Now, how's our Kezie today then?"

Kezia extricated herself from Joanna's embrace and sat up beside her aunt. She gathered her reserves of strength for a smile to flicker round her eyes as she greeted Ruth. "Jabez likes your singing," she said quietly. Ruth beamed at Adah.

"Oh well," she replied, "you got to sing to the babes. Makes 'em talk quicker." She imparted her fact with a confidential nod. Joanna decided it would be tactful to avoid the subject of 'babes'.

"You wouldn't recognise the pottery now." She took Kezia's hand. "Seth's taken on another potter and they've had to build new kilns. I tell you, chicken, I'm losing my home inch by inch. The whole place is stacked with pots! I'll be sleeping in a pot if I'm not careful!" As Joanna threw back her head to laugh, Kezia soaked up the warm normality of her aunt's company.

No-one mentioned the patches of purple black discolouration on her abdomen, thighs and arms. Nor did she voice the aches and pains that wracked her body each time she tried to walk or climb the stairs. Kezia knew full well that Anna had seen them when she delivered the baby. Adah had seen them as she gently washed her body. But not a glance betrayed their thoughts. Not a word was said. Would her mother have joined this conspiracy of silence?

Jared had not been to the house since. It had been Ruth's good-natured husband who had taken the tiny linen parcel and buried it in Leah's grave.

Agony and tears – all those months of carrying – and, now, nothing but a heart numbed by violence and betrayal. Kezia had no tears for her dead son. Jared had destroyed his own flesh and blood and by that evil violation, he had destroyed her heart.

Most nights, since those long, excruciating hours of labour, Kezia had lain staring at the ceiling. At least she felt a measure of relief that Jared kept away from the house. Miriam became the principal messenger from Zebedee's household and, whereas Anna had been in the habit of esconcing herself most of the day with Kezia, since the still birth, her absence spoke volumes. Regardless of the shame, Kezia vowed she would kill herself rather than allow Jared in her bed again.

Whichever way she looked at her life, however many permutations revolved through her head, the conclusion was always the same: she was trapped. Powerless. A woman who refused her husband his marital demands would be divorced. No man would take a divorced woman. Her father would be humiliated and scandalised and she would be ostracised from family and her community. Kezia longed to run away to Sepphoris and live with Joanna but loyalty to her dead mother compelled her to stay and be a mother to Zippie and Jabez. She would never abandon them. Also, she had to keep the home ready for her father's return. Responsibilities weighed on her shoulders like a mill-stone.

The noise within the room washed over her. The chatter between Joanna, Adah and Ruth melted into background. Kezia had the strangest feeling. She knew she was in the room, yet she felt separated from reality. Almost as if her body stayed on the bed with Joanna but her soul had floated away… hearing the familiar voices but disconnected and beyond. Her life, all her hopes and dreams, had ended in this suffering. The force of her grief propelled her into a suspended, surreal state.

What was it that Jesus had said to her on that far-away evening by the lakeside? His dark, handsome features were so fresh in her memory she felt his gaze on her now. His presence was more real than the women in the room. His voice resonated in her heart and she heard his words with painful clarity: '…being a woman is God's choice for you…

to give birth to another life is the most wonderful of all blessings.' A deep breath filtered down her nose in a long sigh and hot tears trickled silently down her cheeks.

'Oh Jesus!' a sob erupted from the dark centre of her being, 'how could you be so wrong?'

***

A month later:

Enthusiastic applause resonated round the open-air auditorium. Whoops and whistles of approval cascaded down the tiered seating as the actors relished their final bows. Little Josh sat wedged between Ben and Nico, high up on the top row of white stone seats. Seth had promised Josh a 'surprise' for being such an industrious, helpful boy and nothing could have thrilled him more than tickets for the Sepphoris Theatre. Little Josh had delivered orders to the theatre's back door but he'd never been inside the actual auditorium. His saucer eyes riveted on the stage as he sat absorbed by this new world. He went wild with his applause.

Seth leaned on Ben to talk over the boy's head to Nico.

"You sure you won't change your mind?" Seth shouted across against the din of clapping. Nico lifted his gaze from the stage, out over the walls of the theatre and down the valley in the direction of Capernaum. He shook his head. Seth stood, pulled on his cloak and secured his trademark purple turban.

"Ah, well," he sighed, "you must do what seems best for you. But," he ruffled Little Josh's hair, "we'll all miss you, you know!" The applause died down and the theatre-goers melted away with uncanny speed. Seth flowed down the steps waving a hand and inclining his turban as he acknowledged friends and customers. With usual aplomb he led his group to the exit.

"My dear boy," Seth continued as they reached the cardo, "you have such talent… the *world* awaits you!" he spread his arms in an expansive gesture. "And from Caesarea you'll be able to export… Tyre… Ephesus… and… and maybe down to Egypt and heaven knows where! There'll be blue pottery from here to Rome!" Nico's eyebrows lifted in grudging pleasure at such a prospect. He appreciated Seth's understanding manner. The pottery had tripled in size over the past year but with his commissioned work complete, he knew it was time to leave Sepphoris.

"Take this young man home, Ben," Seth clapped Josh on the back, "Nico and I have some last things to discuss." Seth steered Nico towards the central plaza where olive trees shaded seats around a fountain. Once the sun had set, shadows of dusk crept over the hills transforming the far valleys into secret, black crevasses. The first bright star of the night shone directly above the plaza like a distant fire-brand. The stone benches still held the day's warmth. Seth sat down and waited for Nico to take the seat beside him.

"Life's a funny old game!" Seth yawned as he stared back at the Theatre's grand facade. "I've just paid good money to see Roman actors perform a Greek play here on my Jewish soil! How's that for irony?" he smiled up at Nico who seemed reluctant to sit down. "Don't know what my old father would've made of it all." Seth flicked a nut up in the air and caught it in his open mouth, a trick Little Josh had just learnt to copy amid great hilarity. A grin played briefly on Nico's lips before the sombre expression returned and he sat down on the apricot coloured stone bench.

"At least you understand now why I... er... why I go." Emotion made his voice thick and gravelly.

"For sure." Seth nodded, his gentle face equally serious.

The previous day, Nico had taken Seth to see the completed mosaic floor in the Magistrate's dining hall. Intricate images of twined vines, figs and pomegranates, created a stunning border of vibrant colour. Various cameos of archers, hunters, gazelles and ibis surrounded the central panel. Seth uttered an audible gasp as he recognised Joanna's striking eyes staring up at him. But then, in a split second, he realised it wasn't Joanna depicted as a glorious goddess in flowing robes, a stylised, roman laurel wreath around her hair. It was Kezia.

Seth stood in silence as he registered the implications of such a picture and Nico's secret heartache. He scratched his ear and bit his lip as he tried to think what he could say. Nico watched the potter's body language from the doorway. Seth took observance of the Jewish religious customs lightly, but he was still a Jew and Nico worried how he would react to the Romanisation of his wife's neice. And, however welcome Seth and Joanna had made him in their home, there was no escaping the fact that the Romans were the occupying power in the land. He worried his picture could be taken as an outrageous defamation of Seth's family. Through his art he had publicly professed a forbidden love.

Seth turned away and walked to the window. Nico interpreted the move as disgust but Seth was far from angry or disgusted. Suddenly he felt a bond between himself and the young artist. Both were gifted in their profession, both enjoyed the admiration and popularity of the city. Seth had the love and companionship of a vivacious, loyal wife and Nico, with his youth and smouldering virility could take his pick of any young girl in Sepphoris. But the mosaic identified a private torture that Seth understood. Deep in his soul, Seth faced the unspoken truth of his own double life. A forbidden love he could never declare. A truth that hurt. A truth he would never admit.

He turned from the window with a flourish, eyes bright with a beaming smile. "My dear Nico. My *congratulations*. She is quite beautiful!" His silence had been a rare lowering of his guard, now he had recovered, Seth the potter was in control. He pushed his fist playfully against Nico's chest. "That mosaic will be the glory of Sepphoris for generations. Finest work I've ever seen…" He strode out of the room still talking, "things to do… kiln to unpack… no rest for the wicked!" They spoke no more about the picture.

"For sure," Seth repeated, lingering on the memory of the previous day. Yes, he understood why Nico had to leave the city. He wrinkled his nose as he considered Nico, even though he was a Roman, would be a far better husband for Kezia than the hot-headed fisherman Jairus had chosen for her.

"My brother, Cornelius…" Nico cut into Seth's thoughts, "he has big house in Caesarea. Big house…big family."

"Is he an artist like you?" Seth enquired. Nico shook his head.

"No, no," he laughed, "Cornelius is army man. A Centurian."

"Oh-ho! The army!" Seth chuckled, "Well, that couldn't be better. Find yourself a good hundred potters and you can supply the Empire with your blue ware."

"You… *best* potter," Nico said with sadness in his voice..

"Yes, yes, I know!" Seth teased. "But there are potters in every town – you'll have your choice. So, come back and see us when you're promoted Governor of all Galilee." Both men laughed. "We're not fussy in Sepphoris, you know," Seth continued, "we don't mind what wastrel becomes governor just so long as we don't end up with that despot Agrippa!" The two men left the plaza and wandered amiably back to the pottery.

***

At first light, a little group gathered at the Akko Gate. Seth, Ben and Ben's mother, who had come to run domestic arrangements in Joanna's absence, Little Josh and the donkey. Individually they embraced Nico, wished him travelling mercies and waved him away from Sepphoris in company with the dozen or so merchants, a contingent of soldiers and various women. Little Josh was the last to turn away from the gate. He watched the travellers until there shapes became obliterated in the rising dust along the valley floor. He wondered if Caesarea was as big a city as Sepphoris. Nico had told him Caesarea was by the Great Sea.

"One day," he promised as he stroked the donkey's nose, "one day *we'll* go to the Great Sea."

Chapter 32

THE great cedar door shut with a mighty crash. Mordecai glowered at the Holy Scroll on the desk in front of him. He rose in temper and strutted into the main body of the Synagogue to remonstrate with whoever it was who dared disturb his study time. The figure walking through the Synagogue to the teaching room dispelled all anger and the old Pharisee's face creased in joy.

"My son!" he threw open his arms in welcome. Jairus gave his uncle the greeting of intimate family without forgetting the respect due to his superior. "Oh, my boy! Come – have some wine."

For the next couple of hours Mordecai sat engrossed in Jairus' news from Jerusalem. He probed for answers to rumours he had heard about Zebedee's boys, James and John. His long white hair escaped from under his prayer shawl as he shook his head in disgust. Jairus confirmed his worst fears. James and John had been exemplary pupils. Mordecai had taught them the Law of Moses and the Prophets, the history and the hopes of their nation. Eager boys they were, but too impressionable for their own good. First they'd gone after some deranged, desert prophet, then, all of a sudden, transferred their allegiance to the Nazareth man. In the same school room where he had nurtured and encouraged the brothers, he received news of how they flaunted themselves around Jerusalem, beguiling ignorant people to hail the crucified Jesus as Israel's Messiah. "Blasphemy!" Mordecai tore open his cloak in shame.

Jairus also brought disturbing news about divisions in the Temple. Friction bubbled within Caiaphas' own family. Hostile confrontations had become commonplace in the Temple courts; even the reveered teacher, Gamaliel, had been heard to challenge Caiaphas' authority. Beneath the pius exterior, the holy Temple had erupted into a hotbed of intrigue and ambitious jostling. Outside the Temple, in the rustic squares dotted all over the city, people flocked to hear unlearned men like James, John and Simon-Peter. Mordecai couldn't believe the strength of the new sect.

"The *Way*!" he snorted, "Is that what they call themselves? 'Followers of The Way'? The only way they're going is the way to Hell!" His fist thumped down on the desk with such venom the Scroll jumped in the air and nearly fell to the floor. The near catastrophe of dropping the Holy Scroll brought the old Pharisee to his senses. Taking a deep breath he changed the subject.

"So," Mordecai nodded, "Caiaphas has honoured you with a seat on the Sanhedrin! Well, well, well." A satisfied smile hovered around his lips and his faded eyes moistened with pride. Jairus brushed the journey's dust from his new and expensive Temple robes.

"I'll not return to the Temple until the feast of Hanukah," Jairus' conversation was oiled by good wine from Mordecai's cupboard. "And, by then, Jabez will be old enough to return with me." Mordecai frowned, puzzled and somewhat alarmed. "Don't worry, Uncle," Jairus reassured him, "I have a good family in Jerusalem to care for him. He will be nurtured in the knowledge and fear of the Lord."

Mordecai suddenly remembered. "Before we go home," he spoke solemnly, "I'm afraid I have to tell you Kezia's child was born dead." A pained expression crossed Jairus' brow. Was this history repeating itself?

"I pray she is not to be cursed with stillbirths like her mother." He sighed.

"This was only the first." Mordecai was defensive. "And, she had a fall… it was all quite unfortunate…but she's strong. She's going about her duties now. She's fine! Joanna is with her." The old man caught the look on Jairus's face. "Oh, but the woman'll soon be going back to Sepphoris, now Kezie's better."

Jairus raised his cup; "Let's drink to that!" he said with feeling.

***

"Am I not good enough to care for my own brother?" Horrified by her father's decision to take Jabez back to Jerusalem, Kezia hunched over the loom in bleak rejection. The shuttle shot erratically across the weave, it's path obscured to her brimming eyes. Joanna's basket lay propped against the door, ready for her early departure in the morning. It had been her suggestion that Adah take Zippie for a walk before bedtime in the hope she would have time for some straight talking with her neice before returning to Sepphoris. It might be months or even years before they had another chance to be alone.

"Don't be harsh on your father, chicken. Remember, you've lost a mother but he's lost his wife." Kezia continued her weaving in silence. Joanna tried again: "He wants what's best for Jabez," she reasoned.

Kezia dropped the shuttle, "I've lost my mother and now

he wants to take away my brother. Zippie and Jabez belong *here,* this is their home…*our* home…together."

Joanna sat on a low stool winding a skein of dyed wool. Calmly she asked, "What about your husband? You will have sons of your own…"

"Never!" screamed Kezia with a desperate emphasis that tore Joanna's heart. She knew she had hit a nerve. Things were not right between Kezia and Jared. She hated the implications of their failed marriage, Joanna longed to protect her neice at any cost.

"Come back to Sepphoris with me, Kezie. Adah and Ruth are more than able to care for the children." Kezia shook her head.

"I can't," was all she could say. Joanna got up, went over to the loom, took the shuttle out of Kezia's hand and, sitting down beside her, took the quivering young wife in her arms.

"Jared will take another wife," she began, "you can live with us at the pottery."

Kezia sobbed into her aunt's shoulder. "I *can't.* I must care for them… and Uncle Mordecai… I *must.*" Joanna waited a few minutes before stating her thoughts.

"You don't have to worry about Mordecai. He'll get by better than anyone. The Synagogue's his life and breath. Plenty of people will feed and care for him." She decided the moment had come for honesty, "It's Nico, isn't it?" she said. The dam to Kezia's emotions breached, the flood of repressed sorrow and pain roared out uncontrollably. At last Joanna whispered, "Hey, chicken, this tunic's been washed already… I need it dry by morning!"

Kezia gave a choked laugh which emerged more like a whimper. Then she said, "Jared'll kill me if he thinks I've seen Nico again."

"Has he beaten you?" Joanna asked softly. Kezia hesitated, then nodded.

"Oh, whatever were your parents thinking about to betroth you to that spoilt thug?" Joanna seethed with anger. Putting everything together, Kezia's bruises, the dead child, the absent Jared and Kezia's emotional state, Joanna completed the ugly domestic jigsaw in her mind.

"Kezie," she whispered, "you don't have to spend your life like this. Let Jared divorce you. Come to Sepphoris. Our home is your home. And Seth... he may not be... well, he is kind and gentle... he wouldn't allow any bully fisherman from Capernaum to harm you." Kezia rocked in the warm security of Joanna's arms. "I too have responsibilities to your mother. I promised to be a mother to you if... if she died." She paused, "If he beats you again, *promise* me you will come to us. At least, think about it... seriously...please."

The door burst open and a exuberant Zippie scampered across the room, her stubby fingers clutching the distinctive black and white check tail-feather from a hoopoe. Adah arrived at the door just in time to witness Zippie launch herself on top of Kezia in a squeal of delight. Zippie seemed to have found a light in the dark tunnel of her bewilderment. Her light was Adah.

***

"Mother says 'could be bad wind tonight'." Debra lay on her stomach, head on her hands as she lounged across Jared's mattress. Her small, inquisitive eyes followed every movement as he dressed.

"What does she know about it?" he scorned. As soon as she'd satisfied him Jared could never wait to get rid of her out

286

of his tent. The girl assumed too much. She took advantage of their secret liaison. She spent too much of her time in his tent. Anna had suspicions of her youngest daughter but preferred to turn a blind eye where Jared was concerned. Salome was just pleased to get Debra out from under her feet. Miriam off-set the coldness she encountered from her mother and sister by spending more and more time over at Jairus' house.

Jared flexed his biceps to his admiring fan.

"Look at this!" he boasted. "Think I'm afraid of a bit of wind? I could crush your skull like a nut!" he sneered cracking his knuckles. Debra preened and giggled at his abusive remarks. She treated his violent insinuations as prized compliments. Jared slunk over to the mattress and with a sudden dart forward, clamped both hands round her neck.

"Scrawny little bitch!" he spat as he squeezed. "You disgust me! Get out before I take your guts for bait tonight." He released his fingers from her throat and swaggered out of the tent.

Down at the harbour Zebedee stood peering into the sky, gauging the strength and speed of the southerly wind.

"We'll not risk the small boats, tonight," he declared. "We'll take the new boat. We'll be back before third watch."

The older men had transferred nets from the harbour onto Zebedee's new boat. Jared could see a dark head moving among the willow baskets on the other side of the boat. He cursed under his breath. Given half a chance he'd throw that Levi overboard…

"Get the main sail up, then. Earn your keep, boy!" Zebedee shouted at his son. Jared leapt on board and immediately began to hoist the sail. The heavy linen flapped loudly against the strengthening wind. "Old Jonah isn't going out, nor his brother, so we corner the market tonight. Make the most of it!"

A white streak of fork lightning tore down through the sky. The earth-shaking, rolling thunder clap that followed gave Salome palpitations. She sat bolt upright on her bed. It sounded as if all heaven was enraged. Rain lashed against the shutters and debris banged along the street outside, the wind whipped rubbish along the gutter running in front of the cluster of homes. A voice inside compelled her to dress and go down to the harbour.

Meanwhile, along the street, an elder of the Synagogue was knocking on Jairus' door.

"Come quick, sir, " he called urgently. "Water's flooding into the Synagogue."

Jairus and his uncle hurried to the Synagogue. Already the water in the street was over their sandals. By the time they reached the Synagogue, water from the lake was slopping in through the great main door and had reached the height of a man's knee. A dozen men with their sons were building sandbags against more flooding and others had brought buckets to bale water out of the back door. Jairus went immediately to the Ark to rescue sacred Scrolls. Mordecai went to the treasury.

***

Out on the lake, Zebedee bellowed into the gale, "Get the sail down! She'll be broke in two if we don't get back." The gusting southerly had turned suddenly to a malicious, easterly gale. Ferocious waves heaved and crashed under lowering charcoal clouds, as the squall roared down from the Syrian hills. The boat lifted and slewed in a drunken dance making it virtually impossible for Zebedee to hold the rudder steady.

His eyes screwed up against the horizontal rain. The rain stung his face with its ferocity leaving him half blind. He cursed his stupidity. He had a life-time's experience of the lake, he knew better than anyone, the speed with which conditions on the water could alter from manageable to nightmare. Only an old fool would imagine his new boat could defy the elements.

"She's taking on water!" yelled the older hired man battling to bale out bilge water with the only battered leather bucket on board. As Jared and his father's other long-serving man brought down the sail, Jared caught sight of Levi vomiting over the stern. His thoughts raced – if he could get to him in the next few seconds he'd hurl the bastard to the waves where he belonged.

"Balance her!" Zebedee bawled at the top of his voice. "Get back in the stern!" Levi staggered away from the side. Jared's chance had gone.

The men rolled and lurched, struggling to hold their footing on the rain-drenched deck. Despite straining every muscle to keep the boat on course for the safety of Capernaum's harbour, the boat bucked and tossed in the darkness making Zebedee feel like he was clinging to a bolting horse.

"If we take her too near," the storm's crescendo drowned out Zebedee's voice, "I'm feared she'll crash 'gainst the harbour wall!" he screamed. His fingers locked round the wooden rudder. A sickening realisation pounded in his chest, he was too old for this; the strength and expertise he had taken for granted over all his years, had deserted him.

Soaked, chilled and exhausted, Zebedee steered the boat close in to shore before another giant wave heaved the vessel aground on the higher side of the harbour. The boat jolted to rest with a tearing, cracking moan of the timber. It tilted precariously on top of the reeds and rushes. The pride of

Capernaum's fishing fleet propelled out of the water like a child's discarded toy.

Shouts of relief rose from Salome and the hired-mens' wives as the large hull beached. Then, as suddenly as the storm had begun, the wind died away, rain stopped and a silver half moon emerged from behind the clouds.

Jared scowled as the empty fish baskets slithered down the deck. He counted. They'd lost half a dozen. Levi came past him with his servile nodding and smiling. Jared stared through him with a cold contempt, then jumped off the boat into the reeds. He was furious with himself. He should have kicked the little bugger over the side to join the baskets. He swore. Next time…he'd get him…

The hired men rushed to their master, slumped over the rudder. The older man gently peeled the gnarled fingers from the wood.

"'ere, we'd best get 'im 'ome," he said. Zebedee staggered silently between his loyal men as they manhandled him over the side, sloshing down into the reed swamp then up onto the narrow shingle beach to where Salome and the women waited.

**

Next day:

"Came to see if there was anything you needed, my friend." Jairus had not been near Zebedee's house in months, but news of the old fisherman's narrow escape from the storm prompted his conscience. Zebedee appeared to have both aged and shrunk overnight. He sat swathed in a blanket, slurping hot broth.

"No fool like an old fool, Jairus!" Zebedee grumbled into his cup. "Never should have gone out… *madness!*" He was livid with himself. Without the cloth he always wore over his head, Jairus noticed the only hair the old fisherman possessed grew in his shaggy beard.

"Bad news from Tiberias," Jairus struggled to keep conversation going. "They say the waves were so high, fifteen houses were swept away and flooding right up to Herod's palace."

"No business to build on the shore like they belong to down there," Zebedee rasped, he had little interest in the suffering of Tiberias.

"Looks like three men were washed away... feared drowned," Jairus persevered. " The Lord had his hand on you, old friend. Nothing short of a miracle you survived last night."

Salome hovered over her husband, adjusting the blanket, offering more broth, touching his arm...

"Away woman!" Zebedee snapped in characteristic mood. "Stop your fussing, do!" He waved her out of the room. "Leave us." He gave Jairus a direct stare. "We have a few matters to discuss." He motioned Jairus to sit on the opposite cushion.

"Good of you to come over, Jairus, but there's nothing I need... unless you can give me back my youth!" Zebedee was gruff. Jairus offered a weak smile. A fleeting surge of pity took the smile away as he saw how the vulnerability of age had overtaken the man, once built like a battering-ram. Pity gave way instantly to a chilling fear as he realised the vulnerability of age to which, one day, he himself would succumb. Jairus made a pitch for the moral high ground.

"I shall be taking my son with me when I return to Jerusalem...I was hoping..." he rubbed his beard as he glanced around the family living room, "well, I'm expecting Jared and Kezia to live in my house..."

"Now, look here." Zebedee jabbed a finger in Jairus' direction, "Your girl's been no wife to my son." The accusation caught Jairus off guard. "Why isn't she *here*?" Zebedee went on, " Don't you see, man…while my boy sleeps in that tent alone, she makes him a laughing-stock."

The cordial atmosphere between the men turned sour.

"She… she took the stillbirth badly." Jairus tried to explain. "She was *very* unwell."

Zebedee snorted. "That's not what my boy's told me!" Jairus raised an eyebrow. What was going on? Zebedee put down his cup and slowly wiped the back of his hand across his mouth.

"Look, Jairus. We've not always seen eye to eye but, I bear you no grudge." He sniffed. "But there's things you need to know before you go scuttlin' back to Jerusalem."

"What things?" Jairus clipped his question.

"I'm goin' to have to tell it to you straight." Zebedee stared at Jairus. "My boy's talking of divorce."

"Divorce!" Jairus shot from his seat as if stung by a scorpion. The very word 'divorce' caused him to sweat in panic. "Why?" he yelped. His family had never been tainted with the scandal of divorce.

"Oh, sit you down, sit you down!" Zebedee shook his head. It was a distasteful subject. "Let's not have the quarrel between *us*." He sighed. "'Tis like this – my boy says… the child wasn't his."

"He's *lying!*" Jairus shouted. "How dare he…" The idea of his Kezia committing adultery was preposterous.

"Just you hear me out." Zebedee barked back. "P'raps I got to spell it out for you – while your daughter was in Sepphoris she mixed with… with…*bad* company."

"What do you mean?" Jairus was flustered. "They were living at Seth's pottery. She was with Joanna, she couldn't…"

"Ah, but has she told you 'bout the gentile in the pottery?" The look on Jairus' face answered Zebedee's question. "Has she told you she was runnin' round with him?" Jairus physically shrank inside his robes. "And has she told you he's been down *here* in our Capernaum market, bold as brass?" He sat back, taking in Jairus' horror. "No! I don't 'spect she 'as."

Jairus's mind went numb. Each sentence Zebedee uttered deepened his daughter's degradation. After an agonising pause, Jairus pulled himself together. "That proves nothing," he remonstrated, "My daughter…"

"Your daughter's a hot-bloodied young filly and, just like any woman, will turn her head for flattery. Now, if she's such a *perfect* wife why does she refuse her wifely duties, eh? Answer me that one."

Embarrassed, Jairus fiddled with the tassle on his prayer shawl.

"She's not well, Zebedee. For pity's sake, man, give her some time," he pleaded. "I'll…I'll speak to her. We'll get this sorted… I give you my word on that." He swallowed hard. "There's um… no need f… for talk of divorce."

With no more to be said, Jairus emerged from the dingey room into the glare of the afternoon sun. He stood for a moment, gulping at the air in shock, before hurrying off to the Synagogue.

Zebedee sat back in satisfaction. He had made Jairus squirm alright! He never did take to those who gave themselves airs; the Synagogue Ruler and his haughty, superior air – like he could smell camel dung on your cloak – well, smirked Zebedee, this little episode has brought him back down to earth… with a fair old bump, too! Yet, however sweet it was to watch Jairus in discomfort, Zebedee had to admit he had no stomach for a scandal. With his elder sons James and

John gone from home, he was desperate for Jared to provide him with a grandson. He had no other prayer than for his boy to carry on the family's fishing business.

Outside the house, below the open window, Salome sat, gripped by morbid trepidation. She crossed calloused hands over her bosom in an effort to still her heart's rapid fluttering. Divorce? Jared hadn't said anything to her about divorce. She gazed up into the few scudding clouds as if seeking spiritual strength. If only James and John would come home…

Chapter 33

"WALK about Zion, go round her, count her..." the boy, standing at his desk, stumbled over the next word. He squinted, cleared his throat and shifted from one foot to the other.

"Towers!" Jairus boomed. "*Towers*, boy. You knew the word last week." The boy continued in a stilted monotone as the silver pointer marked each word on the Scroll.

"...count her *towers,*" he emphasised. " Consider well her ramparts, view her c... cit... um, her cit-a-dels," sweat dribbled tiny streams behind his ears, "that you may tell of them to the next gen-er-a-tion." The boy stopped, the text swimming before his eyes. He prayed for the next boy to take over.

"Next!" Jairus snapped without looking to see if the next boy was ready. The next boy, his star pupil, jumped up and with supreme confidence, rounded off the Psalm like an actor pronouncing the final line of a great play.

"For this is our God for ever and ever;

He will be our guide,... even to the *end!*"

"Good! Very good!" Jairus looked up from his desk at nine pairs of eyes imploring to be dismissed. "The Sons of Korah meditated on the holy word of God within the Temple on Mount Zion. One day, boys," he searched for a flicker of interest in their blank expressions, "when you are men, you too will 'walk about Zion'," Jairus rolled up the Scroll on his desk as he continued, "and it will be my joy to show you the Holy City. We'll count her towers together."

Silence.

Jairus stood up. "Next week we shall read the story of our Father Abraham." For a brief moment he stared at his apathetic class, supposedly the brightest boys of Capernaum. Irritation roughened in his voice as he dismissed them. They rolled up their Scrolls, piled them on Jairus' desk, then pushed and shoved their way to the door… and were gone.

"You're bringing on some good readers." Mordecai had been sitting at the back of the teaching room. The group would be his responsibility when Jairus returned to Jerusalem.

With a heavy heart Jairus returned the Scrolls to the Ark.

"What's the matter with them, Uncle?" he asked in despair. "There's no *love*. Even the bright one, it's all a big game to him. I was younger than any of them when I came to love Torah." He shook his head. The cleaner was sweeping in the main body of the Synagogue and the old Pharisee, sensing Jairus' agitation, decided they should shut the door for some privacy.

"Sometimes," Mordecai began, "it's only as a man grows older that the eternal truths become real…and precious." He poured two cups of water. "They have plenty of time yet. Some of them will grow to love it, but then…" he drew in a deep breath, "for others, maybe most of them, it'll only ever be dry history." He passed Jairus a cup. "You went to see Zebedee this morning?" he prompted.

Jairus leaned against the window. He could see the top of the Syrian hills, shimmering dove grey in the distant haze. In as level a voice as he could manage, he recounted Zebedee's words.

"I don't believe it!" Mordecai thumped a fist on the nearby desk. "Curses on the man to bring shame to your house!"

"Kezia does not sleep with him, I can't deny that." A resigned weariness clouded Jairus' voice.

"Oh, but… the girl will still be unclean. Her time had not come and she had a bad birthing. Circumstances like that… well, she's bound to take longer to get over it than a…than a normal birth. I may be an old man, but I know when a girl is suffering… and Kezie's not ready for the marriage bed yet." He sat on the nearest desk. "Tell the young jack ass to bide his time. She'll be with child again soon enough. Mark my words!"

It hadn't occurred to Jairus that Kezia might still be unclean. But that didn't resolve the rumour of her liaison with a gentile. Divorce would be a disgrace but adultery… total disaster. A gentile from any other nation might be tolerated, especially if he agreed to become a God-fearer, but never a Roman. Never a representative of brutal repression on their nation, God's chosen nation – that was unthinkable. He would have to speak to his daughter. It was something Leah should be doing… his stomach knotted.

Walks along the shore with his little girl had once been his pleasure. He remembered her entranced face as she watched the kingfishers diving into the water near the reeds; the songs they used to sing as a family at the Sabbath meal; the way she would clamber up on his knee… but, now she was a woman, and a wife. He didn't seem to know her anymore. A chasm had opened between them.

***

The caravan straggled through the valley of the doves and began the laborious climb towards Nazareth and Sepphoris.

A group of traders from Jericho took the lead, with their ten camels they were journeying all the way to Tyre. The rest of the travellers comprised a bunch of freelance artisans, basket weavers with laden donkeys, dyers, a blacksmith and his horse from Tiberias, a couple of Saducees, bakers from the garrison and women of assorted ages. Joanna found herself walking in step with two perfumiers, widows from Hippos, a city on the opposite side of the lake from Capernaum.

First light was always the best time of day to travel. As they climbed into the hills, the air soon lost the stifling heat of Capernaum and a welcome breeze cooled their faces. The widows, several years senior to Joanna, had difficulty with the steeper inclines, using their energies to walk rather than talk. This suited Joanna. Her mind was too preoccupied for talking.

Her usual vitality was crushed beneath a nagging guilt. She blamed herself for Kezia's plight. She should have confronted Jared the moment she had seen Kezia's bruised cheek. If only they hadn't returned to Capernaum *she* would have cared for Kezia during childbirth… things would have been so different. For months Joanna had woven idealised pictures of Kezia and her baby at the pottery… she had longed for this baby… she and Seth would have cherished him, lavished him with everything they possessed.

The gradient passed unnoticed. With each stride Joanna's heart wrung with scenarios of 'if only' and 'what might have been'. She laboured under a sickening guilt. She had failed her Kezie. She'd failed Leah, too. Perhaps worst of all, she'd failed the sweet, innocent baby.

When the caravan stopped at noon, Sepphoris was clearly visible on the horizon. At the road-side inn, watermelon vendors turned a quick profit from the thirsty travellers. The widows began to chat to themselves but Joanna sat on the grass by herself. She couldn't wait to get home.

***

"D'you think he'll come back?" Ben asked. He and Seth sat on the bench outside the pottery, resting in the late afternoon sun. The angle Seth leaned against the wall had tilted his purple turban down on the top of his eyebrows. He breathed in slowly then pushed out his lips as he breathed out through his mouth.

"Neo-o," he drawled, "Shouldn't think so."

Ben frowned. "So what about the decorations? I'm no artist."

Seth sat up straight. "Yes, you are!" he adjusted his head gear.

"No, I'm not." Ben protested. "I can't draw vines and… and birds and all the things Nico puts round his plates."

"You don't have to draw the same things as Nico. You're not Nico, you're *Ben*. You decorate with your own designs." Ben remained unconvinced. "Look at the way you use the sponge – and the nib is… well, it's really effective." Seth turned to look at his apprentice. It wasn't like Ben to be negative. Seth put his hand on Ben's thigh.

"Ben," he hesitated, his voice soft and serious, "you won't ever leave me, will you? I couldn't bear it if…" he checked himself, coughed, and lifted his hand. He folded his arms and a twinkle flickered in his eye. "I couldn't bear it if Joanna came home to find her two favourite men had vanished!" Under his clay-spattered shirt, Seth's stomach jiggled with amusement. Ben didn't laugh. He replied in the same earnest tone Seth used.

"I'll never leave you, Seth," he looked directly at the potter. "You're my father and my *dearest* brother…"

Little Josh bowled into the yard under a bale of hay. Their window of intimacy slammed shut.

"Don't forget now… I want my change!" Seth shouted over to the boy who grinned widely on his way to the donkey. Seth sighed. "When I was a humble potter, this place was *vast!* Why, I had to send messages to my dear wife by carrier pigeon! Now that I'm famous, the finest potter in all Galilee, what's happened to the place? No room to swing a mole-rat!"

Ben looked round at the two new kilns, the piles of plates, jugs, ewers and dishes waiting for sale, the donkey's pen, pitchers of water, and the cart Seth had recently bought pushed up against the wall of the house. He had to agree, the yard was pretty much cluttered.

"I know!" Seth announced, "When Joanna gets back, you and I, Ben, we'll go on a business trip. Up north." Little Josh hung on Seth's every word. "We'll take this stock to a new market."

"Where?" Ben was intrigued.

"Mmm. How's about Caesarea Philippi? They say merchants from the east bring all kinds of delights to their market. We can dazzle them with our unique wares!" His eyes lit up, "Shall we?" he pleaded.

Ben grinned, "Yeah! I've never been up there."

"C'n I come?" Josh piped up holding out two shekels change for Seth.

The potter narrowed his eyes at the boy, "We-ll," he frowned, he glanced at Ben with a wink, "what d'you think, Ben…we'll need the cart… that means we'll need some animal to pull it, so… maybe… maybe we'll *have* to take the animal's wretched little keeper!"

Josh leapt in the air with a whoop of joy. "Magic!" he squealed. "You're the *best*."

***

From the flat roof, Jairus watched his daughter hand in hand with Zippie making their way to the shore. Over the last couple of days he had evaded a confrontation with Kezia, thrashing over and over in his mind the best way to approach such a delicate subject. He watched until the pair disappeared from sight. Sickened by the whole business, he grabbed his cloak, threw it over his shoulders and, taking the stairs two at a time, made to follow his daughters.

By the time he caught up with them, Kezia was sitting on a rounded boulder watching Zippie splash in and out of the shallows brandishing a stick in the air. Seeing her father's stern expression, she ran to clutch Kezia's skirts.

Dropping any of his rehearsed preamble he said, "What's this I'm hearing about you, Kezia?" Kezia lifted solemn, brown eyes to her father.

"What have you heard, Father?" she asked quietly. Jairus blustered with a mixture of embarrassment and distaste.

"Jared is talking about a divorce. What have you done to provoke him?" He stood averting his eyes from her gaze.

Kezia stroked Zippie's curls as she replied: "I have been a good wife. I have given him no cause for divorce."

"Then what about this man… this Roman?" Jairus demanded.

"He works with Seth… that's all," Kezia's reply remained composed.

"Do you swear to me the child was not his?" Kezia sighed at her father's lack of trust.

"I swear the child in my womb was Jared's… please believe me, Father, I've not been with any other man." She bent her lips to Zippie's ear, "Go and find me some pretty shells," she patted her little sister's bottom to send her down to the water-line. She wanted direct eye contact with her Father, something he could not bring himself to give. He shuffled awkwardly as he watched Zippie bobbing up and down as she picked up tiny fresh-water shells which spilled in a white curve along the water's edge.

"I'm… er… I've decided to take Jabez back to Jerusalem next week.."

"Next week!" Kezia winced at the sudden decision. She thought her father's return was at least two months away.

"Yes. That will make it possible for Jared to come back to live at the house. You will live as man and wife again… soon." Kezia said nothing. "Do you understand?" Jairus snapped. "I want no more talk of divorce." Kezia remained silent.

"I don't think you realise the *serious* implications of divorce." Silence fuelled his exasperation. "You would be ostracised, girl. No good man will have you." He waited for a response. Zippie ran back to Kezia clutching shells in two tight fists.

"And Kezia," his voice became strained, "if you commit adultery you could be stoned to death." He turned his head away, looked along the shore and up to the imposing outcrop of Mount Arbel. "I could do nothing to stop that." Finally he turned to face her. "I would be so ashamed of you," he said with revulsion. "You would no longer be my daughter."

Kezia held out her hands to receive Zippie's treasures.

In desperation, Jairus reached out and grabbed her arm: "You must promise me… promise you will be a dutiful wife to Jared when I've gone." He gave her an imploring look,

"*Promise* me, Kezie," he urged, "for your dear mother's sake."

Kezia bristled at the mention of her mother. She kept her gaze on the shells and grit in her hands. When at last she felt controlled enough to answer, she spoke carefully. "I promise… when Jared comes back to the house… I will be there."

"Good! That's settled then." Jairus sighed with relief. He turned on his heels and walked briskly back into the village. Whether he went home or to the Synagogue, Kezie neither looked to see nor cared. She had made her promise. She would stand by it. Yes, she would live in the house but no power on earth or in heaven would get her into Jared's bed.

Silently, in sight of the place where Jesus had given her the pouch of stones, she renewed her vow to kill herself rather than be violated by her husband ever again.

Chapter 34

"ANYTHING else to wash?" Kezia's laundry basket was barely half full.

"Surely you'll not go washing till your father and Jabez have gone?" Adah turned from folding the tiny tunics that would be going to Jerusalem, surprise in her voice and concern in her eyes.

"I can't watch Jabez leave this house." Kezia looked at Adah, her words came out in a wail, "I'd've brought him up as my own, Adah. But now… he'll never know me. He'll never know his mother and he'll never know his sister." She hoisted the basket on her headscarf and fled out of the room.

"…Wan go wi' Kezee…" Zippie whimpered trundling to the door.

Adah reached out a restraining hand, "Not this time, my bird. You stay along your Adah…yes?"

Jairus and Mordecai came down the stairs. Jairus looked for Kezia.

"Where's Kezia?" he demanded. "Oh here sh…" but it wasn't Kezia but Ruth entering the courtyard, singing as usual to the bundle on her back. Ruth had volunteered to go as far as Jericho where Rabbi Jonathan's wife would take over the feeding and caring for Jabez. Adah had packed a small basket of provisions for their journey. Ruth said she would be able to buy things in Tiberias and next day in Beth She'an.

"An' there's always sellers by the road-side. We'll do just fine." Ruth had assured Kezia the night before.

Jairus beamed. Although proud of his nephew, Mordecai couldn't quench a degree of hurt at Jairus' excitement. He realised Jairus had outgrown Capernaum. The man had a keen mind and it needed stretching. And, after the upset in the Synagogue a while back, the atmosphere had never recovered. There was an irresistable kudos in working at the Temple, mixing with the High Priest... the old Pharisee understood that. Mordecai regretted his own missed opportunities. The temptation to join Jairus was, even at his advanced age, a mighty strong urge.

"We must go quickly, my son. Don't wait for Kezia... some partings are best made in haste."

Mordecai laid his hand on Jabez' black spikes in blessing before their journey began.

"The Lord make his face to shine upon you, Jabez. The fear of the Lord be the beginning of your knowledge." Jabez twisted his head, wriggling uncomfortably under the old man's rough fingers. Jairus laughed.

"The boy can't even speak yet!" he embraced his uncle, "But he'll be in no better place than Jerusalem to gain wisdom and knowledge. He will be blessed indeed." He picked up the provisions, "Come," he said to the waiting Ruth, "we must go."

Mordecai walked with them to the end of the black stone houses. The two men embraced again before Jairus and his son joined other travellers and disappeared from view down the busy road to Tiberias, and their new life.

A hard lump made it difficult for Adah to swallow. Jabez was a lovely boy, as sunny as Zippie and no trouble at all. She led Zippie out into the sunshine and sat on the bench beside the house. Gathering Zippie up onto her knee, she began to comb tangles from the child's hair with careful, firm strokes. Compared with her brother's thick mop, Zippie's wispy curls floated round her face so that they hardly seemed attached to her head.

"Never mind," she gave voice to her thoughts, "he'll never be more loved than you, my sweet." She combed Zippie's fringe. 'At least,' she said in her mind, 'he won't grow up knowing his father can't be bothered with him.'

Adah was so preoccupied she took no notice as Miriam slid onto the bench beside her.

"She's such a pretty girl," exclaimed Miriam, fascinated by Adah's combing. "Where's Kezie?"

"Down at Job's pool." Adah didn't go into details or explain that Kezia was too broken-hearted to witness her baby brother's departure. The little servant-girl knew Miriam wouldn't understand.

"I've come to help," Miriam smiled. She always said that and both Adah and Kezia did their best to give her simple jobs she could accomplish on her own. They despaired at the way Anna talked to Miriam, criticising and belittling her at every opportunity. It spurred them to encourage her and make Miraim feel they couldn't do without her. Small wonder that the girl spent so much time at Jairus' house.

"Jared's coming back to sleep here ." Miriam disclosed. Adah stopped combing.

"When?" Her eyes widened.

"Not sure," Miriam shrugged. "He's not been well."

"Oh?"

"Belly cramps and… sort of shaking." Miriam demonstrated, holding out her arm and quivering her fingers.

"Well, we don't want that here!" Adah instinctively held Zippie closer.

"Uncle's not well either," Miriam added. Adah looked aghast. "Is it catching?"

"No, no. Nothing like that. It's since the storm. Seems he had a bit of a turn and he's not really got over it." Miriam was in a chatty mood. "Mother says he's too old to take the big boat out." She gave a shrill laugh, for no apparent reason. "There's a new hired hand so it's alright."

"That's good, then." Adah made an effort to sound interested.

The combing session ended, she took a few precious moments to cuddle the placid Zippie before the onslaught of the day's chores. Miriam sat with a contented smile. Furrows deepened on Adah's forehead. Whatever would Kezie say about Jared coming back?

***

A week later.

"We've had word from Magdala." Anna stood with a jug of goat's milk in her hand, bursting to share her news. Kezia kept her eyes on her task of chopping onions and Adah carried on kneading bread dough. "You'll be wanting this for later," Anna lifted the milk jug to indicate what she meant, "Jared always likes a cup of milk before he goes to sleep." Anna sat herself by the fire. "You know Mary from over at Magdala? Well, she's back home. She's been with James and John and all the other 'Believers' in Jerusalem."

"What about Sarah?" Kezia's eyes streamed over the onions.

"Simon-Peter and Sarah have gone to Joppa." Anna gloated over her knowledge.

Kezia dabbed her eyes with a cloth. Anna resumed her

news, "Anyway, Mary says people are praising the name of Jesus and *wonderful* things are happening." She knew the mention of Jesus would give her Kezia's full attention. Kezia's response was internal. She had used the name of Jesus when she laid the stones on her mother. She had prayed…and prayed til she ached, but still her mother died. A wave of heaviness swept over her and she felt as if she was drowning in thick mud.

"Why's Mary come home?" she asked for something to say.

"She's going to have meetings in her house." Anna's small eyes glinted at the idea of seeing inside Mary's prestigous home. "Meetings for *everyone* who remembers Jesus. But…" her voice lowered to a whisper, "she says there's a lot of trouble in Jerusalem. Temple guards spy on their meetings… trying to stir the people against them."

"Sounds dangerous." Kezia was alarmed.

"Oh no!" Anna was so confident she nearly smiled. "Mary says 'the Lord will protect them'." Out of the corner of her eye she saw a lizard scuttle up the wall and disappear out over the windowsill. Kezia turned over in her mind the disturbing fact that her father would soon be at the Temple. If James and John were arrested would they be brought before the Sanhedrin…? She scraped the onions into the cooking pot. She couldn't understand why it was so dangerous to remember Jesus.

"Will you come with us?" Anna quized Kezia.

"What? To Mary's house?" Kezia felt unsure. Her heart wanted to hear everything about Jesus but by doing so she would risk her father and her uncle's anger.

"She said the afternoon of Sabbath. Jared'll take us down by boat. T'is easier going down by boat than all round by road." Anna's stare bore into her as she waited for an answer.

"Zippie can stay with me," trilled Adah. She decided it would be good for Kezie to have more company than Anna, Miriam and that Debra. Kezia gave in to her heart.

"Yes," she nodded, "I'll come."

***

The blue dish Kezia had brought down from Sepphoris especially for her mother lay secretly hidden, wrapped in one of Leah's shawls in the cedar box underneath Kezia's wedding clothes and the kid pouch with the seven gemstones. Jared had smashed the blue dish Nico had given her, she wasn't going to let him find her mother's.

Mordecai and Jared sat at the table together while Kezia and Adah ate in the courtyard by the fire with Zippie. In his effort to make Jared feel at ease, the old Pharisee rolled out endless, inconsequencial anecdotes from his own, distant youth. Jared made no pretence to listen to the dry and dated tales. He picked at his bread and cheese and ignored the special sweetmeats.

Finally Mordecai drained his wine cup. He belched.

"You look tired, boy. You don't have to stay here with an old man." He wiped his fingers on a scrap of cloth. "I've seen Kezia go up to your room." He cocked his head with a knowing twinkle in his eye. Mordecai leaned on the table with an air of self-satisfaction. Jared was back. Kezia was in the bedroom. No more thoughts of divorce!

The bed where Jairus had slept was prepared for Jared. Kezia had perfumed the linen sheet with aloes and cassia and, as Anna had insisted, put a cup of milk and honey on the low stool by the pillow. A single oil lamp flickered on the shelf. As dusk fell outside and the room darkened, Kezia stood motionless by the window. She faced the door, her head held high despite the raging in her breast. She waited for the sound of Jared's sandals on the stone stairs.

The footsteps fell ponderous and irregular as they came towards the bedroom. Jared loomed in the doorway, breathing heavily. He leant against the lintel to accustom his eyes to the lamp-light. Several weeks had gone by since his attack on her, Kezia stared at the figure in the doorway with defiance. Never again would he leave her writhing in agony. As she watched him, her heart beat fast with the memory.

She had not seen him since that day. He looked gaunt and ill. The initial heat of her boiling hatred lowered to a simmering distain. She despised him. She met his uncertain stare with controlled indifference.

"Your bed is ready," Kezia said, a strange calm and strength filled her body and kept her voice even.

"My guts hurt!" Jared flung his shirt on the floor.

"Drink your milk," Kezia suggested. Already the smell of his rancid breath overpowered the sweet odours from the bed. Jared flopped down on the bed and rolled into a foetal position.

"Warm my back," he demanded in a sullen drawl. Kezia went to kneel by the bed so that her face became level with his. With a sudden movement, the weapon she had been concealing flashed in front of his face. Jared recoiled as if he'd been bitten by a snake.

"Give that to me, woman!" he cursed her as she beat his speed to put the knife beyond his reach.

"Not for you, Jared." Her voice intense and brittle, "It's for *me*!"

"What?" He leaned back on his arm, scowling in disbelief. He struggled to focus on the blurred outline of his wife. "What're you babbling about, woman? You're out of your mind." The blade glinted in the lamp-light.

"If I'm out of my mind, you're to blame. You *murdered* our son." Jared had no will to respond. Stunned by her outburst, he stared open-mouthed as she continued. "You've destroyed my life… for all I care your guts can rot in hell!" She took a deep breath. "But, hear this, Jared, son of Zebedee, I will cook and perform all my household duties as your wife, but I will never, never," she stood to tower above him, her voice rising in emphasis, "NEVER lie in your bed. I swear to you, this knife will kill me if you so much as *try* to touch me again."

Jared thrust his body forward raising his arm to strike her but he fell back in acute spasm. He rolled back on the bed, his face twisted in pain. "You make me sick," he moaned, "get out before I throw up!"

"If you've got the colic, I'll make some medicine." Kezia's voice was calm again.

"No." he groaned, "'t'will pass in a minute." Kezia watched him contort in pain. Medicine she would give, but no sympathy.

"Leave me be." He snarled wrenching the blanket up over his shoulders. He shut his eyes.

Kezia tip-toed away to her own room, her heart thumping. A mound in the middle of her bed indicated Zippie was fast asleep. Her hands shook as she undressed. She sank onto Adah's mattress so as not to disturb her sleeping sister. She lay waiting for Adah's slight body to creep in beside her. Kezia sighed with relief. She had expected a screaming row; imagined that Jared would try to beat her again, but she meant every word she said. She would die rather than be a wife to Jared.

Light as a feather, Adah came up the stairs and, without a sound, slipped down beside Kezia.

"What happened?" Adah asked, her body taut with anxiety. For over an hour they lay together, just as they had done as children, whispering and confiding in the darkness, drawing comfort from their mutual love and understanding.

"It was so strange," Kezia shared, "there was a moment… a moment when he seemed almost afraid of me."

"D'you think he'll agree?" Adah whispered, her voice dry at the thought, "You know… to let people think you're man and wife when you're… you know… when you're not." Adah found it all very complicated. Kezia looked up at the window. The bright star she loved had just come into view.

"Tonight he's not well," she replied.

"Miriam said he'd been ill," Adah confirmed.

"He's definitely not himself, but who knows how he'll react in the future? We'll just have to wait and see, won't we!" Adah stretched up and kissed Kezia's cheek. The door banged in the next room.

"That's Mordecai gone to bed," Adah hissed. "We'd better get some sleep."

Kezia propped her head so that she could watch the night sky. After a while, the bright star was swallowed up by thick, pale clouds. The more she gazed the lighter the clouds seemed against the inky patches of sky. Her mind went back to the times when Mordecai had taken her on to the roof and pointed out to her the millions of mysterious lights. She remembered how he had told her God created the stars and God knew all their names. The stars were hidden tonight.

'Why,' she wondered, 'why should stars have names? Were they the souls of the dead?' Lying under the sheet, lulled by Adah's rhythmic breathing, Kezia wondered if her mother 's soul was up there looking down on her...

Chapter 35

THE audience hung on Mary's every word. They all spied the distinctive edges of a prayer shawl visible beneath her elegant cloak. Word went round it was Jesus' prayer shawl which Mary had kept from that terrible night in Gethsemane when he was arrested. By all accounts, she wore the shawl at every one of her 'gatherings'. For Mary, the prayer shawl was not only a momento of love, but a tangible expression that her beloved Master had not left her. She still possessed something of his, which wrapped her in his presence.

"…My brothers and my sisters," Mary concluded, eyes shining with an aura of otherness, "Our Lord Jesus commands us to love one another. When we love one another we obey his teaching…teaching given to us *all*." She glanced around the crowded room, "And I can see people here… people in this room who can testify to his healing touch…" Kezia burned with recognition…yes, she was one of those people, Jesus had healed her.

"…And do you remember…?" Mary held her audience with direct eye contact, "when we sat on the hillside, t*housand*s of us… and Jesus blessed the bread and fish we shared together?" The people nodded misty eyed. "And I was there when he said, 'where two or three are gathered in my name, I will be with them'." She held out her hands in the manner of the Pharisees and Saducees when they bestowed a blessing, "This is the blessing of our Lord and Master Jesus – he *is* with us… *always!*"

***

"Nothing like a message from the Lord's closest followers." Zebedee waved his staff in the air to underline his point.

"Marvellous." Anna simpered holding tight to her brother's arm. She had heard so much about the wealthy Mary's home, and now, she had seen it for herself. Wall-hangings and velvet cushions, ivory inlaid tables, fine glass goblets… Anna was entranced. Salome walked behind with Kezia. Inspiring as the gathering had been, Salome's eyes betrayed the worry she felt for her older sons. Jared walked ahead, whistling, his cousin Debra skipping at his heels. Miriam dared not say a word in case she said something wrong. Kezia, like Salome, felt too emotional to speak. She longed to spend time with Mary on her own before the woman returned to Jerusalem.

Zebedee's boat was among a dozen drawn up on Magdala's beach. As the group approached the beach, Levi stood up, smiling. He held out a basket of sweetmeats and proudly offered the contents to his passengers before they boarded.

"You'd better take some," Jared told his mother. "He spends more time giving out sweetmeats than fishing!" He took two for himself and threw two to Debra; small squares in a delicious, light combination of honey, nuts and gum paste coated with sesame seeds. Kezia took two which she carefully wrapped in her handkerchief; one for Zippie and one for Adah.

"Jared's not well enough to row both ways on his own yet," Zebedee stated in his wife's direction. Jared's jaw jutted in sullen annoyance. Anna's sharp nose pointed towards Kezia in an over worn hint that Kezia should soon be pregnant. Jared was fed up with his aunt treating him like a performing pet. Too interfering by half.

Zebedee and the women boarded; Jared and Levi pushed the boat off the shingle. Once they had the boat well afloat, they too climbed on board.

As Levi pulled at the oars, Jared bit into his snack. He glared at his father's hired-hand, "Sweeter than usual," he conceded as he took his place at the second oars.

"That because it's Sabbath!" declared Debra trailing sticky fingers in the water. Kezia remained silent. Going to Mary's house had set her mind on fire. It had taken her back to the days when Jesus stayed at her father's house, of being in the crowds listening when Jesus told his stories. The atmosphere in Mary's house was reminiscent of how things used to be, full of the peoples' hope and good nature before that wicked crucifixion.

As they passed the low buildings sprawling along the waterfront, Kezia's attention was taken by a flock of egrets perched in the trees like a shower of white blossoms. By the time they reached Capernaum, reds and oranges marbled the sky above the Galilee hills. Kezia's gaze was drawn to the western horizon. Her thoughts flew to Sepphoris, to Joanna and Seth… and Nico. Was he watching the sunset too?

***

The following morning, when Kezia went to collect the cup from Jared's room, she found the milk and honey untouched. Nor had the bed been slept in. She carried the cup downstairs

316

as a treat for Zippie. After rowing back from Magdala, she thought it unlikely he had gone fishing. Her thoughts drifted… Perhaps he'd found another woman. Oh, she hoped so. With all her heart, she hoped so!

So far, Kezia's stipulated 'arrangement' was working. Food was always available for him, his bed was kept fresh, she washed and mended his clothes and, on occasion, cleared up his vomit.

For his part, Jared brought in fresh fish and put money on the table but at no time did he make any marital demands on his wife. After a meal he would slink up to his room and slam the door. More than once, Kezia and Adah had to stifle giggles as they waited for first Mordecai then Jared to bang their doors.

Mordecai found it hard to hold his tongue against Jared's repetitive moans about his guts. He thought it a most unsavoury subject for meal-times. Nevertheless, he endured the surly young man for Kezia's sake, just in case the sceptre of divorce was not entirely lifted.

Over the weeks, Kezia's daily routine managed to become almost Jared-free. He appeared at meal-times and that was it. Increasingly she grew in confidence as mistress in her own house, with the company of Adah and Zippie, Miriam and Ruth.

***

Zebedee squinted from his roof towards the harbour. Pride swelled his chest at the sight of his boat's tall mast, towering over his competitors. A grey mist shrouded the far hills and in the drizzle, the air hung heavy and humid. 'Good light for fishing!' Zebedee rubbed his hands and disappeared into the house. "Go and tell that son of mine he needs to take the boat out this morning," he barked at Miriam.

"I'll go," Debra butted in.

"Oh no you won't my lady!" Anna snapped. "You can stay here and clear the table." Debra flicked her hair and pouted. "And don't look like that… you'll never get a husband with that face!" Anna bustled off to fetch water from the spring. Zebedee wrapped an old sack round his shoulders, grabbed his staff and took himself down to the harbour. He no longer took the boats out himself, but nevertheless, he kept a close eye on all that his men were doing.

The fish shed was a hive of activity. Workers bent over the trays turning batch after batch of the salting fish, women mended baskets and children scurried on errands with rope, willow wands and buckets. Zebedee's hired men sheltered in the doorway mending nets. The old fisherman had the reputation of being a demanding but fair master, which, over the decades, had won him fear and respect in equal measure.

"When the boy comes down, take out the new one," he pointed to his large fishing boat as he spoke to Samuel, the senior of his hired-men. The lake lay flat as a mirror. "The four of you can manage in this calm." He leant a hand on the man's shoulder, "He's still not himself, but it'll do him good to get out on the water." Drizzle glistened on his weathered face, " I'll wager a good catch in this gloom."

Standing in the prow, Jared took a rough count of the other boats dotted across the lake. He could see over twenty, maybe there were more but, through the drizzle, he couldn't see the shoreline around Bethsaida nor over to the far side. Zebedee's boat, by far the biggest out fishing that morning, made stately progress into the middle of the lake, closing in on a patch of water where birds were already squawking and scooping their own catch.

"Cast out!" ordered Samuel. The large net went over the side. The men waited.

"Haul away!" he shouted as soon as he felt the top of the net tug against his hand. Each man hauled and slowly the net lifted into view, fish thrashing and suffocating as they heaved the bulging net into the boat. Levi brought up baskets for the sorting to begin.

The four men worked in silence. When the first catch had been separated and gutted, Samuel looked up;

"Take a break before the next net." He looked to Levi, "C'mon then. What've you got today?"

Levi bent to retrieve his bag from under the anchor ropes. With meticulous care he peeled back the cloth to reveal individual barley baps filled with shreds of spiced goat meat. He offered Jared the first bap.

Jared's nose crinkled in disgust, "Nah! I"m sick of your muck."

"I'll have it, then." Samuel reached out and snatched the bap before Jared could change his mind. Quick as lightning, Levi knocked it flying out of his hand.

" 'Ere, steady *on!*" Samuel protested. Sudden terror, shock and fury exploded in Jared's brain.

"*Bastard!*" he screamed at Levi. "You're bloody *poisoning* me!"

Uttering a blood-curdling howl, Jared hurled himself on the skinny foreigner, arms flailing at the man's chest. Jared tore at his tunic like a maniac. Slippery as an eel, Levi twisted and ducked out of the garment, doubled back under the boom and grabbed his gutting knife. They squared up to each other like two mad jackals, poised and ready to kill.

"Best get out the way," Samuel suggested to his mate, "T'is

not our quarrel." Both older men withdrew to the prow to busy themselves checking the net for the second casting. Secretly, they relished the thought of their master's boy taking a hammering.

"C'mon you little swine," Jared taunted, "I'll beat your guts to pulp!" Levi's smile turned to a menacing sneer of triumph.

"You kill…" he panted through gritted teeth, "my seester." He hyperventilated with the rush of adrenalin, "Now *you* die!" he yelled, launching himself at Jared. The two men crashed their bodies on the wood of the boat's stern as they lunged and sparred with each other, wrestling in a macabre dance. Levi's body, coated with oil, and, combined with the drizzle, was impossible for Jared to hold. Suddenly, he seized Levi's loin-cloth and rammed the smaller man up against the side of the boat. The veins on his forehead pulsated with the effort to force Levi high enough to push him over the side.

"Cast away!" called Samuel. The two men went about their business, their backs to the fight.

As Levi's body inched higher up the side of the boat so his knife flashed ever closer to Jared's neck. Their grunting and panting reached a violent climax as, with his last ounce of energy, and an inhuman roar, Jared exerted one final heave. At that moment Levi's knife ripped across Jared's artery and both men plunged over the stern into the smooth, grey-green water. Jared's blood spurted into the current, fanning out like plumes of scarlet smoke.

Jared's roar caused the two fishermen to turn round. They heard a great splash; they stood, hands on the rope, waiting to haul in the net…waiting to hear Jared and Levi thrashing in the water. But, after the roar and the splash…there was nothing. Only the creaking wood, the rhythmic knocking of the sail rings against the mast and muffled sounds from distant fishing boats to break the sinister silence.

Slowly the hired men registered the enormity of their predicament. Letting go of the net they rushed to the stern, scrouring the water for any sign of the two lads. The boat swayed and turned gently on the current. Gripped by a sickening horror, the hired men stared as gruesome streaks of crimson swirled into the drifting net.

Chapter 36

"MOURNERS are at it again," Adah set down the water pitcher. "Sounds like down by the harbour, who d'you think it can be?" Kezia sat at the loom, a clinging Zippie hovering at her side, shaking her rag doll up and down in time with the shuttle.

"Anna'll soon tell us," Kezia maintained her momentum. "Could be the old man who lives next to Zebedee's house," she surmised. Adah began to sweep the room. A mischievous grin erupted on her tanned face.

"One thing's for sure," she giggled, "it won't be Debra… we'll *never* get rid of Debra!" They both laughed and Zippie chuckled too. A shadow fell across Kezia's weaving. She looked up. Mordecai stood in the doorway. He was pale, drawn and unsteady. He walked solemnly to the table and sat down.

"Kezie, come and sit by me." Kezia jumped up from her work and went to the table.

"What is it, Uncle? Are you ill? What can I get you?" Adah stopped her sweeping and took herself and Zippie out into the courtyard. Mordecai took both Kezia's hands in his. 'It's old Zebedee,' she told herself.

"Kezie, my dear child… " he started but could not finish. He cleared his throat and began again, "Kezie… I'm afraid you are a widow." Kezia heard the news impassively. The words didn't register.

"What do you mean?" she whispered.

"Jared's been in a fight… one of Zebedee's hired men… on the boat… and… it seems both men went over the side." Kezia stared, fearing to trust such good news. "They were out in deep water…it's possible the bodies will never be found." Kezia turned from her uncle in case her face failed to register the required grief. She wanted to scream out the news to Adah, to swing Zippie high in the air, to laugh and cry with sheer relief… Jared was dead… out of her life…she was free.

"You must go to Zebedee's house…" Mordecai's words kept falling, like rain on a tin roof. "You must mourn with Salome. Adah will take care of the little one." Kezia's limbs moved automatically. Dare she believe what her uncle had said? In the cedar box which held all her possessions, she found the black shawl her mother used to cover her head and shoulders in times of mourning. She put it on in a deliberate manner, she realised she was entering a new dimension of womanhood. No longer Jared's wife, treated no better than a mule, but free to be herself. Slowly she walked towards the cacophony of sorrow, unaware that already she held herself taller.

***

"But can you be *sure* he's dead?" Adah fretted, "There'll be no funeral without a body." She stared anxiously into her broth.

"They were out in deep water, they may never be found." Kezia was matter of fact about it as she dipped her bread in Zippi's bowl and delivered the sop into the child's waiting mouth.

"But how will you live?" The startling news of two drowned men had Adah's mind in turmoil, yet her practical nature prevailed. "Your father's in Jerusalem and now you've no husband… what's to become of us?"

"It's alright, Adah," Kezia soothed, "whatever happens, we're *not* going to live under Zebedee's roof." With revived appetite, she helped herself to a chunk of goat's cheese. "I have a plan!" Her cheeks lifted with a hint of a smile.

**

Zebedee hid his grief in rage.

"The fool!" he fumed, "What was he thinking about fighting like that? A life thrown away, that's what it is… a life thrown away!" He beat his staff on the harbour wall until it cracked in two. "I told him his temper would get the better of him." His wet eyes blazed out across the water, "Never listened to his father, that was his trouble… Oi! How can I tell his mother?"

Samuel watched his master, unsure whether he should lead the old man home or carry on sorting the catch.

Salome locked her emotions deep in some internal box. Dry-eyed and silent, she sat furiously carding a fleece as the stream of neighbours and friends came to commiserate. There was no body – why should she believe her son was dead? She would not believe unless she saw his body. Miriam crumpled pitifully in a corner. She snivelled and bubbled her sorrow, overcome by the volume from the professional mourners. Anna cooked. Tight-lipped and drawn, she, like Salome, was not ready to contemplate Jared's death without a body.

Debra took herself out to scour the shoreline, determined to find Jared's body.

Apart from wearing black, widow's garments, and the

neighbours treating her with hushed pity, Kezia went about the daily chores in her normal routine.

Her uncle returned from the Synagogue at midday. As well as the usual bread and olives on the table, Kezia produced Mordecai's favourite pomegranates, and arranged them in her mother's blue dish.

Adah jumped at the urgent pounding on the door. "Anyone would think there was a fire!" she grumbled as she went to open it.

"Must see Mordecai!" Jairus' successor as Synagogue Ruler burst past Adah and came to the table, a small Scroll in his hand. He pushed the scroll towards the Pharisee, "Garrison Commander gave me this... he's back from Jerusalem... came to the Synagogue looking for you... said Jairus asked him to bring you this." He studied Mordecai's expression as the old man began to read.

"I didn't know what to do," the man said, "I couldn't face Zebedee with this." Mordecai's shoulders slumped. The Synagogue Ruler muttered, "I thought... you would um, ..t'would be best he heard it from you."

Mordecai rolled up the scroll, placed it on the table and closed his eyes. "Aaaah!" his anguished cry caused Zippie to run to Kezia. Kezia and Adah paled in anticipation. Mordecai pushed his plate away. "Oh, Great God of Israel..." he intoned lines from a Psalm, " 'I think of days gone by... and remember years of long ago.'"

"What is it, uncle?" Kezia was alarmed by her uncle's palor. Mordecai motioned the Synagogue Ruler to sit at the table. He sighed again, rolling his eyes in disbelief. He picked up the Scroll and read it again.

"Zebedee's first-born, James..." he said slowly, "in Jerusalem... King Herod's men... they've put him to death."

Kezia gasped. She clung to Zippie. It took a few moments before Mordecai found strength to continue.

"And Simon-Peter's in prison!"

"Oh poor Sarah!" Kezia blurted, imagining how distraught poor Sarah would be. Then stark realisation crept over her. In the days the Scroll had taken to be delivered, Simon-Peter might also be dead.

"What about John?" Kezia remembered Jared's other brother.

Mordecai shook his head, "Doesn't say."

He rose stiffly. "I must go to Zebedee. Two sons dead in two days… 'tis more than a man should have to bear." Lifting his prayer shawl over his head, he left the house with the Synagogue Ruler. They made their solemn way to take this greater grief into the fisherman's home.

"Oh, my son, my son…" wailed Zebedee. He tore off his head covering, ripped open his cloak in despair and sat, rocking to and fro, bent and shrivelled with grief. If John didn't return home, he would sell his boats to Samuel. The legacy of generations of his forefathers on the lake… his own lifetime's work… the only security for his old age…wiped out in two cataclismic days.

***

"What's your plan?" Adah was bursting to hear what Kezia had in mind. Kezia brought in the scented sheets from Jared's room to the mattresses where she and Adah slept. The room was in darkness and they could just see each other's shadows.

"We'll go to Sepphoris!" she announced. "We have to earn money, so we can work for Seth in his pottery… out selling or delivering." Adah's mouth opened. "And Joanna would *love* to have Zippie… we'll start a new life." She reached over to Adah, grasped her hand and squeezed it.

"D'you mean…" Adah began, her eyes misting with excitement, "d'you mean you'd take me with you?"

"Of course," Kezia reassured, "my home is your home, Adah, and where I go I want you to come with me." Through a burst of joy the little servant-girl had a sudden thought:

"What about Mordecai?

"Well," Kezia reasoned, "Father's not coming home again so why can't he rent this house to the new Synagogue Ruler and his wife?" she thought a moment. "And they might as well take on Miriam as their servant, she knows where things are here."

"You make it sound easy," Adah sighed. "You sure we can do it?"

Kezia lay back on her mattress. She stared at the ceiling. She linked her fingers behind her head, "I know one thing," she murmured. "I can't stay here."

***

Next morning:

She blinked into the distance, but the southern end of the Sea of Galilee remained shrouded in pre-dawn mist. Debra had walked north of Capernaum, almost as far as the next fishing village of Bethsaida, combing the shallows and reed-beds for any evidence of her cousin. Gripped by a compulsion to find him Debra cultivated a spurious grief, desperate to heighten the drama with a body. Egrets launched themselves from their overnight perches, silently circling above the land, awaiting the first rays of sun. Bull bulls chattered in the tamarisk

327

branches and a pair of kingfishers dived repeatedly into the water a few yards off shore.

A sudden thrashing in the shallows made her jump. She turned in alarm, but it was only the mating gyrations of two gargantuan cat-fish.

Debra's eyes penetrated beneath each over-hanging tamarisk tree, behind each boulder and the mouth of every spring. She hummed as she searched, a tuneful, ancient melody, one that generations of women sang on the threshing floor.

Her sudden scream echoed across the water and up the valley slopes. An ear-splitting scream for attention rather than fear or shock. Caught in the reeds, she glimpsed the back of Jared's head and shoulders. Rushing forward, before anyone came down to see what was happening, she marvelled at his swollen, discoloured body. Bare-foot, she clambered to get a close view of his face. The sight would have revolted anyone else, but Debra's insatiable curiosity devoured every fetid nuance of the corpse. Flies buzzed in and out of his facial caveties. A terrible jagged wound gaped open in his neck. The gash had been widened by fish tearing out shreds of flesh so that part of his jaw-bone lay exposed to the air.

She screamed again in case she hadn't been heard the first time. A putrid stench rose from the reeds. She had found him! She would be the talk of Capernaum. As the first fingers of dawn spun pink clouds across the milky sky, the distant town of Tiberias clarified out of the haze. Debra positioned herself on a boulder facing the body and prepared to be indulged and comforted.

328

Chapter 37

"THIS sounds a hasty decision to me." Mordecai had grave suspicions of Kezia's motives.

"But Uncle, I've got to *live*. There's five in Zebedee's household and no working man... I've no man to support me now, and, don't you see, I know where I can earn a wage for myself...be independent... give Zippie a good life..."

"Hold on, hold on!" Mordecai raised his hand. "Not so fast." He traced his finger round the rim of his wine cup as he considered. "It's a valid argument, I'll grant you that. But," he stared at her sternly, "I'll agree to it on one condition and one condition only." Hope rose in Kezia's heart as she held her breath for her uncle to continue.

"I will accompany you to Sepphoris to make sure Seth and Joanna are prepared to accept this... this arrangement." His tone deepened, "But, Kezia, if I find that the Roman is lurking around the pottery... you will come straight home with me and I will never allow you outside Capernaum again. Is that clear?" Her hesitation confirmed his fears. "I repeat... is that clear?"

"That is clear," she lowered her gaze. Mordecai was unconvinced.

"Listen, child," his patience ran thin, "if you create a scandal, if you form a liaison with a Roman then... Oh Kezie!

You must understand you'll not be welcome in your father's house. Do you hear me? Your father will disown you... *I* will disown you..."

"I'm a widow," Kezia repeated wearily. " My husband's body lies buried on the hillside, my mother is buried, and my father's gone to Jerusalem." She spoke calmly. "Can't you see, Uncle, I need this chance to make a life for myself. I've lived in Sepphoris, it's a good city and, with Seth and Joanna's help, I know I can make a living for the three of us."

"You agree to my condition?"

"Yes. I agree."

"Very well," he sighed. "As you wish. I'll need to find out who's going that way... someone with a wagon to take your belongings." He rose unsmiling, and left the room to climb the stairs to the sanctuary of the roof. As his robes brushed past her, he spoke with his eyes fixed on the doorway, "I fear you are being very selfish, Kezia. Selfish and foolish. Try to think about your mother-in-law. She needs you."

***

Each evening on Mordecai's return from the Synagogue, Kezia's hopes flew sky-high waiting for news of a wagon and a leaving date. Each evening the subject was ignored. By the end of a month, she suspected it was her uncle's ploy to keep her in Capernaum. Kezia had already used one of the coins from her dowry to buy food and a coat for Zippie. She didn't want to use any more of the precious coins.

"We can't wait any longer," her frustration boiled over as she and Adah shook and folded a pile of dry clothes. "I'd rather go with what we can carry and come back later with

Josh and the donkey for the rest." Adah couldn't see how they'd ever be able to leave.

"Tonight," Kezia promised, "I'll tell him tonight. I won't spend another Sabbath here!"

"You won't have to!" startled by the man's voice, Kezia turned to see Nathan the tanner.

"Your uncle sent me to look at your trunk and anything else you want to put on my wagon."

"Are you going to Sepphoris?" Kezia asked, bright with anticipation.

"Sepphoris .. then on to Akko," the genial tanner replied. "Maybe take a ship on from there to Corinth. Donnow yet. Anyways," he grinned, "wife an' me's off in the morning."

***

The ox and wagon stood outside Jairus' house as Nathan went in to collect Kezia's cedar box of possessions. Adah stared at the wagon. Her heart sank. There didn't appear to be any spare space at all, let alone room for the cedar box. Nathan's wife patiently held the ox's rein. She smiled at Zippie who strained to reach up to stroke the animal. The tanner expertly inserted Kezia's box underneath a pile of hides.

"That it, then?" he asked cheerily. Mordecai nodded, looking sombre. Kezia and Adah, laden with as much as they could carry, walked behind the wagon, Zippie skipping between them.

The previous eighteen hours had thrown Kezia into a whirlwind of activity. Her final visit to Salome had been awkward but mercifully brief. Zebedee was out, Miriam looked wistful and seemed reluctant to open her mouth in front of her mother. Anna made her disapproval at Kezia's

331

departure perfectly plain. Her sharp, bird-like eyes flitted up and down the young widow as though she was contemplating a mouldy dish that had to be thrown away. Debra perched on a stool devouring figs.

"You should've seen his face…" Debra's eyes widened for impact.

"That's *enough*!" her mother snapped. Debra, nose in the air, looked in every direction bar Kezia's.

"That girl's not normal," Adah shook her head when Kezia recounted the visit. "Good thing Zippie's getting away from her."

The ox lumbered along the street towards Capernaum's main square. Kezia stole a look at Adah; hardly able to contain her excitement she mouthed, "We're on our way!"

By the time they reached Magdala, the convoy had grown to around thirty people, various carts and wagons, donkeys and a small flock of goats. They climbed the road up through the Valley of the Doves at a tortuously slow pace.

"If we go any slower," Kezia hissed to Adah, "we'll be going *backwards*," Mordecai on the other hand found the pace admirably suited his age and gait. Kezia, unused to carrying such loads, battled with aching arms and heavy legs while Zippie, who had been perched on top of the wagon, chortled happily. Nathan's wife was a woman of few words but kind eyes. At each stop, she saw to it that 'her' young girls had food and drink and made sure they refilled their water bottles upstream away from where animals had polluted it. They gathered grasses to sleep on and, when nightfall came, she huddled with them in the lea of the wagon. Under the endless canopy of the night sky, their woollen cloaks doubled as welcome blankets.

Kezia, who had not bargained for an overnight stop, woke

to the dawn feeling stiff and unkempt. As she helped Zippie feed hay to the ox, and the camp gradually came to life in the morning warmth, even the air she took deeply into her lungs smelled fresh and new.

Just a few more hours and they would arrive in the city of Sepphoris.

***

The towering city walls shimmered in the midday heat like cubes of chrystalised apricot, curds and honey. Kezia's aches miraculously disappeared and her lips broke in a broad smile as the caravan from Capernaum laboured the last couple of miles along the stone roadway into the city. Butterflies chased excitement and apprehension around Adah's stomach. It all looked so big – so different from Capernaum.

Once inside the Nazareth Gate, the caravan dispersed and, with Zippie clinging tightly to her hand, Kezia led Nathan's group to the house of Seth the potter. Adah admired the way Kezia strode through the wide street, unperturbed by the bustle and milling throng of strangers. The buildings were so new and so high, and the pavements were huge slabs of the most beautiful coloured stone. Adah gazed about her, elated and awed by every new sight.

Outside the pottery courtyard, Nathan unloaded the cedar box and Mordecai paid him for his help. The women exchanged cordial farewells and the ox wagon rolled on its way. Adah helped Kezia carry the box into the pottery.

The courtyard had changed – shrunk. Nico had told her about the kilns but she had not expected them to be so tall and wide. They abutted the pottery like two enormous termite mounds. The familiar table alongside the house was still there, packed with items for sale to passing customers, while several precarious piles of pottery stood stacked at the pottery door, waiting either collection or delivery. The donkey's pen at the far end was empty. Kezia called out to Joanna.

Meanwhile, Mordecai walked straight into the pottery. He intended to inspect Seth's workers for himself before they could conspire to avoid him.

"Why! Mordecai, sir!" Seth continued at his wheel. "To what do we owe this great honour?" Mordecai inclined his head in greeting while he took in the two men working with Seth. The old Pharisee had little time for the flambouyant potter with his ridiculous purple turban, but he was amazed at the expansion Seth had accomplished since his previous visit. Another potter sat beside Seth, while a tall young man busied himself emptying a kiln and bringing fired pots to the trestle at the end of the shop.

"I've brought Kezia back to Sepphoris." He spoke with pharisaic dignity.

"Bravo! Splendid news, couldn't have chosen a better time, the more help the merrier!" Seth exuded genuine delight as he skilfully completed a water jug on the wheel.

Mordecai explained Kezia's widowhood and need for employment. He scrutinised Ben and the new potter. He satisfied himself that they, at least, were true sons of Israel.

"My dearest Kezie," Joanna crooned as Kezia found herself engulfed by her aunt's embrace. "Oh, how we've missed you, chicken." When at last she stood to look at her neice, "Well now, you're a different woman than when I last saw you. Good to see some colour coming back to that lovely face of yours." Without Mordecai present, Kezia grasped her opportunity and breathlessly told her aunt how Mordecai was going to take her back to Capernaum if he found Nico.

"No fear of that," Joanna swung Zippie into her arms, "Nico's gone."

Not until that point had Kezia fully realised how desperately she had been looking forward to seeing the gentle artist again. Joanna caught the deflated expression, "Gone to Caesarea. So," her infectious smile lifting the situation, "don't you worry. You'll be staying." With Zippie in one arm she encircled Adah with her free arm, "And you, missy, I can't tell you what a help you're going to be here." Adah's fears subsided. She blossomed under Joanna's warmth like a flower opening to the sun. Kezia juggled her emotions from thwarted dreams to sheer relief – her uncle would have no reason to take her back.

"Now, let's make a start." Joanna returned Zippie to the ground, "I must get a bowl and towel ready to wash Mordecai's feet when he comes across. "And you'd best bring in that great box of yours. If it stays in the yard, Seth'll sell it!"

"Where's Little Josh?" Kezia enquired as she looked in the bread basket.

"He's taken the cart…yes, we've got a cart now! Josh and Ben's mother have gone down by the stream to pick up a load more clay. The boy's a good little worker." Joanna's mind calculated their extra needs for a meal. "Look, chicken," she put some coins in Kezia's hand, "take missy here and go and buy more bread, and… well, whatever vegetables are still fresh."

Kezia and Adah bounced out of the pottery like children off to a celebration.

"*Buy* bread!" an incredulous Adah trilled, open-mouthed.

Kezia grinned, "Yes! *Buy* bread. All different kinds… you'll love it!" she laughed.

***

As he had done on his previous visit, Mordecai arranged to stay at the Synagogue. Seth's house had no adequate room for a senior Pharisee, nor did it have a ritual bath. Since the new potter's wheel had been installed, space in the pottery had become too cramped for Kezia, Adah and Zippie to put down mattresses.

"All things are possible!" Seth quipped. "If we can't build *out,*" his arms splayed in demonstration, "then we can build *up.* I promise, Kezia my dear, as soon as Ben and I return from the north, we'll build a little room for the three of you on the roof."

"For a few nights," Joanna reasurred, "we'll make you comfortable in here... over by the window, and," she mouthed her words in an audible whisper for Seth's ears, "when Seth's out of the way you can all share with me!"

After their meal, Seth walked Mordecai through the wide, stone-paved streets to the newly-completed Synagogue.

"I understand you have an artist working here." The old Pharisee came straight to the point.

"Oh, him," breezed Seth, "yes, this blue glaze was his idea. Good man!" Seth strode along with a nonchalent air, aware of the old man's probing. "I can't keep up with demand now! But," he inclined his head in greeting as the chief collector of taxes passed them, "...he left a while ago... he was only part-time with me. His work was mainly designing mosaics for the grand houses. Afraid he's gone back to Caesarea." Mordecai had to be sure in his own mind that Kezia was safe to leave.

"When do you expect him back?" he enquired. Seth waved across the street to another customer.

"He didn't say anything about coming back," replied the potter, "you see, he didn't come from these parts. Think he said his father's a baker…near Rome." Amused at the distaste on Mordecai's face. Seth added, "Those Greeks and Romans, you know," he teased, playing to Mordecai's mistrust of foreigners, "…even the Egyptians, they're all *very* artistic."

Chapter 38

KEZIA watched her uncle walk out through the Nazareth Gate. This time there had been no emotional parting. Any sadness she expected to feel was eclipsed by rising resentment. She felt hurt that her uncle had been more concerned with family honour than her happiness. She resented being escorted back to Sepphoris like an untrustworthy servant. Also, she knew that if Nico had put a foot inside the pottery, then Mordecai would have forced her back to Capernaum and doomed her to a hateful existence in Zebedee's household.

Holding tight to Zippie's hand, Kezia heaved a great sigh of relief as the group of Pharisees and scribes headed down the road, away from the city. Her uncle was gone.

Leading Zippie down the central street, they made for the market stalls. Joanna needed cheese, olives, eggs and bread, while she and Adah had gone to gather fuel for the voracious kilns.

"*Nook!*" Zippie squealed in delight and pointed. Kezia looked to where the child was pointing. A beggar squatted by an archway, a vivid green parrot tied to his shoulder. Zippie skipped up and down, urging and tugging her sister towards the parrot.

"No, this way Zippie, we must do shopping first," Kezia resisted, "we'll see bird on our way back."

True to her word, and laden with Joanna's groceries, Kezia took Zippie to see the exotic bird, as fascinated by it's garish plumage as Zippie. She stooped to slip some goat's cheese into the beggar's bowl when suddenly a hand grabbed her arm from behind.

"*You*!" a woman croacked, "You've come back then!" Kezia spun round, starled, confronted by the old woman who had first accosted her as a healer. The woman broke into a toothless smile, her massive earrings jangling as she spoke. "I knew you'd come back, my lovely. Knew it! There's need for the likes of you." Kezia's heart pounded but before she could reply the old woman melted into the crowd and was gone.

"Come on, Zippie," she said, her mind whirling, "Joanna'll be waiting for us." The beggar inclined his head in sightless acknowledgement of the cheese. The green parrot leaned forward from the man's shoulder, expecting more treats.

"Birdie! Birdie!" Zippie chanted merrily as Kezia led her by the hand back along the broad cardo, past the Nazareth Gate and back to the pottery. Thoughts raced through her mind... the stones hadn't worked for her mother and she hadn't looked at them since. She was in no hurry to use them again, but...if Jesus wanted her to use his stones again then, so be it. And now, the realisation dawned, there was no Jared to forbid her!

***

Seth glanced up from his wheel. One of the scribes from the Synagogue lurked hesitantly in the doorway.

"Welcome, my friend," Seth hailed the man, familiar by sight but not by name. "Is it plates you're wanting, or cups? Lamps? Take a look along the shelves." The potter concentrated on the bowl spinning into shape. "We deliver heavy orders… Seth the potter is always willing to strike a bargain… for himself, of course!" Seth never missed an opportunity to banter salesman's chatter with a potential customer.

The scribe took a cautious step inside. He inspected the shelves. The stacked wares were interesting, if only for their quantity, but he had not come to buy. Seth slid the completed bowl from the wheel to give his full attention to the visitor.

"All this array and nothing to tempt you?" Seth raised a quizzical eyebrow. He'd seen the stern-faced scribe fluttering around the Synagogue on the odd occasion when he attended. He guessed the man to be about his own age, or older, stocky and very dark.

"My name's Eli," declared the scribe avoiding Seth's eyes. "We had your kinsman, Mordecai the Pharisee stay with us in the Synagogue…" he droned.

"Oh yes. Yes," Seth replied in a light, friendly manner while he waited to know why the scribe was in his pottery. Eli looked around, to the ceiling then back to the open door. Satisfied they were alone he leaned awkwardly against the table.

"Mordecai told me about the young widow-woman staying here ." His voice though educated, piped in a thin, flat line.

"That's right," Seth answered. "She's my wife's neice… all very tragic and er… yes, all very tragic." Some sixth sense warned Seth to be on his guard.

"And is she…" Eli, unused to discussing such things, wrestled with his words before they came out, "does she cook well and… keep herself… clean?" He studied his fingernails.

"Second only to my dear wife. I can vouch for her winsome nature and diligence." Eli shuffled his sandals and adjusted his robe.

"Afraid I've spent too many years in study." Eli's eyes narrowed and his mouth did the same. "I've… there's never, I mean… I've not got around to the question of marriage." He gave a short, self-depricating titter. "And then, suddenly one looks around and things like that have passed one by." Seth waited for the scribe to continue. Eli stood away from the table and pushed his shoulders back in an effort to look tall. He failed. "So, I've decided," he said earnestly, "I'm prepared to take this widow for my wife. You can arrange that, can't you?" At last he looked directly at the potter. Seth was more than a little taken aback.

"But, you've not seen her!" he protested. Eli studied a large, blue dish.

"Oh, from what I've been told, that's not necessary. She will suit me. Mordecai told me her father is a member of the Sanhedrin," he paused, "and so is mine."

Seth frowned, "She cares for her young sister…" he informed the scribe.

"Oh, I won't take the child!" Eli's voice found strength and his eyes widened. He was adamant. "No, I'll take the widow, but I don't want the child." The thought flashed into Seth's mind that Eli's slightly bulging eyes, dark skin and stubby beard resembled the face of a mongoose. Seth smiled.

"Eli, my dear man. I find myself in a *bit* of a delicate situation here. You see, it's not *my* place to give permission for this union. You'll need to ask the young woman's father." By the look on his face, Seth could see Eli the scribe was not used to being denied. "You know how it is…" Seth laughed, "you need to sort out a bride price, and…"

"She's a widow!" Eli snapped. "She should be grateful someone like me is willing to offer her a home," Eli looked churlish.

"Oh, yes, yes, of course," Seth tried to smooth the scribe's prickly dignity, "and I'm sure her father, Jairus, will be *very* grateful...and er... and generous." Seth wiped his hands on the damp rag beside his cushion. "You must eat with us before you make the journey to Jerusalem."

Eli hesitated. Seth coaxed in his amiable way; "Then you will be able to view the widow and sample her cooking!" Eli's eyes wandered as he considered the potter's invitation. Eventually, he nodded in agreement. "Yes, that would seem a sensible idea," he conceded. "And what about a jug? A lamp?" Seth did his best for a sale, but Eli refused to bite.

"I'd be delighted to receive some pieces as a wedding gift," he replied. With a parting smirk, the mongoose slipped out into the courtyard and scuttled away to his Synagogue. Seth got up and stood at the pottery door soaking up the sun. He needed time to think before he discussed Eli's intentions with Joanna. He pulled his nose between thumb and forefinger as if it aided clear thought. Mordecai! The sly old 'fixer'! Seth shook his head. He calculated the scribe would take several days before he would be ready to travel to Jerusalem. 'Jairus would be relieved,' he thought, 'to know Kezia had the chance of another husband.'

But Kezia... hmm! What would she say? The potter pulled a face... she had to realise there was no prospect of a decent life as a widow... and Eli the scribe was a respectable man, willing and able to provide her a home and security. Their children would have education and advantage. It was, Seth assured himself at last, for a young widow in Kezia's position, an ideal solution. Perhaps the only solution.

***

"When're we going up north?" Little Josh whined as he unloaded fuel from the donkey's pannier. Ben took the baskets from him to sort the wood and dung between the cooking fire and the kiln.

"Don't think we'll be going for a while yet, Josh, " said Ben. He wasn't going into details to Josh of how Seth was too busy making provision for Kezia, Adah and Zippie. With that and their increasing orders, he couldn't see that they would ever get away. Business was booming for Seth and, even with the extra potter working alongside, it took them all their time to keep up with customer demands.

Little Josh stretched a disappointed "Oh!" over five swooping syllables.

"Don't you worry," Ben grinned, "we won't go anywhere without you." The boy stroked his donkey's muzzle with a resigned pout.

"Where's your master?" A tall, well-dressed servant ran into the courtyard in high agitation.

"Can't say as I know," Ben gave his honest reply. "What's it you wanted?"

"The magistrate sent me… he wants the healer-woman." The servant stood looking fraught, "D'you know where I can find her?"

"Inside!" Little Josh informed him, pointing to the house. The servant ran to the door and beat insistent raps until Joanna lifted the latch and swung into view.

"Are you the healer?" the man asked, "Please, come with me…" Joanna stood her ground,

"What do you want with a healer?" she asked.

"I come from the magistrate… he's desperate… his wife's dreadful ill and his butler told him about you." Joanna thawed.

"I'm not a healer," she said, "but you've come to the right house. She's here."

"Please, lady, get her to come to my master's wife?" the servant pleaded.

"Wait a moment and we'll both come with you." Joanna closed the door on the servant and turned to Kezia who was in the corner, dressing Zippie.

"Well," Joanna gave a rueful smile, "seems they haven't forgotten you, chicken!"

"The magistrate," gulped Adah, tying the strings on Zippie's tunic in a bow. "Is that the great mansion in the market place?" To Adah, the cream-stoned mansion with its elegant porticos, appeared so vast she would have been afraid of getting lost in some interior labarynth. Kezia felt the warmth of affirmation. Could this be a sign that she was meant to use the stones again? She went up to the roof, to where Seth had erected a temporary tent for what he called his 'sweet refugees'. Kezia extracted the kid pouch from beneath her mother's shawl in her box of possessions. Joanna unhooked her cloak from the door.

"Seth should be back any time now," she said to Adah, "just explain to him what's happened and say we'll be back as soon as we can. You've got Ben here so you'll be alright, won't you." She gave Ada a fond, swift hug, "How wonderful... I can leave everything in your care!" Adah beamed at Joanna, she felt she must be the most fortunate slave-girl in the world.

An imperious guard stood on the steps leading to the magistrate's mansion. The servant hustled Kezia and Joanna through the great double doors and handed them to the sick woman's maid servant. The woman took them up a wide flight of marble stairs and into a room with the highest ceiling Kezia had seen. The magistrate's wife lay on a couch by the open window, another servant stood fanning her mistress with an ostritch feather fan. The senior woman servant addressed Kezia.

"She's been in a coma two days. The Master says if you restore her health he will give you whatever fee you charge." Kezia moved to the bed.

"I make no charge," she said quietly as she opened the pouch and took out the seven stones. Joanna positioned herself out of the way by the door and watched as Kezia placed the stones on the inert woman's throat, chest and stomach. Kezia's hands splayed inches above the beautiful silk bed-gown, her lips moving in silent prayer. Then she made mysterious wiping and wringing movements as though she was getting rid of some unpleasant, invisible material. Joanna sat riveted.

After what she exaggerated to be 'hours' and her back ached with the concentration on her niece's strange activity, Kezia finally leaned against the window ledge.

"Your mistress needs a little warm milk and honey," she whispered. Instantly the woman servant left the room. Kezia knelt by the bed and took the magistrate's wife's slender, manicured hand in hers. General noise from the market place drifted in through the window. The servant returned with a cup of milk and honey. Between them, they raised the magistrate's wife's head and poured a spoonful of the liquid between her lips. Kezia, looking at the luxurious bedding, didn't see the woman open her eyes. The servant darted forward to offer more of the warm drink. The woman wearily closed her eyes again.

"… the floor…" the magistrate's wife moaned in delirium, "on the floor…"

"Quick!" shouted the senior servant to the servant with

the fan, "Go get the Master!" She wiped her mistress' face with a cloth, "There, there," she crooned, "you're safe in your bed, we wouldn't let you fall on the floor."

Kezia returned the stones to the pouch and she and Joanna faded from the room before the magistrate appeared to find his wife restored from her coma and the natural colour returning to her cheeks.

"You've a rare gift, Kezie," Joanna found herself in awe of what she had witnessed. The two women hurried back to the pottery.

"Not me, Joanna," Kezia replied, " I can't explain it… it doesn't always work. I don't understand it, but it's Jesus who heals."

They entered the pottery courtyard to see Adah ladling steaming stew into large bowls for Joanna's hungry men.

"All well?" Seth looked at his wife.

Joanna nodded, "All well!" she smiled. Her smile masked her inner misgivings. Did the healing power belong to Kezia or did it originate from Jesus? Joanna had no difficulty to accept there were powers beyond human logic and understanding, but she was very wary of using the name of Jesus in public. The memory of their flight from Jerusalem still caused her nightmares, yet she vividly remembered occasions when she had heard Jesus teaching. He gave a new slant to everything – to prayer, love, guilt, sickness… She hung her cloak back behind the door. Joanna's mind worked with the ferociousity of a termite nest yet she was no nearer to finding any answers.

Chapter 39

THE table groaned beneath a veritable feast. Half a calf had been turning on the spit for hours, fruits spilled from a bowl, eggs, herbs, nuts and sweetmeats sat appetisingly in their dishes and Seth had bought the best wine from Mount Carmel. However, Eli was hard company. Even the ebullient Seth could not rescue the conversation from dipping into pools of icy silence. Not that Eli was bad company, he was just too aesthete and scholarly for the relaxed banter of working men. As Kezia served the dishes, Eli's gaze followed her every move. He did nothing to hide the fact he found her completely and utterly captivating.

Every time she looked at him, he averted his eyes, a habit Kezia found vaguely amusing. Formality seemed to be his natural zone and she could detect Little Josh was living in fear of an unscheduled tutorial. Joanna's generous verdict on the guest came in two words: 'painfully shy!'

With sufficient wine drunk to loosen his reserve, Eli announced to Seth, "I leave for Jerusalem in the morning. It's four years since I was in the Holy City for Passover." His eyes followed Kezia as her long dress rustled around the table, collecting plates, refilling the wine jar, moving gracefully in and out of the room. He sat sweating at the proximity of such young, flawless skin.

"Perhaps we can arrange the wedding for… shall we say… by Shavuot?" His eyes bulged in anticipation as he looked to Seth to confirm the proposition.

When, at long last, Seth escorted Eli to the courtyard gate, Kezia helped Joanna clear away the food remnants and utensils.

"Who's Eli the scribe going to marry?" Kezia posed the question in all innocence.

Joanna squared her shoulders, "I think it's time we had a talk, chicken," she said. "You'd better come up to my room."

***

The room swam before Kezia's eyes. She bowed her head as the brutal truth sank deep into her soul. Joanna tried to be gentle with her but the harsh reality of her plight was inescapable. She'd never had reason to consider the plight of widows… but now she belonged in that pitiful category of has-beens. Jared was dead. She was a widow. Work in the pottery was alright for a few years but what then? There was no arguing with Joanna's slow unravelling of the situation. It was true. Fact. Seth and Joanna would not be able to care for her for ever. She needed a husband to protect and support her and children to take care of her in age and or infirmity. Without either she was destined to become a mere household appendage, another Anna in Zippie's home, never truly belonging with no child of her own blood. Her prospects were bleak.

From her bloom of youth and vigour, Kezia found it impossible to project into the future and think of herself decrepit and old. Yet, she couldn't argue, she knew Joanna was right. If she was offered another chance of marriage she should accept gratefully, she may not get another.

"And you know I'll take care of Zippie for you," Joanna contined, "she may be your sister, but she's also my dear sister's child. We both feel responsible for her." She knelt in front of her niece, putting a hand to her cheek, "It's not unnatural that Eli won't take on another man's child…"

"I'm going to miss you all… " Kezia sniffed.

"Well, dear me!" Joanna rolled her eyes in mock exasperation. "Anyone would think he's carting you off to Babylon! Eli's house is no more than *ten* minutes walk away… we'll still see lots of each other." Joanna struck a positive tone. "Now look, he's quiet and…" she resisted the word 'dull', "and… dutiful, and… oh, it'll be alright, you'll see."

"That's what you said last time," Kezia reminded her. Joanna bit her bottom lip. Finally she stood up pulling Kezia to her feet as well.

"Frankly, chicken, you have no choice. But, if it helps, the way Eli was looking at you tonight means he'll treat you very different to Jared. And," she laughed, "you lucky girl, you won't have to put up with any critical Anna or dreadful Debra! I happen to know his mother died years ago and his father's a member of the Sanhedrin in Jerusalem."

"With Father?" Kezia's face lifted.

"Yes." Joanna drew Kezia to her in her warm embrace. "Do you still think of Nico?" she whispered. Kezia stalled for a moment then nodded. Joanna's bosom heaved with regret.

"Do you know what would happen if you married Nico?" she left no pause for Kezia's response, "Your father and uncle would disown you for marrying a Roman, and you'd never be able to go back to Capernaum. You'd have to go far away… find a town where that sort of thing is not so frowned upon. And your sons would be Roman citizens… think of that…

uncircumcised…" Kezia had no reply. Joanna continued, "Anyway, Nico's gone from our lives." They heard Seth in the room below them. Kezia wiped her eyes. Joanna studied her face intently before saying:

"Oh, Kezie, you don't have to tell me… I know who you want. But nobody can take away your dreams, and… believe me, we *all* have our dreams…" she held Kezia close again, "we just have to keep them to ourselves. "

***

The tang of seaweed carried on a fresh breeze and Nico could taste salt on his lips. Ships choked Caesarea's port. Galleons lined along one side of the harbour with slaves swarming up and down the gangways like ants, unloading cargoes of volcanic ash, fruit syrups and garments from Italy. Loutish troops waited to board, impatient to return home, swearing at the slaves to get a move on. Nico stood on the deck of one of the dozen or so Liburnias, moored in front of the towering warehouses. The oarsmen were in place and the captain ready to move out of port before the wind and tide changed, but he had to wait on several ships and fishing boats which were scheduled to leave first.

Nico stared back towards the city. The Governor, Pontius Pilate, boasted Caesarea was now twice the size of Jerusalem. To the artist's eye it was massive. Ultra modern with its municipal buildings of limestone and marble, beautiful with its mosaic sidewalks, columbs of marble and pink granite, and scores of larger than life, grandiose statues. A city full of interest but Nico hadn't settled to life in Ceasarea. He decided to return home to Rome.

Since leaving Sepphoris, he had stayed with his brother,

350

Cornelius and his family in the Garrison. Cornelius had done his level best to persuade him to stay in Caesarea,

"You don't want to go back to Rome," he'd said, "there's more than enough work here in Caesarea for two lifetimes." Cornelius begged him to reconsider, but Nico had no heart to remain in this foreign country… he had to get away… to forget the woman in the dusky pink coat.

Cornelius wasn't due to return to Rome for another four years but he seemed surprisingly content to stay in Palestine. The whole household had embraced a new religion which brought them together to sing and pray each evening. Nico was puzzled by their eccentric behaviour. He wasn't really interested in hearing his brother's testimony to his new-found faith. Surely, he thought, there were plenty of gods his brother could have chosen before adopting a new one.

The Liburnia beside him slowly moved to the mouth of the harbour. The double row of oarsmen heaved the ship's bulk towards the open water of the Great Sea. Nico took a swig from his leather water bottle. He looked to the gangway – cargo was still being brought on board. Shouting and swearing escalated from men impatient to depart. A crate of live chickens landed cackling in terror at his feet. The breeze took on the chill of late afternoon. The captain bawled for the anchor to be lifted. Nico picked up his bag and strode down the ship.

***

Joanna looked up from the fire. She recognised the tall figure of the magistrate's servant. Her heart missed a beat – was the woman dead? She willed the servant to go into the pottery to speak first with her husband, but instead, he made straight for Joanna.

"My Mistress wants to see the healer-woman," he said, shoulders erect.

"Is your Mistress recovered?" Joanna ventured to ask. The servant's expression told her all she wanted to know.

"It is a miracle," he beamed. "My Mistress is well." He looked towards the house, "Is she here?"

"You'll find her in the pottery," Joanna nodded her head at the door opposite. The servant turned on his heel and disappeared across the courtyard.

Joanna felt confident Kezia could accompany the magistrate's servant safely on her own. Kezia fell into step behind the servant whose enormous strides made it necessary for her to break into frequent trots in order to keep up. As she mounted the wide steps to the double doors of the magistrate's house, she regretted not putting on her best coat. The marble floors, resplendent wall-hangs and the ceiling frescos over-awed the widow from Capernaum.

They stopped outside the imposing double doors leading to the dining hall. The servant knocked with his staff.

"Come!" the woman's educated voice rang with authority. Kezia followed the servant into the dining hall and stood mute, dwarfed by the high doors, self-consciously waiting for a further summons. A slim, elegant woman, of the same age as Leah had been, reclined on a sofa dressed in a glorious, magenta silk gown. Behind her, swathes of rich material draped across the stone lintel and fanned out each side of the huge window frame. The magistrate's wife lived like a Roman citizen but still retained the modest, Jewish tradition of covering her hair. She stared at Kezia.

"It *is* you!" The woman was incredulous. "Come closer. Let me look at you. Here, sit by the window." Kezia obeyed in silence. The magistrate's wife watched her. Kezia stood silhouetted against the window with the light accentuating the fine bone structure of her face, her dark eyes lowered, hesitant and uncertain.

"I'm *so* grateful to you, my dear," the woman spoke with genuine warmth. "I owe you my life!"

"I prayed in the name of Jesus," Kezia was quick to distance herself from the praise, "Jesus is the healer, not me," she added simply. The name meant nothing to the woman.

"Whatever name you used in your prayers, it was *you* who came to me." Her eyes smiled, "How can I ever repay you?"

"But I…I don't want payment…" Kezia stammered, blushing at the sight of a leopard-skin purse in the woman's hand. The mistress of the house rose from her sofa and moved towards Kezia.

"My dear," she said in an earnest tone, holding out the purse to Kezia, "this is from my husband. He *insists* you take it…"

"Oh, but…" Kezia began

"No 'buts' – we both *insist*." The magistrate's wife planted the purse into Kezia's hands. "I understand you are a widow-woman," she said with sympathy. Kezia nodded. "Well, then, let us put a little extra into your life which, no doubt, you will find useful one day." She put her hand under Kezia's elbow, "But, before you go," she guided her guest towards the centre of the room. "I want to show you something." The two women came to a halt.

"There!" the older woman pointed to the floor.

Kezia's jaw dropped in amazement. There on the floor, surrounded by sinuous vines and pomegranates, her own likeness gazed up. A delicate mosaic picture of herself. Kezia's hand automatically went to cover her mouth. Nico! It had to be Nico, she reasoned inside her head. He had worked in this grand house. The magistrate's wife noted the quickening of Kezia's breathing and the rising colour in her face.

"That," she said, "is a mosaic fashioned by love." A tinge of sadness entered her voice. "Many a woman would envy you that." Kezia was lost for words. The magistrate's wife continued, " Your husband must have loved you very much, my dear. Let that be a comfort to you."

Kezia swallowed hard. She had to escape from the dining hall before the mistress discovered the artist of the mosaic had not been Kezia's husband. She had to escape before tears streamed down her cheeks. Without a word, her heart racing, she turned and fled through the double doors. Blindly she ran across the marble hall, down the wide steps, along the cardo through the market stalls and back to the haven of the pottery.

Was it possible Nicolaus the artist… loved her?

Joanna and Adah were bent over their mending when they heard the sound of sandals padding up the stairs to the roof. They glanced at each other. For some reason Kezia had rushed up to the tent. Zippie heard the footsteps. She dropped her rag doll and made for the stairs.

***

"*How* much?" whistled Seth.

"Gold coins to the value of two thousand talents!" Joanna replied. "In this *amazing* leopard-skin purse," Joanna's hands made a shape to indicate the size of the purse. "I told her, 'we're going straight to the bank with that'." Seth smoothed and folded the purple cloth of his turban and laid it neatly on the shelf below the bedroom window.

"Perhaps God is good after all!" he said. "That'll make

all the difference to her life." He rubbed his eyes and yawned. "The lass deserves it," he rolled under the sheet. "Let's hope it brings her happiness."

Chapter 40

THE road snaked along the Samarian hill ridge. Several miles could be saved for the traveller between Galilee and Jerusalem by taking this route, and although devout Jews found it distasteful to travel through Samaria, the time saved made it worthwhile. Eli kept his head bowed as, with friends from the Synagogue and merchant men from Sepphoris, he strode through the Samarian villages as fast as his dignity allowed. He intended to reach Jairus as swiftly as possible and obtain his permission to marry the widow-woman, Kezia.

The usual crush of pilgrims milled around the gates to the Holy City, with the whole raucous world in microcosm threading their way towards the Temple. Some had lambs strapped to their shoulders, others carried doves in cages, all pressed forward, impatient to get into the Temple courts and make their sacrifices for Passover. As a man who spent his days in the cool, tranquillity of a Synagogue scriptorium, Eli felt overwhelmed by the clamour and smell of the gathered hoards. His previous pilgrimages to Jerusalem had been driven by the expectations of his superiors rather than his own personal journey of faith. He looked around with nervous eyes. How could anyone worship the Lord God of Hosts in this jangling, grating crowd?

As his group of travellers began the steep ascent to the

Lion Gate, their path was blocked. Men jostling to move forward found themselves corralled by bawling, whip-lashing soldiers.

"Two more battalions've come up from Caesarea this week." A surly dove-seller shared his information. "The Romans aren't going to risk no riots this Passover," he grumbled, shuffling with his cart piled with crated birds. Resentment in the ill-tempered queue rose to boiling point and only then did the soldiers grudgingly ease the log-jam at the gate, and allowed the disgruntled human tide to trudge up the final incline and disperse inside the city walls.

Inside the city, Roman soldiers were posted at every corner. Their menacing and oppressive presence cast a tense shadow over the pilgrim crush. Each time Eli lifted his eyes in their direction, he found himself the object of cold, military inspection. His breathing became erratic as, in panic, he realised his own vulnerability.

"Never seen so many soldiers," Eli's friend confided. "They're too thick to see it's *thems* causing all this bother."

"Hush!" scolded another, "You'll feel a spear in your side if you don't shut it!" The men quickened their pace towards the Temple courts.

Apart from a few congratulatory remarks and cursory claps on the back, Eli's father could barely disguise the fact he was eager to return to more important conversations with his fellow Sanhedrin members. They were evidently much exercised over reports of unauthorised healings by some rough fishermen from the north. Eli's father was full of contempt for a small group known locally as 'Jesus People' and was palpably more interested in that particular problem than in his son's proposed marriage.

"Gamaliel's gone senile," Eli heard an aged Sadducee

announce in disgust. "I ask you, brothers, *what* is he thinking about?"

He watched his father's grey-robed figure swish away from him, head bowed in urgent conversation with similar 'grey' men of the Sanhedrin. They moved towards the High Priest's private rooms and disappeared. Eli stood for a few moments, a fish out of water, disorientated and rejected.

Jairus displayed genuine pleasure. He clasped Eli in a fatherly embrace, called him, "my son", and suggested in a vague manner, that they have supper together before Eli's return to Sepphoris after Passover. But he too made it plain he must return to the pressing concerns of his fellow Sanhedrin members. Eli's life was about to be transformed with the blessing of marriage and sons – and no-one was in the slightest bit interested. Deflated, he wandered back to the guest-chamber reserved for visiting scribes. He sensed a chill wind of intrigue pervading the high stone arches of the Temple courts.

***

"Seth…" Kezia loitered in the pottery beside a row of drying pots. Her fingers traced along the shelf as she composed her thoughts.

"That's me," replied the cheery potter. Kezia took a deep breath and plunged in:

"You're a man…" she began.

"Not everyone shares your confidence, my dear," he quipped. Seth's eyes smiled at the jug taking shape under his wet fingers. He knew Kezia would not understand the remark, if indeed she had even heard it. She hovered at Seth's shoulder, preoccupied with her next question.

"How do I tell Eli the scribe that I won't marry him?"

Seth's foot fell off the tredle. The wheel stopped and the jug almost toppled to the floor. He sat back, smile gone. He looked up at her, his eyebrows hitting against his purple turban.

"What do you mean?" Seth queried. "What's the matter with him?"

"Nothing's the matter with *him*," Kezia continued unruffled, "but… Seth, I don't *have* to marry him, do I?"

"Well…" Seth pursed his lips and blew down his nose as he thought. "No… I don't suppose you *have* to. But it would be a *very* good idea if you did!" He looked at her unable to fathom her mind.

"I have my own money in the bank," Kezia had rehearsed her arguement, "I don't have to rely on a husband now." Serious brown eyes stared directly at Seth, "I can be independent, can't I?" There was a pause.

"Is that what you want Kez?" He dipped his right hand in the bucket of water and splashed at the jug. "Have you talked to Joanna about this?" he asked. Kezia shook her head.

"Will Eli be angry?" she turned her face to the doorway as she heard the donkey's hooves in the courtyard.

"*Incandescent* I should think," came the reply. "Disappointed… bewildered… expect he'll be all those things – *and* more! It's not usual for a woman to refuse a man's proposal of marriage, Kez. You'll make him feel foolish… humiliated… and no man likes that."

Little Josh poked his head round the door, "All done, Seth!" he announced the completed deliveries and disappeared.

Kezia nervously fingered one of the glazed jugs; "I *can't* marry him." Kezia had made her decision. Seth returned to complete the jug, waiting for her to say something more. When she didn't, he pleaded:

"Just promise me you'll speak to Joanna… yes?"

"Of course." Kezia flashed a smile of relief. "You're both so good to us. We couldn't manage without you." Little Josh reappeared.

"Adah says 'meal's ready'," he gabbled, turned and rushed over to the house.

"Mmm." Seth finished the jug and placed it carefully on the ledge near his wheel. He'd never heard anything like it. A widow… *refuse* to marry! He frowned. Whatever was the matter with her? He got up, stretched and wiped his hands on a rag. Joanna must talk some sense into her.

***

Passover turned into a miserable chore for Eli the scribe. He longed to be back in Sepphoris to arrange his marriage to Jairus' beautiful daughter. He visualised himself leading his sons to the Synagogue, teaching them to write and follow his own scribal career. The days dragged. His father spent most of his time locked in fierce arguments in the Sanhedrin and Jairus seemed more concerned about his sick friend, the silversmith. Jerusalem heaved with strangers from every corner of the world. Foreign costumes and languages filled the streets around the Temple and soldiers glared down from the city walls like vultures in breast-plates, on guard against any spark of trouble. Amidst so many people, Eli felt totally alone.

At last it was over. Eli packed his bag and, without waiting for the other Sepphoris men, joined a party of tanners and masons travelling north out of Jerusalem. They took the road across the Samarian hills bound for Ptolemais on the coast. Their route would include a stop in Sepphoris before the final stage of their journey to the Great Sea port. Eli enthused over his betrothed and invited the men to stay for his wedding.

Chapter 41

KEZIA took courage from Seth's moral support as they made their way to the Synagogue. A sharp wind gusted through the streets, so much so that, rounding one corner, Seth nearly lost his turban. Eli opened the side door to the visitors and a broad smile wreathed his face at the sight of his betrothed.

Seth stood watching closely as Kezia faced the scribe across the table in the spartan scriptorium.

"I want to thank you, Sir, for your generous offer of marriage," she began formally. Eli inclined his head and licked his lips.

"I hope you will understand, but..." suddenly she realised he detected trouble. His eyes clouded. The atmosphere froze. "I'm afraid I cannot marry you." Kezia faced the scribe with demure composure. The mongoose turned scarlet.

"What does she mean?" he spat, pupils protruding towards the potter. Seth shifted uneasily from one foot to the other.

"I think..." he spoke in a measured tone, "I think, my friend, she means what she says."

Eli's expression switched from incredulity to thin-lipped fury.

"Don't you 'my friend' me!" he snarled, "How *dare* you abuse my kindness... I've *paid* for her!" He thumped his fist on the table.

"You'll be more than reimbursed for your trouble." Seth promised in a vain effort to defuse the scribe's petulance.

"Then take the ungrateful witch out of my sight!" Blood drained from around his nostrils as he yelled, "How dare you... you... *harlot!*" he shreaked at Kezia. "As the Lord is my witness, I'll make you suffer for this. Every man in Sepphoris will *spit* on you. You'll be spurned by the whole city and... and..." The scribe picked up the inkpot from the table and hurled it at Kezia's retreating back with the full force of his fury.

"*Jezebel!*" he screamed. Kezia flinched in pain as the inkpot caught her collar-bone and the stain of dark ink trickled down her dusky pink cloak. Seth grabbed her arm and propelled her hastily through the door. They left Eli ranting and cursing them both as they cut through the alleyways back to the pottery.

"It's alright, Kez," Seth tried to be reassuring as he could feel her body shaking. "I wouldn't want to marry him either!" He grinned in a way so infectious that Kezia had to smile.

"Pity 'bout your cloak, though." He wrinkled his nose at the ugly splash of ink. "Don't think even my Jo can wash that out."

"Not to worry," Kezia regained her composure. "Adah and I'll dye it." She said removing her cloak and inspecting the stain, "we'll dye it *black...* widow's black!"

***

"Can he do that?" Adah sucked in a long breath. She listened in trepidation as Kezia recounted Eli's blustering threat.

"He's angry enough," Kezia whispered. They kept their

363

voices low as Zippie had fallen asleep, spreadeagled across the bottom of the mattress. They had discarded their winter fleeces but were still glad of blankets. The air was crisp and carried the soft scent of night. Adah sat hunched on her bed, arms clasped round her knees.

"But what'll your father say?" the little servant girl queried, quite bamboozled by such goings on. Kezia pulled the comb through her thick hair which now waved half-way down her back.

"I don't think Father cares about anyone except Jabez," her reply held more than a hint of sadness. Adah clucked to herself. She didn't like upsets. The next instant she had another thought.

"But you said 'twas Mordecai who'd planned it, an all?" Adah wasn't too sure.

Kezia nodded.

"He wants you to have a husband to care for you." Adah considered the situation. Kezia put down her comb.

"Uncle Mordecai thinks in terms of his own reputation," she sighed. "It's a blessing we can both work here in the pottery. I've paid Seth half of Eli's dowry for me, and he wants to pay the rest. So, you see, he has bought me to live under his roof." She gave an impish giggle, "I'm a slave-girl like you," she smiled broadly, "but, what better family could we have?" Adah took a sip from her water bottle. Somehow it didn't seem right that Kezia should be a slave. She loved the pottery, being Joanna's servant help, meeting other girls at the well, and, she smiled contentedly to herself, she loved *buying* bread!

Kezia got up from her mattress and parted the tent flap. She walked out onto the roof. Although it was dark, the sky grew lighter the more she stared up into its vast canopy. Distant laughter, then a ripple of applause drifted from the direction of the theatre. Apart from that, for once, the streets of Sepphoris lay still. From the roof she could see flashes of light as soldiers guarding the Nazareth Gate moved around with their torches. She crouched on the rough, flat tiles, lost in thought. Would her mother have been disappointed she had turned down Eli's proposal? Surely she would have wanted her and Zippie to stay together? Subconsciously her fingers closed around the stones in Jesus' kid pouch on her belt.

So much had happened since he had given her that pouch…

***

Seth sat cross-legged on the bed. He watched Joanna put his clean tunic on the stool for the morning, shake their water bottle to make sure they had enough for the night, and then snuff out the oil lamp on the windowsill.

"I've got a suggestion," he yawned. Joanna always knew that when her husband made a remark as if it wasn't of the slightest importance, then he had been giving it days of serious thought. She slipped onto the bed beside him.

"You want us all to go and live in Damascus!" she joked.

"No, no, *no*! Whatever made you think I'd want to do a thing like that!" Seth feined disgust. A slight, uncertain silence elapsed before he said, "No, I was thinking we could start a new pottery in Caesarea!"

"*What?*" Joanna sat bolt upright. She had oiled her arms and neck with sweet ointment and her rapid movement wafted the pleasant scent past his nose. "And when did you decide this?" she demanded.

"Only today, my love." Seth put out a hand to caress his wife's shoulder. Even in the gloom, he detected Joanna's body language did not signal whole-hearted approval. "Just a suggestion," he whispered. Joanna considered in silence before she spoke.

"Could Eli the scribe make things bad for Kezie?" she asked.

"Yes! He was angry. *Livid!*" Seth conceded, "And… can you blame him? Poor bloke's been humiliated." He rubbed his chin, "After all, widows can't be choosey… I don't know what Kez is thinking about."

"I do," Joanna was solemn.

"You do?" Seth sounded mystified. Joanna rearranged herself into a more comfortable position.

"She loves another man."

"She does? Who could that be?" Seth probed. Joanna gave him a sudden, sharp poke in the ribs.

"You *tease!*" she tried to sound annoyed. "You've known all along…" she jumped on him and for a couple of giggling minutes they wrestled on the bed. "That's why you suggested Caesarea, isn't it?"

Joanna lay back. "Isn't it?" she banged her hand down on the pillow waiting for his answer.

"So you might consider it, then?" Seth had won the fight. Joanna settled down for sleep, pulling the crumpled sheet up over her shoulders.

"I *might*," she said airily. It was a typically flippant reply, but even with her face turned away from him in the darkness, he knew she was smiling.

***

Expletives fired into the courtyard from inside the tall kiln. Joseph, the potter Seth had employed when orders for blue pottery escalated, stood inside barking with dismay. Seth jumped up from his wheel to see the cause of such commotion.

"'Tis this last batch…" Joseph growled, "they've gone *green*!" Seth looked over his assitant's shoulder; the rows of fired pots looked in perfect order, just not the expected colour. "Must've lost heat at the vital time," Joseph moaned. Seth retreated from the cramped kiln.

"Well," he breezed, unruffled, "they're not broken, man. What's the matter with you? Green's a perfectly good colour. Don't let's worry about it. Ben'll unpack them while we get on with another batch." He turned to retreat into the pottery, "Green… blue… red… they're all pots… and all pots sell." Ben emerged from the pottery, "Oh, Ben, give Joseph a hand will you?" Seth closed a hand on Ben's arm, whispering as he passed, "Not content with our blue range, we've now gone green!"

Joanna raked ashes from under the fire with her ear to the men at the kiln. Zippie occupied herself dragging her toy mouse up and down the room as Adah tried to sweep behind her.

"I'll sweep mousey away in a minute," Adah's warning only served to send Zippie into convulsive chuckles. The magistrate's servant had called for Kezia again, a summons which had Adah in a dither. Joanna gathered her purse and cloak and left for the market.

Seth the potter looked at his wife with pride. However many sat down to eat at his table, she always produced enough for everyone. He looked at the present company; Ben, Ben's mother, Joseph, Little Josh, Kezia, Adah, Zippie, Joanna and himself: nine hungry souls. An ever-extending family!

***

Kezia had only just returned from the magistrate's house and Joanna was desperate to find out what had been going on.

"The magistrate's wife wants me to be her hand-maid." Kezia said quietly. Suddenly, all eating stopped and all eyes fixed on Kezia.

Seth broke the silence, "What an honour, Kez," he said warmly. Joanna's face betrayed the turmoil in her mind.

"I told her that," Kezia continued, "I said that if she had asked the young wife from Capernaum some six months ago, I would have been pleased to accepted her offer." She paused, she had not shared with Adah or Joanna the fact that Nico had created a mosaic picture of her in the middle of the magistrate's dining hall. "But…" she was hesitant.

"But..?" urged Joanna,

"Things have changed," Kezia said simply. " My place is here now." She looked at Joanna, "If I'm going to be anyone's hand-maid, I'm yours." Tears stung Joanna's eyes as she smiled back.

"The Lord bless you, chicken." She fought to sound cheery.

"Well done, Kez!" Seth raised his wine cup, "Your home is here with us."

Little Josh looked up at Seth, "Me too?" his eyes wide with hope.

Seth put another piece of salted fish into his bread, "You too… and your gruesome donkey!" Seth took a large bite, then, wagging a finger at the boy he warned, "But don't you go bringing any of your brothers and sisters here… or your cousins and their goats… just *you*, d'you understand." Little Josh loved it when Seth pretended to be stern. He cleared his plate.

He had landed in heaven.

Chapter 42

Next day:

THE barley harvest was long over, the barns stacked from the earlier wheat harvest and the small, irregular fields were in the process of being ploughed. Shepherds ushered their flocks to eat up the last of the straw and fallen grains before the new seeds were broadcast.

Seth diagnosed lack of pressure in the kiln as the reason for the batch of pottery turning green. He ordered Ben and Little Josh to double their store of fuel. This meant travelling out further each day in order to fill the cart with kindling, logs, dried dung and any other combustible rubbish they could find. A small copse on the slopes below Nazareth was the furthest they had been but proved an easy source of firewood. However, the Nazareth women, wanting kindling for themselves, shouted and cursed them and banged their iron pots to scare the donkey away from their slopes.

"That's enough!" Ben decided. "Any more and it'll fall all over the road on the way back." He secured the mound of fuel with rope, then they set off, rattling over the Roman road back to Sepphoris. The boy walked by the donkey's head while Ben walked behind to give the cart the odd push if the wheels snagged on any uneven paving. Before the final climb to the

Nazareth Gate, they stopped beside the brook to drink and rest.

"Hey!" They heard a shout. Not expecting anyone, Ben ignored it. The voice came closer. "Hey Ben!" Little Josh scrambled to his feet. He whooped with delight and went careering down the road. Ben stared wearily after the boy and at the traveller Josh was rushing to greet.

"*Nico!*" he yelled, "Never thought… hey! You're back!" Ben leapt up to meet his artist friend. The three embraced.

"We thought you'd gone for good," Ben said looking at the bag on Nico's shoulder. Nico hung his head,

"I was… er going home to Rome, I… I was *not* coming back," he said.

"So what changed your mind?" Ben was intrigued. Nico shrugged.

"Maybe I have some er… some… how you say? Unfinished business." He gave a lop-sided grin.

***

No-one told Kezia that Nico was back. She walked into the pottery to sort dishes for firing. All she could remember was turning round and suddenly he was there. Standing in front of her, melting her with those liquid, dark eyes. She had no recollection of what he said to her or what she said to him, but, as if in a trance, she found herself locked against his firm chest, their lips crushed together. The aromatic scents of the bath-house lingered on his body and two day's growth on his chin bit into hers.

When at last he loosened his arms around her enough to look down into her eyes, he seemed embarrassed. "I'm sorry," he said, in that deep, gravely voice Kezia had so longed to hear again. "I didn't mean to… I… I should have er…" laughter broke out between them and the tension cleared. "No… *not* sorry," Nico began again, "I wanted to… er… to kiss you the first time I saw you." He motioned to the spot by the shelves where they had first met. "Remember?" he asked tentatively. Kezia nodded. Nico looked grave.

"You had husband, then." He lowered his lashes in thought. Not having been so intimate to his face before, Kezia marvelled at the length and thickness of his lashes. She could feel his breath on her nose. He held her close to him once more and their heartbeats thundered in unison.

"He was er… no good… not man for you…" she could vaguely hear Nico speaking but the impression of his lean, muscular contours removed all memories of Jared. Nico carried on not realising Kezia, in ecstacy, was paying no attention.

Suddenly she drew back. "*What* did you say?" she blinked, her full lips open in wonder. Nico repeated himself.

"I sayed, I want you to my wife. But…" he shrugged, "I am a citizen of Rome… I was afraid you would er… hate me." Kezia stared. Colour pounded in her cheeks. "When you goed back to Capnum, I could not stay here without you." He kissed her hands. "I went away, I went to my brother. Then I decide… I was take a ship for Rome… go home… you understand?" Kezia nodded. " But I couldn't go. I *had* to see you again…" His breathing was fast and shallow. "I had to know… could you… could you love me?"

Kezia reached a hand to the side of his short hair letting her fingers trail over his ear and down to his bare neck. "Yes, Nico," she breathed, " I could love you."

Nico fumbled in his tunic. "Look!" he said in triumph, "I have thees ring… make you my wife."

"Does Seth know you are back?" Kezia murmured, not wanting to check his enthusiasm but trying to keep at least one foot on the ground.

"I tell to him last night!" Nico drew her to him one more time as their kisses drowned out the entire creation except the joy of their entwined bodies.

"I see I'm not the only one glad you're back!" Seth stood in the doorway, arms folded, enjoying the scene. Nico and Kezia leapt apart as if a fire-cracker had exploded between them. Joanna stood behind Seth with Zippie in her arms. Nico, beaming with pride, pulled Kezia back into his arms. Seth moved forward to embrace them both.

"I know I'm second best," he quipped into Nico's shoulder, "but I can't tell you how pleased I am to see it was worth you coming back."

"*So* happy!" Nico's full smile showed his strong, even teeth.

"I rather gathered that!" Seth replied. "C'mon, we'll drink wine and then decide what we're going to do." He led the family out of the pottery, across the courtyard and into the house.

***

Two nights later:

Moonlight bathed the courtyard. Adah shivered with excitement as she twined rosemary and wild blossoms into two garlands. She wore the new coat and sandals Kezia had bought her that afternoon. The pottery was in shadow but the moon shone directly on to the house. In the privacy of the Seth's roof, Nico and Kezia prepared to become man and wife.

A public celebration was out of the question for fear of what Eli would do to ruin the event.

"Ah, chicken," Joanna breezed, "a wedding is is only an 'event'. A marriage is something for the rest of your lives."

Kezia, wearing a new cloak of dusky pink, stood beside the tall, Roman artist. Seth put a pitcher of wine at their feet.

"Wine for your blessing, my dears." He beamed.

Nico cleared his throat and lifted Kezia's hands in his.

"I, Nicolaus Marcus Lucanus, take er... Kezia," he faltered with the emotion of saying her name, "Kezia, daughter of Jairus, to my side. You be my wife and er, bear my children."

Tears of joy spilled down Kezia's cheeks. With a tender movement, Nico wiped her tears with his finger. Adah gulped back her own tears as she watched the marriage ceremony from under the vine pergola beside the tent she shared with Kezia. She and Joanna had dressed Zippie's hair with flowers for the ceremony.

"I swear by my father's gods, I protect and provide for you." He placed the ring on Kezia's third finger. Momentarily, her knuckle resisted, but a gentle push and the ring slipped into position. Nico's dark eyes gazed deep into hers. "This... my ring," he whispered, his voice drained of power. He lifted her hand to his lips and kissed the ring. "Now... you my wife."

Right on cue, cheers and applause echoed in the distance from the theatre. The little group in the courtyard laughed at such apt timing and raised wine cups to the health, happiness and fertility of the new husband and wife.

Adah and Zippie slept in the house that night, leaving the tent to Nico and his bride.

His smooth body lay gracefully across the sheet like one of the reclining statues Kezia had seen in the magistrate's mansion. Words were not necessary. Nico's hands and lips patiently unlocked her reticence and gradually obliterated the painful memories of what she had suffered from Jared.

"I won't hurt you..." he promised.

Nico gave her no pain, just immeasurable pleasure and mounting, breathless excitement. Caught in a vortex of passion, Kezia spiralled to heights of exquisite abandon she had not dared believe possible. In their intimacy, time stood still. There was no past... no thought for the future... just the intense beauty of their new-found love.

Chapter 43

"MOMENTOUS day!" Seth sat at the head of his table, wine cup in hand, making his pronouncement. "Today," he nodded round the table, "is the day that Sepphoris loses it's finest potter! This is the last day the famous and beloved purple turban will grace these city streets." Silence fell as each took in the implications of their impending journey. They were leaving Sepphoris for good.

"But," Seth stood with a flourish, rousing their flagging spirits, "today we begin an adventure! A *new* city awaits us! A new fortune!" he winked at Nico. "A new life for us all!" He reached for Joanna's hand, "Are we ready, my love?" he asked.

"You wouldn't be ready this side of next Passover if I hadn't packed your things!" She shook her head and raised her eyebrows to Ben's mother.

Outside in the courtyard, their possessions teetered precariously on the cart. Once more Kezia and Adah shouldered as much as they could carry but Seth wouldn't allow Joanna to carry a burden. Little Josh nuzzled into the donkey's ears,

"Told you one day we'd go to the Great Sea," he whispered to the animal, earnest in his excitement. Ben had bought a hand-cart for his mother's and his own belongings; Seth took Joanna's arm and Zippie rode aloft on Nico's shoulders.

"Let's go, chicken," Joanna wrinkled her nose at Kezia, "best foot forward!"

Slowly the potter's caravan rattled out of the courtyard and into the street leading to the Nazareth Gate. Kezia felt a twinge of guilt as they near the city walls. She had become far more attached to Sepphoris than she was to her birth village, Capernaum. Her mother was dead, her father and brother were in Jerusalem and goodness knows where Sarah had got to… and Uncle Mordecai would now disown her. Kezia gazed fondly at the apricot stone buildings. The city had widened her horizons; its people had opened her mind and eyes to what life was all about. She looked at Zippie wobbling happily on Nico's shoulders and a rush of warmth rippled through her body. Whatever her father or uncle would say, she was no longer Jairus' daughter or Jared's tragic widow, she was herself, Kezia, wife of Nicolaus Marcus Lucanus, citizen of Rome.

Joseph gathered his family to wave Seth's party on their way. Purchased from Seth, the pottery was now his and he couldn't wait to instal his family in the house.

The moment Seth walked out of the Nazareth Gate, a tingle of anticipation stifled any lingering doubts about leaving. He lifted Joanna's hand to his lips. He knew it was harder for her. Joanna's mouth curved in an enigmatic smile. Leaving friends behind was the sacrifice she was willing to make in order to defend Kezia against Eli's vitriol. His slanderous tongue would inevitably affect Seth's pottery as well as undermining Kezia's gift of healing. She squared her shoulders and determined the decision to relocate to Caesarea was best for all concerned.

Stepping out of the city, Kezia felt it was a metaphor for stepping out of her widow's clothes. In Ceasarea nobody would know her as anything but the wife of Nico the artist. No more hideous nightmares of Jared; no more visits from the wisenned Anna and the dreadful Debra; no more flash-backs of Eli's threats. Her eyes shone with an inner light... she felt strong as an eagle. Above all Kezia exuded the glowing happiness of loving and being loved. She looked at Adah, her dear sister and friend, spontaneously they reached for each other's hand and walked smiling down into the valley.

***

Three days later:

In contrast to the city of Sepphoris which covered the high hill-top like a bright, new crown, the city of Caesarea Maratima sprawled along a featureless, coastal plain. Approaching the place it was hard to believe it was a city, as the flat terrain made it impossible to see many buildings except the outline of a high tower and the roof of a Temple. The soil changed from the fertile valley to the brown soil at the foot of the Carmel mountains to a dry, sandy soil of the coast. As they neared the sea, pine trees and olive groves gave way to palms and dust swirled around their feet in the warm wind. Nearing the southern gate, the city buildings rose up before them. The travellers passed a huge hippodrome where, Nico told them, fortunes were gambled at the weekly chariot races.

"We camp here?" Nico suggested. Kezia stared at a sight reminiscent of the encampment on the slopes of Bethany. A tented town of visitors, migrant workers, itinerant traders and travelling bedouins straddled both sides of the Via Maris.

"Here *good* place," Nico pointed to a slightly raised mound nearer to the sea. "They have water for this er… camp. Some not," his mouth turned downwards at the distasteful idea of having no water. "Later, I take you…" he motioned to Seth, Joanna and Kezia, "I take you for… er… for to meet Cornelius, my brother." He placed a hand on his heart at the mention of his brother's name.

With the road from Sepphoris to the coast being a main trade route, there had been plenty of stalls along the way and the women were immediately able to light a fire and begin preparations for their meal. The men pitched two tents, one for the women and one for themselves. Josh, delegated to fetch water from the nearby stone gully, found himself mesmerised by the sight of different ships wedged along the two breakwaters in the harbour. Nico had told him the trade ships sailed in to Ceasarea from every country in the world.

A pitcher in each hand, Josh imagined himself as a rugged sailor carrying water for his thirsty ship-mates. In his day-dream he was sailing the world… amassing vast riches… owning a fleet of galleons… his head whirled with the fantasies until he reached Seth's tents and poured water into the donkey's trough. The grey ears flickered. Josh sniffed as he watched the animal drink deeply. He couldn't go to sea and leave his friend. He wiped his nose on the back of his hand. No, perhaps he didn't really want to go to sea.

After the meal, Seth declared himself in no fit state to go visiting.

"Tomorrow, Nico," he said, concerned by Joanna's tired eyes, "tomorrow would be a *much* better idea. We shall go to pay our compliments to your brother in the morning. Give us time to wash and put on clothes suitable for an audience with an important army officer." He smiled and nodded at the artist. Nico accepted Seth's decision was final.

***

The courtyard walls of Cornelius' house hung with lush vines loaded with plump hands of grapes. From the far wall, a pipe connected into a bronze fish-head spewed water into a shell-shaped pool around which several women chatted in groups. Smells of fresh baked bread and spices carried on the air. Kezia stopped in her tracks.

"*Sarah!*" she cried in amazement. They ran to each other. "Oh Sarah! What're *you* doing here?"

"Kezie, my *dear, dear* girl," Sarah squeezed Kezia in motherly arms, "You're a sight for sore eyes, to be sure."

"You two will have to catch up later," Joanna smiled, as she marshalled Kezia into crocodile behind Seth, Nico and the blonde servant who was escorting them with military precision into the cool of the square, sand-stone dwelling. Kezia turned, waved and raised her shoulders and eyebrows at the unexpected joy of meeting Sarah.

A certain fluttering in Joanna's stomach betrayed her outward assurance. She became accutely aware of where she was, what she was doing and what she had allowed Kezia to do. It was one thing eating with a gentile in her own home, but quite another to find herself walking into a gentile's house. That would be bad enough, but this gentile was a Roman *soldier!* And Kezie… she had promised to be a mother to Kezie and what had she done? Supported her marriage to the Roman soldier's brother. Suddenly, it was all too much for the ever confident and joking Joanna. As she passed the window in the stairwell, her sister's disapproving eyes gazed down on her from the stonework. For a second, Joanna stumbled. She put out her hand to the wall to steady herself.

'Oh! Stuff and nonsense!' she shook her head in silent self-admonishment. Of course Leah would disapprove, *and* Jairus, *and* their parents and just about *everyone* she could think of... but... *they* weren't here. Things were different in this city. *Everything* was different. Joanna vowed that she would move heaven and earth to protect Kezia's new-found happiness. With firm steps, banishing any more extraneous doubts, she arrived at the top of the stairs.

The blonde servant led them into a wide room with windows overlooking the harbour. Striped curtains, which draped to the floor, billowed into the room as the sea breezes gusted. Cornelius, an older and thicker version of Nico, stood proud in his dress tunic and military cloak. At the sight of his brother, he strode forward to greet the visitors from Sepphoris.

Chapter 44

"WHAT was he like?" Adah couldn't contain her curiosity.

"He was really nice," Kezia beamed, surprise and relief in her reply. Sarah had come to the tent to find out what they were all doing in Caesarea. Waiting for Kezia's return she had rolled up her sleeves to help Adah with the dishes. Kezia turned to Sarah, "But, fancy you being here in Caesarea. This is wonderful! Is Simon with you?"

"Yes, he's here. But, oh my dear, everyone calls him Peter now! And would you believe... he's *friends* with that there Centurion you've just been meeting."

"How?" Kezia was bemused that the burly fisherman she remembered from Capernaum would call a Roman centurian a 'friend'. Adah said nothing. It was all a bit beyond her. Sarah settled her skirts in the familiar way Kezia had seen a thousand times when Sarah used to come over to unload to Leah.

"Well, dear, this man Cornelius had a dream about my Peter... we were in Joppa, an' one of his servants came and asked Peter to come here to Caesarea." Kezia listened in amazement as Sarah rattled on, "Well, long and short of it is we came an' Cornelius, he asked my Simon-Peter, to baptise his whole household!"

"Baptise?" Kezia didn't understand.

"Yes! Cornelius is a God-fearer and big follower of Rabbi

Jesus… him and *all* his household… would you believe it!" She lifted her eyes to the bluest of skies. "They're lovely people, you know. Very religious, an' *ever* so generous!" She leaned forward so her words would not be heard by anyone but Kezia, "Never thought I'd say such a thing, Kezie dear, but they're… well, they're almost the same as us!"

Sarah sat up straight to change the subject. "Adah's been telling me of your man…" Kezia blushed, eyes sparkling. "Oh, it's good to see you happy, my love." Sarah prized herself up, "an' he must be a good man mind… to take young Zippie as well," she nodded approval. "But I must be off… make the meal for my man. But I'll be round in a day or so… see how you're all getting on." Sarah picked up her basket and bustled into the labarynth of temporary dwellings.

Kezia opened her arms for Zippie. "Adah," she said in a tone that made the servant girl spin round anxiously, "It's alright," Kezia reassured her, "there's nothing to worry about. It's good news! Until Seth and Nico can buy some land and build a new home, Nico's brother has given us rooms in his house." Adah's furrowed brow registered high anxiety. Kezia explained the hospitable offer; "It's a *huge* house, Adah. Such high windows looking right out over the sea… and the most beautiful drapes… and… oh, the marble floors and *cushioned* benches."

Adah clasped her hands first to her hair, then to her mouth, then wiped them furiously on her apron. "Oh!" she breathed, "Oh! *Me* live in *his* house?"

"Yes,"

"*That* house?" Somehow Adah managed to point back to the Centurion's house with the tip of her nose.

"Yes."

"When?"

"Tonight."

"Oh my!" Adah was severely flummoxed. Kezia clutched Zippie in her arms, swaying her gently and smiling broadly.

"We'll be together, Adah. The four of us." A tug of emotion cracked her voice, "We'll be a new family." As she heard herself say the words she nestled her cheek into Zippie's untamed locks.

Adah's eyes brimmed with a mixture of joy, pride and trepidation. A shy smile quivered on her lips, "We'd best get ready, then," she whispered.

***

Eight months later:

The early evening sun reflected liquid ripples of gold across the water beyond the harbour. Kezia sat, unable to look directly into its seering brightness but allowing the warm rays to penetrate her light clothes. When all the chores were finished, that had always been her favourite time of day. She looked forward to these moments – time to sit with Joanna and Zippie and Adah on the verandah – time to soak up the sounds and smells of their life in Ceasarea.

Seth had chosen a parcel of land with access to good clay and also because it was situated at the edge of the city, on a slight elevation which gave a panoramic view down to the harbour and out over the Great Sea. Nico designed a typical Roman villa with a long verandah facing the sea. Seth and Joanna, Nico and Kezia, Zippie and Adah would share the long wing behind the verandah, with Ben, his mother and Little Josh living in the side wing. Part of the communal courtyard would be covered with vines and already Seth and

Nico had planted tamarisk, almond and olive trees to enclose their property.

Everyone, except for Ben's mother, slogged each day in building the villa with the local, milk-coloured stone.

"It's like a dream," Kezia murmured. She looked at Joanna, patiently teaching Zippie to card wool. Adah had trimmed Zippie's curls that morning and the bobbed hair looked two shades darker than her wispy 'baby' hair. In the months since they had left Sepphoris, Zippie had matured into a responsible child of three and a half. She loved nothing better than to trail behind Adah, copying whatever Adah was doing, convinced her help was indispensible.

Joanna looked up at Kezia, then out over the sea. She grimaced as she answered: "When Seth first mentioned coming to Caesarea, I thought it was one of his pipe-dreams." She put down the wool and hoisted Zippie on to her lap. "Then, the thought of leaving Sepphoris felt more like a nightmare! But," she grinned, "here we are." She looked around at the stone building rising from the deep foundations, the new pottery and the first completed kiln, "And it's not so bad after all, is it? Not so bad at all!"

Pieces of cloth scattered over Kezia's lap and around her bare feet on the floor. The tunic she was sewing for Little Josh was a slow job. "It's like my own promised land!" she replied to Joanna. She gazed out from their courtyard to where the tops of galleons and merchant ships were visible above the red, tiled roofs of the harbour warehouses.

"How can I ever thank you…" Kezia sighed. " You *and* Seth."

Joanna gave Zippie a tight hug. "Och!" she scoffed, "You don't have to thank us. Just to know you're happy, chicken, that's enough for me." Kezia leaned forward to squeeze her hand.

"But… this lovely villa…" she began.

"It'll be lovely when it's *finished!*" Joanna laughed. "Tch! Potters! Artists! I don't know… all their schemes and plans! I've told Seth if he doesn't get a move on we'll still be sleeping in tents when Zippie gets married!"

They stared into the distance in warm contentment.

Seth planned for two walk-in kilns and the first one was nearly ready for the first firing. Shelves lined one wall of the courtyard, stacked with drying pots. At the opposite end, a lean-to served as the donkey shelter.

Impatient to begin his role in delivering Seth's wares, Little Josh had started a business of his own.

"I buys fruit an' stuff, an' sometimes baskets or old wine-skins. Then I loads up the donkey and goes down to where ships is about to leave." The budding entrepreneur unashamedly flaunted his impish charm in pursuit of his new enterprise. Seth was impressed at the profit the boy was making.

The kid pouch of healing stones hung permanently from Kezia's belt. As yet, there had been no call to use them in Ceasarea, but, she knew if she was patient, an opportunity would present itself at the right time. Sarah overflowed with news of how her Simon – Peter and the other disciples were healing people – all in the name of Jesus. Kezia thrilled to hear of such miracles. It meant that each in their own way was keeping his name alive.

Sarah became as frequent a visitor to Kezia and Joanna as she had been to Leah in Capernaum. The last time she called in, she said Simon Peter was talking of returning to Joppa and then going back to Jerusalem.

"It's nice in Joppa," she confided in her friends, "but I don't much want to go back to Jerusalem." She became

earnest, "Simon Peter says the Master's brother, James, is…
well, he's their Leader in Jerusalem." She bit her bottom lip
and shuffled on her cushion in the manner Kezia remembered
so well, "Sometimes they get trouble from Temple guards and
that and.. well, Peter says he ought to be there to give his
support…stand up to the Sanhedrin!"

The word Sanhedrin caused Kezia to catch her breath.
Her father would be actively involved against anyone who
followed Jesus. She realised that meant he would be against
her. Sarah was her nostalgic link with her old life in
Capernaum and Kezia felt saddened she was leaving.
However, in the market and at the washing stream, she and
Adah were beginning to make new friends. And, in Cornelius'
house they met many members of The Way, people who were
convinced Jesus was the Messiah. Jews and gentiles together
went out of their way to help Kezia and Adah integrate with
the cosmopolitan community of the thriving port city.

Initially, Kezia was diffident and self-conscious about
wearing her hair uncovered as Nico wanted, but she soon
found many Jewish women embracing the modern, Roman
ways.

Through his brother's contacts in the Garrison, Nico
landed a prestigious commission for mosaics in the
Governor's residence.

"He cruel man," Nico told Kezia in the pottery, "but not
his house… it's a house for *every* Governor who come to
Ceasarea."

Seth spoke as he man-handled a hefty stone into position.
"From what I hear…" he strained, "Pilate won't be Governor
much longer." He picked up a smaller stone to stabalise the
larger one. "We'd better give him some blue dishes he can take
back to Rome!" he chuckled to himself. Pride welled in Kezia's

heart, Nico was such a brilliant artist and designer, and handsome in a gentle, querky way. At that moment their eyes locked across a consignment of dressed stone... her heart leapt... she responded to her tender lover's gaze.

***

That night, she and Nico walked hand in hand along the beach, a fresh breeze lifting Kezia's hair so that she kept brushing strands from off her face. They walked parallel to the threatre. Tiers of seats rose on three sides facing the sea. As the artist and his wife sauntered past, the theatre stood dark and silent after the noise and euphoria of the afternoon performance.

The waves broke in whispers over the soft sand. In the distance, the harbour warehouses and ship masts were silhouetted against the cloudless skyline like a charcoal drawing. Kezia nestled her head against the hard warmth of Nico's shoulder. They walked slowly, fingers entwined, in perfect step.

Capernaum seemed a life-time away. As her toes sank in the damp sand, she was suddenly conscious of her mother's presence. Disconcerted, Kezia stared up into the deepening sky. With all the excitement of their new villa rising block by block, the distractions of hard work and the pulsating rhythm of the port, Kezia had not thought of her mother for days.

Palpitations! She stood still. What if she was like her mother? What if the life stirring in her belly dropped before its time? What if it was a girl? Would Nico be angry? The questions bombarded her brain, as though a drum-stick was hammering in her head.

"What's wrong?" Nico cupped her chin in his hand. Kezia met his gaze, her lips tremulous.

"What if it is a girl?" her whisper hoarse with dread.

"Then… she will be er… beautiful… like her mother," Nico gave gentle reassurance. But Kezia felt only marginal encouragement, the expectations of her culture being too deeply ingrained to be ignored.

"But… I thought…" she began,

"Oh, you womens!" he let his fingers comb through her wind-tossed hair. "It is…how you say? Boy…girl… not so important for men of Rome. Important things is… the child is er, mine." He bent to kiss her forehead, her neck, then lingered on her lips.

"What will you call your son?" Kezia asked. Nico pursed his lips in the way she had loved from their very first meeting. He looked up at the evening star.

"We call him er… Marcus. Marcus Nicolaus Lucanus!" he gave emphasis to each syllable… Kezia's nose crinkled,

"But… what if it *is* a girl?" she asked, still hardly daring to believe Nico would not mind.

" My mother… her name Corrina." He guided her from the water's edge and they sat further up the beach on dry sand. Sitting side by side, Nico's arm slipped round Kezia's thickened waist. He pulled her close so that their cheeks touched as they looked back at the sea.

"How you like…" he whispered, his hand tenderly caressing the bulge in her tunic, " …we call her Leah Corinna?"